PRAISE FOR *GET EVEN*

"If you're a *Pretty Little Liars* fan, it's safe to say you'll love *Get Even*."—BUSTLE.COM

"A compelling contemporary thriller."—*KIRKUS REVIEWS*

"The suspense that McNeil builds should keep readers curious to discover what happens next."—*PUBLISHERS WEEKLY*

"This suspenseful whodunit is sure to appeal to a broad audience and engage reluctant readers."—*VOYA*

"Ever-enjoyable. . . . McNeil has a screenwriter's instincts."—ALA *BOOKLIST*

"Will engage readers."—*ROMANTIC TIMES*

"*Get Even* expertly mixes suspense and snark, proving once again that Gretchen McNeil is a master of the teen thriller." —HEATHER COCKS AND JESSICA MORGAN, founders of Go Fug Yourself

"Don't get mad, get reading this wild ride filled with twists and turns, revenge and romance, suspense and Shakespeare." —ELIZABETH EULBERG, author of *Revenge of the Girl with the Great Personality*

"A revenge story with murder, mayhem, and Gretchen McNeil's signature snark? Yes, please! Gretchen proves once and for all that revenge is a dish best served deadly."—JESSICA BRODY, bestselling author of the Unremembered trilogy and *The Karma Club*

"*Get Even* is an edge-of-your-seat, sink-your-teeth-into-it mystery filled with vivid, intriguing characters and set against the ruthless landscape of a modern high school."—KATIE ALENDER, author of the Bad Girls Don't Die series

GET EVEN

GRETCHEN McNEIL

BALZER & BRAY
An Imprint of HarperCollinsPublishers

Balzer + Bray is an imprint of HarperCollins Publishers.

Get Even

Copyright © 2014 by Gretchen McNeil

All rights reserved. Printed in the United States of America. No part of this book may be used or reproduced in any manner whatsoever without written permission except in the case of brief quotations embodied in critical articles and reviews. For information address HarperCollins Children's Books, a division of HarperCollins Publishers, 195 Broadway, New York, NY 10007.
www.epicreads.com

Library of Congress Control Number: 2014942342
ISBN 978-0-06-305194-2

Typography by Torborg Davern
20 21 22 23 24   PC/LSCH   10 9 8 7 6 5 4 3 2 1

Revised edition, 2020

For Ginger Clark and Kristin Daly Rens,
without whom there is no there there

Revenge should have no bounds.

—SHAKESPEARE, *HAMLET*, ACT 4

ONE

BREE SAT BACK AGAINST THE CHAIN-LINK FENCE, BOUNCING her tennis racket lightly against the toe of her black Converse. "Why do we still have physical education in school?"

John snatched the racket out of her hand. "It's a political conspiracy to repress the youth of America through enforced humiliation."

A quartet of diligent tennis players trotted past Bree and John to the last empty court and began to hit the ball back and forth over the net with enthusiastic, if not particularly accurate, strokes. They looked lame in their white skirts and sneakers, glistening in the fierce afternoon sun, as they bobbed and swayed like Maria Sharapova in a Grand Slam final.

"You'd think," Bree said, pulling her knees up to her chin, "that a fancy prep school like Bishop DuMaine would have some kind of virtual phys ed. This *is* Silicon Valley. Shouldn't we be high-tech?"

A whistle blared from the other side of the courts. "Deringer! Baggott!" Coach Sampson pointed at them with her racket.

"This isn't break time."

Bree scanned the occupied courts. "We've got next," she shouted, accompanied by an overly enthusiastic thumbs-up.

Coach Sampson slowly shook her head in disgust as she turned her attention to a mixed doubles team.

"First week of school and I already hate phys ed." John tossed Bree's racket onto the court. "Can't your dad get us out of this?"

Bree arched a brow. "Can't your mom?"

"What's the point of having a state senator as my best friend's dad if we don't get any perks?"

"What's the point of having the school secretary as my best friend's mom," Bree mocked, "if we don't get any perks?"

John ran his fingers through his black hair, dyed the only color not verboten by Bishop DuMaine's strict dress code. "At least I'm not afraid to ask."

"I'm not afraid," Bree snapped.

"You will be." John hunched his shoulders and employed his crackly voiced Yoda impression. "You. Will. Be."

Bree rolled her eyes. Most days, John's geeky insistence that there was a *Star Wars* quote for every occasion was relatively entertaining, but today it was about as welcome as a raging case of the herps. All she could think about was tomorrow's supposedly surprise school assembly.

"Did you hear about the special assembly tomorrow?" John said out of the blue.

Bree inhaled sharply. Was he reading her mind? "There's an assembly tomorrow?" she asked, trying to sound indifferent.

John nodded. "Called by Father Uberti himself. Overheard

him talking to my mom about it in the office this morning."

Bree smoothed down her thick bangs and avoided John's eyes. "Why is he calling an assembly?"

"Duh." John turned to face her. "It's gotta be about DGM."

"DGM is going down," a voice boomed from behind them.

Bree craned her neck and found Rex Cavanaugh, flanked by his wingmen, Tyler Brodsky and Kyle Tanner, on the other side of the chain-link fence. They stood shoulder-to-shoulder with tree-trunk arms folded across overly broad chests. All three wore matching royal blue polo shirts sporting the words "'Maine Men," with the Bishop DuMaine crest emblazoned over their hearts.

Part club, part school-sanctioned goon squad, the 'Maine Men had been created by Father Uberti in response to the school-wide wave of humiliating revenge pranks perpetrated by an anonymous group known only as DGM. In an amazing, ironic move, old F.U. had recruited the school's top tier of bullies, poseurs, and power-hungry egomaniacs—the same people DGM targeted—and tasked them with ferreting out the students behind the group.

Much to Bree's delight, the 'Maine Men had been a total bust. In the last year and a half, the score was: DGM—6, 'Maine Men—0.

And she hoped that score held. At least for one more day.

"Did you hear me?" Rex barked.

Bree squinted into the sunshine. "Aren't you a little short for a Stormtrooper?" Next to her, John snorted.

"Huh?" Rex asked.

"What do you want?" Bree said slowly, articulating each word.

"DGM is going down," Rex repeated. Apparently, that was his only talking point. "Once and for all."

"Right," Bree said, narrowing her eyes. "Because you've done such a fantastic job of that so far."

Rex shoved his sweaty face against the fence, so close that Bree could differentiate the individually clogged pores across the bridge of his nose. "We know you're involved, Deringer. Just wait till tomorrow. Even your daddy won't be able to save you."

John was on his feet in an instant, wedging his body between Bree and the fence. "Lay off, Cavanaugh."

Rex shook the chain link back and forth like a caged gorilla. "Maybe you want to be next, Baggott the Faggot?"

Bree threw back her head in a mock laugh. "Ha. Ha, ha. Cuz that joke's never not funny."

"Rex!" A sandy-haired guy with a horrific case of acne trotted up. Bree had never seen him before, but judging by the creases down the front of his blue 'Maine Men shirt, it had recently been removed from its packaging. A new recruit. "Rex, you've got to see this."

"Who are you?" Rex said, his eyes still fixed on John.

"Ronny DeStefano?" the new guy said.

Rex shook his head. "Who?"

Ronny's forehead bunched up in confusion. "We met at Jezebel's house party last week."

Rex pursed his lips as if trying to force his Neanderthal brain to recall the booze-soaked party. "You new here?"

"Yeah," Ronny huffed. "We have a mutual friend, remember?

4

From junior high?" He looked at Rex pointedly. "We both had a weird experience with—"

"Right!" Rex said quickly. "Ronny. What's up?"

Ronny nodded toward the soccer field. "There's some shit going down with Coach Creed. I thought you should—"

"Let's roll," Rex said, cutting him off. He stormed away, Tyler and Kyle close behind, leaving Ronny to scamper after them like a puppy.

Bree looked at John. "Any idea what that was all about?"

"Dunno." John stared over her head toward the soccer field, where a crowd was gathering. "But I have a feeling we're about to find out."

Olivia swept out of the girls' locker room, racket in hand, and straightened her designer tennis dress.

"That outfit looks amazing on you," Amber said, gliding up beside her. "I'm glad you don't mind wearing last season's line."

"Not at all," Olivia said. Half of her wardrobe consisted of hand-me-down items Amber had deemed "last season."

Peanut fitted a baseball cap onto her head, pulling her long ponytail through the back. "Too bad Donté's basketball practice is in the gym," she said absently. "If he saw you in that dress, you'd have him eating out of your hand."

Olivia stiffened. "Why would I care what Donté thinks?"

Peanut's eyes grew wide. "Didn't you tell me last week that you were going to get back together with him?"

That was supposed to be a secret, Peanut.

Amber arched an eyebrow. "Liv, sweetie. We talked about this. You need someone . . ."

"Richer," Jezebel said, lumbering up behind them. She pulled a white hoodie on over her beefy shoulders and shook her head. "*You* broke up with *him*, remember?"

Olivia bit her lip. "Um, yeah."

"If you try to reboot," Amber added, "you'll look pathetic."

"I can't believe we have to wait until Monday to find out what the fall production's going to be," Olivia said, changing the subject. The last thing she wanted was another conversation with Amber about Donté Greene. "The anticipation is killing me."

"*I* can't believe Mr. Cunningham is missing the first week of school," Jezebel said with a shake of her head. "What kind of teacher does that?"

Amber fished a tube of gloss out of the pocket of her new designer tennis dress and lacquered her lips sans mirror. "I'm still putting my money on Mamet."

Olivia smiled. Amber would be the last person to have inside information on the drama department.

"Whatever it is," Peanut said, "there will be a perfect role for you, Livvie."

"You never know." Olivia ran a hand through her pixie cut and laughed. "Maybe with my hair this short, he'll want to cast me as a boy."

Jezebel sighed dramatically. "Only you would shave your hair for a role and have it grow back looking like a supermodel."

The role of crotchety cancer patient Vivian Bearing in *Wit* last spring had been Olivia's crowning achievement. Mr.

Cunningham had offered her a bald cap for the performance, but Olivia had shocked everyone by shaving off her strawberry blond curls for opening night. It was a decision she never regretted—every performance was sold out, and she got at least three curtain calls each night.

"Guess we'll just have to wait and see," Amber said with a toss of her brown mane. "Come on, ladies. Tennis awai . . ."

Her voice trailed off as she caught sight of something on the other side of the yard. Olivia turned and saw Rex blazing across the blacktop at a breakneck pace. He was bookended by Tyler and Kyle, with some skinny guy Olivia had never seen before trailing in their wake.

"Hi, baby!" Amber cooed at Rex. She turned to the side and posed provocatively in her barely there outfit.

"Not now!" Rex shouted, flashing his palm.

Amber's jaw dropped as Rex and his buddies broke into a jog. "What the fuck?"

"What's that all about?" Peanut asked.

"No idea." Olivia eyed the large group of students gathering at the top of the hill above the soccer field, as Rex and his 'Maine Men buddies pushed their way into the throng. That couldn't be good.

Amber sniffed at the air. Like a shark with blood in the water, she could sense gossip-worthy drama from a mile away. A sly smile broke the corners of her mouth.

"I think gym class just got significantly more interesting."

If Kitty had ever doubted that Coach Creed needed his ass handed to him, he was making it real easy for her to get over it.

"Move it, Baranski!" Coach Creed's bark drifted across the all-weather track where Kitty was leading the Bishop DuMaine varsity girls' volleyball team in a warm-up run before practice.

Kitty paused. Below her, students dotted the hillside that stretched down to the soccer field. Clad in their blue-and-gold gym uniforms, they were frozen in various stages of hill charges, eyes fixed on the bottom of the slope and the chubby, panting figure of Theo Baranski.

Coach Creed towered over him, hands on hips, flexing his pecs like an MMA fighter. "It's the first week of school, Baranski, and you're already falling behind."

Theo's face was beet red, and slick with either sweat or tears. Maybe both. He stared up at the steep hillside, his eyes reflecting a mixture of fear and shame. Deep inside Kitty, a memory stirred, so close and so real it was as if she was back in sixth-grade math class, where the numbers and symbols of pre-algebra swam before her eyes, as meaningless to her as hieroglyphics.

Kitty squeezed her eyes shut. The shame of not knowing the right answer. The fear that Ms. Turlow would call on her . . .

How can you be the only Asian kid on the planet who isn't good at math?

"How can you be the only kid on the planet," Coach Creed continued, "who can't haul his ass up that hill?"

Mika jogged up behind her. "That poor kid's got enough problems without Creed jumping down his throat every day."

"I know," Kitty said quietly. Theo had transferred to Bishop DuMaine last spring, and Coach Creed had been on his case since day one.

Mika pulled off her headband and patted her tight black curls into place. "Theo's going to have a heart attack if he tries to charge up that hill one more time. We should do something."

We already have.

As much as Kitty wanted to step in and help, her hands were tied. She'd been hoping Coach Creed would lay off Theo the first week of school, giving DGM enough time to put their plan into motion. No such luck.

"You know," Mika said slowly. "The volleyball team could really use a manager. Do you think I should talk to Coach about bringing Theo on board?"

Kitty smiled. "That's an awesome idea."

A commotion rippled through the gathering crowd, as Amber Stevens pushed her way to the front, smiling gleefully in Theo's direction. "What a pig!"

"Great," Mika muttered. "The Supreme Bitch has arrived."

Amber straightened her neck with the regality of a queen and addressed her subjects. "I mean, have a little self-respect. Back away from the double cheeseburger."

"Move it!" Coach Creed roared. The gathered audience was fueling his rage. "I don't care if it kills you. Haul your ass up that hill."

Without warning, John Baggott emerged from the mass of students. "Screw this," he said, and marched down the hill.

Margot paused midway up the hill, sticky and uncomfortable in her oversize sweats, and gulped huge mouthfuls of air as she tried to calm herself down. Beneath the layers of cotton and microfiber, her heart pounded in her chest, not from the physical exertion of hill charges, but from outrage as she witnessed Coach Creed's latest assault on Theodore Baranski.

"I said, move it!" Coach Creed growled. "Everyone's waiting for you."

Margot understood the degradation, the knowledge that every set of eyes was on him, judging his overweight body, murmuring "fat ass" under their breath while they tacitly assumed the obesity was his fault. Without thinking, Margot touched her forearm through the sleeve of her sweatshirt. She desperately wanted to help Theo, but how could she without ruining DGM's plan?

Suddenly, the tall, lithe figure of John Baggott ambled over to Coach Creed.

"'Scuse me!" he said, his voice light and his angular face all smiles. "Don't mean to interrupt, but are you Theo Baranski?"

Margot started. What was John doing? Why didn't Bree stop him?

Coach Creed whirled around. "What do you want, Baggott?"

John coolly met Coach Creed's glare. "I came from the office," he said, still smiling. "Father Uberti asked me to fetch Theo from gym class. Some kind of emergency."

The idea that Father Uberti had personally requested an errand from John Baggott was ridiculous to the point of being farcical, but short of calling John a liar, Coach Creed had little recourse.

"An emergency," Coach Creed repeated.

"Yep," John said with an affable grin. He patted Theo on the shoulder. "We should hurry."

Coach Creed shook his head in disgust as John led Theo up the hill. "You're pathetic, Baranski," he called out. "You too, Baggott. I'm not done with either of you."

Margot stood rooted in place long after Coach Creed had stormed off across the field and the rest of sixth-period gym class had filtered back to their assignments. It took her a moment to realize that three figures still ringed the top of the hillside, silhouetted against the bright afternoon sunshine: Kitty Wei, Bree Deringer, and Olivia Hayes.

They looked at one another, shifting their glances as if they were all thinking the same thing. An hour ago, a revenge plot against Coach Creed would have generated no obvious suspects. But now, Bree's best friend would be at the top of Father Uberti's list. One degree of separation from an actual DGM member was too close for comfort. Should they abort or not?

All eyes drifted to Kitty. She'd know what to do.

Without hesitation, Kitty drew her hand across her chest, from her left shoulder to her right, giving the signal, then dropped her arm to her side and strode away.

Margot let out a slow breath. The message was clear: their plan against Coach Creed was a go.

TWO

MARGOT GNAWED AT THE STUBBY NAIL OF HER LEFT INDEX finger as she filed into the gym with the rest of her AP Government class for Friday's assembly. The white noise of student chatter punctuated by the occasional squeak of rubber soles against the highly polished maple floor faded into the background as her nerves overwhelmed her. Margot was crawling out of her skin—almost as if it was her first mission with DGM instead of her seventh—and it took every ounce of self-control not to flee campus at a full sprint and beg her parents for a transfer to the local public high school first thing in the morning.

Calm down.

Margot had known exactly what she was getting into when she agreed to join Don't Get Mad. She remembered the moment vividly, as if only two hours had passed instead of almost two years. Freshman religion class, and Kitty, Margot, Bree, and Olivia had been randomly grouped together for a community service project. The four of them had virtually nothing in common: no mutual friends, no shared interests whatsoever. But when it came time to choose an outreach program for the project, all four of them picked the same one—an antibullying awareness group.

No surprise, really. There was a huge disparity between the wealthy students at Bishop DuMaine and their scholarship classmates, between those with privilege and those without. Bullying was rampant—from rich girls who label-shamed poorer students to locker-room fights and lunch-hour shake downs—and Father Uberti had turned a blind eye. All he cared about were high test scores and athletic championships, both of which boosted enrollment.

So during an afternoon study session when the conversation turned toward the latest hazing incident at school, and Kitty half-jokingly commented that someone ought to give the varsity football team a taste of their own medicine, Margot—who had experienced firsthand what happened when an administration allowed bullies to rule unchecked—had agreed. DGM had been born.

Still, the stress of what they were about to do was taking its toll. Margot squeezed her eyes shut and took a slow, silent breath through clenched teeth. *Remember what Dr. Tournay says: panic is a state of mind—quiet the mind, quiet the panic.*

Margot inched her way toward the bleachers; the excitement in the gym was palpable, increasing Margot's antsiness. She had to remember that she was doing something important. She couldn't go back in time and erase the nightmare that had been junior high, but she *could* make sure that no one else had to endure the same bullying, or be driven to the same desperate decision that she had made four years ago.

Just as her nerves began to steady, something heavy barreled into her from behind, knocking her off-balance. Her eyes flew open as her backpack sailed through the air from the force of the impact, hitting the floor of the basketball court so violently the flap ripped open, spewing its contents in all directions.

Her assailant spun around, flipping his own mostly empty backpack onto the ground next to her oversize cargo pack in a display of outrage. Rex Cavanaugh.

"What the hell, freshman?" Rex bellowed. "Watch where you're going."

Margot swallowed the biting comeback forming at the tip of her tongue as she eyed the entrails of her backpack strewn across the gym floor. The remote control! She dropped to her knees, frantically retrieving her belongings. If the remote was damaged or lost, the mission would fail.

Rex snatched his bag off the floor next to her. "Great manners. Not even a 'sorry.' Idiot."

Pens, loose papers, an array of notebooks. But no remote. Margot seized her bag. She ripped open Velcro pockets and unzipped countless organizational compartments, rifling through her supplies in search of the palm-size remote. *Please be there.*

Inside the laptop sleeve her fingers closed around the plastic controller, intact and unharmed. Margot sighed. Crisis averted.

The loudspeakers crackled as the facilities manager set up a microphone. The assembly was about to start.

The near disaster with the remote galvanized Margot's

resolve. She caught up with her class and filed diligently into a row of bleachers, remote gripped firmly in her hand. She didn't dare scan the gym to find Bree and Olivia, but she spotted Kitty right away, on a bench in the first row next to Mika Jones. Kitty looked so calm and composed, dressed simply in jeans and a blue and white Bishop DuMaine running jacket, her long black hair swept up in a tight ponytail, which swished from side to side as she whispered to Mika. Margot wondered if Kitty really felt so at ease or whether it was all a facade.

The side door flew open, and Father Uberti marched into the gym. Short and wiry, the school principal was meticulously groomed as always. His salt-and-pepper mustache and Van Dyke beard were neatly trimmed, his dark, wavy hair—dyed, Margot was relatively sure—tamed with a healthy dose of sculpting wax. He moved quickly; the black capuche he wore over his long cassock fluttered about his shoulders, and the tassels of his cincture whipped back and forth from the ferocity of his stride. His entire demeanor was cocky, and before he got halfway across the floor, Margot realized why.

Two Menlo Park police officers followed him into the gym.

All of Margot's panic returned in an instant. Never in her most far-flung calculations had she anticipated law enforcement.

What if they got caught? She'd get arrested, or worse—kicked out of school. She'd lose any chance at Harvard or Yale and her parents . . . Her parents would kill her.

Margot's right leg bounced up and down on the bleacher so furiously she was sure the entire row could feel the reverberations.

Through her sweater sleeve, she gripped her knee, trying to squeeze it into submission, but her heart was racing out of control, her upper lip already damp with perspiration. Panic attack in three . . . two . . . one . . .

"Are you okay?" a voice said, close to her ear.

Margot let out a strangled squeak as she spun around on the bench and came nose to chin with a boy.

"Are you okay?" he repeated.

Margot opened her mouth to say something, but the capacity for rational thought had momentarily abandoned her. All she could do was stare at the most beautiful face she'd ever seen.

Not that there was anything particularly unique about him. His hair was a typical California blond—streaked by the sun with dark undertones. His skin was tan, and together with broad, muscular shoulders suggested a preference for spending weekends on a surfboard in Santa Cruz. But add in the off-kilter grin and the slightest hint of spicy aftershave, and it set Margot's heart thundering in her chest once more.

"Sorry," he said, with a smile that listed to the left like an unbalanced ship. "I didn't mean to scare you."

"You didn't scare me," Margot forced herself to say.

"Oh!" His eyebrows pinched together in confusion. "Okay. I just . . . It looked like I startled you."

Crap, Margot. Try not to sound like such a jerk. "I mean," she started, "I was just thinking. About classes. I have a big paper due."

"On the third day of school?"

"Um, yeah," Margot rambled on. "It's an extension class. At

16

Stanford. That's where my mind was. Why I was tense. No other reason." *Oh my God, stop talking!*

The boy blinked several times, then smiled again, tilting his head to the right as if attempting to compensate for his crooked grin. "I'm Logan Blaine," he said simply. "I'm new here."

"M-Margot," she said, stumbling over her own name like a halfwit. "Margot Mejia."

"Nice to meet you, Margot."

Margot was about to respond, when a current of laughter rippled through the gym. Coach Creed stood near the top of the bleachers, glaring down at the round face of Theo Baranski.

"Baranski!" Coach Creed barked, louder than was necessary. "Why aren't you in your seat?" He swept his arm across the gym in a grand arc. "The entire school is waiting on *you* to start this assembly. Would you like to tell us why you're having difficulty finding someplace to sit?"

"I . . ." Theo glanced down at the bench. There was a tiny sliver of space left at the end, maybe enough room for a fourth grader to squeeze half his skinny butt onto, and Theo was neither skinny nor a fourth grader. Margot cringed, waiting for the inevitable barrage of abuse from Coach Creed, but unlike yesterday, Theo was spared the humiliation. A freshman girl at the end of the bench stood up and slid into the row behind, leaving enough room for Theo to sit.

"Saved by a girl," Coach Creed said with a laugh. "How sad."

Logan leaned forward, his lips close to Margot's ear. "Is he always such an asshole?"

"Coach Creed?"

17

"Yeah. That guy deserves a public flogging."

Margot glanced at Logan, then fixed her eyes on Father Uberti as he approached the microphone. She squeezed the remote control more tightly.

"Yes," she said softly. "Yes, he does."

THREE

BREE WATCHED FATHER UBERTI PULL THE BLACK LEATHER tassels of his cincture through his hand, letting them slap against his left leg. "Everyone find a seat."

The gym quieted instantly. No one whispered, no one laughed. Even John was completely silent; his eyes, like everyone else's, were fixed on the microphone.

"Thank you," Father Uberti said, without an ounce of sincerity. He cleared his throat with unusual violence, as if to punish his vocal cords for insubordination. "I've called this assembly today to address a threat that has weaseled its way into the very soul of our school."

He paused and placed his hand over the cross that hung around his neck as if to convey the special hurt that had been inflicted upon him. Bree fought the urge to puke in her lap.

"We want to begin this school year on the right foot—free from the constant menace of the anonymous student or group of students known as DGM."

Silence. Bree had expected an outbreak of stunned murmurs,

but apparently the subject of the assembly was about as unforeseen as Liberace coming out of the closet.

"In order to shut DGM down," Father Uberti continued, "we need your help. Your information. We have with us today Sergeant Callahan from the Menlo Park Police Department to discuss the illegal"—he paused again, for special emphasis—"I repeat, the *illegal* actions of this group."

Bree covered her mouth with her hand to hide her smile as Sergeant Callahan stepped to the microphone. She loved the element of danger in each DGM mission, so much so that she usually volunteered for the jobs that might get her in trouble, such as breaking into the school gym over the weekend to install an unsanctioned video playback device in the AV room. In some ways, she almost wished she would get caught. Expulsion from Bishop DuMaine would be a surefire way to piss off her dad. And even if he did follow through on his oft-repeated threat to send her to a convent school back east, it would totally be worth it to see his disapproving face turn purple with impotent rage.

"Good morning." Sergeant Callahan's tone was crisp and efficient. "At the request of Father Uberti, Menlo PD has implemented a hotline for anonymous tips on DGM. We ask that you keep your eyes and ears open. Any clue, no matter how insignificant it seems, could lead to possible suspects."

John rested his chin on Bree's shoulder. "Sounds like a witch hunt," he whispered.

Yeah, and I'm the witch.

"Thank you, Sergeant Callahan." Father Uberti shook his hand, then addressed the student body once more. "We hope these steps will lead to the apprehension of the perpetrators whose mean-spirited attacks on our students have plagued Bishop DuMaine for the past three semesters."

Mean-spirited? Bree closed her eyes to keep from rolling them. Father Uberti could not give less of a crap about the mean-spirited bullying that went on at his school. And if he wasn't going to do anything about it, Don't Get Mad would.

"Now, to introduce a short video presentation by the leadership class, your student body vice president, Kitty Wei."

Six inches taller than Father Uberti, Kitty had to tilt the microphone all the way back and bend forward at the waist to reach it. "Good morning, DuMaine Dukes!" She smiled wide, her voice steady. "Let's face it, there's a part of each of us that kind of envies DGM."

A buzz of whispers swelled through the gym. It sounded to Bree like the students of Bishop DuMaine agreed.

"But we want to make sure our school is a safe, caring environment for everyone," Kitty continued. "So we've put together a short video about what we can do to honor and uphold the name of Bishop DuMaine."

Kitty straightened up. Quickly, casually, she tucked a nonexistent strand of hair behind her right ear. It was an innocuous movement, one every girl in school made a dozen times a day without noticing.

It was the signal Bree had been waiting for.

Kitty smiled. "I hope you'll enjoy our little presentation," she said, and backed away from the microphone.

◆ ◆ ◆

Kitty watched Father Uberti out of the corner of her eye as he pulled an oversize remote control from the depths of his cassock and aimed it at a small window near the top of the far wall. The video player inside the AV room whirred to life, projecting a clear, ten-foot-tall image of the Bishop DuMaine logo on the screen above her head.

Generic Muzak played as a montage of photos faded in and out, depicting students of every shape, size, and color laughing, posing, eating lunch around the outdoor quad. It was the kind of teen utopia adults envisioned for their kids, all perfectly understanding and cooperative and nice, the parental illusion of a modern high school. Only the students at Bishop DuMaine knew better. High school was a vicious place.

The Muzak faded and a light voice chimed in. "At Bishop DuMaine, we're a family, a team working together for the good of our school and of each—"

Kitty's heart leaped to her throat. The image on the screen froze, then blipped as the piggybacked player Bree had installed over the weekend took control of the playback.

As promised, Margot's tech had worked perfectly.

A new image popped onto the screen: a bedroom, messy and disheveled. A sinewy arm yanked a chair into view and the burly figure of Coach Creed plopped down in front of the camera.

"I'm Richard Creed," he said, his best shit-eating grin plastered across his face. "But you can call me Dick." He wore a blue wifebeater two sizes too small, and his bulky arms looked as if he'd oiled them up with an entire tub of Crisco. He jabbed a thumb at his chest. "And I'm here"—he paused and pointed to the camera—"to give you three reasons why I'm going to win *America's Next Fitness Model*."

"Oh my God!" Coach Creed's roar pierced the silence of the packed gym. Kitty couldn't see him, only hear the general ruckus from the upper bleachers as he pounded his way downstairs.

Father Uberti grabbed Kitty roughly by the shoulder. "What's going on?" he hissed. "What is this?"

Kitty looked down at him and desperately wished she had even an ounce of Olivia's acting skills. "I have no idea," she said, trying to sound utterly bewildered. "The video started and then . . ." She let her voice trail off, and her eyes drifted back to the screen.

The video jump-cut to a new scene of Coach Creed seated behind an ornately carved wooden desk. Behind him, full floor-to-ceiling bookshelves flanked each side of a large window. The blinds were open to bright sunshine cascading across the front lawn of Bishop DuMaine Preparatory School.

The entire gymnasium heaved one air-sucking gasp. Everyone recognized that view.

"My office?" Father Uberti growled.

"Reason number one," Coach Creed said, gesturing to the library on either side of him. "I'm not just a fitness guru, I'm an academic." He leaned back in Father Uberti's leather chair and propped a sneaker-clad foot up on the desk next to a framed photograph of the Pope. "Which makes me smarter than the average model, without sacrificing beauty for brains."

"Douche!" someone yelled.

The next scene showed a full-body image of Coach Creed

dangling from a pull-up bar. In addition to the skintight tank top, he also sported a pair of circa-1975 blue running shorts trimmed in gold, so inappropriately short that Kitty was terrified his man parts might peek out through the leg hole as he pulled his chin up over the bar. "Forty-nine," he counted, his voice grunting with fatigue.

The audience erupted into laughter.

"Turn it off!" Coach Creed screamed. He tore across the basketball court and ripped the remote from Father Uberti's hand. He marched toward the booth, pointing the useless device at the window. "Work, you dumbass. Work!"

On the video, Creed strained into another chin-up. "Fifty."

He let his body fall to the floor. "Reason number two: fifty pull-ups," he panted. "One for each year of me. Dick Creed only gets better with age." Coach Creed struck a bodybuilder's pose. "Yeah, you like that?"

Peals of laughter threatened total chaos. Father Uberti grabbed the microphone. "Mr. Phillips," he said. "Get the AV room open. Now!"

The facilities manager was at the door already, searching his ring frantically for the correct key. Kitty smiled to herself. It wasn't there. Olivia had stolen the AV room key, and Bree had disposed of it after installing the video player. After several seconds, Mr. Phillips ran from the gym, probably to fetch the duplicate set.

Coach Creed threw the remote to the ground and sprinted to the locked door, wringing the handle with his meaty hands. "Someone open this fucking door!"

The screen changed again, and the gym quieted as every student and half the teachers sat on the edges of their seats in anticipation. The new setting was a backyard pool. It was an overcast day, but the gray haze didn't stop reality-show audi-tionee Dick Creed. He lounged on a beach towel by the water's edge, his blue tank and track shorts discarded for a pair of swim briefs. His aging, overly tanned skin hung limply from his body, and his stomach resembled a deflated balloon, a combination of taut and flabby that reminded Kitty of Captain Kirk in the old *Star Trek* episodes her dad so dearly loved.

"Reason number three." He cocked his left eyebrow. "Let's face it, Dick Creed is a sexy piece of man meat. The ladies love it, can't get enough of it, and will tune in every week for more, I guarantee." He picked up a glass of sparkling wine and toasted the camera. "Smart, strong, and sexy. Dick Creed is all three and more. Don't you think that's worth an audition?" He winked and the screen went dark.

No one moved. The gymnasium held its collective breath. Father Uberti stopped screaming for Mr. Phillips, his jaw fro-zen midword, and even Coach Creed stopped pounding his fists against the AV room door as one final image faded onto the screen.

Black type against a white background, in an unmistakable custom font that looked like it came from an old-fashioned type-writer.

Compliments of DGM

FOUR

IT HAD TAKEN MARGOT MOST OF THE DAY TO GET HER NERVES IN
check after the assembly. Her hands shook all through the rest of
first period, and her heart was still racing when the bell rang at
the end of sixth-period PE.

Normally, DGM missions weren't so much about public
humiliation as they were about evening the playing field between
the powerful and the powerless, but Coach Creed had been a special case. She'd been half-afraid that he would pop a blood vessel
in his head and stroke out right there on the basketball court,
making her an accessory to murder, but the look on Theo's face
had been worth it. She'd watched in satisfaction as he smiled,
at first tentative and unsure, then swelling with confidence as
the video continued until he was absolutely beaming from ear
to ear. At one point, a classmate two rows behind reached out
and patted him on the shoulder. Then another and another, as if
they recognized that Theo was finally getting retribution for all
Coach Creed had put him through.

Justice had been served.

Even now as she trudged home from school, the memory calmed her. She was doing something good. She was making a difference. That's what Don't Get Mad was for: getting revenge for those who couldn't get it for themselves.

Margot held her breath as she opened the front door, her ears alert for any sign of her parents. Silence. The house was empty.

She closed and locked the door behind her, exhaling slowly with relief. The last thing she wanted to do was answer twenty questions about her day.

Not that her parents ever completely left her alone. There was always a to-do list on the kitchen counter, as if she was a twelve-year-old latchkey kid who couldn't be trusted not to eat ice cream and watch cartoons for three hours until her parents came home.

God forbid.

Today's list was one of her mom's masterpieces.

2:45—Arrive home
2:50—After-school snack (apple or banana and one slice of cheese)
3:00–4:00—Calculus homework (if finished early, move on to the next item)
4:00–5:00—Additional homework as assigned per Bishop DuMaine
5:00–5:15—Break. Perform at least one of Dr. Tournay's meditation exercises, minimum ten minutes
5:15–6:00—Homework for Stanford extension classes
6:00–7:00—Family dinner

*7:00–7:30—Thirty minutes of television, either news or
    Jeopardy!*
7:30–8:00—Shower
*8:00–11:00—If your reading for Stanford extension is
    completed, in addition to all other school projects, you
    may read for pleasure*

Of course by "pleasure" her mom meant she could choose a classic of Western literature, predetermined by the Advanced English Literature course selections from Harvard, Yale, and Stanford. Margot laughed mirthlessly. Nothing more pleasurable than three hours of Chaucer or Hardy to end her day.

And her parents wondered why she'd tried to kill herself.

Margot's suicide attempt almost four years ago had come as a complete shock to her parents. Not that there hadn't been signs; Margot had done all she could to express her unhappiness. She'd cried every morning for weeks, desperate not to go to school. She'd told her parents about the bullying, about how she didn't have any friends, about how she hated herself. But her parents refused to believe it, as if acknowledging that their daughter was in crisis was commentary on their parenting skills. And in the wake of her attempt, they decided that they had been too lenient on their only child, too accommodating of her free will, and so they'd taken a new tack. Margot's days would be übercontrolled, overscheduled, and micromanaged to within seconds. She would have no free time and absolutely no opportunity to ponder how miserable she was. In her parents' eyes, this would be happiness.

For Margot, it was all about maintenance. Seven hundred and twenty-two days until she was off to college, preferably on the East Coast. Then she'd be free of everything—her parents, her past, and the thoughts of both that haunted her.

With a heavy sigh, Margot reached out and dragged her overstuffed backpack across the dining room. Seven hundred and twenty-two days. But for now, calculus.

Margot shoved her hand into the main compartment of her cargo pack in search of her favorite mechanical pencil, but instead, her fingers grazed something slick and hard. She pulled out the strange item and found it was a slim plastic case holding a single DVD.

Probability that it wasn't in her backpack at the start of her school day? One hundred percent.

Curious, Margot slid the DVD from its case. It was homemade, with a note scrawled across its face.

Rex, dude, check this out!

The DVD must have gotten mixed up with her things after her collision with Rex Cavanaugh. A private video for Rex? This had opportunity written all over it.

Margot fired up her laptop.

"Why do we always have to use the back entrance?" John asked, leaning against the doorway.

Bree sighed. "Because my dad monitors the security footage from the front door." She nudged John aside so she could reach the security keypad by the servants' entrance, then keyed in the four-digit entry code, waited for the lock to click, and swung the door open.

John paused, glancing at the two security cameras. "So what are these, decorative?"

Bree shoved him into the house. "No, but he doesn't check the feed."

"Why n—"

Bree slammed the door in his face and hurried back around to the front of the house so her dad would have video proof that she was home, on time, and alone. Not that he cared, particularly, what she did after school, as long as it didn't make the six o'clock news. But the less her father knew about her friends, the better. It gave him fewer opportunities to criticize.

John might fantasize about how cool it would be to have a superstar politician and heir apparent to the governor's mansion for a dad, but for Bree, the reality had been sixteen years of being reminded that she was the black sheep of the family who didn't conform, didn't appreciate her advantages, didn't understand how important it was to maintain her dad's carefully groomed image as the perfect family man.

Bree had never understood why he couldn't leave her alone. He already had one perfect child—Bree's older brother, Henry Jr., an honors student at Columbia. Why did he need two?

"So what shall we listen to today?" Bree called out as she tramped up the stairs. She dragged her army surplus messenger bag behind her and derived a sense of satisfaction from the way it thudded against each hardwood step. "Killers or—" She pushed her bedroom door open, expecting to find John ensconced in the beanbag chair as usual, but the room was empty. "John?"

A heavy thud echoed from her walk-in closet. "Damn," John said, leaning against the closet door. "You've got a lot of shit in here."

"Private shit," Bree said. "What the hell were you doing in there?"

John collapsed into the beanbag chair. "You let me drive your dad's car. I know the security code for the house *and* your locker combination. Why freak out because I'm in your closet? Afraid Senator Deringer will catch me perving through your unmentionables?"

Bree stiffened at the mention of her father. "He's in Sacramento."

"And your mom's with him?"

"Sure," Bree said. That was as good a lie as any.

"Oh."

"Why do you care where my parents are?"

John stretched his long legs out in front of him. "I thought maybe they'd get off your case if they met me."

"A rock musician and the number-one name on F.U.'s DGM suspect list?" Bree copped a snooty accent. "You're hardly a suitable friend for the daughter of Senator Henry Deringer."

John heaved himself out of the beanbag and headed toward the bathroom. "I'd kill to know who's actually behind DGM. They're amazing. Seriously."

Bree smiled as he closed the door. Knowing that her best friend approved of DGM made her feel kind of warm and—

Bree's phone buzzed, interrupting her thought. An incoming text? Weird. The only person who ever texted her was John.

Olivia was bone tired by the time Peanut dropped her off. She'd barely been able to focus on her friend's nervous chatter, and as she climbed the stairs to the one-bedroom apartment she and her mom shared, Olivia felt the weight of her body in every exhausted step.

All she wanted to do was vegetate in front of some bad TV for a couple of hours.

No such luck.

"So! Who drove you home in that gorgeous convertible? New boyfriend?" Olivia's mom leaned back against the kitchen counter, dressed for her bartending job. Her thick, dark hair was pulled back into a severe ponytail, and her makeup was dramatic to match: liquid-liner cat eyes, highlighting shimmer, deep-red lips. Tight jeans tucked into a pair of knee-high boots completed the look, along with a black scoop-neck T-shirt that showed so much cleavage, Olivia had to avert her eyes.

"Aren't you late for work?" Olivia asked, hoping she didn't sound as annoyed as she felt.

Her mom sighed like a peevish child. "Don't be such a mom all the time, Livvie."

Olivia grabbed a can of diet soda from the fridge and sat down at the table. *Someone had to.*

"I wanted to hear about the fall play." Her mom leaned

forward. "Has Mr. Cunningham announced it yet?"

"I told you," Olivia said slowly. "Mr. Cunningham is out all week. He's not back until Monday." Did her mom listen to anything she said?

"Hm. We should probably start prepping your audition over the weekend."

We? "Mom . . ."

"I've already flagged a few monologues. Just a cross section of genres, so you'll be prepared. I realized today that we haven't even touched the classics in months, so we'll start there."

Olivia cocked an eyebrow. Her mom's manic moods were almost always triggered by something acting related, which made Olivia extremely nervous. As excited as her mom got for each and every local theater audition, the depression that overwhelmed her when she didn't get the part frequently left her unable to leave her bed for days. "Did you have another audition today?" she asked warily.

"Yes!" Her mom paced back and forth in the minuscule kitchen. "And you'll never guess what for." She didn't even wait for her daughter to hazard a guess. "Olivia in *Twelfth Night*! My favorite role. Have I ever told you about my performance of Olivia at the Public Theater?"

Only about a million times. "I think so."

"The reviews were amazing. 'June Hayes entranced as Olivia,'" she quoted from memory. "'A fantastic, exhilarating new face at the Public.'"

Her mom's eyes drifted to a framed picture on the wall, showing Olivia's mom in an ornate Elizabethan costume. She beamed in the photo, her eyes bright with excitement and joy. That production of *Twelfth Night* was one of her mom's last stage roles. She'd gotten pregnant soon after and now the only time she saw that spark in her mom's eyes was after one of Olivia's performances.

Olivia could feel her mom slipping into the darkness of lost dreams and unrealized potential. It was not a pretty place. "Aren't you going to be late, Mom?"

Her mom glanced at the clock on the microwave. "Shit!" She gathered up her purse and keys, then planted a hurried kiss on Olivia's forehead. "Study the monologues tonight and we can pick one this weekend."

Olivia didn't realize she'd been holding her breath until the echo of her mom's heels had faded to nothing. She released all the air in her lungs, then slowly stood up and walked to her room. The day bed in the living room was still rumpled, a clear sign that her mom had slept late into the afternoon, but Olivia didn't stop to make it up. She'd do that later. Instead, she glanced out the window and caught sight of her mom's blue Civic turning onto the street.

Confident she was alone, Olivia crouched next to her bed and groped around underneath until her hand rested on a large Tupperware container wedged behind some old shoe boxes.

The smell hit her the moment she cracked the seal on the rubber lid. Sugar. She inhaled deeply, letting the tangy, sweet odor invade her nostrils. She dug past candy bars and dark chocolate peanut butter cups, and pulled out a pack of frosted cupcakes. She'd have to do her Pilates DVD twice to make up for the calories, but she didn't care.

Olivia flopped onto her bed and shoved one entire cupcake into her mouth. The Bishop DuMaine fall theater production seemed so frivolous in comparison to what DGM had accomplished that day. Another bully given a taste of his own medicine. Another victim given a sense of retribution.

A soft chime drifted up from Olivia's purse. A text coming in on her cell.

Olivia sighed as she reached for the phone. Each time DGM pulled off another mission, Olivia hoped it would make her feel better, erase the mistakes she'd made and the overwhelming sense of her own compliance in the reign of terror perpetrated by Amber, Rex, and the rest of the people she called "friends."

It never did.

Kitty's eleven-year-old twin sisters tackled her the moment she came through the front door.

"Kitty!" Sophia screamed as she tore down the hallway.

Lydia was barely two steps behind. "Why are you home so early?"

"Practice was cancel—"

"Play with us," Lydia demanded.

"We're doing Percy Jackson," Sophia added.

"We need you for Blackjack," Lydia said. For some reason, the twins loved to pretend their big sister was a talking Pegasus.

"Okay, okay." Kitty laughed, extricating herself from too many pairs of arms. "Can I drop my stuff in my room first before you guys pull me limb from limb?"

Lydia stuck out her lower lip. "Five minutes, that's all."

"Or we're coming to get you," Sophia said.

Kitty couldn't help but smile as she trekked down the hall to her room. There was something comforting about coming home to her sisters, who were still so innocent, so happy, and so trusting. They hadn't yet discovered that boys were anything other than gross, or that everyone in their world wouldn't always be nice, wouldn't always have their best interests at heart. One of the reasons Kitty fought so hard for DGM was the thought that somehow she was protecting her sisters.

Kitty stashed her duffel bag in the corner of her room. She'd deal with homework later. It was time to role-play a talking, flying horse for her sisters.

She was just leaving the room when her cell phone buzzed.

"Five minutes!" Lydia shrieked from the living room.

"Hurry up, Kitty!" Sophia chimed in.

Kitty grabbed her cell and opened the text message as she walked down the hallway. She paused midstep, immediately recognizing the phone number of the emergency DGM burner phone.

We need to meet tonight.

FIVE

FIVE HOURS LATER, KITTY SAT PATIENTLY ON AN UNFINISHED table in her uncle's furniture warehouse. She took a deep breath. The smell of wood shavings and linseed oil reminded her of childhood, when she'd spent hours playing in the dark recesses of the work space while her mom helped out in the office. She always felt safe here, which is probably why she'd chosen it as the secret meeting place for DGM.

A chair creaked as Margot checked her watch for the fifth time in the last twenty minutes. She sighed heavily, as if Olivia's lateness was somehow unexpected. "She's never this late."

"She's *always* this late," Bree corrected.

"She'll be here." Inside, Kitty was as jittery as Margot, but she tried to keep her voice calm. She was their leader. She had to act like it.

A knock echoed through the warehouse. One rap, a pause, then three more knocks, hollow and deep.

"Finally," Margot muttered.

Kitty threw a steel bolt on the heavy metal door, and

cracked it just enough for someone to slip inside.

"Sorry!" Olivia skittered across the concrete floor, teetering on her sky-high heels. "My bus was late."

"Your bus is always late," Bree said.

Olivia flounced into an open chair and cast a sidelong glance at Bree. "Not all of us get to drive Daddy's brand-new Lexus," she said, her tone icy.

"Cut it out, you guys," Kitty said. "That's not why we're here." Olivia and Bree got along about as well as toothpaste and orange juice, and sometimes Kitty felt like she spent the majority of their meetings keeping them in their respective fight corners.

"Why *are* we here?" Bree asked. She tipped her chair back and propped her boots on the table. "Another target? Please tell me we're going after Amber Stevens."

"No!" The word practically exploded from Margot's mouth.

Bree swung around, clearly taken aback. "Why not? Amber's the biggest cowbag at school. If anyone could use a massive bitch slap, it's her."

"Not yet," Margot said, a tremor in her voice. "I'll tell you when it's time to go after Amber."

Bree opened her mouth to say something, then thought better of it and turned her attention to her fingers, chipping off flecks of blue nail polish.

Olivia raised her hand. "So why did you call the meeting, Kitty?"

"I didn't." Kitty nodded toward Margot. "She did."

Without a word, Margot placed her laptop on the table. The thinnest notebook Kitty had ever seen, it fired up in an instant, and Margot opened a browser window without connecting to a wireless signal.

"Damn," Bree said. "Where did you get that, the CIA?"

"Department of Defense, actually," Margot said. "My parents' new prototype. Three-terabyte solid-state disk, thumbprint identification, bulletproof casing, and a Core i13 processor that won't hit the general marketplace for at least another two years."

Olivia gaped. "That is so hot."

Margot stepped aside so they could see the screen. "Behold, our next target."

Kitty, Bree, and Olivia all leaned in to get a good look at the guy on Margot's computer. He was lanky and blond, and wore an Abercrombie and Fitch sweatshirt and a backward Arizona Cardinals cap. His face was heavily dotted with acne, his smile wide and angular.

"Who is he?" Olivia asked.

"Ronny DeStefano."

Olivia shook her head. "Never heard of him."

"I saw him at school yesterday," Bree said. "In a 'Maine Men shirt. Looked like a new recruit."

"He is," Margot said. "Just transferred."

Kitty glanced up at Margot, suddenly on guard. "How can he already be on our hit list if he just got here?"

Margot toggled to a video player. "Does *she* look familiar?"

The jostling video clip started up as Margot hit the space bar, revealing a face so close to the screen you could see the crocodile pattern of his skin. It pulled away and revealed Ronny, smiling ear to ear. He talked to the camera in a raspy whisper. "Dudes, you're not going to believe this fucking hot chick in my bed."

He stepped aside to reveal a half-naked girl in the bed behind him. She lay on her back wearing only a pair of jeans, the dark skin of her breasts bare to the camera. Her eyes were half-open, mascara and liner smudged to full-scale raccoonage.

All the warmth drained out of Kitty's body. "Oh my God," she whispered, her throat constricting as if it didn't want to say her name. "It's Mika."

"Mika?" Ronny asked, his voice slimy. "Do you want to make out with me?"

Mika nodded, reaching up for him. "Mm-hm."

"What's that?" he asked. "I didn't hear you."

"I want," Mika panted. "Make out."

Ronny pushed his lips to hers, planting a sloppy kiss all over her face.

Totally fucked up as she was, Mika kissed him back and pulled his body down on top of her. After a second, Ronny pushed himself up, and Kitty half-hoped he was going to do something decent, like cover her up and take her home.

Instead, he turned to the camera and gave an exaggerated thumbs-up while Mika began to paw at his shirt. "And that, gentlemen, is a wrap. You said I couldn't bag a Cali girl within three months of getting here and I totally faced you. The bet is won. I believe you owe me a hundred dollars each, payable in cash. Suckas!"

Then he switched off the camera and the screen went blank.

SIX

KITTY FELT AS IF ALL THE AIR HAD BEEN SUCKED OUT OF HER lungs as she stared at the computer, dumbstruck.

"Asshole!" Bree said, taking the word out of Kitty's mouth. "Is that shit on the internet?"

Margot shook her head. "It was just a DVD. But it's only a matter of time before it gets around."

"How did you find it?" Olivia asked.

Margot tugged at the sleeves of her sweatshirt. "It was meant for Rex. He rammed into me at the assembly, and our bags went flying. The DVD must have gotten mixed up with my stuff."

"We should call the police," Kitty said through clenched teeth. "Can't he be prosecuted?"

"He was smart," Margot said. "Got Mika to ask him to make out with her, and didn't film anything more incriminating than that. If she'd gone to the police or the hospital that day, maybe they could have done something. But as it is, I'm not even sure she knows the video exists."

Kitty shot to her feet and started pacing the warehouse floor. "We can't let that video go public. We have to do something."

"Whoa," Bree said. "I thought we had a rule? At least six weeks between missions to let the heat die down."

Kitty raised her eyebrows. "Since when do you care about the rules?"

"Since never." Bree walked up to the computer screen and clicked on Ronny's Facebook page. "'Ronny DeStefano,'" she read out loud. "'Bishop DuMaine Preparatory School,' blah-blah-blah." She glanced up. "Oh, this guy's a winner. 'Religious views—chicks. Political views—lots of chicks.'"

Olivia recrossed her legs. "Well, this shouldn't be too hard."

"My thoughts exactly," Margot said. She pulled a file folder out of her bag and handed it to Bree. "Address and personal information. Ronny moved in with his dad and stepmother last spring after abruptly leaving his old school in Arizona, a private reform institution called Archway Military Academy."

Bree's head snapped up. "Archway Military Academy?"

"You've heard of it?" Kitty asked.

"Yeah." Bree paused. "Probably on the news or something." She turned her focus back to her chipped polish.

Despite the casual action, Kitty noticed that Bree's shoulders were tense and her breaths came more quickly than a moment before. Why had the name Archway bothered her?

Kitty filed the thought away for another time. It wasn't important at the moment. If they were going to move against Ronny, they needed to get the ball rolling as soon as possible. "Time'll be short on this one and we've got two main goals:

delete the video and find a way to make Ronny pay."

Margot nodded. "It'll have to be done from his home computer, like we did with Coach Creed." She glanced at Bree. "Which means you'll have to break in."

Bree rolled her eyes. "What else is new?"

"Margot will figure out the DeStefanos' home security situation and I'll start with background research," Kitty continued rapidly. "Bree, do some recon. Find out where he hangs out and who his friends are."

"Yay," Bree said unenthusiastically. "You two get to sit at home on your computers while I hide in the bushes again."

Kitty ignored her. "Olivia, initiate contact. Get his interest and keep it."

Olivia squinted at Ronny's profile photo. "Why can't we ever have hot targets?"

"I'll go with you," Margot said. "I can try to clone his phone while you keep him occupied."

"So we're going to do this, right?" Kitty asked. "We're all agreed?"

Olivia and Margot nodded, but Bree didn't move.

"We *all* have to be on board," Kitty said, more pointedly. "Breaking our timeline rule will make this mission even more dangerous." She thrust her right hand forward.

"I, Kitty Wei, do solemnly swear, no secrets—ever—shall leave this square."

Margot was beside her in an instant, her right arm extended.

"I, Margot Mejia, do solemnly swear, no secrets—ever—shall leave this square."

Kitty grasped Margot's wrist through the thick layer of her XXL sweater as Olivia extended her right arm with a ballerina's elegance.

"*I, Olivia Hayes, do solemnly swear, no secrets—ever—shall leave this square.*"

Margot linked Olivia into the square, then all three of them turned to Bree. The square was incomplete without her presence—her wrist linked to Olivia, her hand grasping Kitty—and she knew it.

"Tell me something," Bree said, her eyes suspicious. "Would you be asking us to do this if the victim wasn't one of your best friends?"

"Honestly?" Kitty asked.

"No, lie to me."

Kitty sighed. Bree was right: it was risky planning another mission this soon after their plot against Coach Creed, and she needed to remind everyone—herself included—of the stakes. "There's a lot on the line if we get caught," Kitty said. "We could get kicked out of school."

"That wouldn't be so bad," Bree muttered.

"But we started Don't Get Mad for a reason—to seek justice for classmates who are too scared to speak up for themselves." It was good to hear, good to remind herself why they put themselves on the line. "So I'd like to think that if I saw a video this horrific, victimizing someone I didn't know, I'd have the same reaction."

Bree stared at her for a moment, then without a word, she thrust her arm forward.

"*I, Bree Deringer, do solemnly swear, no secrets—ever—shall leave this square.*"

The square was complete, everyone was in agreement about the plan, but Kitty still looked each of them in the eye, just to make sure. She didn't see a hint of doubt in anyone.

"Ronny's a predator," she said. "And we can stop him from hurting someone else." Kitty thrust out her chin. "Don't get mad!"

All four girls answered in strong, solid unison.

"Get even!"

SEVEN

OLIVIA SCANNED THE QUAD, TRYING TO LOOK CASUAL. THE outdoor area teemed with groups of students enjoying lunch on a sunny Monday afternoon, and the air was filled with carefree giggles and chatter. It was a relaxed atmosphere for everyone except the four members of DGM.

Kitty sat on the edge of a planter beneath one of the enormous elm trees that dotted the grassy landscape, joined by Mika and several of their volleyball teammates. She seemed calm, but Olivia noted she avoided looking in her direction. Bree and John leaned against the wall of the science building, watching the crowd with their usual aloofness, but even from the other side of the quad, Olivia could see Bree's foot tapping nervously against the concrete. Only Margot was nowhere in sight. She was scouting Ronny's location, and as Olivia sat on the bench, sipping her diet soda, she kept her eye out for Margot's signal, which would put the plan into motion.

"Is that *all* you're eating for lunch?" Jezebel asked.

Olivia's attention was pulled back to the lunch table, where

46

Peanut had laid six celery sticks on a napkin and portioned out the contents of two slabs of low-calorie cheese spread among them. She topped each with a sprinkle of *fleur de sel*, produced from a tiny noncarcinogenic glass container, and a sprig of parsley.

Peanut picked up the nearest celery boat. "Yes. Mom says it's the perfect balance of negative calories and good fats."

Olivia was officially concerned about Peanut's newest diet. "Won't you be hungry in like an hour?"

"Mom says hunger pains are good." Peanut took a dainty bite, chewed it at least a dozen times, then swallowed.

"I don't know," Olivia said. "I'm not sure that's good for you."

Peanut glanced at Olivia's midsection. "Not all of us were born looking like a ballerina."

"Yeah," Jezebel said. "Some of you were born looking like a sumo wrestler."

"Ha, ha," Peanut mocked. She pointed at the prepackaged salad covered in cheese and thick dressing that sat in front of Jezebel. "Do you have any idea how many calories are in that thing?"

"Don't know," Jezebel said, taking a massive bite. "Don't care."

Peanut tucked her long, straight hair behind each ear. "Whatever. But I don't want to hear you bitch when Mr. Cunningham casts you in a male part again."

Olivia started. She'd forgotten that Mr. Cunningham would be announcing the play in fourth period.

"Better a man," Jezebel said, her low voice more masculine

than usual, "than no part at all."

"Ladies!" A gleam of braces and a whiff of strong and probably needless aftershave were the only harbingers of the skinny sophomore who spun onto the bench between Peanut and Jezebel. He slipped an arm around both of them. "How are my first, fourth, and twelfth favorite juniors?"

"Hey, Ed." Olivia couldn't keep her eyes from lingering on his bulging backpack as she wondered what contraband he was peddling today.

"Twelfth?" Peanut pouted. "Which of us is twelfth?"

Jezebel refused to look at him. "Ed the Head. What ladies' room did you crawl out of?"

Ed ignored her. "I've got a new shipment of junk food." He glanced at Olivia and pumped his eyebrows. "Including those salted caramel chocolate balls *someone* is addicted to."

Olivia gave Ed the Head a look that said, "Shut up before I pull your tongue out." The last thing she wanted was for Jezebel and Peanut to find out about her junk food addiction. She'd never hear the end of Peanut's lectures against processed food and Jezebel's warnings that someday Olivia would get fat from all the crap she ate.

"Or if you lovelies are all maintaining your girlish figures," he said, changing the subject, "I've also got a new batch of homework. Fresh off the nerd press. If you don't have the cashola, I also accept"—he leaned into Jezebel—"sexual favors."

"Ew?" Olivia said.

Jezebel elbowed him in the ribs. "Do you have any mind bleach to wipe that image from my brain?"

Ed the Head grinned broadly, flashing his full mouth of steel. "It's called tequila. And I'm all out. Sold the last of it to your mom."

Before Jezebel could formulate a response, Amber bounced onto the bench next to her. "What is that?" She sniffed the air, then wrinkled her nose like she'd entered a raw sewage treatment plant. "It smells like . . . dweeb."

"That's Mr. Dweeb to you." Ed the Head straightened his shoulders. "Don't you know it's the age of the geek?"

Amber's gaze was cold as ice. "Why are you here?"

A formidable shadow fell across the lunch table. "Yeah, why *are* you here?"

Ed the Head leaped to his feet as Rex, Kyle, and Tyler ringed the bench.

"Rex! Dude. Buddy." Ed the Head twittered nervously.

Rex folded his arms across his chest. "You have ten seconds."

"Er, right." Ed the Head eyed Kyle and Tyler. "I've been looking for you guys all weekend." He held out his hand expectantly. "Pony up."

Without a word, Kyle and Tyler reached for their wallets. Each fished out several bills and reluctantly slapped them into Ed the Head's palm.

Rex turned to Kyle. "What the fuck is going on?"

Ed the Head shoved the bills into his pocket and started to back away from the table. "Just a little bookmaking. I was running ten to one odds on DGM going balls out in response to our fearless leader's assembly Friday. Kyle, Tyler, and several of your dutiful 'Maine Men bet against it. Oopsie."

Rex balled up his fists and started after the retreating bookie. "You little shit."

Olivia had seen enough. She stepped in front of him and laid her hand on his chest. "Let him go, Rex."

Ed the Head saluted. "I am considerably out of here."

It took a few seconds for Rex to wrest his gaze away from the rapidly departing figure of Ed the Head, but eventually his eyes strayed to Olivia's hand.

"Fine," he said softly. His body relaxed like a rubber band gone limp. "You know as well as I do, Liv, that I'd do anything you want."

Olivia snatched her hand away. Seriously? He was flirting with her right in front of his girlfriend?

And Amber didn't miss a second of it. Her expensively crafted nose was wrinkled in disgust as Olivia returned to the bench. "Going after Ed the Head, Livvie? Yeah, I'm sure that'll bring Donté running back to you."

"Don't be jealous," Rex said. He reached out to massage Amber's shoulders, but she jerked away from him. "Come on, why are you pissed at me?"

Amber clenched her jaw but refused to answer.

"I'm not the bad guy here," Rex said sharply. "We need to focus on the real enemy."

"Which is?" Amber said without looking at him.

"DGM." Rex leaned back against the lunch table. "We weren't tough enough on them last year, and look what happened. First week back and *bam!* They hit us." He slammed his fist into the tabletop. "We need to take matters into our own hands. Do whatever it takes to protect the school."

Olivia didn't like the anger in Rex's voice.

"How?" Kyle asked.

"We can start by targeting possible suspects." Rex stared across the courtyard. "Someone who consistently breaks the rules, even brags about it. Someone who has absolutely no respect for the name Bishop DuMaine and what it stands for."

Olivia followed his line of sight across the courtyard to Bree.

EIGHT

BREE EYED THE LUNCH TABLE ON THE OTHER SIDE OF THE grassy quad, where Rex and his band of 'Maine Men fucktards pointed in her direction.

"In the pandemic of douchebaggery," she said thoughtfully, "Rex Cavanaugh is Patient Zero."

John slowly glanced up from his comic book. "Did you think up that line yourself?"

"As a matter of fact, I did. Like it?"

"A little forced," John said. "But you get points for originality."

Bree smirked, but there was something about the intensity of Rex's conversation that made her nervous.

Out of the corner of her eye, Bree caught sight of a small, huddled figure moving quickly through the shadowed edge of the quad. Margot. She paused briefly to readjust the enormous backpack she had slung over one shoulder, then tucked a piece of hair behind her ear and disappeared into a hallway.

Bree's eyes darted back to Olivia, who quickly gathered up

her things, muttered something to her friends, and hurried after Margot.

Phase one of Mission Ronny DeStefano was in motion. Now Bree could turn her attention to more important things. . . .

A quick sweep of the quad showed that her "more important thing" was nearby. Shane White sat on a bench beneath one of the giant elms.

Perfect.

Bree pulled out a copy of Nietzsche's *Thus Spoke Zarathustra*, opened it to a random page about two thirds of the way through, and leaned back against the wall, propping the book up on her knees so everyone could get a good look at the title while she pretended to read.

She glanced up occasionally to see if Shane had noticed her. He seemed so normal and clean-cut hanging out with his friends at lunch, the perfect image of an everyday, unassuming DuMaine senior.

But Bree knew better.

She knew what Shane was like onstage, singing lead vocals in a local indie punk band called Bangers and Mosh. She'd seen him in a tight tank top, skinny jeans, and combat boots, guitar slung low across his waist. She'd seen the full-sleeve tattoos on his left arm, and when he peeled off his shirt, drenched in sweat from a performance, she'd seen the tattoos that covered his stomach as well.

Bree knew everything there was to know about Shane White, and most importantly, she knew that he was a huge Nietzsche fan. She'd heard him asking the school librarian about Nietzsche last spring, and she'd been waiting all summer to flaunt her new collection of his works, hoping Shane might notice, might talk to her, might . . .

"Are you even listening to me?" John asked.

"Of course," Bree lied.

John folded his arms across his chest. "Then what was I saying?"

Bree had no clue. "You were telling me how hot you think Amber is, and if I thought she'd dump Rex for you."

John stared at her for a second, blinking rapidly; then his body convulsed, once, twice. His hand flew to his mouth as he leaned over and made a fake puking sound.

"Oops. Guess that wasn't it after all."

John wiped his mouth with the back of his hand. "I said I can't meet you at the Coffee Clash tonight."

"*Pourquoi?*"

"Band practice."

Bree dropped Nietzsche to the ground. "Clearly, I'm hallucinating. I thought you said band practice. *Clearly*, you didn't though. Because that would mean you'd finally auditioned for a band. And if you'd finally auditioned for a band, *CLEARLY* you would have told your best friend."

John smirked. "Band. Practice."

"Deets," Bree said, snapping her fingers. "Stat."

John sighed. "Let me try a practice first, okay? They may think I suck balls and cut me loose."

"Doubtful." John constantly downplayed his talent, but Bree knew how amazing he was with a bass in his hands.

He nodded toward Shane. "If they keep me around, maybe I'll be as famous as your boyfriend."

Bree scowled. "He's not my boyfriend."

"True," John said, with a cold gleam in his eyes. "But not for lack of trying. Maybe you should have gotten a large-print Nietzsche so he could actually see it from over there."

"Ha, ha."

"Or . . ." John pushed himself to his feet, surprisingly nimble for his gawky frame, and stuck his thumb and middle finger in his mouth, emitting a whistle that would have stopped traffic on Market Street at rush hour.

"What are you doing?" Bree hissed.

John ignored her. "Shane!" he called out, waving his arm over his head like a lunatic.

"Oh my God!" Bree grabbed his pants leg and tried to pull him down before Shane noticed. Too late. To Bree's horror, Shane returned John's wave and trotted over to them.

"I hate you so much right now," Bree whispered, trying to control the blush rushing up from her chest. "So much."

"Bagsie," Shane said. He held up his hand and John embraced him like an old friend. "We still on for rehearsal tonight?"

John nodded. "I'll be there."

"Sweet. Can't wait to get you up to speed. We were blown away by your audition."

Bree blinked. Holy shit, did her best friend join Bangers and Mosh?

NINE

OLIVIA KEPT HER DISTANCE AS SHE FOLLOWED MARGOT through pockets of lunching underclassmen, past the science building, to the courtyard outside the boys' locker room. It was completely deserted except for one person.

Ronny stood at a vending machine stocked with nonsugary waters and diet sodas and, much to Olivia's eternal dismay, devoid of all candy or pastries deemed unhealthy by the administration.

Margot slipped into an alcove behind the water fountain and left Olivia to it. Show time.

"Looking for something?" Olivia asked.

Ronny glanced at her out of the corner of his eye, then slowly turned. "Um, I . . . er . . ." His face flushed red as he tripped over his own tongue.

"I know, it sucks." Olivia leaned against the vending machine, stroking the glass with one pink fingernail. "F.U. won't allow any junk food." Olivia giggled as Ronny stared at her blankly. "Sorry, that's what we call Father Uberti."

"Oh."

Olivia tilted her chin. "Are you new here?"

Ronny nodded vigorously, his eyes fixed somewhere near Olivia's cleavage.

"I thought so!" Olivia batted her eyelashes. "I'd have remembered you." She stepped closer, and Ronny dropped his backpack to the ground, instantly forgotten. Now all she had to do was lure him away from it for a few minutes. . . .

"So," Olivia said. "What's your name?"

"R-Ronny," he stuttered.

Olivia grabbed him by the hand and circled halfway around, spinning his body away from his backpack. "Ronny!" she squealed. "I love that name. I'm Olivia."

"Olivia Hayes, right?" he said, clearly wanting to make sure he was talking about the right person when he bragged to his new 'Maine Men buddies.

"That's me."

Margot snuck up to Ronny's discarded backpack and fished out his cell phone, quickly attaching the cloning device, which would copy all its information, including his passwords.

"So, Ronny," Olivia began, keeping one eye on Margot. "Where did you come from?"

"Arizona."

"Do you miss it?"

"No."

Olivia bit her lip. At this rate it was going to be hard to keep him talking long enough for Margot to clone his phone. She needed to amp up the charm factor. "I've never been to Arizona," she said, squeezing his hand. "But I hear it's . . . hot."

Her performance seemed to be loosening Ronny up. "Yeah," he said with a slight laugh. "It's wicked hot in the summer."

"I bet," she said, grazing the back of Ronny's hand with her finger. "Since you're new here, maybe I could show you around sometime?"

"That would be cool." Ronny smiled.

Now she just needed to set a date with him so Bree would have a chance to break into his computer. "What are you doing after school tomorrow?"

"Giving you a tour of my bedroom," Ronny said, arching his left eyebrow in what he probably thought was some kind of subtle way.

Olivia made a mental note to never be alone with Ronny. Ever. "Why don't we start with the Coffee Clash tomorrow? Say, four o'clock?"

"Are you sure that's all you want to do?"

To Olivia's relief, she saw Margot slip Ronny's cell phone back into his bag and silently disappear into the hallway. Time to escape.

"It was so good to meet you, Ronny," she said, blatantly ignoring the question. She stepped around him and began to follow Margot out of the courtyard. "I'll see you tomorrow at four, okay?"

Ronny grabbed her hand. He wasn't gentle. "Wait," he said. He tugged her back to him. "Running away so soon?" He slipped his arm around her waist, holding her firmly in his grip.

Olivia tried to wiggle free. "I'm going to be late," she said, searching the courtyard for any sign of people. Why did this have to be the most secluded part of the entire freaking school?

"That's okay," Ronny whispered in her ear. His breath smelled like banana and Altoids. "It'll be worth it."

Was this guy seriously going to assault her right there on campus in the middle of a school day? Mission or no mission, she was going to start screaming in ten seconds if he didn't—

"Olivia!"

Ronny stopped at the sound of Olivia's name, dropping both hands innocently by his sides as if he hadn't been attempting to paw through her clothes.

Olivia stumbled back as Ed the Head trotted toward her.

"Olivia," he repeated, eyes darting back and forth between her and Ronny. "You okay?"

"Fine," Olivia said. She wanted to hug Ed. "Have you met Ronny?"

"Transfer student from Arizona, right?" Ed the Head asked. His tone was steely.

"How did you know that?" Ronny asked.

Ed took a step toward him. "It's my business to know everything about everyone." He was a head shorter than Ronny and probably thirty pounds lighter, but Olivia appreciated the chivalric effort nonetheless.

"Right." Ronny checked his watch. "Well, I gotta go." He winked at Olivia. "I'll see you later."

Olivia forced a smile as he turned and disappeared around the corner.

Ed the Head stared after him. "Sure you're okay?"

"Yeah," Olivia said. "But . . ." She eyed Ed the Head's backpack. "You don't happen to have any donuts in there, do you?"

TEN

"ERIK BIENKOWSKI," MIKA SAID, NODDING TOWARD A GROUP OF senior lacrosse players at a nearby table.

Kitty shook her head. "I heard him bragging the other day in the weight room that he's never read a book voluntarily."

"At least he's tall enough," Mika said.

At six foot two, finding a guy Kitty didn't tower over in flats, let alone heels, had been somewhat of a challenge. "Good point."

Mika shifted her gaze to the table Olivia had recently left. "Tyler Brodsky?"

Kitty chortled. "You want me to date a 'Maine Man?'"

"Fine." Mika nudged her. "You know, if you had come with me to Jezebel's back-to-school blowout, I could have introduced you to some hotties. The place was crawling."

"Parties aren't my thing."

"It was pretty wild," Mika admitted. "I got hammered. Don't even remember how I got home."

Kitty stiffened. That must have been the night Ronny

assaulted her. "Really?" Kitty fished. "Do you remember anything?"

"Not really." Mika shook her head sharply, then forced a laugh. "Just the usual: hangover, fuzzy memories. Don't worry about me, Kitty Cat."

"If you say so." Kitty supposed it was a good thing that Mika didn't remember the specifics of her assault, though Ronny had clearly taken advantage of her when she was too drunk to say no. Kitty clenched her jaw as the video flashed before her mind. DGM would make him wish he'd never laid eyes on Mika Jones.

Mika continued to scour the quad before she landed on a large group of juniors clustered around the outdoor amphitheater. A smile spread across her face. "Ah, I've got it."

Kitty followed Mika's gaze. Lounging in the middle of the group, taking up four rows of concrete seats with his massive frame, was Donté Greene.

Mika turned, her face beaming. "I know the perfect guy for you. Smart, handsome, and, most importantly, recently single."

Kitty felt her face burning. Mika had to be talking about Donté. When Olivia broke up with him at the end of last year, it had been the biggest gossip to hit Bishop DuMaine since DGM. What Mika didn't know—what no one but Kitty's journal knew, in fact—was that Kitty had a long-standing crush on the star forward of the basketball team. And there was no way in hell she'd have the courage to ask him out.

"Don't you want to know who it is?" Mika's smile was wicked.

Not really. "Don't you want to tell me?" Kitty replied, taking a sip of water to hide her embarrassment.

Mika took a dramatic breath. "Ed the Head."

Kitty spewed water all over the lawn. "Ed the Head?" she sputtered. He was at least a foot shorter than Kitty, not exactly what she had in mind as a boyfriend.

"Sorry!" Mika buried her head in Kitty's shoulder. "Couldn't help it."

"If he could help me pass Algebra II," Kitty said, "I'd consider it."

Mika cracked up and Kitty joined her, snorting out loud as she laughed, an uncontrollable reaction that had plagued her since childhood.

"Hey, Kitty."

Kitty froze as all the warmth drained out of her face. Donté Greene towered above her. His blue 'Maine Men polo shirt must have been custom ordered to fit his basketball player's build. His eyes were wide, practically glowing in contrast to his dark brown skin, and the dimples that had puckered his cheeks a second before vanished as a look of concern washed over him.

"H-hey," Kitty stuttered, horrified that he'd witnessed her snort-filled spaz-out.

"You okay?" he asked.

Kitty nodded, unable to find her voice.

"Hi, Donté," Mika said, her voice full of mischief. "What's up?"

Donté's eyes never left Kitty's face. "You have fourth-period algebra, right?"

Kitty nodded. So that was it. Donté needed help with his math homework. Too bad he was talking to the only Asian kid in school who wasn't good at it.

Donté jerked his thumb toward the math building. "I'm, er, heading that way. Can I walk you to class?"

"Absolutely," Mika answered for her. She jumped off the edge of the planter box and grabbed Kitty's duffel bag, shoving it into her arms.

Donté's entire face lit up. "Great!"

Kitty glared at Mika as she slid to her feet, tossing her bag over her shoulder. "I'll see you later," she said, trying to sound as menacing as possible.

"So how's the volleyball team looking this year?" Donté asked, falling into step beside her.

"Good." Kitty was happy for the small talk. "Not sure we can repeat as state champs, but we'll definitely be competitive. How about the basketball team?"

"Awesome." There was a softness in Donté's voice that was completely out of place with his boulder-like physique. "A solid group of guys. I'm lucky to play with them."

The warning bell rang as they approached the door to Kitty's algebra class. "So," she started, pausing with her hand on the knob, unsure why Donté had taken the time to walk her to class. "Was there some—"

"Would you like to go out with me?" Donté said abruptly.

Kitty caught her breath. Donté Greene was asking her out on a date. Fireworks exploded in her brain as all of her Donté day-dreams replayed themselves in her head, no longer the fantasies of a secret admirer. Could this really be happening?

She smiled and opened her mouth to say yes, when she

remembered Olivia. Even though she'd dumped Donté months before, going out with Olivia's ex-boyfriend probably wasn't good for the DGM group dynamic. As she wrestled with her answer, her eyes strayed to the 'Maine Men logo on Donté's shirt. Not only was he Olivia's ex, but he was a member of the 'Maine Men, sworn enemy of DGM. She couldn't go out with him, not now, not ever.

Say no.

"Sure," Kitty said. "I'd like that."

Margot plotted a roundabout route back to her locker after cloning Ronny's phone. Overly paranoid? Perhaps. But it was better to be safe than sorry.

Not that she'd ever been hauled into Father Uberti's office for questioning. She was too anonymous at school, too quiet and unimportant to elicit suspicion. And yet, as she wove through the hallways, she couldn't shake the feeling that someone was watching her, following her. She glanced over her shoulder several times and even doubled back through the arts building to make sure no one was trailing her.

Still, as she hurried to her locker, she could have sworn she heard the squeaks of shoes on the tiled floor, as if someone was—

"Margot!" Ed the Head cried as she rounded the corner.

Margot jumped.

"You okay?" he asked, pushing himself off the row of lockers.

"Fine," Margot said breathlessly.

Ed the Head followed Margot to her locker.

"How's my favorite smartest girl in school?"

Margot dialed in her combination. "Smartest *person* in school."

"That's what I said."

"No, you said smartest girl. But I'm the smartest person at DuMaine, not restricted by gender, or by age."

Ed the Head laughed. "And so modest."

Margot opened her locker and pulled out her calculus textbook. "What do you want?"

Ed the Head scanned the hall, then crammed his hand into his pocket and pulled out a wad of cash. "That tip you gave me about the assembly paid off huge. I thought you were entitled to a cut."

"Keep it."

Ed the Head dangled the money in front of her face. "There's like three hundred bucks here. You could buy yourself a shiny new protractor." He smirked. "Or some friends."

"Friends are overrated," Margot snapped. "You should know."

"And yet," Ed the Head continued, "despite your lack of social standing, you're the one who always seems to have the most dirt to share. Game spreads, Oscars predictions, who's gonna make the homecoming court. Half my bookmaking business comes from your tips. How?"

"Educated hypotheses based on empirical data."

Ed blinked. "Was that English?"

Margot wrinkled her mouth. "I read minds."

"Fine, Uri Geller. Don't tell me. Just give me one good reason why you won't take this money."

Margot sighed. There was only one thing she wanted from

Ed the Head. "We have a deal, Edward. Remember? I help your business and in return you find me some traffic-stopping dirt on Amber Stevens. Any news on that front?"

Ed dropped his eyes to the floor. "I'm working on it."

Margot needed something big on Amber, something that would put an end to her queen bee status for good and inflict the same level of pain and suffering that Amber had doled out to Margot for so many years. Nothing she'd been able to discover on her own had been damaging enough: a tip on Amber's liposuction last summer, a rumor about her mom and a massage therapist in Santa Barbara, possible proof that her dad bribed her kindergarten teacher not to retain her. Hell, Amber would probably brag about the last one. So she'd struck a bargain with the only person at school as skilled at ferreting out information as she was: Ed the Head.

"Keep your money," she said, turning to leave. "And work harder."

"Hey!" Ed jogged after her. "Look, as turned on as I am at the idea of pocketing all this cash for services rendered, I'm worried it's going to fuck up my karma, so . . ." He tried to shove the cash into Margot's backpack.

"Cut it out!" Margot whirled and knocked the money out of his hand.

Ed the Head stared in disbelief as the bills fluttered to the ground. "That is the unsexiest thing I have ever seen." He dropped to his knees and snatched at the discarded cash.

"I doubt that," Margot said under her breath.

"Hey, is the green up for grabs?" Logan Blaine bounded out

of the men's room and halted in his tracks.

"No." Ed the Head didn't look up as he palmed the last of the twenty-dollar bills. "No, it is not."

Logan clicked his tongue. "Too bad. I need to get my board waxed and . . ." His voice trailed off as he noticed Margot standing behind Ed. "Margot, right? From AP Government?"

Margot felt her throat constrict. He remembered her? "Yeah," she managed to choke out.

"Logan, my man." Ed the Head held his hand up for a high five, realized he was double-fisting wads of cash, and quickly shoved the loot into his pockets.

Logan looked confused. "Have we met?"

"Nope." Ed the Head hiked up his backpack on his shoulder. "Well, kids, it's been awesome. Catching up, sharing memories. A real special moment for all of us, but I am considerably out of here."

Logan stared at Ed the Head as he disappeared around the corner. "Weird dude."

Margot nodded. *Weird but useful.*

ELEVEN

OLIVIA WAS STILL FRAZZLED FROM HER ENCOUNTER WITH Ronny when she walked into drama.

"Liv!" Peanut called from the front row the moment Olivia started down the aisle. "Where have you been?"

"Secret meeting with your new boyfriend, Ed the Head?" Amber asked. She was all smiles, but there was an edge to her voice.

Olivia dropped into the empty seat next to Peanut and attempted to compose herself. "I wasn't feeling well."

"Miss Hayes," Mr. Cunningham said from the stage, his lilting British accent at once casual and commanding. He ticked her name off the roll sheet. "Lovely to have you back this semester."

As if his only scholarship student would miss it.

Olivia felt the row of seats bounce as a blond guy in cargo shorts and Timberlands plopped down next to her. Mr. Cunningham used his clipboard to shield his eyes from the heavy stage lights and stared at the front row. "And you are?"

"Logan Blaine," he said.

Mr. Cunningham checked Logan off the list. "Do you have

any theatrical experience, Mr. Blaine?"

"Sure do." Logan flashed a boyish smile but didn't elaborate.

"O-kay," Mr. Cunningham said slowly. The late bell rang, and he took one last scan of the roll sheet while he waited for the echo to fade. "Looks like we have everyone but—"

The back door to the theater flew open, banging against the wall with a violence that made Olivia jump. She turned her head and her fingers dug into the cushy armrest as Donté jogged down the aisle.

"Sorry I'm late," he said.

Mr. Cunningham consulted his clipboard. "Mr. Greene?"

"Yes, sir."

"I understand that Advanced Drama is considered an easy elective for some of you athletic types." He paused, pursing his lips. "Which is why Father Uberti forces me to take you. So understand this: being on time for my class is a prerequisite for a passing grade."

Donté joined drama? Excitement rippled through her. She'd have an entire semester with him. It was too good to be true.

"Sorry," Donté repeated, holding his head high. "Won't happen again."

Mr. Cunningham nodded, seemingly satisfied. "Apology accepted, Mr. Greene. And I'd like to thank all of you for your patience while I was out of town last week. As you will soon learn, the delay was well worth it."

Olivia leaned forward. It sounded as if Mr. Cunningham had a surprise for them. Celebrity coach? Field trip to Broadway?

"We have a few new people this semester." Mr. Cunningham

nodded to Donté and Logan. "Mr. Greene, Mr. Blaine, and Mr. . . ." He pointed toward the house left seats. "What was your name again?"

"Shane White."

"Yes, Mr. White. If I'd known we'd have so many males in the class, I'd have picked one of the *Henry the Sixth*s to do." He chuckled at his own joke. "Regardless, we'll be moving very quickly into advanced scene study, focusing on Shakespeare, and I expect the newcomers to keep up."

Amber let out a strangled sound, somewhere between a squeak and a growl.

"Speaking of the Bard . . ." Mr. Cunningham walked to the edge of the stage and sat down with his legs dangling into the orchestra pit. "Due to the generosity of Mr. and Mrs. Stevens"—he gestured to Amber—"we are mounting a brand-new production of *Twelfth Night* this semester."

"What?" Olivia turned to Amber, who stared fixedly at Mr. Cunningham, refusing to meet her eyes. Amber's parents were funding the fall play? That didn't make any sense. Not only was Amber ambivalent about theater, but she wasn't very good at it, possessing a remarkable inability to remember her lines. Why this sudden interest?

Olivia's hands went cold as another realization dawned upon her. If Amber's parents were paying for this production, then she'd known for a while that the fall play would be *Twelfth Night*, even though she'd steadfastly told Olivia all summer that she thought it would be Mamet. Why had she lied?

"So brush off your monologues," Mr. Cunningham continued.

"Because auditions will be Wednesday after school."

"Wednesday?" Peanut gasped. "But that's in only three days!"

"Two, Miss Dumbrowski," Mr. Cunningham said. He sounded almost sad. "Two days to prepare a soliloquy from the Shakespearean catalog. I know that seems impossible, but there is a method to my madness. I want your auditions to be spontaneous. Uniquely individual. And so, for this audition only, I'll be allowing you to read from the script."

Was it Olivia's imagination or had Mr. Cunningham's eyes rested on Amber for a brief moment as he dropped that bomb?

"I've saved the best for last. The reason for my absence at the beginning of the semester. I was in Bath, attending a performance of *As You Like It*, directed by the great Fitzgerald Conroy."

Olivia sat straight up in her seat, the shock of Amber's involvement in the production forgotten. *The* Fitzgerald Conroy? Former director in residence at the Royal Shakespeare Company and current artistic director of the Oregon Shakespeare Festival, Fitzgerald Conroy was the godfather of modern Shakespearean productions, a world-class director who had literally worked with every leading stage actress of the last two decades.

"Fitzgerald is an old friend and colleague," Mr. Cunningham continued. "And I am pleased to announce that he will be attending our opening-night performance and will be evaluating members of our cast for an internship position in this summer's Oregon Shakespeare Festival."

Olivia's jaw dropped. An internship at Ashland? Working with Fitzgerald Conroy? This was the chance Olivia had been waiting for.

Amber squealed and grabbed Peanut's hand. "Can you imagine? Me performing at Ashland?"

"You?" Olivia said. She couldn't help herself.

Amber turned on her. "Why not? You're not the star of the show around here anymore."

Anymore?

Mr. Cunningham clapped his hands again, and the class quieted down. "There is one catch, so listen up. Due to Fitzgerald's calendar, we need to open this production in three weeks."

Olivia gasped again, this time simultaneously with almost everyone in the theater. Three weeks to mount an entire Shakespearean play? That was the most insane production schedule she'd ever heard.

"I realize that three weeks is a compressed rehearsal period, which means I must have a full commitment from everyone involved. For those of you not cast in the play, there will be important roles to fill: stage crew, costumes, lighting. This is a brand-new production with a great many moving parts, and it's going to take all of us to pull it off. We'll also need more behind-the-scenes crew than usual, so recruit your friends. Sound good?"

He didn't wait for a response.

"So let's start with some warm-ups. Everyone onstage." He pointed at Amber. "Miss Stevens, would you like to lead? We can see how those private lessons over the summer paid off."

Amber pranced up the stairs onto the stage, preening like a peacock. "I'd love to."

Mr. Cunningham asked Amber to run the warm-ups? That was Olivia's job, had been for four semesters. She was practically

Mr. Cunningham's TA, a de facto position based on her status as the only student at Bishop DuMaine on a drama scholarship.

Olivia slowly followed the rest of the class onto the stage, moving to the far corner as the class loosely formed rows behind Amber. Her mind reeled. Amber had taken acting lessons during the summer. Amber had lied to her about what the fall play would be. Amber had conned her parents into donating the funds to mount the new production. Amber had known about the internship with the Oregon Shakespeare Festival all along and decided she wanted it for herself. Why?

"We'll start with some stretches," Amber instructed.

"Olivia," a voice whispered.

Olivia turned her head sharply. Mr. Cunningham stood in the wings, beckoning her over. As Amber began a windmill drill, Olivia ducked behind the leg curtain.

"*Twelfth Night*," Mr. Cunningham said quickly. "I'm sure you want to play Olivia. It was your mother's greatest role, and your namesake."

Olivia was confused. "No, I don't. I want—"

Mr. Cunningham held up his hand, cutting her off. "I need you to audition for Viola."

"Okay."

"And don't tell anyone that's what you're doing."

"Uh, okay."

He placed a hand on her shoulder. "Things are going to be a little different this semester. I . . ." His eyes faltered from her face. "I need this production. Fitzgerald's looking for original stagings to fill next summer's lineup. It would be my own production, a huge directorial role for me. Do you understand?"

Olivia had no idea what he was talking about but nodded anyway.

"I'll do everything I can for you." He squeezed her shoulder.

"Mr. Cunningham?" Amber called out. "We're ready!"

Mr. Cunningham whipped his hand away. He straightened his shoulders and stepped past Olivia onto the stage.

"Excellent. Shall we start with some *Hamlet*?"

TWELVE

OLIVIA MADE SURE SHE WAS AT THE COFFEE CLASH EARLY for her date with Ronny. She picked a small table in the corner, obscured by the dessert counter, where she ran minimal risk of being seen by . . . anyone, and opened her copy of *Twelfth Night* to study one of Viola's monologues. Mission or no mission, she needed to be prepared for the audition.

One hour, that was all she needed to give Bree. One hour spent dodging Ronny's octopus hands and avoiding anyone she knew.

Thankfully, she had an exit strategy this time. Kitty would be showing up precisely at five o'clock. It made her feel better, somehow, knowing she had Kitty there looking out for her.

"Babe!" Ronny yelled from the front door of the café.

Ugh. It took all of Olivia's acting ability to plaster a demure, flirtatious smile on her face as Ronny sat down opposite her.

"Hi," Olivia said in return. "I'm *so* glad you could make it."

She glanced at her cell phone. One hour started now.

◆ ◆ ◆

Bree crouched behind a large green wastebin and stared at Ronny's house. She'd been huddled in the backyard for half an hour; her knees dug into the gravel, her back ached, and the stench of rotting leaves and manure was starting to make her nauseous.

She tapped the Bluetooth device in her ear. "You still with me?"

"Don't do that," Margot grumbled. "You're going to make me deaf."

"Sorry." She could hear the clack of Margot's keyboard on the other end as she worked to disable the DeStefanos' security system. "Almost done?"

"I'll tell you when I'm done."

Bree shifted her weight to her heels and arched her back. "Easy for you to say," she muttered. "You're not the one hanging out with the garbage."

"You know I can hear you, right?"

Another few seconds of manic typing, and then Margot let out a long breath. "Okay," she said. "Try it now."

Bree crept out from behind the bin and ran swiftly to the back door. The crunch of the gravel beneath her boots sounded cartoonishly loud in the silence of the afternoon, and she paused at the door, listening for any signs of life.

Why was she so paranoid? Ronny was safely engaged at the Coffee Clash, and his dad and stepmom wouldn't be home from work before six o'clock. She had plenty of time to break in, download the contents of Ronny's hard drive and email using the passwords cloned from his phone, delete the video, and hustle out of there before Kitty rescued Olivia from her date.

Easy.

"Are you inside yet?" Margot asked.

"Patience is a virtue." With a deep breath, Bree inserted her skeleton key gingerly into the lock and gave it a jiggle. The back door swung open. "In!" she said. "Heading to Ronny's room now."

Blackout shades were drawn over the windows, but the screen saver on Ronny's computer was bright enough to light Bree's way into the darkened room. Which was a happy accident because his bedroom was a freaking pigsty.

Clothes were strewn about the bed, desk, and floor like they'd been churned up by a tornado and were left where they fell. Several food-stained plates were piled up on the nightstand, and at least a dozen glasses of half-consumed mystery liquids christened every available surface.

"Must be the cleaning crew's day off," Bree said, wrinkling her nose.

"They come Wednesday and Friday," Margot said.

"Damn, he did all this since Friday?"

"Bree, the computer," Margot prodded.

"Yeah, yeah." She had an hour, after all. It would only take about twenty minutes to download Ronny's hard drive.

Bree picked her way toward Ronny's desk, avoiding a pizza box with unknown contents and several pairs of dirty tighty-whities that made bile gurgle up the back of her throat.

"What an incredible smell you've discovered," she murmured.

"Did you just quote *Star Wars*?" Margot asked.

"No," Bree said quickly. "Maybe."

John was clearly wearing off on her.

"Okay," Bree said, forcing herself to focus on the task at hand. "Logging in to his computer now."

Kitty swung through the door of the Coffee Clash right on schedule.

Ronny's back was to her as she approached the register, but Kitty watched as Olivia quickly drew her hand across her chest from left shoulder to right, signaling that she was ready for extrication.

"Can I help you?" the barista asked.

Kitty reluctantly pulled her gaze away from Olivia and Ronny. "I'll have a small—" Kitty started as she recognized the barista. "Barbara Ann?"

"Hi, Kitty." Barbara Ann smiled; her eyes did not.

Kitty stared at her former teammate, unsure what to say. Barbara Ann Vreeland had been a sophomore at Bishop DuMaine when Kitty was a freshman, and had been captain of the junior varsity girls' volleyball team until she was expelled from school after being implicated in a grade-fixing scandal. The last time Kitty had seen her, Barbara Ann had tried to recruit Kitty into the scheme by offering her a passing grade in geometry. The scandal had broken two days later, and Kitty hadn't seen Barbara Ann since.

"How are you?" Kitty said lamely.

Barbara Ann shrugged. "Good, I guess. I'm at Gunn now."

Kitty tilted her head to the side. If Barbara Ann was at Gunn, they should have played each other at volleyball.

"I don't play anymore," Barbara Ann said, as if reading Kitty's mind.

"But . . . but you were amazing," Kitty stammered. "Pro level. I thought—"

"Oooooooh," Olivia groaned from her table. She grabbed her stomach, doubling over in pantomimed pain.

The Coffee Clash was half-empty, but several patrons glanced in Olivia's direction.

"Babe?" Ronny said nervously, not moving from his seat.

"My stomach," Olivia cried. She writhed in her chair.

"Are you okay?"

Olivia stumbled forward out of her chair, bracing herself against the dessert counter. "I think I'm going to be sick."

That was Kitty's cue. She wanted to talk to Barbara Ann, find out why she wasn't playing anymore, and if that was somehow her fault. But they were on a tight schedule. With a weak smile at her old teammate, she stepped toward Olivia. "What's wrong? What hurts?"

Olivia jabbed at her stomach below her rib cage. "Here. It's like I've been stabbed."

"I didn't do anything," Ronny said, slowly rising to his feet. "I never touched her."

Kitty fought to keep from rolling her eyes.

"It must be your appendix," Kitty said instead, sounding like an extra on a medical drama. She snatched Olivia's purse off the back of her chair. "We need to get her to the hospital. Now."

Ronny's eyes practically bugged out of his head. "Right. Um, should I take her? Or, I mean, do you have a car?"

"It hurts!" Olivia sobbed.

Were those real tears streaming down her face? Wow, she really was an amazing actress.

"Come on," Kitty said, putting an arm around Olivia. "I'll take you."

Kitty took one last glance over her shoulder as she escorted a groaning Olivia out of the café. The rest of the patrons had returned to their conversations, but three heads were turned in their direction. Barbara Ann's stare was hard; Ronny's, dumbfounded. And in the back of the café, Theo Baranski gazed at her, eyes wide, watching their retreat.

"How much longer?" Margot asked. Bree could picture her, manically checking the clock every thirty seconds, paranoid that they were behind schedule.

"Two minutes."

"Finally," Margot said sharply.

"Not my fault his ancient laptop was so slow. Freaking PCs."

A soft chime echoed through Bree's earpiece. "Kitty just texted," Margot said. "She and Olivia left Ronny at the Coffee Clash. His drive time is approximately sixteen minutes in rush hour traffic."

"Then I'll be out of here in five."

Bree stared at the download progress bar, which kept changing its mind as to how much time was left. It taunted her, jumping from thirty seconds, to sixty, to ninety, then back to thirty. *Come on.* Her fingers tapped impatiently against Ronny's desk as she glared at the screen, mentally threatening it with physical harm if it didn't hurry up and finish.

"Cut it out," Margot said, her voice edgy. She was losing her cool.

"Cut what out?"

"Tapping your fingers against the desk."

Bree paused. "How can you possib—" She stopped midword as a faint creak broke the silence of the room, followed by an almost imperceptible patter, like bare feet retreating down the hall.

"What's wrong?" Margot asked.

"Sh!" Bree sat frozen, listening, but the sound of footsteps had vanished. Silently, she swung Ronny's desk chair around to face the bedroom door, which was closed.

Did she close the door? She was pretty sure she'd left it open. Maybe a breeze swung it shut? Or maybe the DeStefanos had a cat?

Or maybe it was a person.

"What happened?" Margot whispered. "Bree, are you—"

DING! The download was complete. Finally.

"Nothing," Bree said, quickly ejecting the flash drive. "Just thought I heard something."

"Okay," Margot said slowly. "Did you delete the video of Mika?"

Bree swirled the mouse across the screen and with a few deft clicks, the video was erased from Ronny's computer permanently. "Done," she said. "Now I'm getting the fuck out of here."

"You have twelve minutes," Margot said.

Bree's hands trembled as she eased Ronny's desk chair back to the exact spot she'd found it. Why was she so skittish? If anyone had been in the house and actually seen her at Ronny's desk, they would have either confronted her on the spot or called 911. A distinct lack of blaring sirens in the distance meant it had all been a figment of her imagination.

She carefully threaded her way back to the bedroom door and was about to swing it open with her foot when something caught her eye. Taped to the back of Ronny's door was a list of names.

Coach Creed
Rex Cavanaugh
Theodore Baranski

What possible connection could exist between a dickwad teacher, the biggest douche at school, and a bullying victim?

"Ten minutes," Margot said. "Are you done yet?"

Bree shook her head and nudged the door open. Whatever the reason, it didn't affect the mission. "Exiting the house now."

As soon as her car rounded the corner at the end of the block, Kitty held up her hand for a high five. "Nice job."

Olivia slapped Kitty's hand with all the ferocity of a butterfly. Oh well, at least she was getting into the spirit. "It felt *so* good. I mean, it's like those interactive theater shows in New York. The exhilaration is absolutely amazing and . . ." She paused midthought. "Hey, did you know that barista?"

"No," Kitty lied.

"Oh. I thought I saw you guys talking," Olivia said, still chattering away at a mile a minute. "Sorry if I interrupted, but I couldn't take another second of Ronny."

"Did you see Theo in the café?" Kitty asked, desperate to change the subject. She didn't want to talk about Barbara Ann.

"Theo Baranski?"

Kitty nodded. "In the back corner."

"Huh," Olivia said.

Kitty pictured the look on Theo's face as she escorted Olivia from the café. He wasn't concerned or worried, he was confused, as if seeing Kitty and Olivia together was as strange and out of place as a polar bear in the desert, which might be a problem if he remembered seeing them together with Ronny after their revenge against him went public.

Kitty's cell phone buzzed. She waited for a stoplight, then checked her incoming text. "Margot says that Bree successfully downloaded his hard drive and deleted the video," she said. "I'd say, phase one accomplished."

Olivia sighed as Kitty rolled up in front of her apartment building, visibly relieved that her role was over. "I'll see you at school tomorrow?"

"Absolutely." Kitty nodded. "Don't get mad."

Olivia smiled. "Get even."

THIRTEEN

KITTY WAS FIDGETY AS SHE DROVE TO SCHOOL THE NEXT morning, unable to get Ronny DeStefano out of her head.

Phase one was complete—they had Ronny's hard drive. Now they just needed some juicy tidbit of a secret on his computer that they could use against him. But time was short. How long would it be before he realized his video had been deleted? Maybe it had been a mistake to jump so quickly into this mission without a complete plan of action? It was so unlike her to do so, but with Mika's reputation on the line, she hadn't really had a choice.

Kitty turned onto DuMaine Drive, and instantly all thoughts of Ronny DeStefano faded away.

At least half a dozen police cruisers lined the streets around campus. An officer stood sentry at the main entrance, and as she pulled into the upperclassmen's parking lot, she found another officer at the side door.

For a split second, Kitty thought about fleeing the scene. She could pretend to be sick, tell her mom she had food poisoning, fake a migraine, anything that would get her out of school for the day. There could only be one reason for the police, one thing that could bring them to campus for the second time in less than a week. Father Uberti had found out who was behind DGM.

Logic kicked in almost immediately. Why would they wait to arrest her at school? Wouldn't they show up at her house and bring her in for questioning? Taking a deep breath, Kitty pulled into her usual parking spot.

Four police officers ringed Mrs. Baggott's desk as Kitty entered the office to prep the morning announcements. Their eyes were alert and the walkies attached to their shoulders crackled with unceasing chatter.

Father Uberti pointed his finger menacingly at the school secretary. "I don't care what the Archdiocese says. If they won't do anything, I'm taking matters into my own hands."

"Of course, Father," Mrs. Baggott said, eyeing the police officers.

Father Uberti's head whipped around as soon as Kitty approached. "No announcements today," he barked. "I'm taking care of it."

John was already at his desk for first-period religion when Bree plopped into her chair.

"Why does school have to start so early?" she asked, stifling a yawn. She hadn't slept well after her experience in Ronny's bedroom, unable to shake the feeling that someone had seen her in the house. She'd tossed and turned most of the night, convinced the cops would kick down her door any moment and take her into custody.

"Think of it this way," he said, tossing a lock of hair out of his eyes. "Every day when you mosey in five seconds before the bell, I've already been here for half an hour."

"Bite me," Bree said.

The final bell rang and, much to Bree's surprise, Sister Augustinia, their perpetually late religion teacher, was already at her desk, looking pale and fretful.

"Settle down, class," she said, the usual airy-fairiness gone from her voice. She sounded almost hoarse, as if she'd been screaming. Or crying. "We have a special announcement coming from Father Uberti."

Bree went rigid. A special announcement? Did that mean he'd gotten credible information on Don't Get Mad?

There was no time to speculate, no time to worry or even plan an escape route. The loudspeaker buzzed to life.

"Attention, students of Bishop DuMaine Preparatory School," Father Uberti began. "Last night, a member of our student body was found dead in his home. The scene is being investigated as a homicide. The victim's name is Ronny DeStefano."

FOURTEEN

MARGOT STARED UP AT THE LOUDSPEAKER. IT WAS AS IF the world had fallen away, swallowed up by a dark void, leaving only the voice of Father Uberti filtered through a box on the wall.

The room began to swim around her, fading in and out of view. Her hands tingled, her neck and chest broke out in a heavy sweat, and her breaths came in frantic gasps, as if an invisible hand were choking her.

Margot clamped her eyes shut. *Quiet the mind, quiet the panic.*

The world went silent. Occasionally, a word or phrase would jump out in Father Uberti's sharp, nasal voice. "Investigation." "Police presence." "Interrogation." It seemed so far away, and yet as her brain labored to internalize the words' meaning, the reality of what was happening overwhelmed her with a new emotion: fear.

"Crazy, huh?"

In an instant, Margot was back in the world. Back at Bishop DuMaine. Back in AP Government, gazing at Logan.

"Yeah," Margot managed to croak. "Crazy."

"Did you know him?"

Margot shook her head. "I never met him." Technically, it wasn't a lie.

"Tall guy?" Logan continued. "About my height? Sandy blond hair with too much gel and bad acne?"

That described Ronny to perfection. "I don't know."

"Right. Sorry." Logan smiled sheepishly. "You just said that."

There was something comforting about the affable face, the blue eyes that immediately calmed her down.

"We have reason to believe," Father Uberti continued, "that the group known as DGM was involved. Once again, if you have any information as to the identities of those behind DGM, we ask that you come forward as soon as possible."

The loudspeaker fell silent.

Margot stared blankly at her desk. They couldn't seriously think DGM or anyone at Bishop DuMaine had a hand in Ronny's death, could they?

Logan cleared his throat. "You're vibrating."

Margot opened her backpack and rooted around for her cell phone. "Sorry. Getting a text."

The very words were foreign to her. No one ever texted her except her parents, and absolutely never during school. Considering the bomb that had just been dropped on Bishop DuMaine, Margot wasn't the least bit surprised to see that the text was from Kitty.

We need to meet ASAP. Lunch today by the baseball field?

Margot paused. It was a bad idea for the four of them to meet on campus, but Kitty was right. Something horrific had happened, and they needed to get to the bottom of it.

She texted back.

Computer lab at lunch. I have a key. Regular greeting.

Kitty stood next to the water fountain, trying to look as casual as possible. The hallway in front of the computer lab was deserted, but Kitty was taking no chances. If she was pacing by the door to the lab, that might appear suspicious, but using the water fountain, checking the time on her watch, was innocent enough.

She was being overly cautious, but after what had happened that morning, she needed to be.

The door at the far end of the hall creaked and Kitty immediately bent over and pushed the bar on the front of the water fountain, as if she'd been passing through and just happened to need a drink.

Kitty looked up, relieved to see Margot hustling down the hall.

Without breaking stride, she yanked a key out of her pocket and unlocked the door. Margot ducked inside, and after a quick glance down either side of the corridor to make sure they were alone, Kitty followed.

The computer lab was dark, lit only by the dull glow of screen savers from a wall of monitors. The whole effect was surreal, and Kitty felt the skin on the back of her neck prickle.

"Are you sure no one will find us in here?" Kitty asked, desperate to fill the uncomfortable silence.

Margot pulled out a chair. "Only the yearbook class uses this lab anymore. The rest of the time the door's locked."

"You didn't answer my question."

Margot looked up at her coldly. "No one's ever bothered me in here."

Knock. Pause. *Knock. Knock. Knock.*

"Am I late?" Olivia asked breathlessly as she dashed into the lab. "I had to give Amber the slip and then I couldn't find the room." She ran a hand through her short hair. Before Kitty could stop herself, she pictured that hand caressing Donté's face, his bare chest. . . .

"Bree's not here yet," Margot said. She glanced at the clock on the wall. "Thirty seconds or we start without her."

As if on cue, the doorknob shook, then the DGM knock sounded on the lab door. Forceful and strong, the kind of announcement that said Bree didn't care who heard her.

Kitty whipped open the door and Bree stepped unhurriedly inside.

"I'm here," she said. "Let's get this over with so I can finish my lunch."

"This isn't a joke, Bree," Margot snapped.

Bree walked to the nearest chair. "If you say so." She deposited her cell phone on a desk, propped her combat boots up next to it, and tilted the chair back.

From beside her, Bree's cell phone rang. She silenced the call and tossed it back on the desk. "It's just John," she said without being prompted.

"Does he know where you are?" Kitty asked.

Bree arched an eyebrow. "We're not attached at the hip."

The phone rang again. This time Bree sent the call to voice mail.

Olivia cocked her head. "Are you sure about that?"

"Are you sure," Bree said drily, "you like your face that way? Because I could rearrange it for you."

"Guys," Kitty said, stepping between them. She kept her eye on the phone, wondering if the third time was the charm. "No fighting. We've got enough problems."

"Have you heard the rumors?" Olivia asked, switching gears. "Rex said Ronny had 'DGM' carved into his chest."

Bree rolled her eyes. "How can you take anything Rex Cavanaugh says seriously? The guy has a set of gonads for a brain."

"I thought maybe he'd heard it from Father Uberti?" Olivia pouted.

"Even if F.U. knows," Kitty said, trying to keep everyone calm, "which I doubt, there's no way he'd be allowed to share that information with anyone, especially not a student who might be a suspect."

Olivia's blue eyes grew wide. "Rex is a suspect?"

"Wake up, Princess," Bree said. "We're all suspects."

Kitty held up her hands. "We don't know that yet. Ronny's death could have been an accident. Or suicide."

Margot glanced up but didn't say a word.

"Come off it, Kitty." Bree kicked her feet off the table. "The police wouldn't show up at school for an accidental death. Ronny was killed, plain and simple. They must suspect someone at school is involved or they wouldn't be here."

"Poor Ronny," Olivia whimpered.

Bree snorted. "Poor Ronny? The guy's a sexual predator. I'd say he got what he deserved."

Olivia sucked in a sharp breath. "Don't say that. Don't ever say that."

"I think what Bree means," Kitty said, with a cutting look in her direction, "is that maybe it's not a surprise Ronny was murdered?"

"Murdered . . ." Olivia jumped to her feet. "We have to get out of here. Right now. What if they find us? We'll get sent to juvie. Oh my God, do you know what happens to girls like me in prison?"

"They become someone's wife?" Bree suggested.

Olivia started for the door. "I have to go."

Kitty intercepted her. "Olivia, we are not going to juvie, okay?" If Olivia panicked, Margot melted down, or Bree went rogue, they'd all be screwed. "We need to go about our lives like nothing's happened."

"Like nothing's happened?" Olivia's eyes were glassy, a clear indication tears were on the way. "I have an audition tonight for the fall play. How am I supposed to focus on Shakespeare when Ronny is . . . is . . ." Her eyes faltered as she wiped stray droplets from her cheeks.

"It's just one more role, Olivia," Kitty said. "Consider it an acting challenge."

"I'm glad you've got your priorities straight," Bree said. "Audition over murder. I'll keep that in mind."

Olivia whirled on her, her eyes wet. "What about you? You don't seem to care at all that Ronny's dead."

Bree stuck out her chin. "I don't." Only Kitty could see that her lower lip trembled.

"Where were you last night?" Margot said from out of nowhere. Her voice was calm. Too calm.

Olivia caught her breath. "Me?"

"All of you."

Turning on one another wasn't going to help. "Hold up," Kitty said. "We can't go pointing fingers."

"One of our targets is dead," Margot said. Her lips flattened as she pressed them together, and she looked more angry than scared. "No one else knew we were going after Ronny. That makes us the most likely suspects."

"Maybe we should go to the police?" Olivia said. "Tell them we didn't do it?"

Kitty nodded. "That's not a bad idea. It's not like they have proof DGM was involved."

Margot stared at her. "Don't they?" She wrenched her spy-caliber laptop out of her bag, entered a password on the screen, and pulled up a browser window. Within seconds, she was reading from a newspaper article. "'Authorities are searching for suspects involved in the fatal bludgeoning of a seventeen-year-old Bishop DuMaine high school student. Officers responded to an anonymous 911 call in the early hours of Wednesday morning near the Menlo Park neighborhood of North Fair Oaks. The victim sustained multiple blunt force trauma injuries to the head and was pronounced dead at the scene. He is believed to have been in bed at the time of the attack. No signs of forced entry. The entire household appears to have been asleep at the time and heard no sign of a struggle.'"

Olivia bit her lip. "Anonymous call?"

"It means identity unknown," Bree said with a smirk.

"I know what it means," Olivia snapped.

"'The apparent murder weapon was found at the scene,'" Margot continued. "'Along with a moniker for a local organization. No suspects are being held at this time. Anyone with information about the incident is asked to call detectives at the Menlo Park Police Department.'"

Kitty shrugged. "I don't see how any of that points to DGM."

Margot swung around in her chair. "The moniker for a local organization? That would be us."

FIFTEEN

"WE CAN'T BE SURE OF THAT," KITTY SAID QUICKLY. WHY WAS Margot so intent on placing the blame on a member of DGM?

Margot sighed, clearly frustrated. She spun back to her laptop, fingers blazing over the keyboard, then pulled away to reveal a photo on the screen.

It was a long metal baseball bat, the bottom third of which was thickly coated in a dark red substance. It stood leaning against a dresser, and the same reddish-brown liquid had seeped into the beige carpet, staining it.

Kitty's brain refused to process what she was seeing. It dawned on her slowly, painfully.

"You hacked into the police database?" she asked.

Margot didn't answer.

"Oh my God," Olivia gasped. "Isn't that illegal? Can't they find you and track you down and send us all to . . ." Her voice choked off.

"Juvie," Bree said. "We get it. You're obsessed with juvie."

"I've randomized the IP address," Margot said simply. "Even

if they could trace us through the satellite modem, the search won't lead them here."

Bree arched an eyebrow. "Not gonna lie, Margot. You're freaking me out a little bit."

Margot ignored her. She clicked the mouse rapidly, scrolling through several photos of the crime scene, then stopped. This time, all three of them gasped at the picture on the screen.

The photo was of a male hand, palm down on a bed. Blood splatter coated the gray-and-white striped bedspread like a Jackson Pollack, redder and more violently eye-catching than it had been on the bat or the carpet. Tucked beneath the hand, a white note card with three letters printed in a neat black font, reminiscent of an old typewriter: DGM.

"So much for going to the po-po," Bree said, slumping against the wall. "They'd never believe us."

"They have to," Olivia squeaked.

"Who has the rest of the DGM cards?" Kitty asked.

Bree slowly raised her hand. "But I didn't kill Ronny."

Kitty sighed. "Of course not. I'm wondering who might have had access to your room." She stared at the photo on Margot's computer. The DGM moniker might be the key to finding the killer. "It must have been stolen. How many people have actually seen one of those cards up close long enough to have been able to create an exact replica?"

Margot looked right at her. "You mean besides the four of us?"

"Stop it!" Kitty cried. "We've got to stick together if we're going to figure out who killed Ronny and why."

Margot turned her steely gaze on Kitty, so implacable it

made her uncomfortable. "Is that what we're going to do?" she said softly.

"I . . ." Kitty's voice trailed off. Twelve hours ago, Don't Get Mad had been a united front. Suddenly, in the wake of Ronny's death, Kitty could see the cracks forming. Blame, guilt, distrust, fear. She couldn't let that happen.

"Look," she said. "If we want to avoid getting blamed, we need to find out who actually killed him."

"Fine," Margot said. She clasped her hands in front of her. "If we assume that one of us didn't do it, then there are two logical possibilities: either someone wanted to kill Ronny and used DGM as a scapegoat, or someone wanted to frame us for murder, and killed Ronny to do so."

"But why Ronny?" Olivia asked. "And who would want to frame us for murder?"

"You mean other than Coach Creed?" Bree asked.

Bree had a point. After DGM's public humiliation of Coach Creed, he'd definitely be a suspect. Kitty nodded. "Creed runs first-period leadership. I can keep an eye on him."

"Rex," Olivia added. "He said at lunch the other day that he'd do whatever it took to bring down DGM."

"Good," Kitty said. "Then he's your assignment."

"I think Rex and Ronny knew each other," Bree said. "Or had a mutual friend. They had a weird conversation in phys ed on Thursday that made Rex twitchy."

"Even better," Kitty said. "Olivia, look into it."

"I'll go through Ronny's hard drive," Margot said. "Maybe I'll find a clue."

Bree sat up. "I saw something in Ronny's room."

"Yeah?" Kitty prompted.

Bree tilted her head to the side as if suddenly confused; then she rushed over to Margot's laptop. "Scroll back," she ordered. "Through the crime scene photos. I want to see something."

Everyone's eyes were locked on the screen as Margot clicked back through the photos. Most of them were mundane, photos of a messy room meant to document its exact condition when the body was discovered. After two dozen or so photos, Bree straightened up.

"Stop!" she shouted, then tapped the screen. "It's not there," she said. "Someone took it."

Kitty peered at the photo. It showed Ronny's bedroom door, half-open, with dirty laundry shoved into the corner behind it. "What's not there?"

"A list," Bree said quickly. "There was a list on his door with three names: Coach Creed, Rex Cavanaugh, and Theo Baranski."

"Removing evidence from a crime scene is against the law," Margot said.

Bree clicked her tongue. "So is murder."

"You think the killer took the list," Margot said. It wasn't a question.

"It's the only thing that makes sense," Bree said.

"Any idea what those names have in common with Ronny?" Kitty asked.

Bree shook her head. "Nada."

"Okay." Kitty glanced around the room. "Everyone keep

their eyes open on that one. If the names are all connected to Ronny, it might point us toward his killer." Kitty smiled. They were thinking like a team again.

"Anything else?" Bree asked, checking the time on her phone.

"You can make a list of who had access to the DGM cards," Kitty said, her voice stern.

"And keep an eye on John Baggott," Margot added.

Bree whirled on her. "He's got nothing to do with this."

Margot remained unnervingly calm. "He's your best friend, he has access to the DGM cards, and he's Father Uberti's number-one suspect. I'd say that makes him very much involved."

"I'm sure he's got nothing to do with Ronny's death," Kitty said, trying to pacify Bree. "But if Father Uberti's on his case, it might not be such a bad idea if you kept an eye on him. For his own safety."

Bree turned her back. "Fine."

"We'll lie low," Kitty continued. "No contact at all unless there's an emergency, okay? And let's meet at the warehouse one week from tonight to see what we've come up with. If we can't trust F.U. or the police to give us the benefit of the doubt, then we'll have to find Ronny's killer ourselves."

SIXTEEN

MARGOT HASTENED DOWN THE HALLWAY WITHOUT A BACKWARD glance. The last to leave the computer lab, she waited a full two minutes after Kitty's exit before she slipped out of the room, and she was halfway across campus before she slowed her pace.

As cool and collected as she'd tried to appear in front of the girls, Margot was freaking out on the inside. Ronny had been murdered, and even if she hadn't been the one to take a baseball bat to his head, what if by choosing him as the next DGM target, she'd unwittingly signed his death warrant? Wouldn't she be just as guilty as the murderer himself?

Margot kept her eyes glued to the floor as she hurried to her locker. The hallways were filled with students eating lunch, but the usually boisterous mood was significantly subdued. Cliques huddled closer than usual and spoke in hushed tones, and Margot couldn't help but think that everyone was staring at her with suspicion in their eyes.

You're being ridiculous.

There were exactly six students at Bishop DuMaine who

even knew her name. She was invisible at school, a ghost who moved through the hallways with anonymity, and she estimated her chances of being a named suspect in the investigation at approximately 572:1. No one even gave her a second thought, let alone suspected her of being involved with DGM.

She rounded the corner to her locker and stopped short at the sight of someone leaning against it. No, she was wrong. There was one person who suspected her.

Ed the Head.

"Dude," he said, eyes wide. "I can't believe it."

"Believe what?" Margot elbowed him aside and dialed in her locker combo without looking at him.

"Are you mental?"

The panic of Ronny's murder washed over her afresh. "I heard the announcement." Why couldn't he leave her alone?

"How can you be so casual?"

Margot gazed at him coolly. "It has nothing to do with me."

Ed the Head shoved his arm across her open locker, barring her from retrieving any books, and dropped his voice to a whisper. "Margot, we're talking about murder, and your friends in DGM are at the top of the suspect list."

"I don't know what you're talking about." Margot swallowed hard and tried to keep her breathing steady. She couldn't let him see her fear.

"Look." Ed's voice softened. "Personally, I don't give a shit about Ronny. Cruel? Maybe. But he'd only been at school for like a hot minute and he'd already stiffed me on a half-dozen Snickers bars, joined up with the 'Maine Men, and I caught him face raping Olivia Hayes outside the boys' locker room. Kinda hard to mourn his loss."

Margot had to appreciate his bluntness.

"But shit just got real. I mean, maybe you should tell them to just turn themselves in? Let the police figure it out?"

Margot looked up at him sharply. "I do *not* have any connection to DGM." For some reason, she desperately needed him to believe her. "It was a guess about the assembly, based on their previous exploits. An educated guess. Don't think I'm their secret keeper all of a sudden just because I predicted their last move."

"Sorry." Ed the Head dropped his eyes to the floor, suitably chastised. "I didn't mean to freak you out."

Margot took a deep breath and tried to center herself. "I'm going to be late to class."

Ed leaned forward and his usual mask of cocky glibness fell away for a second. "Be careful, okay? There's something rotten in Denmark."

Margot nodded. She'd never seen Ed the Head drop the clown act before, and she realized that despite their business arrangement, he actually cared about her. No one at Bishop DuMaine cared about her, and Ed's moment of kindness touched her so deeply she wasn't even tempted to correct his misuse of the *Hamlet* quote.

"Right." Ed the Head straightened up, his old self again. "Watch your back. That's all I'm saying. Because if anything happens to you, my earning potential at this school is going to take a serious nosedive. Speaking of, I've got new odds on the murder investigation. Three to one they never find out who did it. You in?"

"Am I ever?"

"Touché, *mon frère*. I am considerably"—he snapped and gave Margot two finger pistols—"out of here."

Margot pressed her head against the open door of her locker and closed her eyes. She'd been careless to let Ed the Head have a glimpse into her association with DGM. Unless he was significantly stupider than she gave him credit for, Ed didn't buy her proclamations of innocence for a nanosecond. While he couldn't know she was directly involved, Ed believed she had some connection to DGM. She just prayed he'd keep that hypothesis to himself.

It was so unlike her to trust anyone with anything. But she'd needed his help to dig up dirt on Amber Stevens, and she'd been blinded by hatred where that goal was concerned.

Margot sighed. There was nothing she could do about it now. The best way to protect herself was to find out who actually killed Ronny before the police and Father Uberti uncovered the truth about DGM. She pulled her calculus textbook out of her locker, grunting with the weight of the college-level tome, and froze.

A large manila envelope tumbled to the ground.

She stared down at the yellowish brown envelope on the tile floor. A white address label had been printed with her name, centered on the front. The print-and-peel label was the standard one inch by two and five-eighths, thirty to a sheet. The font was Times New Roman, also standard, and the envelope appeared to be the generic brand sold in every office supply store.

Margot gingerly picked up the envelope, handling it with care as if it were made of porcelain, and examined the back side. It had been sealed with a single piece of tape, meticulously positioned dead center on the flap.

Who would go through the trouble of leaving this envelope in her locker? And why?

There was only one way to know. Margot forced her finger under the flap and broke the seal.

Inside was a photograph.

Margot clenched her jaw so fiercely she thought she might crack a tooth. It had been years since she'd laid eyes on that photo, years since the humiliating image of her twelve-year-old self had made life no longer worth living. And yet she remembered every nuance of the image, because she had seen it every single day of her life for the last four years, burned into her memory. Eyes open or closed, she saw that image, like the single dot of light branded into your retina after looking directly at the sun.

It had been taken from outside her house four years ago, long after sunset, when the light from her bedroom window cast an orangey glow on the large sycamore tree. Her bedroom, less austere and more childlike, her stuffed animals and toy shelves not yet replaced by bookcases packed to the brim with academic texts. Her bedspread of bright flowers instead of plain gray, and the walls covered with teen idol photos instead of framed certificates of merit.

Even the girl in the photo was a different Margot. She stood in the middle of her room, dressed only in a training bra and panties. A roll of fat blossomed from either side of her belly button, her lumpy thighs looked like overstuffed sausages, and her bubble butt was so enormous and out of place, it looked as if it was artificially enhanced.

Twelve-year-old Margot held something in her hand, a roll of plastic wrap, which she was twisting around her midsection.

That photo had made Margot the laughingstock of junior high. It had almost killed her.

So why had someone left it in her locker?

SEVENTEEN

BREE PLUGGED HER IPOD INTO THE CENTER CONSOLE OF Mrs. Baggott's minivan and scrolled through her playlists. It was safer to focus on picking out a song than to just sit there, trying to pretend that nothing out of the ordinary had happened when in reality all she could think about was a douchey seventeen-year-old bludgeoned to death in his bedroom. Bree had been in that room just hours before. It was as if she'd ventured too close to death and now it haunted her, tainting every moment of her day.

"Would you play something already?" John sprawled on the middle bench seat, head propped up on his backpack, munching on Smartfood while he perused his newest comic book. "The silence is oppressive."

"I'm looking for the perfect hiding-in-your-mom's-minivan-while-we-ditch-sixth-period-gym soundtrack."

"We're not hiding," John said, flipping a page. "That new kid is dead, and F.U. and the cops think DGM is involved, which means the 'Maine Men will be on the lookout for the two of us."

He lowered his comic book. "I don't know about you, but Baggott the Faggot is simply not in the mood for his adoring fans this afternoon."

"I don't blame you." Bree landed on her favorite Bangers and Mosh song—"Bangin' Love"—and cranked the volume.

John groaned. "You've got to be kidding me."

"What?" Bree smiled innocently. "It's a great song."

"A great song I played until my fingers bled last night."

At the mention of rehearsal, Bree perked up. "You going again tonight?"

"Yep," he said. Then, as if he could read her mind, "But Shane won't be there. He's got an audition for the school play."

"Oh." Play auditions? She pictured Shane surrounded by a bunch of pain-in-the-ass girls like Amber and Olivia. He'd be trapped in that theater for fourth period every day, sitting all by himself in rehearsals, bored and snarky.

This was an opportunity. Maybe if Bree joined the drama class, he could get to know her and realize how freaking perfect they were for each other. . . .

"Stop daydreaming about Shane and change the damn song already."

Bree started, irritated by the fact that he could read her so well. "Fine." She paused "Bangin' Love" and searched for something else that would needle him, pausing at a New Wave playlist she'd recently created for just such an occasion.

John arched an eyebrow at the opening synth line, stark and lonely. "Seriously?"

"Relax and let it happen," Bree said as the drum track

kicked in, so utterly eighties it made Bree want to wear an off-the-shoulder sweatshirt and leg warmers.

"Why are we listening to this?" John asked.

"Cuz it's awesome." Bree sang along with the vocals. *"And if I had to walk the world, I'd make you fall for me."*

"This blows."

"Come on. You're supposed to be the open-minded musical genius. How do you know you don't like it if you don't try it?"

"You think I don't know this song?" John cleared his throat. "'The Promise' by When in Rome. A one-hit wonder from the British New Wave scene of the eighties. 'The Promise' was their biggest hit in the U.S., charting in 1988."

Bree stared at him. "You're like a music savant or something."

"It's what I do." John cracked open an energy drink.

"It's a little—" Out of the corner of her eye, Bree saw a pack of blue-shirted 'Maine Men turn the corner of the gym and wander into the faculty parking lot. "We've got bogies, ten o'clock."

John flattened himself against the bench seat while Bree crouched behind the headrest. Looking like a gaggle of overgrown Smurfs, four 'Maine Men strode purposefully into the parking lot as if hunting for something specific. They scanned the lines of cars; then, satisfied that there was no one to harass, they marched back inside.

"Clear," Bree said, unpretzeling her body.

John rolled onto his side to face her. "So where were you at lunch?"

Bree picked up her iPod and pretended to search through its contents. She'd known this question would be coming and she'd prepared an answer, gone over the delivery in her mind, trying to make it sound credible. But she didn't want to look at John while she lied to him. "I had an appointment with Mr. Niemeyer."

John snorted. "Since when do you actually show up for appointments with your guidance counselor?"

"Why would I lie about going to the guidance counselor?"

"I was worried you'd been hauled into Father Uberti's office."

Bree chuckled. "Yeah, right. F.U. won't risk the wrath of Senator Deringer without proof."

"Don't be too sure," John said. "This is a murder investigation. The rules have changed."

A chill passed over Bree. Murder. Someone had deliberately and intentionally killed Ronny. She remembered the creak of the door and the faint patter of footsteps outside his bedroom. Had she been in the presence of a killer without knowing it? And if so, would he come after her next?

"I've been thinking," John said, pushing himself upright with sudden energy. "If it's not us perpetrating these crimes on douchebag humanity, then who is it?"

"*If* it's not us?" Bree smiled. "You mean *since* it's not us."

John shrugged. "Sure."

Bree didn't like John's body language. *Sure?* Could he possibly believe, even for a second, that Bree was involved?

"Whoever it is," John said, staring out the window, "they're smart."

Thank you. "So that rules out Rex's brain trust."

"Not necessarily." John leaned forward. "What better way to gain insider information? I mean, think about it. That dance-recital footage of Tammi Barnes last year? You and I wouldn't have known anything about it. But someone from Tammi's inner circle might have."

Like Olivia. "Okay," Bree said, playing along. "Let's say it *is* one of them. I know the rich bitches aren't the sharpest arrows in the quiver, but don't you think someone would have figured it out by now?"

The right side of John's mouth quirked into a half smile. "If there was only one person involved, sure. But my guess is that DGM is a group. Three, maybe four members. That way, no one person would be the source of all their information, or responsible for every aspect of their pranks."

"You've thought *way* too much about this."

"If you're accused of a crime you didn't commit, you get curious about who's really to blame."

A wave of guilt passed through her. It was, after all, partially her fault that John was a suspect.

The bell rang, signaling the end of the school day, and Bree stretched her arms over her head. "If F.U. had you working for the 'Maine Men," she said with a yawn, "this case would be solved by now. Maybe we should get you one of those polo shirts and you can crash their next meeting?"

"Hell no," John said, sliding open the van door. "If I did know who was involved with DGM, Father Uberti would be the last person I'd tell. I'd want to give them a hug, that's all."

John locked the minivan with the key fob as he walked toward the school. Students were already pouring out of the side door as Bree fell into step beside him. "Or join them."

"Nah," John said. "They don't need Prime Suspect Number One hanging around. I'm pretty sure F.U. thinks I'm a killer at this point."

Bree laughed. John couldn't hurt a fly.

"I've gotta hit my locker," he said. "Meet you at the bus stop?"

"Okay," she said to no one. John had already bounded off down the hall.

Bree couldn't help but sigh as she wove through the crowded hallway toward her locker. She'd known for a while that John had a man crush on DGM and their antics, but she hadn't realized exactly how much energy he'd spent contemplating their identities.

Bree shook her head as she dialed in her locker combination. If John really started to dig around, would all of DGM's carefully planned subterfuge hold up to his scrutiny? Maybe Kitty and Margot were right. Maybe she *did* need to keep a close eye on him, in case he decided to ramp up his investigation.

The idea of spying on her friend made her nauseous: not only would she be betraying his trust, but in doing so, she was implicitly admitting that he was some kind of threat to DGM. But the idea that both of them could be implicated in a crime of which they were totally innocent was even worse than jeopardizing their friendship.

Bree reached into her locker to grab some homework. If spying on John was a way to keep him safe, it was a risk she had to take.

As she stood on her tiptoes to grab a binder in the back, she saw something that wiped all thoughts of John from her mind: a manila envelope with her name on it, carefully placed on top of her history textbook.

Bree was damn sure the envelope hadn't been there before lunch.

Which meant someone had been in her locker.

With a trembling hand, Bree picked up the envelope and broke the seal.

A crumpled piece of notebook paper fluttered out into her open palm. It was soft and wrinkled, as if someone had balled it up and thrown it away, then changed their mind and reclaimed it from the trash, and it was covered in frantic, almost manic handwriting.

Bree scanned the scrawled words and her heart nearly stopped.

DGM
Dare Go 'Maine
Dare God and 'Maine
Damn God and 'Maine
Damn Good Men
Do Good Men
Do Good and Mad
Do Get Mad
Don't Get Mad!!!!!!

The last was punctuated with a half-dozen exclamation

points, underlined several times, and circled, just in case the writer didn't remember which version he liked the best.

Worst of all, it was a handwriting Bree recognized only too well.

It was John's.

EIGHTEEN

KITTY FELT A PANG OF DISAPPOINTMENT WHEN THE ALARM ON Donté's phone went off. "Damn," he said, silencing it. "I can't believe it's already six o'clock."

"I know." It had been a fantastic date, the kind that Kitty had believed existed only in romantic comedies and chick-lit novels. Two hours of conversation over burgers and sodas had never flown by so quickly, and she didn't want it to end. They'd talked about everything, and found out they had a ridiculous amount in common. They both had two younger sisters, two working parents, and had been playing team sports all their lives. Two hours flew by without any awkward pauses or weird faux pas, and she was sorry to see it end.

"I'm sorry I had to bail on the movie tonight," Donté said after he flagged down the waitress. "But play auditions are mandatory for drama class, and I kinda need the easy A."

"It's okay," Kitty said.

"Kinda weird, us going on a date today, isn't it?" Donté said.

Weird? Had their date been weird and Kitty hadn't even realized it?

"After what happened at school," Donté continued.

Kitty bit her lip. Ronny. That's right. In the midst of her amazing date with Donté, Kitty had completely forgotten that a murder had been committed that may or may not be partially her fault. "Yeah," she managed to say, her throat dry. "Awful."

Adele's "One and Only" came on the PA system, and Kitty jumped at the opportunity to change the subject.

"I love this song," she said awkwardly.

Donté stared out the window, his eyes far away. "It was our song. Olivia's and mine."

"Oh." Was he trying to tell her that he was still hung up on Olivia? Was this his way of telling her they were just friends? "I guess she was pretty special?" She couldn't hide the question mark at the end of the sentence.

Donté sucked in a breath. "Crap, I'm sorry! I totally didn't mean it like that. I mean, I wasn't trying to bring up my ex."

Kitty sat utterly still. Was she supposed to say something? Ask him to explain it to her? Dammit, why was she so indecisive all of a sudden?

Donté reached across the table and touched her hand. "I wasn't thinking about Olivia at all. I promise. We broke up. It's over."

Kitty snorted. "Please, everyone knows she dropped you like third-period French."

As soon as she blurted out the words, Kitty's hand flew to her mouth. "Oh my God!" she squeaked, her voice muffled by her palm. What did she just do? If Donté hadn't lost interest before, he'd hit the eject button now for sure.

But instead of getting defensive, Donté tossed his head back and laughed. "I know, I know," he said. "That was the rumor and I didn't correct it. I think Livvie's friends were putting pressure on her to dump me." He stopped laughing and leaned back against the booth, smiling. "The truth is I broke up with her."

"But you guys were the perfect couple."

Donté shrugged. "I guess that's what people thought, but Olivia and I never really gelled. We were always going to parties or out with her friends. It was never just the two of us, and I felt like I was always acting, pretending to be the kind of boyfriend she wanted."

"Oh." Kitty couldn't think of anything else to say. The most beautiful girl at school getting dumped by the boy who just took her on the best date of her life was a difficult concept to wrap her head around.

"But it's not like that with you." Donté passed his hand over his closely shaved head and leaned toward her. "I had an awesome time today."

"Me too." She'd half-thought she was imagining that the date was going well, especially since she jabbered away like a lunatic most of the time, and it was a relief to know that despite her lack of social experience, she wasn't the only one who'd had a good time.

"And you won't get in trouble with Coach Miles?" he asked, his eyebrows raised.

Kitty shook her head. "We get to miss one practice each

semester, no questions asked."

Donté laughed again. "Me too! This was the best use of my free pass ever."

The check came and Donté slapped some bills on the table, then stood up and offered Kitty his hand. "Can I walk you to your car?"

Neither of them said a word as they approached Kitty's hand-me-down Corolla, the first time that day there had been silence between them. Kitty wasn't sure what it meant. Was Donté bored with her? Or was he debating whether or not to ask her out again?

Please ask me out again. Please, please, please.

They reached the door, and Donté turned to face her. "So, how would you feel about doing it again? Maybe this weekend?"

"I'd like that," she said, trying not to sound relieved.

"Good." Donté cupped her chin with his hand and tilted her face upward to meet his. Simply gazing into his enormous brown eyes made her legs turn to jelly. He traced her lips with his thumb and they buzzed beneath his touch; then he leaned down and kissed her.

Donté touched Kitty as if she were fragile but not frail. One hand held her firmly at the small of her back, the other was behind her neck—his fingers laced into her thick hair. The effect was electric, charged like a thunderstorm rolling across her body. Her mind turned to putty and her heart skipped a beat as if it too was having a hard time keeping its mind on what it was supposed to be doing.

Donté was the first boy to kiss her since Marty Heffernan in sixth grade, who had to stand on a stepstool to reach her face, and who'd mistakenly thought that "slipping her the tongue" meant licking Kitty's cheek. The Donté version was less sloppy and significantly sexier.

He pulled his lips away. "Damn," he whispered.

Damn? "Is that good?" she asked.

"Yes," he said softly.

"Oh. Okay."

"You're cute."

Kitty sighed. Well, if she was going to act like a total spaz on their first date, at least he found it adorable.

Donté leaned toward her. "I wish I didn't have to leave."

"But you do." Kitty unlocked her car door and swung it open. "Good luck at the audition."

"Break a leg," Donté corrected. "That's what the actors say."

Kitty headed straight to her room the second she got home and flopped down on her bed, her head spinning. Donté Greene had kissed her! She'd dreamed about that moment for months, but he seemed so out of her league. Homecoming court, captain of the basketball team, member of the 'Maine Men.

Donté was a 'Maine Man.

Kitty sat straight up as her stomach dropped. She and Donté—it could never work. He was part of the 'Maine Men, specifically created to bring about the downfall of Don't Get Mad. A group that she started. Even if he hadn't been Olivia's ex-boyfriend, they were on opposite sides of the net.

She needed to stop now before she got in too deep. She'd text Donté and tell him she couldn't see him anymore. Blame it on her parents, her grades, anything. She dug through her duffel bag, searching for her cell phone, and halted abruptly. Shoved between her spiral notebook and pencil case was a large manila envelope.

It looked like the kind of envelopes that piled up in her in-box on the leadership desk, used by Mrs. Baggott to convey official administrative memos. Only those were generically addressed to "Student Leadership." This one had Kitty's name on it.

She broke the seal on the flap and turned it upside down.

Kitty watched a newspaper clipping flutter out of the envelope and rest faceup on her bedspread. It was a short article, simply titled "Archway Student Goes AWOL."

Archway Military Academy. Had Margot found new information on why Ronny left Archway?

She scanned the article. Yes, an Archway student had gone AWOL.

Only it wasn't Ronny DeStefano.

Who the hell was Christopher Beeman?

NINETEEN

ACT NORMAL, OLIVIA REPEATED TO HERSELF AS SHE SLOWLY walked across the quad. Peanut jabbered at her side as she'd done almost incessantly since they'd left her house. She'd asked Olivia at least a half-dozen times if she'd known Ronny. Each time Olivia had told her that she'd seen him around, and then Peanut had launched into a nervous, meandering stream of consciousness about how she had first-period English with Ronny and how she'd known the moment Father Uberti came on the PA that something had happened to him.

Olivia had listened patiently, letting Peanut ramble on, even though the mere mention of Ronny's name was enough to make Olivia's stomach clench up with a confusing mix of sorrow, guilt, and fear.

Meanwhile, all Olivia wanted to do was to run home, climb into bed with a king-size pack of Ho Hos, and pull the covers over her head until the horror of the day disappeared.

But Kitty's words ran through her head on an endless loop: *We need to go about our lives like nothing's happened.*

In the face of Ronny's death, the fall play suddenly seemed trivial, but if she bombed her audition, it might look suspicious. And that would be disastrous.

She had to keep it together.

The theater was buzzing with excitement by the time she and Peanut arrived. It was an odd feeling, as if events outside the theater door hadn't happened at all. Inside, it was all business.

"Everyone needs to sign up," Mr. Cunningham directed from the stage. He pointed to a clipboard at his feet. "Then take a seat so we can get started."

"Olivia!" Amber waved from the foot of the stage. Her light brown curls were radiant in the glow of the overhead lights, her face smiling. "I signed you up right after me."

"What about me?" Peanut asked.

Amber pointed to the sign-up sheet, then grabbed Olivia's hand. "Won't it be fun to go back-to-back? Both reading for Olivia?"

Why was Amber so adamant that they both audition for Olivia? She remembered Mr. Cunningham's cryptic warning and forced a smile. "How do you know I'm not auditioning for Viola?"

Amber laughed. "Why would you do that? She spends the whole play dressed like a boy."

So that was it. Amber wanted to play the pretty role, the girl who got all the attention, and assumed Olivia did too.

Olivia nodded sagely. "Right."

As everyone settled into their seats, Mr. Cunningham sat on the edge of the stage for a little tête-à-tête. "It's been an emotional day here at Bishop DuMaine," he began, his face sympathetic. "We've lost one of our own, a star whose light will never have the opportunity to shine."

Olivia had to force the images of Ronny's smarmy face and octopus arms from her mind.

"And though Ronald wasn't a member of the drama program," Mr. Cunningham continued, "we will be dedicating our opening-night performance to his memory."

Amber placed her hand over her heart. "For Ronny," she whispered dramatically.

Ew?

After a suitable pause, Mr. Cunningham picked up his clipboard and got back to business. "We'll start with the gentlemen, since there are significantly fewer of you. When I call your name, please take the stage, announce yourself and the role for which you are auditioning, then you may begin." He cleared his throat and consulted his sign-up sheet. "I'll be posting the cast list at lunch tomorrow and we'll be jumping into rehearsals immediately. So let's get started. Mr. Greene, if you please?"

Olivia inched to the edge of her seat while Donté walked down the aisle. She was more nervous for his audition than she was for her own.

Needlessly nervous, it turned out. Donté wasn't half-bad. He read from the script, but there was finesse to his performance, a spark that elevated him above the average high school student reading Shakespeare out loud in English class, as if he'd absorbed some of Olivia's skills from watching her perform.

Olivia sighed as he exited the stage, her heart warm. Clearly she'd given Donté something during their relationship, ignited the acting bug in him. She'd gained so much from their time together: confidence, security, and a sense that she deserved to be treated well. But after he dumped her, she'd always wondered if she'd given him anything in return. Donté's audition was proof that she had.

Shane White was next, auditioning for the clown, Feste. Then a steady flow of Sir Toby Belch monologues, probably due more to the character's name than anything else, and several nervous auditions where Olivia swore she could see the script pages shaking in the actors' hands. She was beginning to worry there would be no decent Orsinos, until Logan.

"I'm Logan Blaine," he said, then paused and gazed around the stage, eyes wide with wonder. "Awesome acoustics, dude. This theater is tight."

Laughter rippled through the house. Mr. Cunningham cleared his throat pointedly and everyone fell silent.

"I'm glad it meets your approbation, Mr. Blaine," he said, sarcasm dripping from every syllable. "Will you be gracing us with an audition today?"

"Oh yeah! Sorry." Logan ran his fingers through his long blond hair. "I'm auditioning for Orsino."

He had no script in his hand.

"I cannot wait," Mr. Cunningham mumbled.

Logan's voice was strong and passionate as he gave Orsino's desperate final speech to Olivia. Anger and spite radiated from every word, every crisp consonant and phonated vowel. He filled the stage with his presence, the house with his voice. As the monologue ended, it took all of Olivia's self-control not to applaud.

"Wow," Amber breathed next to her.

Wow was an understatement. The only people who commanded such an unwavering commitment to character were highly trained thespians and sociopaths, and Logan didn't seem to be either.

"Mr. Blaine," Mr. Cunningham said, rising to his feet. "That was astounding."

"Thanks!" Logan said. "I watched the movie last night. The one with Gandhi and the chick that's married to Tim Burton. It was awesome."

"I see." Mr. Cunningham sounded utterly confused.

The girls were next, and it took about a dozen or so auditions before Olivia realized that something weird was going on.

Every single girl was reading for Viola.

Granted there were only three actual female roles in the play, and even though Mr. Cunningham was planning some creative casting with several of the supporting male parts, there should have been at least a fair distribution of auditions for Olivia, Viola, and Maria the maid.

Nope. One after another, girls announced that they'd be auditioning for Viola, and one after another they all gave one of Viola's main speeches.

Even Peanut and Jezebel both read the "I am the man" soliloquy, with about as much enthusiasm as if they'd been reciting Spanish verb conjugations. As Peanut sat down after her audition, she steadfastly refused to look at Olivia.

"Miss Stevens."

Amber sprang to her feet, barely able to contain her excitement. "Here I go!" she said as she shimmied past Olivia and Peanut into the aisle.

As soon as she'd left the row, Peanut gripped Olivia's hand. "Sorry," she mouthed.

"What?" Olivia whispered. "Why are you sorry?"

Peanut shook her head and looked away.

Why was everyone acting so weird about this production? She remembered Mr. Cunningham's warning, Amber's insistence that they'd be vying for Olivia, an endless parade of Viola auditions . . .

Olivia's hands shook so violently she had to sit on them to keep from vibrating the entire row of chairs. Suddenly it all made sense. Amber's parents had bought her a role in this production, but they hadn't been able to guarantee that she'd win the internship. And what was the best way to do that? Eliminate the competition.

Olivia's stomach flip-flopped with a mix of betrayal and anger.

Amber didn't just want the lead in the school play; she wanted to make sure that Olivia wasn't cast at all.

"My name is Amber Stevens and I'll be auditioning for the part of Olivia."

Amber was cocky. Olivia could hear it in her voice, see it in the way she held her body. Olivia knew that attitude. It was the same posture Amber had copped when she waltzed into the winter formal last year wearing a thousand-dollar Badgley Mischka, or when she got "elected" prom queen in eighth grade after her dad rented out the Corinthian Ballroom for the dance. It was a cockiness that came with knowing the outcome in advance.

Amber read from the script, though her audition had been heavily coached. It wasn't bad, per se. She used the stage, following obvious choreography with stock hand gestures. But it was lacking in any real depth, any sense of what the stakes were for the character. Still, it was better than any performance Olivia had ever seen her give. Mr. Cunningham's private lessons were paying off.

Amber finished her short audition, curtsied, and literally bounced off the stage as Mr. Cunningham called the last audition of the day. "Miss Hayes."

Olivia slowly rose out of her chair, her eyes fixed on Amber, seeing her for the first time in a new light.

"That was amazing," Amber said, breezing past her. "I wasn't nervous at all!"

Olivia didn't respond. She needed to focus. The walk down the aisle took forever, as if the distance was elongating before her. Her ballet flats were noiseless on the thick wooden stage, and as the audience disappeared into anonymity behind the ferocious lights, Olivia suddenly felt very small and very alone.

You can't let her win. This is your chance. Take it.

"My name is Olivia Hayes," she said. Her bell-like voice rang out through the theater. "And I'm auditioning for Viola."

Olivia was still on an audition high when Peanut dropped her off at home. Gone were the panic and anxiety that had oppressed her from the moment Father Uberti had broken the news of Ronny's death. The audition had driven everything else from her mind, and as she sauntered up the stairs and into the dark apartment, she was practically drunk from the adrenaline.

She switched on the light in the hallway and leaned back against the door. One day she'd be a famous actress. Her mom would be able to quit her crappy job, and Olivia could get them a real home instead of a cluttered one-bedroom apartment bordering a sketchy neighborhood. Today's audition was the first step toward that goal.

But now, she needed to decompress. With a heavy groan, Olivia swung the Burberry tote that doubled as her school bag onto the sofa, spilling the contents across the plush cushions.

On top of the pile of monologue anthologies and textbooks sat a plain manila envelope with Olivia's name on it.

It must be from Mr. Cunningham. He often sent her home with Xeroxed scenes, acting worksheets, and character exercises. In the confusion of the auditions, he'd probably left the envelope near her bag and forgotten to tell her.

Eager to see if it had something to do with *Twelfth Night*, Olivia tore it open.

Inside was a newspaper article.

It was from the *San Jose Mercury News*, dated almost two years ago and detailing the Bishop DuMaine grade-fixing scandal that had rocked the school during Olivia's freshman year.

She hadn't paid much attention at the time. The suspensions and expulsions had only affected a handful of student athletes, no one from Olivia's circle. All she remembered was that several coaches had bribed teachers to give members of their teams inflated grades, keeping them off academic probation. As she read through the article, Olivia learned that the authorities had been informed by an anonymous tip, and when the details of the conspiracy came to light, several students were expelled for recruiting others into the grade fixing, and a handful of faculty members—including Coach Creed's predecessor—were fired outright.

She glanced through the list of students who had been expelled, trying to see if it had any bearing on the drama program. She recognized a few names, but the rest were unfamiliar. So why did Mr. Cunningham want her to read the article?

Research maybe? Mr. Cunningham did say that this would be an original production of *Twelfth Night*. If he was gunning to sell it to the Oregon Shakespeare Festival, it would have to be an off-the-wall setting, maybe the background of a high school scandal?

Olivia smiled to herself. No one knew more about high school scandals than a member of DGM.

With a yawn, Olivia stuffed the newspaper clipping into her drama notebook and grabbed the remote from the table. She'd deal with it later.

TWENTY

KITTY WASN'T SURE WHAT SHE WAS EXPECTING TO FIND WHEN she turned into the upperclassmen's parking lot the next morning. A return to normalcy? A full reset, as if Ronny's murder had never happened? Totally unrealistic, she realized, but still, unconsciously, she'd hoped that life at Bishop DuMaine would go back to its regularly scheduled programming.

No such luck.

The police were still out in full force. In fact, it didn't look like they'd left their posts at each of the main school entrances since yesterday. Kitty's heart sank as she realized that there would be no reprieve from suspicion and anxiety at Bishop DuMaine any time soon.

An SUV pulled into the spot next to her, and Donté stepped out.

"Hi!" Kitty said, swinging her door open. She felt a surge of excitement she immediately tried to suppress. She needed to stick to her guns: she and Donté could never be together. "What are you doing here so early?"

Donté jogged around the front of his car. "I couldn't wait to see you again." He slipped his hand into hers, and Kitty's stomach did a backflip.

"Come on," Donté said, tugging her toward school. "I'll walk you to the office. You need to prep those announcements."

Not one but two officers barred their way into the administrative building—one male, one female—and they each carried a clipboard.

"Name?" the female officer said to Kitty.

"Kitty Wei and Donté Greene." Her eyes grew wide. "I mean, not that we're together. Not like that. Er, I mean, we came through the door together, but it's not what you're thinking." Kitty could feel her face growing hot. What was it about Donté that turned her into a total dork?

"I'm sure it's not," the officer said with a smirk, crossing two names off her list. "Next?"

"It's okay, you know," Donté said quietly as they hurried to the school office.

"The security checkpoint?" Kitty asked.

"I meant people thinking we're a couple. It's okay, right?"

"Right," Kitty said. Only she didn't hear herself speak over the sound of her brain screaming *OH MY GOD, DONTÉ THINKS WE'RE A COUPLE!* on an endless loop.

They turned the corner and found Mika waiting by the office door. As soon as she saw Kitty with Donté, a sly smile spread across her face. "Hi, Donté," she said coyly. "Aren't you here early this morning?"

Donté laughed lightly. "It's like the airport—gotta leave time for security."

"For reals," Mika said, instantly serious. "Can you believe that? What's next—locker searches? Pat-downs?"

"It's pretty jacked," Donté said.

"A student was murdered, Mika," Kitty said, trying to be the voice of reason.

Mika threw up her hands. "They haven't proved anyone from Bishop DuMaine was involved. Are they going to take away all of our rights while they search for the killer?"

If it kept someone from killing again, Kitty wasn't so sure that was a bad thing.

But she couldn't say that to Mika, for whom the security checkpoint had clearly touched a nerve. Instead, she glanced at her watch. "I've got to get the announcements ready," she said, then looked at Mika. "Did you need me for something?"

Mika shook her head. "Nope, it can wait. Come on, Donté. You can tell me all about your date yesterday on our way to leadership class." She dragged Donté down the hall before Kitty could protest.

Donté barely managed a wave over his shoulder as Mika hustled him out of sight.

"Good morning, Kitty," Mrs. Baggott said as Kitty walked into the office. It was her usual greeting, but Mrs. Baggott's voice lacked her characteristic cheerful, singsong quality. Instead, both the words and the sentiment seemed forced, and her smile, usually so genuine, was tense, her face lined with worry.

"Morning, Mrs. Baggott," Kitty said. "Still crazy around here today?"

Mrs. Baggott pushed her wheelie desk chair across the floor to a short file cabinet and nodded toward Father Uberti's office. "You can say that again."

The blinds in his office were open, and Kitty stole a glance inside as she shuffled through the in-box. Father Uberti paced in front of the window, arms clasped behind his back like a man deep in philosophical thought. Sitting on the other side of the desk, arms waving erratically as he spoke, was Coach Creed.

Coach Creed and Father Uberti in conference? Perfect opportunity to find out what they knew about Ronny's murder. Feigning a visit to the filing cabinet next to Father Uberti's office, Kitty pretended to search for something, her ears straining as she eavesdropped.

"Bullshit!" Coach Creed barked. "Uh, sorry, Father." He cleared his throat. "I just mean, we've got a dead student. Murder is still a crime, isn't it?"

Father Uberti gritted his teeth. "Yes, Dick. Murder is a crime. But there's no evidence that they're guilty."

Coach Creed pounded his fist against the desk. "We can't let John Baggott and Bree Deringer get away with it!"

Kitty stiffened. Bree and John?

"Shh!" Father Uberti hissed. "Maureen will hear you. And you can't go around throwing out murder accusations willy-nilly."

"But they're guilty!" Coach Creed said.

Father Uberti shook his head. "Maybe of being behind the

DGM pranks, but of murder? I'm not willing to go that far."

"Fine," Coach Creed mumbled. "But we can't let them get away with it."

Father Uberti smiled. "You mean murder or making you look like an ass in front of the entire school?"

Coach Creed scowled but didn't answer.

Father Uberti renewed his pacing. "We need probable cause."

Coach Creed's head snapped up. "How do we do that?"

"Weren't you at some military academy before you came here? Out in Arizona?"

A military academy in Arizona? The list Bree saw in Ronny's room popped into Kitty's mind. Could that be the connection? Could Coach Creed have taught at Archway?

"Yeah," Coach Creed said slowly. "What about it?"

Father Uberti sighed heavily. "Use your brain, Dick. Bishop DuMaine has its own army of peer enforcers."

It took Coach Creed a full ten seconds to grasp the priest's meaning. "You mean the 'Maine Men? You want us to—"

A massive bang ripped through the office as the door burst open and Rex sprinted into Father Uberti's office. "They got him!"

Kitty froze. *Him?*

Coach Creed vaulted to his feet. "Baggott? They've arrested him?"

In the lobby, Kitty watched the color drain out of Mrs. Baggott's face.

Rex shook his head. "No. He confessed. And you're never going to believe this, the killer is—"

Before Rex could answer, the two police officers who had been manning the side entrance marched into the administrative lobby, half-dragging a student between them. Kitty's jaw dropped.

It wasn't John Baggott who had confessed to Ronny's murder. It was Theo Baranski.

TWENTY-ONE

"TELL ME AGAIN WHY WE'RE EATING LUNCH IN THE LIBRARY?"
Bree asked.

John snuck a bite of his turkey sandwich, clandestinely hidden in his backpack. "More comfortable than my mom's minivan."

"Is it? Is it really?"

John sniffed the air. "Well, the library doesn't make my lunch smell like car freshener, so yes."

"Point taken." Bree slouched in her chair. Shane was out in the quad eating lunch with his friends, while she was stuck in the library, hiding. "But why can't we eat in the quad like normal pariahs? You heard the news: Theo confessed. The 'Maine Men have been called off. Isn't that the end of it?" Bree hoped more than believed that the case was closed.

"Please," John sputtered through a mouthful of turkey. "He didn't do it."

Bree stiffened. The moment the rumor swept through school, Bree had felt a tremendous weight lift from her shoulders. If Theo had killed Ronny, it meant that the list she'd seen in

Ronny's room had everything to do with his death, and DGM was totally innocent. Now John was bursting her bubble, and she prayed that he was wrong. "How do you know?"

John chewed thoughtfully. "Theo confessed to protect DGM. It's pretty obvious. Probably feels he owes it to them after what they did to Coach Creed."

"Confessing to a murder you didn't commit is kinda overkill on the payback, don't you think?"

"I bet he has an alibi," John said. "Ten-to-one odds he's back in school tomorrow."

Bree wasn't sure how she felt. Part of her wanted to believe that Theo had killed Ronny. His name was on the list that had disappeared from Ronny's room—clearly they had a connection no one knew about.

On the other hand, Bree cringed at the thought that Theo had only confessed to protect DGM. She couldn't let him go down for a crime he didn't commit, could she?

While thoughts of Theo and Ronny did a square dance in her head, John pulled a crumpled piece of notebook paper out of his bag and studied it closely. From what Bree could see, it was a list, in John's frenzied scrawl, and the anonymous envelope in her locker rushed back into her mind.

If someone other than John had slipped that envelope into her locker, it could only be a warning: someone's on to you. Thankfully, since Bree and John were the prime suspects on Father Uberti's DGM short list, such a warning wasn't totally off the wall.

The other option was significantly more terrifying. If John

had left her the envelope, was he trying to tell her that he suspected her involvement with DGM? Of course, he could simply be showing off his deductive powers. But if that was the case, why all the cloak-and-dagger crap?

Bree didn't even realize she was staring at the list in John's hand until he snapped his fingers in front of her eyes.

"It's a set list," John said, patting her hand. "It won't hurt you."

"I take it they haven't kicked you out yet?"

"No," John said with an exasperated sigh. "Your boyfriend hasn't kicked me out yet."

Bree rolled her eyes. "Give it a rest."

"Are you seriously trying to tell me that you don't have a crush on Shane White?"

"I don't know where you get the idea—"

John interrupted her. "Stay on target."

"I mean, how can you—"

"Stay on target!"

Bree took a deep breath. "Look, Shane White doesn't even know my name. And that's the beginning and the end of it." It was painful to admit, but it was almost as if Bree needed to hear herself say the words out loud. She hadn't told John that she'd transferred into fourth-period drama, and suddenly the reality that she'd changed her class schedule in order to chase a boy who barely knew she existed felt simultaneously pathetic and embarrassing.

John stared at her for what felt like an eternity, then slowly turned his attention back to the set list. "If you say so."

♦ ♦ ♦

Peanut wrung her hands as she and Olivia approached the the-ater. "I'm so nervous," she said, glancing at Olivia. "Aren't you?"

"It's just a play, Peanut," Olivia lied. "It's not a big deal."

"I know, but what if . . ."

Peanut's voice trailed off, but Olivia knew exactly what she was going to say: *What if you don't get cast?*

Olivia pushed the thought from her mind. She had to trust that her audition, coupled with Mr. Cunningham's assurance that he'd do everything he could for her, would be enough to counterbalance whatever power Amber currently wielded over the theater department.

Now that Ronny's killer had confessed, Olivia could turn her attention back to the Oregon Shakespeare Festival. This cast list could make or break her.

A crowd of drama students had already gathered around the door; their voices drifted across the courtyard.

"Can you believe it?"

"Duh, she practically told everyone she'd get it."

"Who's that?"

"The smoking new guy."

"Gang Member Number Two? Do I even get any lines?"

Peanut made a beeline for the door, but Olivia paused as Jeze-bel and Amber appeared at the far side of the courtyard. Jezebel raced up to the cast list and practically danced a jig in front of it.

"You got it!" she squealed. "You're playing Olivia."

Amber breezed through the crowd, looking as nonchalant and uninterested as possible. "Logan as Count Orsino," she read aloud, starting at the top of the list. "Excellent. Our acting styles are remarkably complementary."

Olivia suppressed a gag.

"Donté as Sebastian? Intriguing choice." Amber continued down the list. "Oh look, Peanut. Even you got a part!"

Peanut squeezed her head in front of the cast list. "I did?"

"Fabiana. Originally Fabian, a male role," Amber lectured. "Mr. Cunningham confided that he'd be taking some liberties with the play."

"Look!" Peanut squealed, her head still lodged in front of the cast list. "Olivia got Viola." She stood on her tiptoes and waved. "Liv! You got it!"

"What?" Amber roared.

A wave of relief engulfed Olivia. "I did?"

Peanut rushed up and hugged her, and soon other members of the drama class gathered around, offering their congratulations.

Everyone except Amber. She stood in front of the door, her fists balled up so tightly her hands were turning white. After a moment, she grabbed Jezebel and dragged her into the theater.

Olivia didn't need to hear what Amber was saying. Her body language implied enough. She was furious that Olivia had been cast in the play, and a pissed-off Amber was a dangerous Amber. Olivia would need to watch her back.

It was going to be a long three weeks.

Bree was practically in front of the theater before she realized that John was still at her side.

"Where are you going?" she said with a nervous laugh. "You'll barely make it to art history before the bell."

"I'll be fine." John just stood there, without making the expected dash across campus.

Bree didn't open the theater door. After the conversation at lunch, she didn't want John to see that she'd transferred into drama class with Shane. At least not yet.

"The bell's going to ring any second and . . ." She was getting impatient.

"Didn't I tell you?" John said. "I transferred into drama."

"What?"

"Yeah, I know. But Shane asked me to." John yanked the door open and smiled over his shoulder as he ducked into the darkened theater. "See you later?"

Bree stood outside the theater as John let the door close in her face. Well, crap. For some reason, the idea of flirting with Shane in front of John made her uncomfortable. Maybe she should march herself to the office, say she made a mistake, and go back to fourth-period French?

Bree sighed and opened the door. No, she was going to do this, John or no John.

TWENTY-TWO

BREE STOOD IN THE BACK OF THE HOUSE, TRYING TO ACCLIMATE her eyes to the low lighting. She wasn't sure what to do. Introduce herself to the foppish British guy who appeared to be running the show? Eh, she wasn't there to kiss ass. He'd figure out who she was eventually. Besides, it wasn't as if she could hide from John all semester. Better to take the bull by the horns.

She scanned the auditorium and saw John sitting between Shane and some redheaded senior chick Bree had never met. *Here goes nothing.*

"Hey," she said, slipping into the row in front of them.

John started as if he'd seen a ghost. "What the hell are you doing here?"

"Same thing you are."

John planted a boot-clad foot against the back of her seat. "I seriously doubt that."

Bree didn't like the clouded look she saw on his face. What right did he have to be pissed off?

The redhead leaned on John's arm. "Who's your friend?"

Bree eyed the girl. She wore heavy purple lipstick and more black eyeliner than the lead singer of KISS, and the way she touched John's arm—so familiar and comfortable—rubbed Bree the wrong way. "Shouldn't I be asking you that?"

"It's Bree, right?" Shane extended his hand.

Holy shit, he knew her name? "Yeah." She shook his hand, praying her palms weren't gross and sweaty.

"Are you joining drama?" he asked.

The redhead rolled her eyes and nodded toward Amber and Jezebel, posing on the stage like they were auditioning for a Madonna video. "I don't know why anyone would want to join this freak show."

"When you gaze long into the abyss, the abyss also gazes into you," Bree said, carefully quoting Nietzsche. She'd memorized a dozen or so of the philosopher's best, just in case she got the chance to drop one in front of Shane.

But instead of smiling in recognition, Shane tilted his head to the side. "Huh?"

John snorted. "I believe she's quoting Nietzsche."

"Oh!" Shane's eyes grew wide. "I had to do a report on him last spring. Didn't understand most of it."

John grinned from ear to ear. "Yeah, Bree's a huge Nietzsche fan."

Bree wanted to slap the smugness off his face.

Shane smiled. "I'm Shane, and this is Cordy," he said, thumbing at the redhead. Bree noticed that her knee was touching John's leg. What the hell was that about? "Cordy does the promo and shit for Bangers and Mosh. She's sitting in on class today to get the DL on the gig."

Bree had no idea what gig he was talking about, but clearly Shane thought John had filled her in, so she flashed Cordy a shit-eating grin and played along. "So you're a groupie."

Cordy wrinkled her nose. "Look who's talking."

"Dude," Shane said, slapping John on the shoulder. "Glad you could transfer in. This gig is going to be epic for us." He stepped into the aisle. "I'll go tell Mr. C. that you're here."

Cordy climbed over John and followed Shane, assiduously avoiding Bree's eyes as she went. Bree waited until they were halfway to the stage before she turned to John, eyebrows raised. "Cordy seemed really friendly," Bree said. "Why haven't I heard about her?"

"Why haven't I heard about your sudden interest in the theater?" John countered.

"You weren't exactly sharing that little nugget either," she said, suddenly embarrassed. "And what the hell is this about a gig?"

Instead of answering, John linked his fingers behind his head and crossed one combat-boot-clad foot over his knee.

Bree narrowed her eyes. "Are you going to tell me what's going on or am I going to have to rip that boot off your foot and beat you senseless with it?"

"Pay attention, Miss Charming," he said with a nod toward the stage. "Class is starting."

With a series of cringe-inducing squeaks, Shane helped Mr. Cunningham wheel a massive television across the stage. "All right, everyone. We have a lot to cover today, so let's start with a few announcements. Thank you, Mr. White."

Shane saluted, then jumped off the stage in one bound and took a seat in the front row next to Cordy.

"Um, right," Mr. Cunningham said, eyeing Shane suspiciously. "First off, congratulations to everyone who was cast in our fall play. I was impressed with your auditions, and I believe we're going to have a fabulous production. Now, I want to share with you the concept for this semester's production of *Twelfth Night*." He plugged his phone into an auxiliary jack and connected it to the screen. His browser appeared, showing a photo gallery marked "Twelfth Precinct."

"Thanks to the generosity of our donors, we are building this production from scratch, based on my own original concept." He tapped on the gallery and opened a slide show. The first image was a watercolor mockup of the stage, portraying a run-down urban landscape: New York–style brownstones pockmarked with boarded-up windows, a burned-out hulk of an old sedan peeking out from the wings, and graffiti plastering every available surface.

"This is our main set. It's a near-future dystopian landscape, based on New York City as depicted in the 1979 cult classic"—he paused and swiped to the next photo—"*The Warriors*."

Mr. Cunningham waited, clearly expecting some sort of reaction to the production still of several shirtless dudes in brown leather vests, open to show their glistening torsos, hairless like Ken dolls. It was a seventies explosion—afros and feathered headbands, beaded necklaces, and ridiculously low-slung jeans.

"What the hell is that?" Bree said, out of the corner of her mouth.

"Oh, come on, guys," Mr. Cunningham said, practically pleading. "*The Warriors*? 'Can you dig it?'"

Giggles erupted from somewhere near the front of the theater. Mr. Cunningham ran a hand through his thinning hair and sighed. "No matter. We'll be watching it in class tomorrow." He cut off the groans with a wave of his hand. "Be thankful I'm not assigning it for homework. The point is that we are recreating a gritty, dangerous gangland. Think *West Side Story* on steroids. And we'll be going all out—original sets, costumes, even an original score." Mr. Cunningham waved Shane to his feet. "This is Mr. White, who performs in a local rock band."

Bree glanced at John. "You're kidding me."

"Mr. White will be performing the role of Feste, the fool, and will be composing and performing original music for our production."

"Hold up," Shane said. "I play guitar and sing, but I'm crap at writing songs." He pointed at John. "My bassist Bagsie is the epic songwriter."

Every head in the theater turned around to face Bree and John, a backlit amalgam of shock and awe.

"Yes. Right." Mr. Cunningham fussed with his phone and flipped to another screen. "Moving on."

The rest of his presentation was lost on Bree. John had kept yet another secret from her? She turned fully around to face him. "You're composing songs for the school play? And you were going to tell me this when?"

"You're not my mother, Bree," he said without looking at her. "I can go to the men's room without you there to wipe my ass."

His jaw was clenched; the tendons below his cheek rippled back and forth as he ground his teeth together. John rarely got angry—either at Bree or anyone else—but when he did, it was not something to be taken lightly.

Why was *he* pissed at *her*? Shouldn't it be the other way around? Twice in one week she'd found out he'd been keeping major life decisions secret from her. What kind of friend did that?

John leaned forward and whispered in Bree's ear. "What do you see in him?"

"Mr. Cunningham?" Bree asked.

"Shane."

"Oh." It wasn't a question Bree had an answer to, even if she'd been inclined to give it. "I don't know. He's cool, I guess."

"Cool?"

"Who can resist a rock star?" she half-joked.

The class began to stand up and move toward the stage, the presentation apparently over. John slowly rose to his feet. He looked down at her, his hair hanging in front of one eye. "We'll see about that."

TWENTY-THREE

OLIVIA'S MIND RACED WITH CHARACTER POSSIBILITIES AS Mr. Cunningham wheeled the television off the stage. She'd be playing Viola in a futuristic 1970s New York gangland. She needed to get the movement and the feel of the character just right, without sacrificing the language and tradition of the Bard. It was a unique opportunity to reimagine a classic character, exactly the kind of off-the-wall setting that had made the Oregon Shakespeare Festival famous.

"These are your rehearsal schedules." Mr. Cunningham plopped a stack of papers on the edge of the stage. "I want them in your smartphones before the end of the day, understood? We've got three weeks of regular drama class plus evening and weekend rehearsals to bring this entire production together."

"That sounds hard," Peanut said, wringing her hands in her lap.

Olivia patted her arm. "Hard but fun. Don't worry, I'll help you with your lines."

"Actually," Amber said, leaning over Peanut possessively. "*I'll* help you, Peanut."

Mr. Cunningham picked up his clipboard and stood center stage. "Today, we'll be working on backstory for your characters. Those of you without a role, we'll need your input as we brainstorm who and what these people were before the beginning of the play. Backstory will be remarkably important to this production, since we are colliding two universes: Shakespeare and *The Warriors*."

Olivia listened attentively as Mr. Cunningham continued.

"We all know who Viola and Sebastian are. We know Olivia and Count Orsino, Feste the fool and Maria the maid. But this is *Twelfth Precinct*, not *Twelfth Night*. The twins are no longer Viola and Sebastian, but Violent and Stab, leaders of the Warriors gang, stranded in enemy territory miles away from their Coney Island home. Feste becomes Fist, the biker wing nut from the Rogues. Olivia is transformed into Live Wire, female warlord of the fedora-wearing Hurricanes. And then we have the Count, an enigmatic figure, attempting to unite the gangs under one banner, who mistakenly thinks that the Warriors tried to assassinate him."

Mr. Cunningham paused dramatically. "I'd like the entire cast onstage."

Amber sprinted up the stairs like an Olympic hurdler. She preened and posed, clearly excited to be the star of the show.

"Okay," Mr. Cunningham said, once everyone was onstage. "Let's pair up into our backstory components: Live Wire and the Count. Belcher, Antman, and Holy Mary. Fist and his band.

Violent and Stab. The rest of you, separate by the gang affiliations you were assigned on the cast list."

The cast milled around the stage, forming small groups. Amber grabbed Logan by the hand and spun him around like a disco dancer, while Shane White and John Baggott stood awkwardly in the back, clearly confused by the direction.

Olivia forced herself to stay calm as Donté approached. This was just the beginning of hours and hours of time they'd be spending together over the next three weeks. He'd have to have known that when he auditioned for the production. Maybe spending time with her was his intention all along? Maybe he'd been having the same second thoughts about their breakup?

"Hey, Livvie."

Olivia took a deep breath. "Hey."

"You, as actors, need to know who your characters are," Mr. Cunningham lectured. "What drives them? What scares them? What are they trying to hide from others? From themselves? I want you to discuss your motivations with your group. Ten minutes, starting now!"

"So," Olivia began, testing the waters for normal conversation. "How have you been?"

"Good. Really good. You?"

"Same, for the most part."

Donté smiled and Olivia fought the urge to throw herself into his arms. There was something so comfortable and warm about Donté's smile, and Olivia missed basking in it.

Donté dropped his voice. "I know we haven't really talked much since . . ." He swallowed. "Well, you know."

"Since you broke up with me." It was the first time Olivia had said it out loud.

"Er, right." Donté grinned sheepishly. "I'm sorry about that. I didn't know you'd take it so hard."

Olivia winced. Nothing worse than your ex-boyfriend feeling sorry for you. "I didn't take it that hard."

Donté glanced up, smiling wryly. "Is that why you made out with Rex Cavanaugh right in front of me at the bonfire?"

Olivia's face burned. "I . . ."

Of all the things she wanted to forget, making out with Rex Cavanaugh at the spring sing bonfire was second on Olivia's amnesia list. It had only been a few days since Donté had dumped her, and when they both turned up at the bonfire, Olivia saw an opportunity to try to make him jealous. It had seemed like a good idea, especially with half a bottle of wine clouding her judgment, but at the time she thought Donté hadn't noticed.

Wrong again, Liv.

The only upside of the evening was that Rex was too drunk and too high to remember any of their spit swapping, and no one else—especially not Amber—had witnessed the pathetic display.

"It was a long time ago," Olivia said at last.

"Livvie." Donté leaned in and dropped his voice. "Don't settle for someone like Rex. There's a special guy out there for you."

Like the one standing across from me? "I guess so."

"I know so. Your one and only."

He remembered their song! Was he trying to tell her that he was the only one for her? Because she already knew that.

Mr. Cunningham clapped his hands. "All right, class. Everyone grab a seat in the house and we'll start with the Riffs gang—"

The PA system popped to life; then an electronic shriek tore through the theater. Everyone onstage groaned, and Olivia's hands flew to her ears, attempting to block out the horrible sound.

The shriek stopped abruptly, and the shy voice of Mrs. Baggott came through the speakers. "Sorry!" she squeaked. "I'm so sorry."

The sound of shuffling papers filled the theater and Olivia lowered her hands.

"Right," Mrs. Baggott said, clearly locating the correct page. "Attention, faculty. Father Uberti requests that all members of student leadership be excused from class for the remainder of fourth period. They are to report to the office immediately. Thank you."

Mika and Donté, along with most of the leadership class, were already gathered in the office by the time Kitty arrived. They stood together near Mrs. Baggott's desk, and Kitty quickly made her way over to them.

"What's going on?" she whispered.

"No idea," Donté said. Obscured by the large desk, his hand found hers.

"Father Uberti's been on the phone in his office the entire time," Mika said. "I can't hear anything, but he sounds pissed off."

As if to punctuate her point, the door to Father Uberti's office flew open and the diminutive priest swept into the lobby.

"I'm sure you've all heard the rumor," he began unceremoniously. "That Theo Baranski confessed to the murder of Ronny DeStefano."

"Hell yeah!" Rex said. He turned to Tyler and gave him a high five.

Father Uberti's eyes were steely. "Premature celebration, Mr. Cavanaugh. I've just had confirmation from Sergeant Callahan that Mr. Baranski has an alibi for the night of Ronny's murder. He has been released from custody."

Kitty felt as if she'd been kicked in the stomach. All the air was sucked out of her lungs. Theo was innocent? Somehow she'd known all along that he wasn't the killer. The look on Theo's face when the police had hauled him into the office that morning had been one of defiance, not fear.

"In light of this news," Father Uberti continued, "I'm releasing you all from fourth period today. You are to report to the leadership classroom, where you will work with Coach Creed on a solution to this problem."

"You want our help to find a killer?" Mika said incredulously.

"I want your help," Father Uberti said coldly, "to find DGM."

TWENTY-FOUR

COACH CREED STOOD AT THE FRONT OF THE LEADERSHIP classroom, arms folded across his 'Maine Men shirt as Kitty and the rest of the class filed into the room and took their regular seats.

"So it turns out," he started, as if they'd just walked into a conversation already in progress, "that little twerp Baranski was trying to protect those DGM criminals, which should be a crime itself. But the police have let him go."

Mika leaned forward. "I'm going to talk to Coach Miles today," she whispered. "See if we can get Theo in as manager before Creed tries to kill him with hill charges."

"Good idea," Kitty said out of the corner of her mouth.

Coach Creed began pacing the room. "The authorities have no leads at this time. They've failed, which means it's up to us to find Ronny's killer."

Mika raised her hand. "I thought we were here to find DGM?" she said without waiting to be called upon.

"Same thing, Jones," Coach Creed snapped. "Where there's pirates, there's booty."

Kitty didn't like the sound of this. At. All.

"So listen up!" Coach Creed continued. "'Maine Men, we'll be upping your patrols. I want you around campus during class, before class, after class. All the time, got it?"

"Got it!" Rex said.

"And I want lists of students who have been exhibiting any kind of suspicious behavior," Coach Creed continued. "Nervous tics, unexcused absences, isolationist tendencies. Work in groups. I want a comprehensive suspect list by the end of the period."

Kitty turned around to face Mika. "Want to work togeth . . ." Her voice trailed off and her eyes drifted toward the back of the room, where Donté was waving at her.

Mika turned to see what Kitty was looking at, and smiled wickedly. "I see you already have a partner." She winked at Kitty. "You can fill me in later."

Donté swung a desk around for Kitty as she threaded her way to the back of the classroom, and the two of them huddled up, pretending to work on their suspect lists.

"This school is getting weird," Donté said under his breath.

Kitty nodded, keeping an eye on Coach Creed. "Big Brother is watching you."

"Creed's totally off the rails," Donté said, glancing at the coach. "He didn't used to be like this, I swear."

That's right. Creed coached the men's JV basketball team. He would have been Donté's coach last year. Kitty recalled the conversation she'd overheard that morning between Creed and Father Uberti. Maybe it was time to do a little fishing?

"Oh yeah?" Kitty asked.

Donté shook his head. "Dude was always strict. Kind of old-fashioned. He was at a military school before he got the job here and I think he sort of preferred the discipline at his old job."

"What school was it?" Kitty asked.

"Don't remember. Somewhere in Arizona, I think."

Kitty stared at Donté, her suspicions confirmed. Arizona. Could there be more than one military academy in the state? Possibly. But the link between Coach Creed and Ronny was feeling more tangible every moment, and all roads seemed to lead to Archway Military Academy.

"Got anything for me?"

Coach Creed loomed above them. Instead of creating his list, she'd been staring at the notebook page on her desk, pen in hand, while her brain grappled with anonymous clues and military academies in Arizona. Without even realizing it, Kitty had written a single word: Archway.

"Not yet," Kitty said, trying to cover the page with her arm. "I haven't noticed anything—"

"Let me see." Coach Creed whisked the notebook out from beneath Kitty's arm and held it up to his nose. "What the hell is this?" he roared.

Shit. "Nothing," Kitty said, trying to laugh it off.

Coach Creed shoved the notebook in Kitty's face. "What the hell did you hear, huh? What are people saying?"

Kitty flinched away from the page. "I don't know what you're talking about."

"None of it is true, do you hear me?" He stepped closer. "None of it."

"Coach!" Donté said. He was on his feet, his massive frame towering over his former coach. "Leave her alone."

"Greene, focus on your own list." Creed glanced down at Donté's page. "I see you haven't done any better than our vice president here."

Donté didn't back down. "I don't think this is an appropriate use of class time."

"Appropriate use of class time?" Coach Creed said incredulously. "I thought you understood the severity of the threat to our school, Greene."

"Maybe I don't see it that way."

Coach Creed looked as if Donté had slapped him across the face. He pointed at the 'Maine Men emblem on Donté's shirt. "Greene, you're a 'Maine Man. You swore an oath to protect the reputation of Bishop DuMaine Preparatory School. Are you telling me that means nothing to you?"

Donté stared at Coach Creed for a moment, the muscles around his jaw rippling. Finally, he nodded. "You know what, Coach? That oath does mean something to me." Then he reached over his head, grabbed the collar of his 'Maine Man shirt, and pulled it off. "And this is the best way I can think of to protect our school." Without another word, a shirtless Donté left the classroom.

Coach Creed stormed after Donté. "Greene! Come back here. I'll fail you. I swear to God!"

As his voice faded, Kitty battled the urge to cry. She'd tipped Creed off about Archway, plus Donté had gotten into trouble on her account. Not exactly a stellar start to her detective career.

"You okay?" Mika asked, taking the seat Donté had vacated.

"Yeah."

"Kitty Cat," Mika said, smiling wickedly. "What have you done to poor Donté?"

Kitty slumped forward on her desk. "He's going to fail leadership and it'll be all my fault. He'll hate me."

"Are you kidding me?" Mika laughed. "You've got that boy whipped. What did you do, put out on the first date or something?"

Kitty's head snapped up. "No, I just—"

The bell rang without Coach Creed or Donté having returned to the classroom. Mika slowly rose to her feet. "Well, whatever you did, share it with me when I meet Mr. Right, will you?"

Kitty absently packed up her bag and slung it over her shoulder. She'd been so panicked by Creed's reaction to Archway, she'd kind of missed the fact that Donté had come to her defense and dropped out of the 'Maine Men.

"You forgot this," Mika said, handing Kitty an envelope.

Kitty was about to say it didn't belong to her, when she caught sight of the familiar label with her name on it.

"Oh, thanks." She hoped Mika couldn't see her hand shaking as she grasped the envelope to her chest.

Kitty waited until Mika had headed off for her chemistry class before she dared to peek inside. She walked slowly, scarcely aware of the throng of bodies bustling through the hallway around her. She paused at the top of the stairs and slid the contents of the envelope into her hand.

It was a photo.

There were two people. One of them—a boy, by the outfit—was missing a head. It had been cut clean out of the photo. The other definitely had a head, and she looked familiar. Her hair wasn't styled like a twenties flapper, cropped short in the back with a heavy fringe of bangs, and the clothes weren't thrift-store chic, but there was no doubt in Kitty's mind that the smiling girl in the photo was Bree Deringer.

She turned the photo over and saw a caption scrawled across the back.

Best friends and Fighting Jesuits: Bree Deringer and Christopher Beeman.

TWENTY-FIVE

"AND WE'LL BE TEAMING UP IN PAIRS FOR THIS ASSIGNMENT."

Margot's head snapped up. Short of "I'm accusing you of murder," Mr. Heinrich had just spoken the words Margot dreaded most in her school experience: "teaming up."

Whether it was kickball on the elementary school playground or a presentation for first-period AP Government, Margot would inevitably be the odd girl out, paired up with whomever was unlucky enough to still be standing in the game of musical chairs once the iPod shut off.

"Pick your partners," Mr. Heinrich continued, "and remember, this will count for twenty percent of your final grade."

Alarms bells went off in Margot's head. She was in a class full of seniors, which is what happens when your parents insist you enroll in summer semester every year so that you can load up on AP classes before you even start applying for college. She only knew one person in the room, and despite the fact that she was probably the smartest student in the class—a niche that occasionally meant a classmate with failing grades would beg her to be their partner on an assignment like this—it was only the second week of school, so no one knew that about her yet.

Someone tapped her on the shoulder. "Margot?" Logan asked. "Do you have a partner yet?"

"No," she managed.

He paused, looking embarrassed. "Do you want to pair up with me?"

Margot could have hugged him. "Sure," she said simply, hoping it sounded somewhere between "OMG THANK YOU FOR SAVING ME" and "I might be more terrified of pairing up with you than being left unpartnered."

"This looks like a lot of work," Logan said, flipping through the packet of materials Mr. Heinrich handed out. "What are your nights and weekends like?"

Totally open as long as my parents think I'm doing schoolwork. "I can work something out."

"Okay." Logan's eyebrows drew together. "Mine are a little wonky. I've got rehearsals for the school play almost every night for the next three weeks."

"Why so intense?" Margot asked.

"We've got this special performance of *Twelfth Night* for some Big Kahuna director."

"'If music be the food of love,'" Margot said softly, quoting the opening line of *Twelfth Night*, "'play on.'"

"You know Shakespeare?"

Margot dropped her chin, hoping he wouldn't notice the blush creeping up her neck. "We did a Shakespeare module in AP English last year. I'm good at remembering things."

Logan pointed at her. "You know, Mr. Cunningham is totally overwhelmed with this show. I bet he could use someone like you to help run lines with the actors."

Slipping out of the house once in a while for a Don't Get Mad meeting couched as a study group was one thing, but hanging out in the theater department every night for the next three weeks? Margot wasn't sure her parents would buy it.

"Come on," Logan said. He bumped her shoulder playfully. "We can work on our AP Government project whenever I'm not in a scene, so it's academic *and* extracurricular. They keep telling us it looks good on college apps, right?"

He had a point, but Margot wasn't sure she could sell her parents on it. "I'll think about it."

"Good enough."

The bell rang, and the class began to pack up. Logan laid his hand lightly on her arm. "Do you think . . ." He blinked several times. "Um, do you think I could get your phone number? So we can coordinate?"

It's just for school, Margot told herself, trying to suppress her excitement. "Sure."

She rattled off her cell phone number as Logan typed into his phone. "Sweet. I sent you mine. So you have it."

Margot sat at her desk, dumbfounded, as she watched Logan bound out of the classroom. Had that really just happened? In the course of an hour, had Margot agreed to join a theater production and given her phone number to the cutest boy she had ever met in her life?

Margot slipped her hand into her backpack and pulled out

her cell phone. She needed to see Logan's text, to make sure it was real and not some elaborate practical joke engineered by Amber Stevens. There was an incoming text on her screen.

It's Logan! Now you have my number. ☺

Nausea. Fear. Excitement. Panic. It all swamped her at once. Part of her wanted to text Logan back and say, "No! I made a mistake. Can't do this!" But fear had motivated so much of her life, Margot refused to give in to it this time.

Margot was still in a haze as she walked down the hall, but as she swung her locker door open, all thoughts of Logan evaporated.

Sitting on top of her textbooks was another manila envelope.

Margot had never been late to a class in her entire academic career, but she didn't regret the decision to duck into the ladies' room before second period, even with the 'Maine Men patrolling the halls during class. Whatever was in the mysterious envelope was not something that could (a) wait for the break, or (b) be opened in a crowded classroom.

And while a toilet stall wasn't exactly her first choice for privacy, it was the only place she was likely to get it.

She was oddly calm as she studied the envelope in her hands. It was exactly like the first—a generic office supply with a single piece of tape meticulously centered on the flap— and left in exactly the same way. And though part of Margot cringed at what she might find, her hand was steady as she popped the tape and peeked inside.

More photos. Three of them.

But unlike the first, Margot had never seen any of these.

She thought of the first photo, the one of her overweight body wrapped in plastic.

It had all been part of Amber's plan. But Margot was too naive to realize that it had been a setup when she overheard Amber in the locker room, telling Peanut and Jezebel about this amazing new weight-loss sensation. All you had to do was bind yourself in plastic wrap before bed each night, and you'd sweat the pounds off in your sleep.

It had sounded like the miracle she'd been waiting for. As soon as she was free of her parents for the night, she'd stripped down and swaddled herself before bed.

It wasn't until the next day, when the photo of her chubby body encased in plastic wrap was infecting every phone in school, that Margot realized the whole thing had been a horrible joke.

As if that wasn't bad enough, a group of eighth-grade boys had come to school with plastic wrapped around their arms and legs and stomachs. Wherever Margot went, someone was mocking her, pointing, laughing. It had been too much. Margot had left school at lunch, walked six miles home, and taken her dad's straight razor with her into the bathtub.

She would have succeeded, too, if the cleaning lady hadn't shown up.

For four years, Margot had nursed a secret hatred of Amber Stevens. Amber, who had set her up, taken that photo, and circulated it to the entire school.

Margot stared at the photos in her hand, cycling through them slowly. The first two were from outside Margot's house, but too far away from the bedroom window to see what was inside. The third was closer, probably taken from behind the sycamore tree outside Margot's window. It showed Amber standing near the windowpane, turning to the camera with a wicked smile on her face and flashing two thumbs up. But there was a second figure in the photo, reflected in the darkened window. The flash from the camera phone obscured the photographer's face, backlighting her to a vague, monochromatic silhouette. All Margot could make out was that she had long, curly hair.

The realization made Margot's hands turn ice-cold. Amber wasn't alone that night.

And Amber didn't take the photo.

TWENTY-SIX

"ANY IDEA WHAT MR. CUNNINGHAM'S GOING TO DO WITH US non—acting types?" Bree said as she and John trudged across the quad.

"Personally," John said, holding the door open for her, "I'm hoping you get put on wardrobe detail. I'm sure Amber Stevens and Olivia Hayes would love to have you as a dresser."

Bree gagged. "Barf."

"Everyone take a seat," Mr. Cunningham called from the front of the house. "I've got crew assignments to hand out before we jump into staging act three."

John leaned down so his lips were inches from Bree's ear. "Wardrobe," he whispered.

The feel of John's breath against her neck sent a chill racing down Bree's spine. What was that all about? She laughed uncomfortably as she spun away from him. "Yeah, perfect."

"We'll begin with the set crew," Mr. Cunningham said, consulting his clipboard. "Does anyone—"

"Mr. C!" Shane raised his hand.

"Yes, Mr. White?"

Shane shot to his feet. "Can I make an announcement?"

Mr. Cunningham sighed. "I don't know, can you?"

"Um . . ." Bree cringed as Shane scratched his chin, missing Mr. Cunningham's grammatical commentary.

"Proceed, Mr. White."

"Awesome." Shane turned to face the class. "There's a Bangers and Mosh show next Sunday night at the Ledge. All ages, and we'll be premiering the new songs for the play." He looked at Mr. Cunningham. "Cool?"

"Absolutely cool, Mr. White. I think that will be a mandatory field trip for all drama class members."

Bree elbowed John in the ribs. "The Ledge? Seriously?"

"I didn't choose it."

"John." Bree turned to face him. "Stop downplaying this. A gig at the Ledge is a big deal."

"If you say so."

Bree narrowed her eyes. "I do. Enjoy it for once in your life, okay?"

John's face softened. "Okay," he said. "I'll try."

Now it was Bree's turn for a smart-ass comeback. "Do or do not," she said, throwing the *Star Wars* in his face. "There is no try."

"Crew assignments," Mr. Cunningham said, picking up where he left off before Shane's announcement. Olivia tuned out as he rattled off a bunch of names, appointing people to sets, props, wardrobe, lighting, and sound duties.

While she waited for her first scene to be called to the stage, Olivia wandered around the expansive wings, basking in production glory. A graveyard of old stage lights had been removed from the rafters, their aging color gels awaiting replacement before they were remounted. Carpenters assembled set pieces, the cacophony of drilling and staccato hammering more sublime to her ears than a Mozart symphony. A group of student crew members gathered around scenery flats, paintbrushes in hand, ready to turn empty canvases into retro Harlem.

Olivia leaned against a wall behind the electrical grid and smiled to herself. This was home.

Footsteps clacked against the concrete floor and Olivia instinctively pressed herself into the shadows.

"I don't understand," Jezebel said. "Why do I have to lie?"

Amber tsked her tongue. "I told you, my dad might ask where I was. Just tell him I stayed at your place."

Jezebel stopped and folded her thick arms across her chest. "You didn't answer my question."

"I don't want Daddy to know where I was that night."

"Fine." Jezebel sighed. "What night?"

"Tuesday," Amber said.

"You slept over at my place Tuesday night," Jezebel recited, her voice intentionally monotonous. "Good?"

Amber turned and dragged Jezebel onto the stage. "Perfect."

Olivia stayed in the shadows, confused. Amber bragged all the time that her parents didn't care where she spent the night, implying that her sleepovers at Rex's house were frequent and condoned. So why would she be suddenly worried about a cover story for Tuesday night?

Olivia stiffened. Tuesday was the night Ronny was killed. Could the two things be related?

Bree stared at the anarchy of stage lights in dismay. "We have to do all of these?"

"I think so," John said.

The heavy black lights were all coated with dust and grime, and several of them were so corroded, they looked as if they'd been buried in a swamp for a decade. "This makes wardrobe look like fun."

"You want me to go tell Mr. Cunningham?" John asked playfully.

"No!" She peeled off her hoodie and plopped herself in the middle of the chaos. "This kind of dirty is much more palatable, thank you very much."

They worked in silence. For each light, Bree had to unscrew the gel frames from the rig, then extricate the little square of colored plastic from its holder. Some slid out easily, while some had melted to their metal holsters and required a vigorous scraping and tearing in order to dislodge. There was something mind-numbing about the process that Bree found soothing, and after half an hour, the backstage looked as if a piñata had exploded, littering the floor with its multicolored skin.

"I heard the police will be on campus indefinitely," John said, apropos of nothing. His eyes were fixed on his pile of lights.

"Whatever," she said dismissively.

John sat up straight. "You do realize how serious this is, right? If Father Uberti tries to frame us, there will be real consequences. There's more at stake now than forcing Daddy to pay attention to you."

Bree winced. Is that really what he thought of her?

John sighed. "You know, there are better ways to piss off your dad than getting arrested, Butch Cassidy."

Bree seriously doubted that.

"Your dad would probably freak the hell out if he knew you had a guy up in your room three days a week"—John struck a laughably sexy pose and tossed his hair out of his face like Fabio at a romance-novel cover shoot—"without parental supervision."

Bree burst out laughing.

John swung around onto all fours and crawled through the sea of lighting rigs toward her. "That's right. I make you laugh with passion. We're the hottest couple in school."

"Oh my God," Bree managed, blurting out the words between heaves of laughter. "No one thinks we're a couple."

John stopped his gyrations. "No one thinks we're a couple," he repeated. He planted his boots on the floor and pushed himself to his feet. His face was drawn as he looked down at her. "Especially not you."

Without another word, he slipped through the curtains onto the stage.

Bree sat there, staring at the empty space that John had vacated. "Shit," Bree said to no one in particular.

Was Mercury in fucking retrograde or something? Her entire world seemed to be falling apart. What would be next:

Earthquake? Meteor strike? Seven hours of religion homework?

She wasn't sure which she'd prefer.

Maybe she should text John? But what would she say—*sorry people don't think of us as a couple, we're still cool, right?* Yeah, no. She felt as if a chasm had opened up between herself and her best friend, and she had no idea how to bridge it.

She sat on the cold concrete floor, her eyes searching the backstage wings as if an answer to her problem might magically appear amid the discarded light gels. Eventually, they landed on her ammo bag. The flap was open, and something was sticking out.

Something flat and long and antique yellow in color.

Manila envelope? Back the truck up. No way had Bree put that in her bag.

The fine hairs stood up on the back of Bree's neck. She glared at it, no longer a mundane office supply but a harbinger of doom.

Really, Bree? Ridiculous didn't even begin to cover it. Like the last one, this envelope was probably from one of the girls, trying to tip her off on John's investigations into DGM without telling the others. Nothing ominous. She whipped it out of her bag and popped the seal.

A piece of computer paper slid out onto the floor. It was a printout of an email to John from an anonymous account.

Bree quickly scanned the contents, and her stomach dropped.

There's a photo of DGM if you know where to look.
Check the school library.

◆ ◆ ◆

Olivia was halfway to fifth period when Peanut came tearing after her. "Liv! You forgot this."

"What?" she asked, turning around.

Peanut shrugged. "Dunno. It was under your purse in the theater. You left it on the seat."

"Oh." She reached out and lifted the object from Peanut's hand. It was a plain manila envelope.

Olivia stared at the envelope as Peanut ran back down the hall. It was exactly like the first one. With a shaky hand, she broke the Scotch-tape seal and peeked at the contents.

It was a photo of Kitty and another girl, both in volleyball uniforms and knee pads. It was definitely a younger version of Kitty, taken a year or two ago. The other girl looked familiar, but Olivia wasn't sure why.

There was no note on the photo, no hint as to why it had been sent to her. One thing was for sure—this photo had nothing to do with *Twelfth Precinct*, which meant Mr. Cunningham hadn't left it for her.

What the hell was going on?

TWENTY-SEVEN

OLIVIA LAMINATED HER SHOULDERS WITH SPF 85; THEN, confident every square inch of her skin was adequately protected from the bright September sun, she pulled a wide-brimmed hat over her short curls and snuggled back into the chaise longue.

Jezebel sniffed the air disapprovingly. "What's the point of sunbathing if you wear all that crap?"

Olivia tightened the halter straps on her cherry-print bikini top. "I like the way the sun feels."

"See, Jez," Amber said, "I'm not wearing any sunscreen. You know why? Because I noticed when I watched *The Warriors* that the women were all amazingly tan." She had reclined the lounge so it was completely flat and lay on her stomach to work on her back tan. "As a serious actress," Amber continued, turning her head toward them, "I think it's important to fully embrace my character."

Behind her enormous sunglasses, Olivia rolled her eyes. "As a serious actress," she said, effortlessly mimicking Amber's tone, "I think it's important to fully protect my skin so I don't look like a shriveled old prune by the time I'm thirty."

Amber lay on her stomach for a moment longer; then, without a word, she reached out and dragged over a large umbrella, engulfing her lounge chair in its shadow.

"It's good to have priorities," Jezebel said, picking up a fashion mag.

They sunbathed in silence while Peanut prepped some nibbles in the kitchen. The conversation Olivia had overheard between Amber and Jezebel was still fresh in her mind, and she realized this might be the perfect time to do some digging.

"Can you believe," Olivia began in an offhand manner, "it's only been like four days since Ronny was killed?"

"Three and a half," Jezebel said, flipping through an article on fall makeup trends.

"Are you trying to ruin my Saturday?" Amber asked.

"It just feels so strange," Olivia continued, undaunted. "Tuesday night when we all went to sleep, we never imagined that someone we knew would be dead the next day."

"I didn't know him," Amber said.

Out of the corner of her eye, Olivia saw Jezebel and Amber exchange a glance. What secret were they hiding?

"But I thought," Olivia said, pushing herself to a sitting position, "Ronny and Rex knew each other? I heard—"

"Snacks!" Peanut trundled out through the patio door, her arms laden with bowls and plates.

Perfect timing as always, Peanut.

Peanut flicked the screen closed with her big toe and waddled over to the outdoor table. "It's Mom and Dad's new health-food line," she said, laying out the spread. "Rhubarb oatmeal bars, veggie bacon-wrapped Tofurky skewers, savory quinoa cakes, and kale chips."

Olivia scanned the plates of organic, vegan, gluten-free snacks that were the staples of Mr. and Mrs. Dumbrowski's fresh-food-delivery empire, and was secretly thankful she had half a pack of crumb cakes squirreled away in her bag.

Amber leaned over the table and wrinkled her nose. "It looks like dog food. Can't we order a pizza or something?"

Peanut's face fell. "Oh, I . . ." Olivia might worry about the never-ending string of bizarre diets Peanut's mom inflicted on her only daughter, but Peanut was proud of her parents' business.

"I think it looks fantastic." Olivia picked up a fake-bacon-and-Tofurky skewer and took an enthusiastic bite. "Mmmm." She plastered a smile on her face as she forced herself to chew.

"Why not?" Jezebel grabbed a rhubarb bar, but Amber turned up her nose.

"At least the boys will be here soon," she said.

Peanut caught her breath. "The boys?"

"Of course." Amber readjusted her bandeau top. "What's a pool party without boys?"

"Pleasant?" Jezebel said.

Peanut stared at the kale chip in her hand, then gently laid it on a napkin. She turned to the patio door and fussed with her swimsuit in the reflection, pulling at the retro polka-dot one-piece. "I wish you'd told me you'd invited them." Her voice cracked. "I didn't even put on makeup."

"Lesson learned," Amber said. "You should always put on makeup."

Olivia stood behind Peanut and looped her arms around her waist, squeezing her tight. "You look amazing. Kyle's going to swallow his tongue when he sees you."

Peanut flashed Olivia a clandestine smile. "Thank you," she said under her breath.

Amber returned to her shaded lounge chair and propped it into an upright position. "Kyle's got his eye on some junior at St. Anne's, so you might as well let it go, PeaPea."

Peanut shook herself free of Olivia's embrace and raced inside the house without a word.

"Really, Amber?" Olivia was tired of seeing Amber stomp on Peanut's dreams. "Could you be a little less tactful?"

"I'm trying to help her," Amber said. "Better she gets it into her head now that Kyle's not interested. So pathetic to see your friend chasing after a boy who doesn't give a shit about her, don't you think?"

There was something sly in Amber's tone that made Olivia question whether she was talking about Peanut and Kyle or Olivia and Donté.

"Same way I feel when I see my friend dating a douchebag," Olivia countered. "Unless they deserve it."

"What are you—"

"Cannonball!"

Rex tore around the side of the house in his swim trunks and leaped into the pool, hugging his knees to his chin.

Water exploded from the pool, splattering in all directions

from Rex's impact and dousing Amber from head to toe.

"Asshole!" Amber screamed the moment Rex's head broke the surface of the water. "Look what you did."

Rex tossed his hair out of his face and freestyled to the side of the pool. "What? You're in a swimsuit. Aren't swimsuits supposed to get wet?"

"Swimsuits, yes," Amber growled. "Hair and makeup? No."

"Lame." Rex hauled himself out of the pool as Kyle and Tyler dragged a cooler through the sliding door.

"Brew!" Rex called out. "Stat."

Tyler tossed a can to Rex, who caught it midair like a center fielder.

Before he could crack it open, Amber bogarted the beer from his hand. "Why yes, thank you. I'd love one." She swiveled her hips as she returned to her lounge chair.

"You could have asked," Rex sneered.

"You could have offered," Amber said, matching his tone.

Aha, the bickering had begun. "I'm going to check on Peanut," Olivia said, and quickly slipped into the house.

The bathroom door was closed, but Olivia could hear the gentle sobbing from inside. She knocked lightly. "Peanut? You okay?"

"Yeah!" Peanut said, so overly perky it was clearly an act. "I'm fine. Just, um, fixing my makeup."

"You should come back out," Olivia said. "The boys are here and . . ." Olivia paused, grasping for a ploy that might get Peanut to rejoin the party. She had to start showing Amber that the bitchy comments didn't bother her, or Amber would never let up.

"And?" Peanut prodded.

176

Olivia swallowed. "And Kyle was asking where you were." Okay, it was a lie, but just the white kind. The good kind.

"I'll be out in a minute," Peanut said after a pause.

It wasn't always a grand DGM gesture that made a difference. Sometimes, it was the small things. Olivia smiled to herself as she padded down the hallway in her bare feet, but she stopped in her tracks as she neared the family room.

"He's dead," Rex said. "Nothing we can do about it now."

Olivia flattened herself against the wall. Was he talking about Ronny?

"This had better be worth it," Amber whispered. "I want DGM fubarred, got it?"

"Calm down," Rex said, using that silky-smooth voice that always reminded Olivia of a serial killer.

"What did that guy have on you anyway?" Amber asked, slyness creeping into her tone.

"N-nothing," Rex stuttered. Only Rex never stuttered, was never unsure of himself for a second. Whatever Ronny knew about Rex must have been epically damaging.

"You sure about that?"

"It doesn't matter now," Rex said through clenched teeth. Then his voice relaxed. "You talk to Jezebel about Tuesday night?"

"She's on board," Amber said. "And no, I didn't tell her why."

"Good."

"But I swear to God," Amber said, her voice steely, "if anyone finds out I was with Ronny that day, I'll tell them—"

"Babe," Rex said through a laugh. "I've got everything under control."

"You'd better," Amber pouted.

"Listen." Rex dropped his voice and Olivia couldn't hear what he said. She crept to the edge of the living room and caught the last few words. "We'll make sure DGM goes down for Ronny's murder. I promise."

Thirty seconds of slobbering sounds indicated that an Amber–Rex make-out session was in full swing. Olivia was beginning to wonder how long she'd be trapped there when the patio door abruptly slid open, and Olivia heard two sets of flip-flops snapping onto the concrete outside.

She stood in the hallway, her mind racing. Amber was with Ronny the day he was killed. Rex was plotting to make sure that DGM went down for Ronny's murder. And Rex's connection to Ronny made him incredibly nervous.

Was it enough to kill for? Olivia wasn't sure. Rex and Amber had been raised with unlimited money and freedom—they always got what they wanted when they wanted it, and that kind of arrogance and entitlement could possibly lead them to murder. A plot to frame DGM might be a stretch, but it was possible, especially if it got Ronny out of the way in the process.

Olivia would have to keep her eyes and ears open when it came to Amber and Rex. If they did kill Ronny, there must be proof, and if she could find it, she'd exonerate DGM entirely. She cringed at the idea of buttering up Rex, and maintaining her friendship with Amber was proving more and more difficult.

She'd just have to figure out a way.

TWENTY-EIGHT

AFTER BEING SIDELINED BY THEO'S FALSE CONFESSION, Menlo PD was back in full force Monday morning. The interrogations started first period.

Bree had just slumped into her desk when a blue-shirted 'Maine Man arrived in the room with a list of students. Unsurprisingly, she and John were at the top.

They were herded into the teacher conference room, where each interrogee was paired with a police officer. Bree's Grand Inquisitor looked as if she needed a second cup of coffee: she stifled a yawn as she opened her notebook to a new page and poised her pen for action. "State your name for the record."

"Bree Deringer."

"Age?"

"Sixteen."

"Home address?"

Bree rattled off her address while the officer diligently transcribed the information. But she kept an eye on Father Uberti, who slowly strolled around the conference room, hands clasped behind his back, like a prison warden patrolling the cell block. The yellowish glow of the fluorescent lights in the conference room gave his skin an unusual pallor, accentuating the sunken cheeks and the dark, hollow spaces below his eyes. Well, at least DGM was causing Father Uberti some sleepless nights. That was something.

The officer finished writing down Bree's address, then pulled a sheet of paper out from beneath the notebook and recited a prepared statement with all the enthusiasm of a DMV employee.

"You are not being accused of a crime, and this is not a custodial interrogation. We are merely gathering information that might be relevant to the case, in regards to the victim, Ronald DeStefano. There is an interested adult present, and you may refuse to answer any questions and/or leave the interview at any time. Do you understand?"

Bree arched her brow as she eyed the back of Father Uberti's head. "Interested adult?"

The officer sighed. "An interested adult is present to ensure appropriate protection of your rights as a juvenile, pursuant to California law."

"Oh." She seriously doubted if old F.U. was interested in protecting the rights of any of his students. Especially not hers.

"Do you understand?" the officer repeated.

Bree smiled. "Sure."

"Nothing to be afraid of, Olivia. We're just trying to gather as much information about Ronny DeStefano as we can, okay? We're all on the same side here."

Olivia *was* afraid. Terrified, in fact. Why was she being questioned about Ronny's murder? As far as school was concerned, they barely even knew each other.

"I understand that you and Ronny had coffee last Tuesday. Is that correct?" Sergeant Callahan asked.

Olivia was on guard in an instant. They knew about her date with Ronny? It was in a public place, so of course there were witnesses.

Or a member of DGM had told them.

She didn't quite believe anyone in DGM was a snitch, but then again, why was Olivia being questioned? Someone must have tipped them off. Either way, Olivia needed to be very, very careful.

Sergeant Callahan smiled, big and broad, and softened his eyes as he leaned in, attempting to cultivate an atmosphere of friendship and camaraderie. But his eyes were sharp and shrewd, and not the least bit friendly. His smiles and winks were an act to gain her confidence.

Olivia was too experienced an actress to fall for affected body language.

Two could play that game.

She looked up at Sergeant Callahan, her eyes wide with fear, and tensed her lower lip so it quivered, as if she were desperately holding back tears, and nodded tentatively.

"At the Coffee Clash," she said, her voice catching. "That was the day . . . the day he . . ."

"Don't think about it," Sergeant Callahan said. "I don't want to upset you."

Olivia forced a weak smile.

Sergeant Callahan poised his pen over a blank notebook page but didn't break eye contact. "What time did you leave the Coffee Clash?"

Olivia bit her lower lip and scrunched her brows together as if she was thinking hard. "A little after five."

A few deft strokes from his pen while he maintained his friendly smile. "And I understand you had an attack of some kind?"

She and Kitty had discussed the plan so long ago, she just prayed she remembered it correctly. "Actually," she said, dropping her voice, "I wasn't sick at all."

Sergeant Callahan's eyes grew wide in mock surprise. "You weren't? But I have a statement from the barista at the Coffee Clash that you were doubled over in pain and had to be assisted from the café."

"This is embarrassing," Olivia said. She pressed her hands to her cheeks. "But Ronny was . . ." She paused and waited for Sergeant Callahan to prompt her.

"It's okay. Go ahead."

Olivia sighed. "He kept trying to grab me. He wanted me to go back to his house with him. It made me really uncomfortable." Olivia shook her head as if trying to shake off a bad memory. "I was trying to be nice, you know? Ronny was new at school, so when he asked me out, I thought I should at least have coffee with him. But he wouldn't take no for an answer, so . . ."

"So you pretended to be sick." Sergeant Callahan looked down at his notebook while he transcribed her account of last Tuesday. Her act was working.

"Mm-hm."

"And a patron at the café helped you outside, right?"

Olivia nodded.

"Do you know her name?"

Olivia didn't have time to wonder whether or not their stories would match up. She had to hope they'd be on the same page.

"Kitty Wei."

Kitty swallowed and considered the question carefully. Sergeant Callahan continued to watch her, his eyes sweeping her face for any sign that she was lying. "Everyone knows Olivia Hayes," she said simply. "She's like the most popular girl in school."

"You saw that she was having an attack and you jumped in to help." It wasn't a question.

"She was grabbing her stomach, low on the right side. My dad's appendix burst six years ago and it seemed like the same kind of pain. Everyone stood around watching her, not doing anything. So I did."

"I see." He wrote something down on his notepad and looked up at her again, his pale gray eyes locked on her own. "And did you know who she was having coffee with?"

Kitty shook her head. "I'd never met him before." At least that wasn't a lie.

"What happened after you helped Olivia outside?"

This was the tricky part. She and Olivia had agreed on a story last week, but they hadn't gone over it since. A stupid mistake, but Kitty had to hope that Olivia remembered the original plan.

"She seemed fine the second I drove out of the parking lot. Said she didn't need to go to the hospital, and I drove her home instead."

"And she didn't mention it to you at school the next day?"

Oh, how little adults understood the intricacies of high school social life. "We don't exactly hang out with the same people," she said. Then she added, "Besides, we got the announcement about Ronny's death first thing in the morning. That's all anyone's talked about since."

"Did you realize at some point that the guy at the Coffee Clash was the victim?"

Kitty shook her head. "I never got a good look at him."

"I see." He scribbled some more notes, then nodded to himself. "Thank you, Kitty. You've been very helpful."

But Kitty didn't let down her guard until she stepped outside into the courtyard.

TWENTY-NINE

MARGOT HAD BEEN DEBATING WHETHER OR NOT TO ASK FOR help in finding the identity of the faceless girl in the photo. Though it appeared to have no bearing on Ronny's murder, the timing was suspect. The first envelope arrived the day Ronny's death was announced, and though logic suggested this was simply a coincidence, Margot could not dismiss a connection out of hand. If the envelopes were somehow connected to Ronny's murder, she needed to find out.

She'd spent a significant amount of time trying to figure out who had taken the photo, exhausting all of her own resources, which despite her access to high-grade equipment, were relatively meager. She didn't have the kind of freedom that would allow her to drive all over town, employing photo experts who might be able to sharpen the contrast or lighten the exposure. If she wasn't at school, she was at home, and her leash was a short one.

But there was one person Margot knew she could trust.

She found Ed the Head at lunch outside the boys' locker

room by the health-food vending machine, selling candy bars to freshmen.

"I know they're only a buck at the grocery store," he said. "But you see, I'm a businessman. And as such, I have meticulously studied the supply and demand of my various products here at Bishop DuMaine, and right here, right now, this Snickers bar is worth exactly three dollars to you. But, if your mommy didn't give you that kind of cash in your lunch box today . . ." He slipped the candy bar back into his bag. "You can wait until after school to taste the magical sugar rush that is—"

"Fine!" the freshman said. He fished three wadded-up dollar bills out of the pocket of his gym shorts and handed them over. "Anything to shut you up."

Ed the Head smiled broadly as he exchanged the contraband for the money. "It was lovely doing business with you."

He turned to leave and spotted Margot lurking near the water fountain. "Margot, my own true love. Did you get hauled in for questioning today?"

"Of course not," Margot snapped, eyes darting around the courtyard to make sure they were alone. "I told you, I have no connection to DGM."

"If you say so." He winked. "To what do I owe this honor?"

"I need you," Margot began.

Ed the Head leaned into her. "Do you have any idea how long I've waited to hear you say those words?"

Margot wasn't about to be sidetracked. She whipped the manila envelope out of her backpack and held it between them. She pulled out a single photo, handed it to Ed the Head, and pointed to the silhouette of the photographer reflected in the darkened window. "I need to know who this is."

"Hmm." Ed the Head scanned the photo from top to bottom. His eyes settled on Amber first, then he squinted at the figure in question. "Well, we know it's not Amber Stevens."

"Cute."

"When was this taken?"

"Four years ago."

"Interesting." Ed the Head flipped the photo over. "No developer's watermark. Looks like DIY photo paper, generic, the kind my mom uses to print digital photos for her scrapbooks."

That made sense. Whoever was behind the manila envelopes had been taking great pains not to leave a paper trail, which included the use of the most generic, nondescript materials available.

"Do you have the digital version?" Ed the Head asked.

"Just this."

"Can I keep it?"

Margot nodded. She'd already scanned a high-res copy at home.

Ed the Head contemplated the photo. "Okay," he said at last. "I can probably figure out what kind of phone it was taken from, maybe run the hard copy through some filters and see if I can sharpen the image. Can't promise anything, and"—he glanced up at her—"this won't be cheap."

"How much?"

Ed slipped the photo into his backpack. "Let's say, a concert? Next Sunday night?"

Margot arched an eyebrow. "You want me to buy you a concert ticket?"

"No, babe. I want you to go to a concert with me."

Margot swallowed, completely taken aback. "Like a date?"

"You can call it that if you'd like as long as you're there."

Ed the Head was asking her on a date? Did he really think of her that way, or was this part of some elaborate scheme? It was confusing and, odd to admit, kind of flattering.

Ed took her silence as an answer and hastily unzipped his backpack. "If you can't afford the price tag, I'll just give this back to you."

Margot sighed. "Fine."

Ed smiled broadly. "And don't think you can weasel out of this one, Margot."

"Then your information had better be worth it."

As much as Bree hated the idea of following an anonymous lead left in her bag, the temptation to find out what was in the library was too much. Besides, she couldn't shake the niggling idea that the envelopes were somehow connected to Ronny's murder. She needed to follow the trail and see where it led, and with any luck, she could uncover a murderer.

The first chance John would have to get into the Bishop DuMaine library would be lunch, and Bree made sure she was there, staking out the reference stacks, before he arrived.

They hadn't spoken all weekend, and John had pointedly ignored her through first-period religion, even after they returned from the police questioning. She'd half-hoped the friction between them would have eased over the weekend, but no such luck. If anything, the gap had widened.

And now here she was stalking him. What was wrong with her?

It's for his own good. That's what she kept telling herself. Someone was leading John down the primrose path, and though the who and why escaped her, Bree felt the overwhelming urge to protect him, especially with a murder rap hanging in the balance.

John had already figured out the meaning behind the DGM acronym. How long before he discovered their identities as well? If the police tried to pin Ronny's murder on John, would he give up what he knew about DGM? Would he, unwittingly, put Bree in danger?

And would she let him take the fall if he didn't?

A desk bell rang, a silvery ding that pierced the silence, and the librarian shuffled out of her office. "Can I help you?"

"I'm looking for yearbooks," John said.

"Any volumes in particular?"

"The last two."

There's a photo of DGM if you know where to look. Check the school library.

Two years. DGM had started two years ago.

A loud thud signaled that the librarian had deposited the requested materials on the circulation desk.

Bree keenly remembered the day freshman year when she, Olivia, Margot, and Kitty had all been assigned to a group project in religion class where Don't Get Mad had been born. She was pretty sure no one else at Bishop DuMaine even remembered that project, let alone connected the dots between the four of them, but was it possible that a photo of them together existed? Could the anonymous tipster be right?

"Find what you're looking for?" the librarian asked impatiently, clearly ready to get back to her work.

"Not really," he said absently. "You don't happen to have copies of the *DuMaine Dispatch* in the library, do you?"

The librarian sighed. "Of course. We keep hard copies going back several years; the rest are scanned and archived in the database." She pointed to a filing cabinet near the magazine rack. "Knock yourself out."

The library fell silent once more except for the sound of Bree's heart thundering in her ears. She'd never been particularly religious, but at that moment she prayed that John wouldn't find what he was looking for, and that he'd give up the wild DGM goose chase for good.

As if in answer to her futile prayers, John suddenly gasped. Bree peeked around the bookshelf and watched as he fished his cell phone out of the pocket of his black jeans and took a photo of an issue of the *DuMaine Dispatch* spread out across the top of the cabinet. He quickly stuffed the issue back into the file, closed the drawer, and started to walk away.

He seemed energized, excited about something; then he suddenly paused midstep. He hung there a moment and appeared to be having some sort of conversation with himself, then swung around and returned to the file cabinet. He pulled out an issue of the *Dispatch* and cast a furtive look at the librarian, who had retreated to a back office; then, without a second thought, John ripped a section of the page clean away and shoved it into his notebook.

It took every ounce of self-control for Bree to keep still until the library door clicked shut behind John before she sprinted to the file cabinet.

Back issues of the *DuMaine Dispatch* hung in file folders, labeled by date. Bree's eyes were immediately drawn to one issue, which sat askew, sticking up from the overstuffed drawer. She flipped through, and it fell open to a page where the lower half had been hastily torn away.

Bree scanned the vandalized page, looking for some hint as to what John had removed. The top half was still intact, and it appeared to be an article on community outreach programs at Bishop DuMaine. Bree's breath came in quick gasps. The project in religion class that had brought DGM together? Community outreach. Shit, shit, shit. Could there possibly be some mention of their names in that article? Some hint of the carefully protected secret of their connection to one another?

She turned to the front and checked the date—spring semester of her freshman year at Bishop DuMaine.

Bree was at the circulation desk in an instant. "Excuse me?" she said impatiently, tapping the bell several times in an erratic tattoo. "I need some help."

The librarian slowly appeared at the office door. "Yes?" she said, making no attempt to mask her annoyance.

"I was wondering, do you have any additional copies of the *DuMaine Dispatch*? Other than what's in the file cabinet?"

"Why is everyone so interested in the school paper today?"

the librarian muttered. She shook her head. "We archive issues after ten years. Only hard copies of the newer issues are in the file cabinet."

"Oh." Crap. She needed to know what was in the photo John had ripped out of the paper. "What about online?"

"Well, of course," she said, as if stating the obvious. "All the recent issues are online. This isn't the nineties." Without waiting for another question, she disappeared back into her office.

Bree sheepishly retreated to a table and pulled up the school website on her tablet. It took several minutes before she could find the correct issue, then agonizing moments as each page loaded with such painful slowness Bree felt like she was being punished. She bounced her foot under the table, silently cursing her cell network. *Hurry up and load!*

Finally, she was able to scroll through to the article. The photo was tiny—all she could make out were students grouped around tables. But when she zoomed in, her stomach dropped. There, sitting at a table together, were the soon-to-be members of Don't Get Mad: Kitty, Margot, Olivia, and Bree.

THIRTY

COACH MILES BLEW HER WHISTLE WITH A FEROCITY THAT froze the entire Bishop DuMaine varsity girls' volleyball squad in their tracks. Kitty snatched the scrimmage ball in midair and spun to face her as she blazed across the court.

"Annabelle!" Coach Miles said. "If I ever see you half-ass a kill like that, I'll bench you for an entire match, you hear me?"

Annabelle's beet-red face flushed even deeper. "Yes, Coach."

Coach Miles swung around to the scrimmage team on Kitty's side of the net. "And, Zoe, I have no idea what you thought you were doing with that last dig. The goal is to keep the ball in play, not launch it into orbit. Come on, guys. It's only Tuesday. I'm not used to seeing this much lazy ball handling so early in the week."

Kitty knew Coach was right, but her approach to motivating her players wasn't exactly what Kitty would have done in her place.

Two short blasts on the whistle signaled a change of drill. "Accelerations," Coach Miles said. "Eight balls."

The entire team groaned in unison and skulked to one side of the court for the hated drill. Coach was about to throw the first balls, when Mika walked into the girls' gym with Theo Baranski close behind.

Coach Miles tooted on her whistle again. "Water break. Ten minutes." She pointed at Kitty. "Wei, come with me."

"Coach, this is Theo," Mika said, her hand on Theo's shoulder. "He's interested in the team manager gig."

Coach Miles examined Theo up and down. "You're the first in and the last out," she said curtly. "You're on the bus for every away game, and I expect stats on my desk first thing the next morning. Can you handle that?"

"Yes, sir!" Theo barked.

Kitty bit her lip to keep from smiling as Theo's eyes grew wide, instantly realizing his mistake.

"I mean, ma'am," he squeaked.

"Sir is fine," Coach Miles said. She pointed at the two girls. "Get him up to speed."

Theo hustled after Kitty and Mika as they strode to the athletic lockers across from the main gym. He had to take three steps for every two of theirs.

"All the team sports keep their equipment in these lockers," Mika explained. "Volleyball, basketball, soccer, water polo, whatever."

"Coach Miles is kind of a hard-ass about keeping the equipment organized," Kitty added. "If you can manage that, you'll be golden."

They gave Theo a tour of the locker, explained the setup for practice versus home and away games, then stopped by Coach Miles's office to retrieve copies of the team rosters and schedules.

Theo took prodigious notes throughout, scribbling away in a pocket-size spiral notebook. He seemed eager to do a good job, motivated by the luxury of avoiding Coach Creed in sixth-period PE, and soaked up everything Kitty and Mika spilled out. By the time they ducked into the main gym where the team played their home matches, Theo had picked up enough of the lingo to anticipate what they were going to say. It was kind of adorable.

As they started to leave, the far door of the gym opened and the varsity boys' basketball team meandered in, sweating like they'd just spent an hour in the weight room.

"Kitty!" She jumped at the sound of Donté's voice. "Hey, Mika," he said, jogging up to them. He took Kitty's hand. "What are you doing here?"

Kitty gestured to her new recruit. "Theo Baranski, this is Donté Greene. Theo is going to be the volleyball team manager this semester."

"Right on, man." Donté held out his fist to Theo, who, with a look of delighted surprise, readily returned the bump. "Don't let these ladies run you ragged. They're a tough bunch."

"Please," Kitty said. "We're way less demanding than those divas on the boys' basketball team."

"Kids," Mika said, cutting off their banter. "You guys have plans tomorrow night?"

Donté glanced at Kitty. "Not that I know of. What's up?"

Mika dropped her voice. "There's a meeting at the Coffee Clash. Kind of an organizational thing."

What was Mika up to? "Organizing for what?"

Mika glanced from side to side, then leaned closer to Kitty and Donté. "For an on-campus rally. We're going to protest the way old F.U. and his 'Maine Men have been treating the students around here."

Theo was at Mika's side in the blink of an eye. "Can I come?" he asked eagerly.

Mika's face lit up. "Of course. Everyone's welcome."

"Thank you," Theo said. "I'll do whatever you need. Paint signs, recruit people. You name it."

Mika turned to Donté and Kitty. "What about you guys?"

"Count me in," Donté said.

Kitty swallowed. She had a DGM meeting scheduled for tomorrow night, and that wasn't something she could change even if she wanted to. "I can't," she said. "I have a family thing."

"Can't you get out of it?" Mika pleaded.

Kitty shook her head. "Sorry."

"How about Friday night?" Mika pressed. "We're doing some prep work after Ronny's vigil."

Mika wasn't going to let her out of it. Dammit. She'd be on F.U.'s blacklist if she took a leadership role with this rally, but Mika would be suspicious if she avoided it.

"That'll work," Kitty said, forcing a smile. Out of the frying pan, into the fire.

Mika grinned. "I knew I could count on you guys. I organized one of these in junior high to try and get the school to change their mascot so we didn't have to wear a stupid fighting Jesuit on our jerseys."

Fighting Jesuits? Kitty recalled the photo of Bree with the cropped-out image of Christopher Beeman.

"Where did you go to junior high?" Kitty asked.

"St. Alban's," Mika said.

With the exception of the article about Christopher Beeman going AWOL from Archway, there were no other hits on him when she'd Googled his name. Was it possible that her best friend knew him?

"We played against you guys," Donté said, stroking his chin. "Helluva blowout each year."

Mika pursed her lips. "Yeah, but the girls' volleyball team rocked."

"Hey," Kitty began, hoping she didn't sound as anxious as she felt. "Did you know a student at St. Alban's named Christopher Beeman?"

Out of the corner of her eye, Kitty saw Theo start.

Mika scrunched up her face, trying to remember. "Short, kinda chubby, thick glasses?"

Kitty had no idea. "I think so."

"I didn't really know him," Mika said, shaking her head. "He left in sixth grade. Suddenly, I think."

"Got it," Kitty said. She stole a glance at Theo, whose ruddy face seemed to have blanched several shades paler. Mika might not have known Christopher Beeman, but apparently Theo did.

The squeak of athletic shoes and the thundering of a half-dozen basketballs signaled that the varsity team's practice was under way. Donté glanced over his shoulder, then squeezed Kitty's hand. "Gotta go. We still on for Saturday?"

"Absolutely," she said, wresting her gaze away from Theo.

"Sweet." He leaned down and kissed her cheek, while Mika prominently rolled her eyes.

"Thanks for taking me in," Theo said as they walked back to the girls' gym.

"No problem," Kitty said. "We need a manager, so it's win-win."

"Coach Creed has it in for me," Theo said bluntly. "I think he blames me for what happened at the assembly."

"That's ridiculous," Kitty said. "He can't hold you responsible for DGM."

Theo shrugged. "Father Uberti threatened to expel me if I didn't tell him everything I knew about DGM."

"See?" Mika said, throwing her hands in the air. "This is what I'm talking about. Creed bullies students right and left, and Uberti doesn't do jack about it. Then he blames the victim. Total bullshit."

"Even if I knew anything about DGM, I wouldn't have told him," Theo said with a grin. "They're the only ones who've ever stood up for me."

"Is that why you confessed to the murder?" Mika asked.

Kitty watched Theo. She was curious about him, touched and saddened by his confession to Ronny's murder, as if it was the only way to show his gratitude for what DGM had done.

Theo nodded. "I just wanted them to know how much I appreciate them."

"But what if you'd gone to jail?" Kitty asked. The idea that someone would have voluntarily suffered on her behalf made her sick to her stomach.

"My parents have a security system," Theo said. "The kind that monitors all the doors and windows. My dad had the records pulled up immediately and it showed there was no way I could have left the house that night during the time Ronny was killed."

"It's a good thing your parents had that," Mika said, pausing at the girls' restroom. "I'll catch up with you guys in a bit. Glad to have you on board, Theo."

Theo and Kitty continued back to the gym in silence. She was about to bring up Christopher Beeman again when Theo beat her to the punch.

"I could have killed him," Theo said, suddenly pensive.

"Ronny?"

Theo nodded.

"But you said—"

"I mean," Theo interrupted, "that I could have if I wanted to."

Kitty remembered the list Bree saw in Ronny's room. Theo's name was on that list. What connection did he have with Ronny? And could it possibly have anything to do with Christopher Beeman?

"Did you know him?" she asked.

"Not really," Theo said, without elaborating.

Theo reached the door to the girls' gym and paused. Then he turned and looked Kitty directly in the eye. "He wanted something from me. Something I knew."

What could Ronny have wanted from Theo?

"Ronny DeStefano was not a good person," Theo continued. "And I'm not sorry he's dead."

Without another word, he yanked the door open and disappeared inside, leaving a stunned Kitty in the courtyard.

THIRTY-ONE

MARGOT STARED OUT THE WINDOW OF THE LOCAL BUS AS it lumbered through the streets of western Menlo Park. She passed tree-lined parks and fancy houses with highly manicured lawns, but she didn't see any of it. The only image before her eyes was a photo of a twelve-year-old Amber Stevens posing outside Margot's bedroom window.

The mystery of who had sent her the photos paled in comparison to that of the identity of the photographer. Peanut and Jezebel were the prime suspects—they'd been Amber's toadies since junior high. Wendy Marshall and Christina Huang were just as horrible, though a year ahead of them. Rex went to a different school, Tyler and Kyle hadn't morphed into mindless sychophants yet, and Olivia didn't start hanging out with Amber's crowd until eighth grade.

Would Ed the Head be able to help? She certainly hoped so. While she could still hate Amber for putting her through three years of junior high hell, apparently there was someone else who deserved Margot's enmity. Someone else who deserved revenge.

"Atherton Avenue," the bus driver cooed in a chipper tone more appropriate to a conductor on the Disneyland Railroad than public transit.

Margot forced thoughts of Amber and the photograph out of her mind as she hopped off the bus and trekked up the street to the public library. She had more important things to worry about.

Margot was a familiar fixture at the West Menlo branch; other than home, it was the only after-school destination preapproved by Margot's parents. The librarians all knew her by name, all recognized that she was a diligent, hardworking student who wasn't there to cause any trouble. She'd earned a reputation as someone who could be trusted to, say, borrow the keys to the special collections room without damaging, stealing, or otherwise defacing the contents therein.

Which meant she could get away with murder.

Margot winced. *Horrendous choice of words, subconscious.*

Perhaps not so ironically, murder was the reason Margot had spent three out of the last five afternoons parked at a table in the far corner of the main reading room, her back to the wall, poring through the personal computer files of Ronny DeStefano.

"Why hello, Margot," Mrs. Shi said with a beaming smile as Margot approached the circulation desk. "How are you this afternoon?"

"Tons of research to do today," Margot said, laying the honor roll student routine on thick.

Mrs. Shi clicked her tongue in concern. "They do load you up so at Bishop DuMaine."

Margot nodded. "*And* my Stanford extension classes."

"My, my." Mrs. Shi patted Margot's hand. Her elderly skin was tissue-thin. "You need to make sure you have a little fun, too, dear. Can't be all work and no play."

Margot forced a smile. "I'm volunteering for the theater production at school. That should be fun."

Mrs. Shi winked at her. "And an excellent place to meet cute boys, yes?"

Margot blushed. She didn't even need to fake it.

"Now, what can I do for you?"

Margot tried to look suitably embarrassed. "I hate to ask this, Mrs. Shi. . . ."

Mrs. Shi leaned forward with a conspirator's grin. "Yes?"

"Would it be possible to get into the special collections room? I know it's like the third time in a week, but I desperately need to double-check my notes against the Filoli archives. I'll be sure to leave everything as I found it."

Mrs. Shi winked again as she reached into her pocket and retrieved a set of keys. "Our little secret."

The library was one of Margot's favorite places in the world. A converted manor house with a modern wing added on for the lobby, study hall, and computer lab, the bulk of the library's collection was housed in a series of winding interconnected rooms stretching from the old wine cellar to the slanted-roofed servants' quarters. Part haunted mansion, part M. C. Escher print, there were areas that could only be accessed by rickety spiral staircases, adjacent rooms with no connecting doors, and nooks and crannies that looked as if they hadn't been fully explored since World War II.

As a child, Margot would wander off from her parents and instantly find herself happily lost in a labyrinth of books.

The special collections room was actually an alcove bored into the bedrock next to the wine cellar, accessible only by a metal spiral staircase that shook precariously when used. The special collections room was locked 95 percent of the time behind a thick glass door, except when the special collections librarian kept brief office hours every other Thursday. There really weren't any books of note in the collection, so it was a rare occasion that someone actually requested access, and Margot guessed that no one else had gone through the collection in over a year.

Which made it the perfect hiding place.

Immediately after Ronny's death, Margot realized two things: (a) being caught in possession of the stolen contents of his hard drive was as good as an admission of guilt, and (b) said hard drive might be even more useful than she'd expected. If there was a clue as to why Ronny was killed, it might be on his computer. That said, she couldn't exactly keep it in her bedroom. So she came up with the perfect plan: the special collections room.

The pungent aroma of moldering wood hit her the moment she unlocked the door. As usual, the room was empty, but Margot locked the door behind her anyway.

She kept the stark overhead lights off as she padded across the room, just in case there was a library patron perusing the infrequently visited yearbooks and city council records housed in the wine cellar. She had chosen her hiding place carefully. A bookshelf in the corner held tomes of livestock records from the estate that used to encompass most of the area, massive old ledgers with six-inch-thick spines crammed onto each metal shelf. Margot squeezed her arm between the bookcase and the stone wall, and her fingers immediately found what they were looking for: a magnetic box, attached to the back side of the second-to-last shelf.

Margot was just about to pry the box from the metal shelf when she froze. Outside the glass door, something moved.

It was just a flash, a half second of shadow and light, but in that moment, Margot could have sworn she saw a figure peek into the special collections room, then disappear back into the wine cellar.

Margot fought to keep her nerves in check. Even if someone *was* out there, they wouldn't be able to see her in the darkened interior of the room.

Unless they'd followed her down there.

She inhaled slowly, eyes fixed on the glass door, waiting to see the figure again. One minute. Two minutes. There was no motion except the steady rise and fall of Margot's chest.

Margot needed to get a grip on her paranoia. She'd imagined it, obviously. She was tense and stressed and her brain was on alert.

She shook her head and pried the magnet from its prison, then grabbed a couple of boring volumes on the Filoli estate for cover and hurried upstairs without looking back.

After three days of searching, Margot wasn't particularly optimistic that she'd find anything of value on Ronny's computer. So far, his personal files contained the most comprehensive collection of pornographic photos, videos, manga, erotica, and product site screen grabs than she'd imagined possible. The pursuit of sex seemed to have occupied at least 75 percent of Ronny's brain. She'd been through all of his files and downloads, forcing herself to scan through increasingly graphic thumbnails, just to make sure she didn't miss anything important, and breathed a sigh of relief when she realized she only had about thirty thousand personal emails left to sift through before she could call Ronny's hard drive a bust.

Two hours of tedious school and family emails later, Margot's diligence was finally rewarded. An email response to Ronny from a friend named Chris.

To: rd@ama.mil
From: cb@ama.mil

Dude, that's crazy. Old Creed turned up at your dad's alma mater? What are the odds? I doubt he'll be there for long. Only a matter of time before they fire his ass. If he couldn't cut it at Archway, no way some fancy prep school will put up with his bullshit. Maybe we can hurry that probability along like last time? BWAAAAAAAHAHAHAHAHA.

Margot went rigid in her chair. Based on the evidence before her, not only did Ronny know Coach Creed from their mutual time at Archway Military Academy, but Ronny might even have had a hand in getting Creed fired from that position.

Which gave Coach Creed a strong motive for murdering Ronny DeStefano.

Margot had blown the investigation wide open.

Fingers tearing across the keyboard, Margot executed a keyword search for all emails from cb@ama.mil. There had to be more information about how and why Coach Creed was fired from Archway. Three hundred and forty-seven emails and chat logs popped up right away. Margot's hands trembled with excitement as she scrolled down to the oldest email, dating from Ronny's eighth-grade year. She was about to double click on the file when her cell phone buzzed.

Incoming text from her mom.

I'm almost there, mija. Be outside in the parking lot in five minutes.

Margot stared at the thumb drive. Maybe she should take it home with her and comb through the emails during the "reading for pleasure" portion of her evening schedule? The temptation was intense: it would be Saturday's library study session with Logan before she got a chance to access the files again. But even the .05 percent chance of her room being searched for a connection to Ronny was a risk not worth taking.

With a heavy sigh, Margot ejected the drive and trudged it back down to the special collections room with the untouched research books. At least she'd have a solid lead to share with the girls at tomorrow night's meeting, but the 347 emails to and from the mysterious Chris would have to wait until the weekend.

THIRTY-TWO

EVERYONE WAS ON TIME TO KITTY'S UNCLE'S WAREHOUSE FOR Wednesday night's DGM meeting. Well, everyone but Olivia.

This time, even Kitty couldn't resist the urge to check her watch every few minutes. Nearly half past eight and still no Olivia. While tardiness ran in the girl's blood, she'd never been this late to a meeting.

Margot paced the warehouse floor. "Where is she?"

"Maybe she got stuck in rehearsal," Kitty offered, hoping a harmless but logical solution would counterbalance whatever wild fantasies were running through Margot's brain.

"Or maybe," Bree said, stretching her arms over her head, "Coach Creed got her."

"What?" Margot squeaked, pausing midpace.

"Bree . . ." Kitty said through clenched teeth.

Bree ignored her. "Maybe he found out Olivia is involved with DGM. Maybe he's interrogating her right now." She stood up and in one fluid motion flipped the chair around and straddled it. "Maybe the 'Maine Men are massing their forces outside the warehouse as we speak, ready to burst through the doors like a Catholic school SWAT team and put us all on double secret probation."

Kitty fought the urge to strangle Bree. "Cut it out, will you?"

Bree threw her hands in the air. "I'm kidding. Sheesh, you guys used to be able to take a joke."

One rap followed by three sharp knocks at the door made Kitty jump in her seat. *Finally.*

"Sorry," Olivia said, as she scurried across the warehouse. "Mr. Cunningham needed me to go through a scene one more time. I couldn't get out of it."

"See?" Kitty said with a sideways glance at Bree. "No big deal."

Margot continued to pace, her face twisted in irritation. "Couldn't you tell him you had study group?"

Bree snorted. "Yeah, like anyone would believe that."

"Let's get this meeting started," Kitty said, trying to head off the potential catfight. "Olivia, you start. Anything to report?"

Olivia nodded as she unscrewed the lid of her metal water bottle and took a long sip. "Amber was with Ronny the day he was killed."

"What?" Kitty, Margot, and Bree said in unison.

"And she asked Jezebel to lie about where she was that night."

Bree laughed. "That's just awesome."

"Any idea why Amber saw Ronny that night?" Kitty asked.

Olivia shook her head. "I'm working on it." Then she added, "And Bree was right about Rex and Ronny. They had some kind of history that made Rex nervous. He and Amber are trying to frame DGM for Ronny's murder to make sure we're put out of commission before they end up as the next target."

"Motive and opportunity for both Ronny's murder and framing DGM," Margot said, gnawing at the nail of her right index finger.

"Case closed," Bree said. "Amber and Rex killed Ronny."

"Not so fast," Kitty said. "There could be other suspects."

She had to admit, the case against Amber and Ronny was strong, but she'd discovered her own set of incriminating coincidences that needed to be explored.

"Like who?" Bree asked.

Kitty opened her mouth to tell them about Coach Creed but Margot beat her to it.

"I found something interesting in Ronny's computer files," she said quickly. "An email from last year, to Ronny from a friend at Archway, mentioning Coach Creed."

Olivia scrunched up her face. "How would Ronny know about Coach Creed? Didn't he just transfer to DuMaine this year?"

Kitty leaped to her feet. "Coach Creed used to teach at Archway," she said excitedly. "I heard him talking to Father Uberti about it."

"No way," Olivia said.

Bree's combat boots clunked to the floor. "And his name, like Rex's, was on the list in Ronny's room."

"According to Google," Margot continued, "Coach Creed was fired from Archway, but I don't have details yet. Still searching."

"Damn." Kitty kicked the leg of her chair lightly with the back of her sneaker. Another suspect with motives for both killing Ronny and framing DGM for the murder. Who knew so many people wanted Ronny dead? Apparently, there was a lot about Ronny they didn't know.

"Any idea who Ronny was emailing?" she asked.

"Someone named Chris," Margot said. "The email address was 'cb,' which I'm assuming are initials."

Kitty caught her breath. The newspaper article, the photo of Bree from St. Alban's. "Christopher Beeman!"

Bree stiffened. "What did you say?"

"Who?" Olivia asked.

She spun around, facing Bree. "He went to St. Alban's. Didn't you go there, Bree?"

"No!" Bree stumbled back. "I mean, yes. A lot of people did. Mika, Rex . . ." She ran her fingers through her bangs, plastering them back against her head. "Why are you asking me about Christopher?"

"He was a student at Archway," Kitty began. "I—" She stopped midsentence. Should she tell the girls about the anonymous envelopes? Part of her wanted to be completely open and tell them. Maybe together they could figure out who had sent them and why.

But something Margot had said the other day in the computer lab stuck with her. *The most logical explanation is that one of us killed him.* Kitty had tried to fight against it, but even with Rex, Amber, and Coach Creed emerging as prime suspects, Margot's logic was sound. Until she knew more about the envelopes—who sent them and why—perhaps it was better to keep them to herself.

"What?" Olivia prompted, clearly exasperated. "What were you going to say?"

"I did some research on Archway," she lied, "and I came across an article on a student who went AWOL last year. Turns out, he's from around here. He went to St. Alban's." Kitty glanced at Bree, who sat unmoving in her chair, eyes locked on the floor. "His name is Christopher Beeman."

"It can't be a coincidence," Margot said.

"So that means we're off the hook, right?" Olivia said, inching forward on her stool. "If Coach Creed, Rex and Amber, or this Beeman guy killed Ronny, then it wasn't one of us."

Margot shrugged. "It's possible, but we still have some major snags."

"Such as?" Bree asked.

Margot stared at her coldly. "Such as the DGM cards."

"No one broke into my house," she said. "So whoever killed Ronny made their own."

"Unless John Baggott took one." Margot's innocent smile was at odds with the sarcastic lilt to her voice.

"Why do you keep bringing John into this?" Bree asked. "He didn't have a motive to kill Ronny."

Margot raised her chin. "Are you sure about that?"

"John didn't even know Ronny," Bree said. "Let alone kill him."

Bree's anger flared when Margot brought up John. It seemed

212

over the top, considering he was the most likely person to have access to the DGM cards. Why did Bree so adamantly refuse to consider that he could be a suspect? "Did he tell you he didn't know Ronny?"

Bree pursed her lips. "Well, no, but—"

"They had a fight," Olivia blurted out.

"How would you know?" Bree snapped.

Olivia smiled sweetly. "You've been avoiding each other in drama, and he's been eating lunch with Shane White all week."

More secrets. What else was Bree hiding?

"There are plenty of real suspects," Bree said slowly. "Coach Creed, Rex and Amber." She paused and swallowed. "Christopher Beeman."

"And Theo Baranski," Kitty added.

Margot raised her eyebrows. "Theo?"

"He told me that Ronny was trying to bully some information out of him. And that he wasn't sorry Ronny was dead."

"He had an alibi, though," Olivia said. "Didn't he?"

Margot chewed on another fingernail. "Records from the security system at the Baranski home showed that he didn't leave the house that night." She shook her head. "But that's easy to get around, if you know how."

"But if Theo killed Ronny," Olivia began, clearly confused, "why would he confess?"

Margot shrugged. "If he knew he had an airtight alibi, why not?"

Silence descended over the warehouse. Instead of struggling

to find one credible suspect, they'd managed to find a half dozen or so. How were they going to figure out who killed Ronny before the police closed in on DGM?

"We should tell the police," Olivia said. "About all of it."

"How?" Bree asked. "Just waltz into the station and say, 'Hi! We're DGM! We're not the killers, but maybe you should check out these upstanding members of society who might be!' Yeah, that'll go down well."

Olivia glared at her. "Why not? I get the feeling someone's already been telling the police more than they need to know."

Margot wrapped her arms tightly around her body as if suddenly uncomfortable with the turn in the conversation. "What are you implying?"

"The cops knew about my date with Ronny."

Bree shook her head. "So what? Weren't there like a half-dozen patrons there plus the barista? Any of them could have pointed the finger at you."

"Or it could have been one of you," Olivia said.

"No one in this room would narc," Kitty said solemnly. "We swore an oath."

"Princess has a point," Bree said. "All of us had the opportunity to save ourselves. Go to the cops, turn ourselves in, and point the finger at the rest."

The skin on the back of Kitty's neck prickled. Was Bree threatening them?

Olivia narrowed her eyes. "All of us, or just you?"

Bree rocketed to her feet. "I'm putting all the options on the table. Isn't that what this meeting was for? Margot's got Ronny's hard drive. Olivia and Kitty were seen with Ronny the day he died. And I was in the room where he was murdered. There's evidence against every one of us. How long before someone chooses to save their own neck?" Bree scooped her surplus bag off the table and bolted for the door. "Sleep on that, kids."

Kitty realized, as the door clanged shut behind Bree, that she'd left without saying the pledge.

The square was now a triangle.

THIRTY-THREE

THE LAWN IN FRONT OF BISHOP DUMAINE WAS TEEMING WITH people by the time Kitty and Mika arrived. Hundreds of candles flickered in the twilight, as they joined the mass of students and parents gathered to commemorate the death of Ronny DeStefano.

Kitty felt like a hypocrite as she selected a candle from a box on the front steps and carefully lit it from Mika's. Wasn't she responsible for Ronny's death? Even if she hadn't stood over his sleeping body with a baseball bat, even though it looked more and more likely that his murder had nothing to do with DGM, the opportunity to frame DGM for his murder might have tipped the killer's hand toward homicide. And for that, Kitty was responsible.

"Lot of people here," Mika said hesitantly. "You know, considering he was kind of a douche."

That's an understatement.

More people flooded the front lawn, pressing in around them like it was church on Easter Sunday. Kitty searched the crowd fleetingly, hoping to catch a glimpse of Olivia, Bree, or Margot, but the sun's rays were rapidly fading, and in the flickering light of several hundred candles, every face looked like a jack-o'-lantern leering at her from the darkness.

"He's over there," Mika said. She pointed to the far side of the lawn. "With the drama class."

Donté towered above the theater crowd, his candle held waist-high, and Kitty couldn't help but notice that Olivia stood at his side.

"Hey, Mika!" Theo pushed his way through the crowd. His eyes sparkled with excitement, his hands conspicuously candle-free. "I've got twenty people showing up at the park tonight to help make signs for next week's rally. Is it still happening?"

"Shh!" Mika hissed. "Not so loud, Theo."

"Sorry," he mouthed silently.

"Acorn Street park," Mika whispered. "Right after the vigil."

Theo nodded and gave Mika an exaggerated A-OK, then backed slowly into the crowd.

"Someone's excited," Kitty said, watching Theo disappear across the lawn.

Mika let out a slow breath. "I think I've created a monster."

"Theo?"

"Kid's gone ballistic. Organizing people, supplies. Who knew he had . . ." Mika paused as she caught sight of something over Kitty's shoulder. Her eyes grew wide. "Barbara Ann!" she cried.

Kitty froze.

"Hey, Mika."

Mika grabbed Kitty by the arm and spun her around. "You remember Kitty, right?"

"Hey!" Kitty said, turning around to face Barbara Ann with the biggest smile she could muster.

"Long time, no see." Barbara Ann's face was implacable in the gathering darkness, illuminated by the fluctuating candle flame. But unlike at their meeting at the Coffee Clash, Barbara Ann's voice sounded sharp, each word tinged with attitude.

"I haven't seen you in forever," Mika said. "How have you been? What are you up to? Are you still playing club ball?"

"I'm good," Barbara Ann said. "I'm at Gunn now, but I don't play anymore."

"What?" Mika exclaimed. "What the hell? Girl, you're too good to not be playing."

Barbara Ann shrugged. "Don't want to. Not after what happened."

Barbara Ann stared right at Kitty, her eyes teeming with hostility. Something had changed since their last meeting. Barbara Ann had been reserved that day but not hostile. Now she looked as if she wanted to tear Kitty limb from limb.

"I'm sorry," Mika said. "Father Uberti is a dickwad for kicking you out of school."

"*You* have nothing to be sorry about." Barbara Ann's gaze never faltered. "It's amazing the things you find out about people you thought you could trust, you know?"

"Don't worry," Mika barreled on. "F.U.'s going to get what's coming to him. Call it payback."

Mika might have missed the pointedness of Barbara Ann's comment, but Kitty did not. Barbara Ann's face was tense, her nostrils flared. "Payback," she said slowly. "I like that."

If Kitty had ever had any doubt that Barbara Ann blamed her for getting kicked out of school, it vanished in that instant.

Kitty thought of the anonymous envelopes, full of someone else's secrets. Could it be that someone knew hers? Could the same person who pointed her toward Bree and Christopher Beeman have spilled her dirty secret to Barbara Ann?

Olivia stood silently by Donté's side. She tried not to smile. That would be totally inappropriate at a somber occasion like a candlelight vigil, but standing there with him, she could almost pretend that they were still a couple.

That sensation was short-lived. The crowd swelled and shifted, Donté was shuffled away, and suddenly Olivia felt someone press up behind her.

"Liv," Rex whispered in her ear. His voice was thick and she could smell the alcohol on his breath. "You're looking fine."

"Uh, thanks?"

Was he really hitting on her at a memorial service?

"You wanna explain to me why we've never hooked up?"

Because you're my best friend's boyfriend? Olivia opened her mouth to tell Rex to piss off, when she paused. Rex had definitely been drinking. And one thing Olivia had learned about a drunk Rex was that he wouldn't remember anything the next day. It was the perfect opportunity to troll for information on his connection to Ronny. Swallowing her comeback, Olivia turned to Rex and smiled sweetly. "This vigil is so sad, don't you think?"

"Totally." Rex leaned closer. "Totally sad."

"I heard you and Ronny went way back," she said, her voice low and soothing.

Rex swayed. "Nah. Only met him twice."

How could Rex have had a history with Ronny if they'd only met twice? Olivia racked her brain, trying to think what other connection they might have had. "Didn't you know him in junior high or something?"

"Junior high . . ." Rex abruptly stopped swaying. His eyes flitted over the crowd. "Goddamn homo. Is he here?"

Who was he talking about? Olivia took a stab in the dark. "Do you mean Christopher?"

Rex's head snapped back to her. "You know about him?" He grabbed her arm, digging his fingers into her flesh. "What do you know? Tell me what you—"

"Rex!" Amber hissed. Rex released Olivia's arm as his girlfriend wedged herself between them. "What are you doing?"

Rex glared at Olivia. "Nothing."

"Uh-huh," Amber said. "Sure." She dragged him away, shooting Olivia a look that would have flayed the skin off a lion.

So, something happened between Christopher Beeman and Rex in junior high. Ronny must have known about it somehow. Kitty said that Ronny had tried to bully information out of Theo; had it been about Rex? And if so, would it be enough to kill for?

The key seemed to lie with Christopher Beeman. Who was he?

◆ ◆ ◆

Bree leaned against the side of the school, hands shoved deep into the pockets of her hoodie, and gazed out over the assembled crowd. She wondered how many of them had actually known Ronny. A handful, she guessed. So why had so many people gathered to mourn his loss? Curiosity? A sense of duty? Community support? Or was it just the sort of thing you did when one of your classmates was murdered? Bree had no idea. Hell, she had no idea why she was there, other than that something had drawn her to the vigil.

The front door of the school opened, and Father Uberti walked out onto the steps, followed by a bull-chested man and a bleached-blond woman, both dressed in black. They held hands and stood at Father Uberti's shoulder as he addressed the crowd.

"Thank you all for coming tonight," Father Uberti began. "In the face of a senseless tragedy, it is comforting to find such tremendous support in the community." He gestured to the couple behind him. "Mr. and Mrs. DeStefano have asked me to convey their gratitude for all the sympathy you've given over the last few days." He turned and shook Mr. DeStefano's hand.

Bree felt her throat catch. However much of a jerk Ronny might have been, his parents looked absolutely devastated, and Bree couldn't help but wonder if her own parents would feel such overwhelming sadness at the loss of their only daughter, or if that degree of sorrow would be reserved only for the death of Henry Jr.

Father Uberti turned back to the crowd. "And now I'll lead us in a prayer of remembrance." He bowed his head. "Let us pray."

As Father Uberti began his prayer, Bree caught sight of Shane hanging out near the back of the crowd. He was standing by himself, checking his cell phone. Bree hastily wiped a stray tear from her cheek with the back of her hand and slowly made her way toward him.

"Hi!" Bree whispered.

"Bree!" His eyes strayed to her hands. "You don't have a candle."

"Oh." Right, it was a candlelight vigil and she was the only person there without a candle. Good job, Bree.

"It's okay. I don't think Ronny will mind." He elbowed her in the arm as if he'd just made a tremendous joke.

Bree started. Making a joke about a dead kid at his vigil was borderline tasteless, and it made Bree vaguely uncomfortable.

"Amen," Father Uberti said.

The entire crowd replied in unison. "Amen."

"I know many of you are concerned about the safety of your children," Father Uberti began. "But I want to assure you that both the Archdiocese and the Menlo Park Police Department are doing everything they can to protect the students of Bishop DuMaine. In addition to the continued police presence on campus, in the coming days, we'll be implementing a new peer monitoring system."

"Peer monitoring?" Shane asked. "Does he mean like TV cameras?"

"I think he's talking about the 'Maine Men," Bree said. The idea that those cavemen would be given even more power made Bree nervous.

"Hey!" Something caught Shane's eye across the lawn. "There's Bagsie," he said. "Damn, Bree. Cordy's trying to muscle in on your territory."

"Huh?" Bree followed Shane's line of sight and saw John standing with his mom, Cordy hanging off his arm.

"She's such a groupie," Shane said with a sigh. "Not a bad kisser, though."

As Bree stared at John and Cordy, she couldn't decide which image was more disturbing: Cordy making out with Shane or Cordy making out with John.

"And on Monday," Father Uberti continued, "there will be an announcement of a new school-wide safety policy. Details will be emailed to parents via the contact network, so please be sure to read the email carefully. I know you will find the information"— he paused—"interesting."

Bree was skeptical. The last time F.U. had implemented a new school-wide policy he'd given birth to the 'Maine Men.

This couldn't be good.

THIRTY-FOUR

LOGAN SAT DOWN AT MARGOT'S LIBRARY TABLE AT EXACTLY nine o'clock Saturday morning, as promised. "Hey!" he said, his voice respectfully subdued but still upbeat. "Ready to hammer out this project?"

Margot smiled and shut her laptop, forcing Ronny's email correspondence with the mysterious Christopher Beeman to the back of her mind. "Absolutely." Logan only had two hours to spare before rehearsal. Ronny's files could wait.

They got right to work, sketching an outline and divvying up the assignment. Logan was surprisingly knowledgeable about congressional committees, and even made some impressive suggestions on the logistics of the project.

"I didn't see you at the vigil last night," Logan said, as they settled into research.

"I had one of my extension classes," Margot said, stealing a glance at him.

"One of? How many are you taking?"

Margot swallowed. He was going to think she was some kind

of psychotic overachiever. "Just two."

Logan was silent for a moment. "And you're taking how many AP classes?"

"Three." Margot's voice sounded very small.

"No wonder you don't have any time for the school play. Your schedule is too packed. Forget I even brought it up."

"No!" Margot blurted out, more forcefully than she would have liked. "I mean, the school play actually sounds like fun."

Logan looked at her sidelong. "Are you sure? If you have an aneurysm due to lack of sleep, I'd feel hella guilty."

Margot smiled. "I'll be okay."

"Promise?"

Her smile widened. "Promise."

"Okay." He checked his watch. "Rehearsal in thirty minutes. You coming with?"

Margot grimaced. "I can't," she said. "My parents are expecting me home."

"Later this week?"

"Um . . ."

"Don't worry. It'll be cool." He shoved the last of his books into his bag and zipped it up. "Besides, we're going to need to work on this project again at some point. Kill two birds with one stone?"

"Tuesday," Margot said. Oh God, how was she going to clear it with her parents?

"Perfect." Logan pulled out his cell phone and added her to his calendar. "Oh, and what are you doing next Sunday night?"

"For rehearsal?"

"No," Logan said slowly. "Actually, some of the dudes in the cast are in a band and they're doing a show at this all-ages club in town. . . ."

"The Ledge?" Margot said, her mouth suddenly dry.

"That's it! Anyway, we're all supposed to support them, like a drama class field trip, and I was wondering if you'd like to go."

Holy Mary, Mother of God, had Logan just asked her out on a date?

Logan must have seen the fear in her face, because he immediately backpedaled. "I mean, you don't have to just because you're in the production. I thought it might be fun."

"Yes," Margot said.

Logan's lopsided smile crept across the right side of his face as he slung his bag over his shoulder. "Awesome."

Awesome. Yes, it was awesome. And horrifying, and terrifying, and mortifying all rolled up into a ball of anxiety. Not only was she going to have to get out of the house for rehearsals, but now for a concert at a club? This was going to take one epic con job on her parents.

"So, I guess I'll see you Monday morning in class," Logan said, clearly loitering at the table.

"Monday." The word floated out of her mouth dreamily.

Logan touched her hand with the tips of his fingers. "Bye." Then he was gone.

It wasn't stalking. That's what Bree kept telling herself. Staking out John's apartment building to see where he went on his Saturday afternoon was totally and completely not stalking. Not really.

She had a good reason, of course. John was on the brink of figuring out who was involved in DGM, if he hadn't already. Thankfully, his free time was scarce. Between the school play and band rehearsals, John's weeknights were packed. Which meant Bree really only had to stalk him on the weekends.

It's not stalking, she repeated to herself. *You're just keeping an eye on him for his own safety.*

Sure she was.

So when she followed Mrs. Baggott's minivan to the public library, Bree was immediately suspicious. John didn't have any school projects that required outside research, and he hated studying with people around. What was he up to?

A sobering thought hit her. Maybe he was meeting Cordy? Fine, whatever. She and John weren't dating. He could study with another girl if that's what he wanted. Bree totally didn't care.

Didn't she?

Margot returned to Ronny's emails and chat transcripts with a sigh of resignation. So far, most of his communication with Christopher Beeman had been of the regular dude variety—chicks and school and bands and sports. They'd met in eighth grade when Ronny's mom sent him to Archway, discovered they both had parents in Silicon Valley, and struck up a friendship. But as she moved deeper into their freshman year, hints of a problem with Coach Creed crept into their conversations, and soon they were plotting to get him fired.

Which apparently had worked. It was a simple plan, lacking in the kind of finesse and extensive preparation that was the hallmark of DGM, but an effective one. Both Ronny and Christopher claimed that Coach Creed had made inappropriate advances, and that he'd showed them lewd images from gay pornography. When his office was searched, the offending materials were found, and though Coach Creed professed his innocence and official charges were never filed, Creed was fired.

There was something abhorrent about the whole incident. DGM was in the business of revenge, but it was never manufactured. They never lied about anyone or anything, merely used people's hypocrisy against them. But falsely accusing a teacher of sexual misconduct, even one as awful as Coach Creed, was hitting below the belt. Margot had never met Ronny or Christopher Beeman, but she was liking them less and less by the second.

After Creed's dismissal, Ronny and Christopher's friendship took a turn. They were obsessive friends, attached at the hip and chatting online for hours each night from their dorm rooms. That's when Christopher started dropping hints about an encounter he'd had with a boy back home in sixth grade, and his growing feelings for Ronny. Romantic feelings.

Then all hell broke loose. Something must have happened between them sophomore year because by spring, Ronny had left Archway and moved in with his dad and stepmom in California, where he stopped responding to Christopher's increasingly desperate emails.

To: ronnydonnydingding@mail.com
From: cb@ama.mil

You can't run away from what happened between us. Don't you understand? We're soul mates. Think about what we could accomplish together. You can't cut me out of your life. I won't let you.

I know you felt something when I kissed you. Don't even try to deny it.

I'll keep fighting for you, Ron. Don't think I'll just go away. We can start fresh in California, far away from here.

The article Kitty had mentioned about Christopher going AWOL was easy to track down, and the dates fit perfectly. Christopher jumped the wall last spring a mere two weeks after his last unanswered email to Ronny. Had he followed Ronny to California?

If so, he could literally be anyone. He could be working at the Coffee Clash, or the gas station. He could be posing as a freshman at Bishop DuMaine, a new face no one would look twice at. Or a transfer student, like Theo Baranski or . . .

Margot's eyes involuntarily flew to the chair across from her, so recently occupied. Or he could be Logan.

She pulled up an internet browser window, desperate to find out what Christopher looked like. *Please don't be Logan.* He could be Theo, or John—anyone but Logan. Or maybe it wasn't Christopher they were dealing with at all, just someone who knew about him and Ronny?

Google wasn't much help; aside from the AWOL article, there was nothing at all about Christopher Beeman on the internet. No information, no mentions, and no photographs. But he'd gone to St. Alban's with Bree. There must be a yearbook photo of him somewhere.

Margot snapped her laptop closed. And she just happened to be in a public library with a whole collection of yearbooks.

She was packing up her bag when she noticed two unusually tall people walk through the main entrance of the library, hand in hand. Margot dropped her head to the table, hiding her face behind her oversize backpack as she realized who it was.

Kitty and Olivia's ex-boyfriend, Donté Greene.

"I'm sorry a morning date is all I could manage this weekend," Donté said. "Between rehearsals and practice, my schedule is whack."

"It's okay," Kitty said. She'd had ulterior motives for suggesting the library. "I'm sorry I had to drag you along with me here, instead of the Coffee Clash." Not that she'd ever set foot in there again after her run-in with Barbara Ann. "I know this isn't exactly the best place for a date."

Donté squeezed her hand. "Any place with you is the best place for a date."

As much as she wanted to pull him behind a stack and attach her face to his like a cyclone-powered vacuum cleaner, she was at the library for a reason. Christopher Beeman.

The public library was Kitty's last shot.

Since making the link between Christopher Beeman, Coach Creed, and Ronny's death, Kitty needed to know more about him. The internet had been a waste of time—it was as if Christopher Beeman didn't exist in any files, search engines, or databases online. She needed to know who he was and who had left her clues about him. His connection to Bree seemed to make her extremely uncomfortable, and why had his head been cut out of the photo of the two of them? Somehow, she felt if she could just see a photo of Christopher, everything would fall into place, so she'd trekked over to St. Alban's after practice one day to check out the yearbooks they kept in their school library.

Slight problem. The page that should have contained Christopher's photo had been torn out.

Thankfully, the public library had its own collection of yearbooks from local schools. It was her best chance to find him.

Bree kept her distance as she followed John into the library. She waited until he disappeared through the main doors before she rounded the front of the building and dashed up the stairs, where she was just able to catch a glimpse of his floppy black hair winding through the magazine racks.

By the time she made her way back, John had disappeared. Bree gazed down the wrought iron spiral staircase leading to the old house's wine cellar, which held the forgotten archives. He must have gone down there. But why?

The good news was that Cordy was nowhere in sight. The bad news was that she couldn't risk following him. She'd been in the old cellar once; the stairs were noisy and the room was small. It was a miracle John hadn't already caught Bree spying on him—if she followed him into the cellar, she'd get busted for sure.

So she waited. Five minutes tops, though it felt like an hour, hiding behind an old filing cabinet, waiting for John to come back. He did, eventually. Was it Bree's imagination or was he practically running toward the entrance?

She had to think fast: Should she follow him or try to ferret out what he was looking for?

As Bree picked her way down the rickety staircase, she couldn't shake the feeling that she'd made the wrong choice.

Much to Margot's relief, Kitty and Donté disappeared into another area of the library seconds after walking through the front door. Margot was 99 percent sure Kitty hadn't seen her.

This is not good. What was Kitty thinking? She was dating Olivia's ex, endangering the team at a time when they needed to be as low profile as possible. There was a murderer on the loose, someone who was trying to frame Don't Get Mad for a brutal crime. Romance should be at the bottom of the priority list.

Hypocrite. Hadn't she just spent two hours pursuing her own romantic interests? She was turning into Olivia.

Time to refocus. She had work to do. Without another thought of Kitty or Donté or Olivia or Logan, Margot shoved her laptop into her bag and headed down to the cellar.

A peaty mix of age-old dust and wet newspaper tickled Bree's nose. The row of overhead lights could barely muster enough wattage to illuminate the eight-foot-tall bookcases arranged in makeshift rows throughout the cellar. It seemed so anachronistic in comparison to the mega-modern, LEED-certified, tech-heavy structure attached to the older building above, and Bree wasn't surprised that this seemingly forgotten basement housed local school yearbooks—things no one wanted to see in a place no one wanted to go.

Bree strolled through the aisles, wondering what John could possibly have been searching for down in the moldy old cellar. She pulled a volume from the shelf. An old yearbook from Gunn, the local public high school. From the layer of dust on top, Bree guessed it hadn't been looked at since the day it became property of the library. She shoved it back into its longtime home and continued to scan the shelves. No wonder the cellar was so abandoned. Not exactly the most popular books in . . .

A yearbook caught her eye. There was something odd about it. The uniform coating of dust that adorned every other volume was smudged with fingerprints, like it had been handled recently.

Hardly daring to breathe, Bree slid out the volume and tilted it so she could see the title. St. Alban's.

Bree's sixth-grade yearbook.

A giggle from the other side of the stacks startled her.

Bree stood still for a second, yearbook balanced precariously against her index finger, and listened. A girl laughing. It cut off abruptly, and was immediately followed by a soft, slobbering sound that could only mean one thing: kissing.

So the library basement was the local make-out spot? Great.

Dilemma. Should she clear her throat? Signal that she was there and risk being found with the yearbook? Depended on the culprits. Bree noiselessly slid the yearbook back into its slot, then pulled two heavy volumes off the opposite shelf and peered through to the adjacent aisle to see who she was dealing with.

The guy she recognized right away: Donté Green, Olivia's ex-boyfriend. She saw his face in profile as he kissed the cheek and neck of a tall girl. The girl arched her head back as he ran his fingers through her thick, black hair, and he pulled the V-neck of her shirt aside so he could kiss the exposed area of her chest.

The girl took a deep breath and righted her head, eyes closed, lips parted as if expecting a kiss. That's when Bree got a clear look at her face.

It was Kitty.

THIRTY-FIVE

BREE GASPED. SHE COULDN'T HELP HERSELF. AND THOUGH she clapped her hand over her mouth the instant the sound escaped her lips, it was too late.

"Did you hear that?" Kitty asked in a harsh whisper.

Bree ducked down and held her breath.

"No." Donté's voice sounded thick and heavy.

"Someone's here," Kitty said.

"No one ever comes down here," Donté said. "Trust me."

Kitty paused as if considering Donté's reassurance, then checked her watch. "Don't you have to be at rehearsal?"

Donté groaned. "You had to remind me."

There were more kissing sounds before the two lovebirds finally separated. "I'll call you tonight," Donté said. "Bye, baby."

"Bye."

Bree heard shuffling footsteps, then the sharp metallic ring of the spiral staircase as someone ascended from the cellar.

Had they both left or just Donté? After a few moments, she

heard another set of footsteps on the stairs. Kitty was leaving as well. Phew.

Bree peeked out from behind the book stacks. That was a close one. Kitty and Margot already had John in their headlights. How suspicious would Kitty have been if she found Bree checking out her junior high school yearbook after trailing her best friend to the library? She was glad she wasn't going to have to explain that one.

She slid the yearbook from the shelf and jumped back, her heart in her throat, as an eyeball stared back at her from the empty space.

"Bree?" a voice said.

Bree shoved the yearbook back onto the shelf once again and ducked around the bookcase, coming face-to-face with Margot.

"What are you doing here?" Margot asked, suspicion in her eyes.

"What are *you* doing here?" Bree countered.

"Margot?" Kitty came around the end of the last row of shelves. "Bree?"

Margot and Kitty stared at her—awkward and confused and ever so slightly combative. Really? She was the one under suspicion?

"I was doing research," she said at last.

"Me too," Margot and Kitty replied in unison.

Okay. So everyone was keeping secrets. Just what they needed while being framed for murder.

"Whatever you guys say." Bree pushed past them both toward the staircase. She'd check out the yearbook later when there wasn't so much traffic. "I'm out of here."

She'd just gripped the railing when the whole staircase rattled. Someone else was coming down.

"If that's Olivia," Kitty said calmly, "I'm going to scream."

By way of an answer, a soft singing descended into the wine cellar. The song was familiar. Too familiar. *"And if I had to walk the world, I'd make you fall for me."*

"It's John!" Bree whispered. She sprinted away from the staircase, looking for a place to hide.

"He can't see us together," Margot said.

Kitty glanced around helplessly. "What do we do?"

Margot pulled a key out of her pocket and sprinted to a glass door on the far side of the cellar. "Follow me."

In an instant she had the door open. They ducked inside the darkened room, and barely had time to close the door before John's head descended into the cellar.

Without pausing, he disappeared into the row with the St. Alban's yearbook.

It seemed as if they waited an eternity huddled on the floor of the special collections room before Kitty heard John's heavy footsteps on the stairs. She let out a controlled breath as Margot cracked the door.

"Why do you have a key to the special collections room?" Kitty asked.

Margot turned on her. "Why were you holding hands with Donté Greene?"

Kitty flushed pink. "I don't know what you're talking about."

"I saw less holding hands," Bree said with a snide grin, "and more sucking face."

Kitty set her jaw. "It's none of your business."

"He's a 'Maine Man," Margot said. "That makes it our business."

"Not to mention he's Olivia's ex-boyfriend," Bree added.

"He dropped out of the 'Maine Men," Kitty said coolly.

Bree rolled her eyes. "Yeah, cuz that makes it better."

Kitty whirled on Bree. "And what were you doing spying on us?" She made air quotes. "Research? Or maybe I should ask why you're hiding from your boyfriend?"

"He's not my boyfriend," Bree said, throwing her arms wide in exasperation. "And that's rich, you accusing *me* of keeping secrets."

That was it. Kitty'd had enough of Bree's attitude.

"You want to talk about keeping secrets?" she asked, turning toward the library stacks. "Fine." She scanned the call numbers at the top of each row, looking for the yearbook section. She realized with a start that it was the same row John had just visited.

"What are you doing?" Bree asked, her voice sharp.

Kitty's eyes landed on one volume, curiously askew on the shelf as if someone hadn't pushed it all the way back in. It was also the only yearbook whose thick coating of dust had been marred.

"What is it?" Margot asked, following close behind her. Bree lingered near the end of the case.

"A yearbook," Kitty said.

Margot sucked in a breath. "St. Alban's?"

Kitty eyed her. "How did you know?"

Margot stared at the book in Kitty's hand. "That's what I came down here looking for too."

"Christopher Beeman," Kitty and Margot said in unison.

Out of the corner of her eye, Kitty saw Bree flinch.

"Let's see what he looks like, shall we?" Kitty said. She opened the yearbook with a flourish.

Only the page with Christopher's photo had been removed.

"Gone?" Bree blurted out. "His photo is gone?" She stared at the page in disbelief. Had John ripped Christopher's photo out of the yearbook?

Margot lifted the book from Kitty's hand and examined the page in question. It had been torn cleanly from the spine, leaving a minuscule flap of paper. "Whoever did this," she said, handing the yearbook back to Kitty, "used a straight-edge razor or paper cutter, which implies that the act was deliberate and premeditated."

"Not just this one," Kitty said. She returned the impotent yearbook to the shelf. "The copy at St. Alban's, too."

Bree felt her entire body go cold, as if she'd been plunged into an ice bath. Her brain felt sluggish, not quite grasping the reality. "Someone ripped the same page out of both yearbooks?"

"Looks like it," Kitty said.

Christopher Beeman. Archway Military Academy. She couldn't keep ignoring the signs, especially if John had already figured out that both of them were connected to Bree's involvement with DGM. She needed to face her past. She needed to face Christopher.

"Do you remember what he looks like?" Kitty asked.

Bree stared at the shelf. "Short, kinda chubby, brown hair, brown eyes. Generic."

"Do you think you'd recognize him?" Margot asked.

Bree shook her head. "I barely recognize myself from junior high."

"Really?" Kitty asked. "You wouldn't recognize your best friend?"

"Best friend?" How did Kitty know that? "Who said he was my best friend?"

"Oh." Kitty's eyes faltered. "I . . . I thought Mika said you were."

"Uh-huh." Kitty was a horrible liar. Who had she been talking to about Christopher Beeman?

Kitty cleared her throat. "Well, at least we know who tore the photos out."

Margot shook her head. "John didn't have anything in his hand when we left."

He was down here before. Only Bree didn't share that out loud. If John had ripped the pages out of both yearbooks, did it mean he'd discovered what she'd done to Christopher all those years ago? And if so, could he ever forgive her for it?

"I'm late for theater rehearsal," she said, heading for the stairs. She had to get home as soon as possible. There was one more yearbook that needed to be checked.

"Bree," Kitty said, "we have to—"

But Bree didn't hear her. She was already up the stairs, sprinting through the library.

Bree dragged a chair over to her closet and used it to reach a series of boxes shoved onto the uppermost shelf. She deposited the first two on the floor, but the third was significantly heavier. With a grunt, she heaved the box off the shelf and dropped it onto the carpet.

Bree hadn't gone through her junior high crap since, well, junior high. The collection was embarrassing. Tickets to concerts by bands she now loathed. Cutouts from fashion magazines featuring clothes she wouldn't be caught dead in. Friendship bracelets from people she no longer spoke to. Damn, a lot had changed in four years.

With a shake of her head, Bree hauled three yearbooks out of the bottom of the box. The St. Alban's Fighting Jesuits, complete with a sword-wielding priest as a mascot. The yearbooks from seventh and eighth grades she discarded, leaving just her sixth-grade keepsake. Without giving herself time to change her mind, she whipped it open and flipped to the alphabetical beginning of her sixth-grade class.

She froze.

An entire page had been ripped out of her yearbook.

Bree had a moment of panic as reality hit her: while she could have explained away the missing page of her own book as some kind of repressed guilt memory or forgotten moment of prepubescent rage, there was no way in hell she would have forgotten the defilement of the yearbooks in two different libraries unless she'd had some sort of psychotic breakdown in the last few years that she'd forgotten about.

Which meant someone else had torn out those pages.

Someone like John, who'd been rummaging around in her closet just last week.

"No!" She refused to believe he would have gone through the trouble. He didn't have any motive for hiding Christopher's identity.

Because that was the logical reason the yearbooks had been defaced. Someone didn't want anyone to know what Christopher Beeman looked like.

Bree tried to think back. She remembered a short, chubby kid with mousy brown hair and glasses who looked five years younger than the rest of the boys in their class. He was quiet, but smart. Only spoke when he had something important to say, and preferred reading in the library to athletic activities of any kind.

But his face . . . Bree squeezed her eyes closed and tried to picture it. Brown hair, brown eyes. He looked like every kid, Harry Potter–generic without the telltale scar.

Bree opened her eyes and sighed. She wasn't getting anywhere.

Okay, who would want to make sure all traces of Christopher Beeman were erased from the world? If Bree assumed that she was not, in fact, losing her mind and hadn't ripped out those pages herself, then someone else had been in her room, dug through her things to find her sixth-grade yearbook, and vandalized it.

The suspect list was short, as very few people had ever been in her room: aside from herself and her parents, there was only the cleaning lady and John.

John, who spent plenty of time in her room. John, who knew how to gain access to the house. John, who had been holding the yearbook at the library an hour ago. John, who was clearly on a mission to unmask DGM. Could he have discovered Bree's secret, and her reason for joining DGM in the first place?

And if he had, what would he do next?

THIRTY-SIX

DONTÉ WAS WAITING FOR KITTY AT THE SIDE ENTRANCE OF school Monday morning. His face was pained, and Kitty immediately knew something was wrong. "You aren't going to believe this," he said, holding the door open for her.

Kitty halted the moment she set foot inside the building.

The rows of dull, metallic lockers that lined both sides of the wide hallway had been plastered with neon pink fliers. Each taped below a locker number, hundreds of fliers fluttered in the breeze like a blinding fringe.

"What the . . ." Kitty's voice trailed off. Her eye caught the letters printed in massive, boldface type on the top of the fliers:

REWARD: DGM

Kitty pulled a flier off the nearest locker. Her hand shook, her throat closed up, and her brain only took in about every other word.

"'Reward: DGM,'" Donté read over her shoulder. "'The

administration of Bishop DuMaine Preparatory School hereby announces the following reward: any student who supplies information that leads to the identification of DGM will have their tuition fees waived for one full year.'"

"A bounty," Kitty said, her voice raspy. "He's offering a bounty on DGM."

"'In addition,'" Donté continued, reading more quickly, "'by special directive from Father Uberti, the student service organization known as the 'Maine Men is now under the direct command of Coach Creed. You will offer them every support and compliance during this time of crisis.'"

"You . . . you don't think anyone will actually go for this, do you?" Kitty paused, as if afraid of the answer. "I mean, with all the rich kids at this school, it seems kind of silly."

"Maybe for the Rex Cavanaughs," Donté said. "But once word gets out to the parents, you can bet your ass they'll be pressuring their kids to squeal."

Bishop DuMaine was about to morph into a school of DGM bounty hunters, complete with their own gestapo, the 'Maine Men.

Donté reread the flier and shook his head. "When I signed up for the 'Maine Men, it seemed like a good way to help the school, you know? But now . . . I don't know. The stuff they've been doing lately makes me really uncomfortable. I'm glad I dropped out."

Kitty wanted to throw her arms around Donté's neck and kiss him right there in the hall, she was so elated. Instead, she just nodded. "Me too."

He squeezed her hand. "Look, try not to let all this bother you, okay?"

Kitty closed her eyes and took a deep breath. "I'll try."

"How about we do something fun this weekend? Something to take our minds off the drama around here?"

"Like what?"

"There's a show at the Ledge Sunday night. That band everyone's talking about? The lead singer goes to our school?"

"Bangers and Mosh."

"Right! They're in the school play and we're all supposed to go and support them." He pulled her close. "What do you say? Ready to make our relationship DuMaine-official?"

Coach Creed was addressing the leadership class—beefy hands planted on his hips, legs shoulder-width apart like he was a drill sergeant instead of a second-rate gym teacher—when Kitty entered the classroom after prepping the announcements. He paused, clearly annoyed at the interruption, and glared at her while she took her seat.

"It has been one hundred and twenty-five hours since a member of the 'Maine Men was cut down in cold blood," Coach Creed continued. "And there are still no suspects in custody. So we're taking matters into our own hands." He was wearing a blue 'Maine Men polo shirt two sizes too small, tucked into a pair of camo pants. A complex flowchart drawn in multiple colors adorned the whiteboard behind him.

A smattering of applause rippled through the room. It made Kitty's skin crawl.

Coach Creed pulled a laser pointer from his pocket and aimed it at the whiteboard. "Based on your assignment from last week, I've assembled a profile of the most likely perpetrator. Our primary suspect—the DGM ringleader—is male, between the ages of sixteen and seventeen. He's a loner, quiet. Maybe with a dangerous, artistic temperament. He's got a smart mouth, but for the most part he keeps it shut. He doesn't have many friends, maybe one or two at most, and he feels safe here at Bishop DuMaine, almost like he's an insider or has a relative who works on staff."

Kitty licked her lips, which had gone bone dry despite a layer of balm. Coach Creed wasn't describing some anonymous profile of a suspect, he was describing one person quite specifically. He was describing John Baggott.

Coach Creed smiled wickedly. "Last of all, he's cocky." He leaned forward on his desk. "I think we all know the kind of student I'm talking about."

"Hell, yeah!" Rex said. Tyler reached out and high-fived him.

"That's what I thought." Coach Creed straightened up and began to pace behind the desk. "We must be diligent. If we put enough pressure on him, he'll cave." He paused. "Did everyone see the fliers around campus?"

"Yes, sir," Rex said.

"One year of free tuition," Coach Creed said. "To whoever can force our suspect to confess to his involvement with DGM."

Force our suspect to confess? This couldn't be good.

Coach Creed folded his arms across his chest. "It's time to take back our school."

A cheer went up, as Rex and a group of 'Maine Men rushed

to the whiteboard, where Coach Creed was diagramming the school, circling certain target areas like the quad and the baseball field, as if they were planning an attack.

Coach Creed had whipped the 'Maine Men into a frenzied mob that was about to be unleashed.

She needed to warn Bree.

THIRTY-SEVEN

BREE SPIED KITTY COMING TOWARD HER IN THE HALLWAY AND was careful not to make eye contact. Those were DGM rules, of course, but after their run-in at the library on Saturday, Bree wanted nothing to do with her de facto leader. And she was pretty sure the feeling was mutual.

Which made it even weirder when Kitty pretended to trip and fall directly into Bree.

"Sorry," she said, turning back to look at the tiled floor. "I slipped."

Bree felt something being pressed into her hand. A note.

Kitty was gone in a flash, disappearing through the door into the courtyard. Bree palmed the folded piece of paper, then shoved both of her hands into the front pockets of her hoodie while she continued down the hall.

She ducked into the ladies' room, moving slowly and calmly, like she hadn't a care in the world, and didn't pull the note from her pocket until she was safely locked in a stall.

MM are coming for JB. Be careful.

As the warning bell tore through the restroom, Bree hastily flushed the note down the toilet, standing over the bowl until the tiny paper square spiraled downward into the sewage system.

This was all her fault.

John had been keeping secrets from her, had replaced her with Cordy, and had maybe even discovered her long-buried secret about Christopher, yet suddenly all of Bree's resentment evaporated, replaced by blind panic. She needed to protect him, no matter what.

Lunch. That would be the most dangerous time. If Rex and the 'Maine Men found John alone on campus, especially someplace secluded . . . Bree's stomach lurched at the thought of John getting pummeled by Rex Cavanaugh in an attempt to beat a confession out of him.

She needed to find him first.

Bree whipped her phone out of her pocket and texted John.

Hey.

Bree paused. How was she supposed to break through the gigantic iceberg that had settled over their friendship?

Can we talk? At lunch today?

No response.

Meet me in the library, or your mom's car?

This time, her phone buzzed as a text came through.

The party you are trying to reach is unavailable. Please try again later.

Well, at least he still had a sense of humor. She quickly responded.

This is serious. There's some drama going down you need to know about.

John's response was so fast he must have copied and pasted it.

The party you are trying to reach is unavailable. Please try again later.

The cell phone equivalent of plugging his ears and chanting, "I can't hear you! I can't hear you!"

John was still mad at her. Fine, she'd deal with that later. For now, the important thing was keeping the 'Maine Men from kicking his ass. If only she had friends on the wrestling team, or some big biker dudes who could create a perimeter around him during lunch. But she and John didn't have friends like that.

Or did they?

Bree opened the Facebook app on her phone and located Shane White's page.

Shane? This is Bree. She paused. *John Baggott's friend,* she added.

This is going to sound crazy, but I think there's a group of 'Maine Men going after John at lunch.

Could you keep an eye out for him?

Bree held her phone in a death grip as she swung her surplus bag over her head and hurried to class.

Third-period trigonometry lasted an eternity. She kept her phone in her pocket, set on vibrate, and every time someone so much as moved at their desk, Bree was convinced she'd gotten a response.

When the bell finally rang, Bree discovered she was wrong.

No notifications on her cell phone. Total radio silence.

Bree sat in the empty classroom, staring at her phone. She double-checked to make sure the message to Shane actually went through and wasn't caught in some sort of Facebook messenger app purgatory, but it had a timestamp. The message had been delivered.

She'd just have to find John herself and drag him into hiding.

Students were already in the quad eating lunch when Bree exited the building. The same cliques of friends sat at the same tables in the same corners of the courtyard as they always did, that unspoken territorialism that was only ever challenged in teen movies and antibullying PSAs. She looked around for Shane. John had been eating lunch with him all week, but other than the sour-faced Cordy and some of her goth friends, none of Shane's gang was in sight.

Which might be a good thing. Wherever Shane was lunching, maybe John was with him? That should keep the douches at bay.

Bree hurried across the quad. She'd better keep searching, just in case. Small groups of blue-shirted 'Maine Men roamed campus, questioning students—a militia on a manhunt.

But unlike those Smurf-shirted idiots puffing aimlessly around school, Bree knew John better than anyone.

When John was in a shit mood, the first thing he turned to was music.

The music building was silent, eerily so. Usually there was at least one neurotic string player sawing out arpeggios on a cello during lunch. She peeked into each of the practice rooms through their small, double-paned windows, passing empty room after empty room. Until the last one at the end of the hall, where John sat on a piano bench, leaning against the wall with a book propped up on his leg.

"Dude," she said, swinging the door open unceremoniously. "There you are."

John glanced up at her, then slowly lowered his eyes to the book. "These aren't the droids you're looking for."

With a pang of embarrassment, Bree noticed that he was reading Nietzsche.

"Save it," Bree said. She tried to act like there was nothing wrong, like there had never been a rift between them. She desperately hoped he'd take her cue and do the same. "There's important shit going down today."

John read in silence, or at least pretended to, but Bree wasn't about to give up. "Coach Creed has gone off the rails. Did you see the flier? He's in direct command of the 'Maine Men."

Flip went another page. *Flip, flip.*

253

"I heard through the grapevine," she continued, planting her hands on her hips, "that they're looking for you."

John's eyes never left the book. "And you felt some great parental need to come save me, is that it?"

Bree threw her hands in the air. "Would you cut it out? I came to find you because you're my best friend. And I'm definitely not going to sit around and let you get hunted down by some douche nozzle like Rex Cavanaugh."

"You rang?"

Bree spun around. Three blue shirts blocked the practice room hallway. Tyler and Kyle flanked a sneering Rex.

John settled against the piano lid. "And I thought they smelled bad on the outside."

Rex glanced at Tyler. "Huh?"

"We've entered the eye of the douche-icane," Bree said, folding her arms across her chest.

"I think you jumped the douche shark on that one, Fonzie," John said.

"Too much?" Bree asked, acting as if Rex and his boys weren't even there.

John held up his thumb and forefinger a half inch apart. "Tiny bit."

"Enough!" Rex roared. "You two are nuts, you know that?"

"What do you want, Rex?" John said. He stood up and angled his body in front of Bree. "Music lessons? I charge by the hour, and the clock is ticking."

"Music lessons? Is that what you queers call it?"

Bree snickered. "Do you hear yourself? You're like an eighties bully cliché."

"We're not here for you," Tyler said.

Rex elbowed him. "She's as guilty as he is."

"Guilty of what?" Bree asked.

"Dude," Kyle said, his face suddenly serious. "I don't beat up girls."

Bree clasped her hands together. "Such a gentleman."

"I've got three words for you," Rex said, holding up three fingers. "D. G. M."

"Those are letters," John said calmly. "Not words."

Rex clenched his jaw, and beside her, John tensed himself, as if preparing for a punch in the gut. Instead, Rex laughed. "That's funny." He turned to Tyler. "Funny guy, right? Always thinks he's so smart. So much better than us." In an instant, Rex was serious again. "But you're not. This time, we outsmarted you."

John remained absolutely still. "I have no idea what you're talking about, Rex."

"I'm going to give you one chance, Baggott. Just admit you're the one behind DGM and . . ." His voice trailed off.

"And what?" Bree laughed drily. "You'll leave him alone? You seriously expect us to believe that?"

"You're here to kick my ass, right?" John said. This time, Bree noted the slight tremor in John's voice. "That's how you outsmarted me, by finding me here to beat a confession out of me?"

Tyler and Kyle exchanged glances, but Rex's eyes never left John's face.

"Admitting to a crime I didn't commit will get me a beating either way." John took a step to his right, distancing himself from Bree. "But, as you said, you're the smart one here. So get on with it, Sherlock."

Bree balled up both of her hands into fists. How was she going to protect John from all three of them? Kyle and Tyler might be squeamish about beating up girls, but either of them was strong enough to hold her back while the other two went to work on John. It wasn't far enough through lunch yet for the fourth-period music students to start wandering in for class, and even if they did, would Rex care? He clearly felt he was above the law at Bishop DuMaine. And he was probably right.

"What's wrong, Rex?" John's face was steely as he stared Rex down. "Suddenly not so sure I'm guilty?"

"Of course you're guilty," Rex sneered.

"Why haven't you pummeled my face to a bloody pulp yet? You scared? Or too much of a pussy?"

The last taunt sealed it. Bree watched as a red wave of rage washed over Rex. He reared back his arm, ready to punch John squarely in the face, when a hand appeared on his shoulder. "What's up, guys?"

Rex flinched and spun around. Behind him, Shane and five of his friends crowded into the hallway.

"You okay, Bagsie?" Shane continued, nodding in John's direction. "Seems like there's some kind of problem here."

"A misunderstanding," John said. Bree saw his body relax. "Right, Rex?"

Rex eyed Shane's crew, as if calculating his odds in a fight.

Then he turned to John, defeated. "This isn't over, Baggott." He pointed at Bree. "And next time, you won't have your little bitch here to protect you."

John opened his mouth to say something, but Bree never gave him the chance. Without thinking, she jerked back her arm and punched Rex in the face.

THIRTY-EIGHT

BREE RUBBED HER ACHING WRIST AS SHE LOOKED AROUND Father Uberti's office. She'd never actually been inside, and as she gazed at the overly polished wood and pristinely arranged bookshelves, she was struck by the fakeness of it all. This office had been designed to intimidate students and parents alike. But Bree knew that the ostentatious display was an attempt to over-compensate for insecurity and insignificance.

"I'm waiting," Father Uberti said. His fingers were laced in front of him on the desk as he stared at Bree.

"What was the question?" Bree asked.

"Why," Father Uberti said, with the utmost calm, "did you punch Rex Cavanaugh?"

"Oh, right," Bree said with an easy smile. She flexed her wrist back and forth, as if loosening it up. "Because he threatened to kick my friend's ass, and then called me a bitch. True story. I have witnesses."

"So you think you were justified in your assault on a fellow student?"

Bree nodded. "Absolutely." She knew damn well that F.U. was trying to scare her, but she wasn't going to give him the satisfaction. The worst he could do to her was kick her out of school, and hey, would that really be so bad?

Father Uberti leaned back in his chair and stroked his pointy beard. Bree noticed for the first time how weak his chin was, perfectly camouflaged by his facial hair. "You realize that using violence against another student is grounds for expulsion, do you not?"

Bree's smile widened. She was prepared for this one. "Except in cases where the student fears for his or her immediate personal safety."

Father Uberti tilted his head. "Where does it say that?"

"Third page of the student code. Paragraph two."

She half-expected him to look it up, but Father Uberti didn't bother. "That clause is not applicable to this situation."

"Isn't it? Have you interviewed my witnesses?"

Father Uberti slapped both of his hands on the table. "I've talked to three upstanding members of the 'Maine Men student patrol, none of whom corroborate your story."

Bree shrugged. "Because they picked the fight."

She was really enjoying this. He kept trying to intimidate her, and Bree was cool as a cucumber. It was only a matter of time before her continued indifference really pissed him off.

"I don't believe that for a second," he said.

"Of course you don't."

Father Uberti rose to his feet. "Bree Deringer, I have no choice but to expel you from Bishop DuMaine Preparatory

School for physical assault against a student, effective—"

The door of his office flew open, banging violently against the wall. "Good afternoon, Father Uberti."

Bree cringed. How the hell did her dad get there?

"Senator Deringer," Father Uberti said. A jagged row of sweat beads materialized on his forehead. "I didn't realize you were in town."

"I'm sure you didn't," he said, closing the door behind him. "Or you wouldn't have tried to expel my daughter without due process."

Father Uberti pointed at Bree like a petulant child placing blame on the playground. "But she hit a student. Punched him in the face."

"After he threatened her and her friend." Bree's dad looked down at her. "Did you feel your physical safety was in jeopardy, Bree?"

Bree put on her best "I'm a victim" face. "Yes," she said through a sniffle. "I was terrified."

"That is absolutely not true!" Father Uberti cried.

Bree's dad remained utterly calm. "Really? Were you there, Father Uberti?"

"Well, no." The priest smoothed down the shoulder flaps on his capuche. "But I have an eyewitness who says—"

"I've spoken to six eyewitnesses," Bree's dad said, cutting him off. The sternness in his voice made Bree feel like a naughty five-year-old again. "Six eyewitnesses who state that Rex Cavanaugh, Tyler Brodsky, and Kyle Tanner purposefully sought out John Baggott and my daughter during the lunch hour, cornered them in a confined space, and threatened them with bodily harm unless they confessed to their involvement in a murder." He strolled to the window and gazed out onto the lawn. "I also understand that these boys operate under your orders. Is that correct?"

"Senator Deringer," Father Uberti started. His voice shook with a mix of fear and anger. "Perhaps you're not aware of the situation at Bishop DuMaine, considering how frequently you're away in Sacramento."

"I am well-informed of all the goings-on at Bishop DuMaine, Father Uberti. *All* of them."

Father Uberti straightened up. "If you're accusing me of authorizing student-on-student violence, I suggest you contact the Archdiocese directly."

Bree's dad glanced sidelong at Father Uberti. "I already have." He returned his gaze to the manicured front lawn of Bishop DuMaine. "However, I might be willing to withdraw my complaint about your obvious lack of good judgment in this matter, if all charges against my daughter are dropped, and she *and* her friend John Baggott are protected against any and all retribution in this matter."

"I . . ." Father Uberti's mouth worked up and down like a codfish in its death throes. Then he slowly sank back into his chair, defeated.

"I'll take that as a 'yes.'" Bree's father strode to the door. "Bree? We're leaving."

Bree's stomach dropped as she followed her dad out of the office. She detected the icy tone in his voice, the one reserved for the minority leader in the Senate and for reprimanding his youngest child.

"Dad, I can explain," she said, as soon as they were clear of the school building.

He didn't even look at her, just continued to storm toward the car. "I don't want to hear it."

"But—"

"Bree!" Bree spun around and saw John jogging toward them across the front lawn of the school. "Bree, wait up."

Crap. This was not going to go well.

"What happened?" John asked, panting slightly. "What did F.U. do?"

"Nothing," Bree said quickly. "It's okay." She glanced at her dad, who had turned his critical eye on John. She could practically see the judgment telegraphed across his face as he registered John's jet-black hair and his beat-up Doc Martens.

"Oh," John said. Then he quickly turned to Bree's dad. "Senator Deringer, I'm John Baggott. What happened today wasn't Bree's fault at all. She was trying to help me and . . ."

Bree kicked John's foot with the toe of her boot. "Shut up," she mouthed.

"John Baggott," her dad said. "You called me this afternoon to inform me of the situation at lunch, correct?"

"Yes," John said. He swallowed, then added, "Sir."

Bree's jaw dropped. "You called my dad?"

"And you're the boy my daughter sneaks into the house through the servants' entrance."

Bree groaned.

"Yes, sir."

"Are you dating my daughter?"

"No!" Bree said quickly. Sheesh, why did everyone think they were dating?

Her dad looked from Bree to John and back. "I see. Well, understand this, both of you. Today was the last time I intervene on your behalf. I've given you nothing but the best advantages in life, Bree, but I will not continually bail you out and become the laughingstock of California parents. Next time, you're on your own."

"Fine," Bree mumbled. And she meant it. She'd never ask for his help again.

"I understand, Senator," John said.

"Very well, then." Bree's dad grabbed her by the arm and escorted her to the passenger door of his SUV. "Nice to finally meet you, John."

THIRTY-NINE

BY THE NEXT MORNING, BREE'S FIGHT WITH REX WAS FRONT-PAGE news. Olivia wished she'd been there to see the look on Rex's face when a girl kicked his ass.

It was hard to hide. Even sporting a pair of Ray-Bans, Rex's left eye was a disturbing mix of purples and reds, and the swelling hadn't completely gone down yet.

Unfortunately, she couldn't spend too much time fantasizing about Rex's humiliation. Olivia had other problems to deal with. Like the mysterious envelopes. A cheating scandal and a photo of Kitty with some random chick—what did they have to do with her? Absolutely nothing, as far as Olivia could tell.

But after the blowup at the DGM meeting the other night, Olivia realized just how vulnerable she was. One of the girls could turn on her at any moment. Maybe whoever had sent her the clues was trying to warn her? He or she clearly thought the information was important, but Olivia had no idea why.

Thankfully, she knew someone with a talent for ferreting out information.

She found Ed the Head at lunch, lurking in the courtyard outside the boys' gym.

"Olivia," he said with an exaggerated frown. "I'm all out of Ding Dongs today."

Olivia shook her head. "I'm not here for a fix."

Ed the Head arched an eyebrow. "Really?"

"I need some of your, um, other services."

A wide grin swept across his face, crinkling his eyes into thin slits. "Olivia, baby doll. So word of the Head's love machine has finally reached your ears?"

"Huh?"

Ed the Head placed his hand over his heart. "I'm honored, truly. A fox like you coming after me? It's the chance of a lifetime."

"Have you lost your—"

He held up his hand for silence. "Wait! I want to savor this moment." Ed the Head closed his eyes and bobbed his chin back and forth as if dancing to an imaginary techno track.

Olivia cocked her head. "Really?"

Ed the Head opened his eyes and sighed. "That was magical. However, I'm sorry to disappoint, but the Head's heart is already engaged. I wouldn't want to lead you on."

"Stop!" Olivia cried. "You're making my stomach hurt."

"I've got some Tums in here somewhere. I'll sell them to you retail."

Why could he never engage in a normal conversation? Olivia shook her head and tried to refocus. "I need your help."

Ed opened his mouth to respond, but his attention was

caught by something behind her. His face instantly lit up. "Margot!" he cried. "Hey, why are you running away?"

Olivia turned slowly. Margot had stopped in her tracks, hesitating between fight and flight.

"I've been looking for you all day," Ed said.

Margot reluctantly walked toward them. "I've been around." She studiously avoided Olivia's eyes.

"Do you know Olivia?"

"I know who she is," Margot said.

Ed the Head laughed. "Right. Who doesn't? Anyway, I just wanted to confirm that we're still on for Sunday night. I can pick you up around seven? Your parents might want to meet the future son-in-law."

Margot's eyes grew wider and wider during Ed's speech, until Olivia was afraid they were going to pop right out of her head. "I can't go Sunday night."

"What? But we had a deal!"

Margot winced. "I know. I'm sorry. I can do any other night but Sunday."

Ed the Head eyed her. "Fine," he said reluctantly. "Maybe we could—"

But Margot had already turned on her heel and was scurrying down the hall as fast as her legs could carry her.

So Ed the Head asked Margot on a date? How freaking adorable was that?

"Okay," Ed said, staring after Margot. "What can I do for you, Olivia? Apparently, I'm free Sunday night if you need a date."

"Not a chance," she said clearly, leaving no room for innuendo. "I need your detective skills. I have a photo and I need help figuring out—"

"A photo?" he asked. "You too?"

"What do you mean, me too?"

Ed the Head shrugged. "You're the second person who's asked me to help them with a mysterious photo."

The second person?

"You got it on you?" he asked.

Olivia slipped the manila envelope out of her bag and placed the photo in his hand.

Ed the Head immediately flipped the photo over and examined the back side. "Weird."

"Um, the image is on the front."

Ed the Head ignored her. "Same photo paper."

"Same as?"

He turned back to the image on the front and held it close to his face, studying it intently. "Interesting."

Olivia's patience was wearing thin. "Look, can you help me or not?"

Ed the Head smiled. "You haven't told me what you want."

That's because I don't know. "I need to know who it is," she said.

"Kitty Wei, our student body vice president."

"I know that," Olivia snapped.

"And Barbara Ann Vreeland," he continued. "Former captain of the junior varsity girls' volleyball team, kicked out of Bishop DuMaine as part of the grade-fixing scandal two years ago."

As soon as Ed the Head recited her bio, Olivia realized where she knew her from. The barista at the Coffee Clash.

Ed the Head beamed at her. "Anything else?"

"I wonder what it means?" Olivia mused more to herself than to him.

"It means you owe me ten bucks," he said.

Olivia sighed. "I need more information."

"Like what?"

"Like . . ." Olivia's mind raced. "Like how Kitty might be connected to the grade fixing," she heard herself say. It was the only reason someone would have sent her both the article and the photo.

Ed the Head nodded. "Twenty bucks. Unless you have another form of payment in mind?"

Olivia was starting to think asking for Ed the Head's help was a bad idea. "You know what? Never mind." She snatched the photo out of his hand. "I'll take this to someone else."

"Really? Who?"

She blurted out the first person who popped into her head. "Margot Mejia."

Ed the Head's eyes grew wide. "That would be interesting."

"Why?"

"Because that other photo I told you about? It came from her."

FORTY

OLIVIA STARED AT ED THE HEAD AS IF HE'D SPOKEN IN tongues. It took her brain several seconds to grasp his meaning.

"Are you telling me that Margot got an envelope like this with a photo in it?"

Ed the Head flashed his braces. "That's exactly what I'm—"

He hesitated and flitted his head back and forth, like a hawk who'd been alerted to prey. "Do you hear that?" he whispered, even though they were utterly alone.

Olivia listened, expecting to hear sirens or screaming or something violently horrible, but all she heard was the wind rustling through the elm tree in the middle of the courtyard.

"What am I supposed to be hearing?" Olivia asked.

"Sh!" Ed the Head hissed. His eyes scanned the sky, then his head began to bob up and down rhythmically. "Bah. Bah. Bah *bah*, bah *bah*," he chanted. Then louder. "Bah. Bah. Bah *bah*, bah *bah*. Bah. Bah. Bah *bah*, bah *bah*."

Olivia thought Ed the Head had finally lost his mind, until

she heard a faint cheer in the distance, like a crowd at a sporting event.

"What is that?" she asked.

"That, my darling Olivia, is the sound of public uprising. And where there is social unrest, there is money to be made." He bolted from the courtyard. "To the Bat Cave!"

Olivia had to jog to keep up with Ed the Head as he wove through the hallways. The chant got louder and louder with every step they took, and positively exploded the moment they burst into the quad.

Ed the Head stopped short. "Holy shit."

The amphitheater at the far end of the quad was packed with students, some holding signs with slogans like "'Maine Men = Gestapo" and "Down with Uberti!" Others punched their fists in the air to articulate the beats of their chant. "Hey! Ho! 'Maine Men must go!" they cried in rhythmic unison. "Hey! Ho! 'Maine Men must go!"

And smack in the middle of the stage, megaphone in hand as she led the rally, was Mika Jones, with her best friend, Kitty Wei, by her side.

Holy shit indeed.

Kitty stood stiffly next to Mika, a tight smile plastered on her face, while her friend engaged the crowd.

"Are you tired of their reign of terror?" Mika cried into the megaphone.

"YEAH!" the crowd answered.

"Are you tired of bag searches?"

"YEAH!"

"And interrogations?"

"YEAH!"

"And bribes to get us to turn on each other?"

"YEAH!"

"Can I get a 'hellz yeah' on that one?"

"HELLZ YEAH!"

"That's what I'm talking about!"

So much for keeping a low profile.

Mika handed the megaphone to Theo, who started up the chant with as much if not more enthusiasm than Mika.

"This is pretty amazing," Kitty shouted above the cheers.

"I'm just tired of the bullshit," Mika said. "Seeing people like Theo get hurt. DGM made me think that I could be doing more to help people."

Kitty wanted to hug her. DGM had inspired the protest, had galvanized a movement toward tolerance and freedom. Never in her wildest dreams did Kitty think people would actually be influenced by DGM, but this rally? This was proof. DGM may have been in a shit ton of trouble, but they were doing the right thing.

"Break it up! Break it up!"

A swath of blue shirts forced their way through the sea of students that inundated the quad. Right in the middle of them, his bald head the color of an overripe tomato, was Coach Creed.

The crowd fell silent as he approached the stage, less out of respect and more from curiosity.

"By the authority of Bishop DuMaine Preparatory School,"

Coach Creed began, spittle flying from his mouth in all directions, "I demand that you cease and desist this illegal gathering and submit yourselves for punishment."

Power had clearly gone to his head, and Kitty was seriously beginning to question Coach Creed's mental stability.

"We're exercising our First Amendment right to free speech!" Mika cried. The crowd roared in agreement.

Creed leaped onto the stage and got right up in Mika's face. "There are no rights at this school!"

"You can say that again," Kitty said without thinking. She didn't even realize the words had come out of her mouth until Coach Creed swung his sweaty face in her direction.

"Traitor!" he growled. "You are a traitor!" He stuck his index finger right in her chest. "I'll have you impeached for this, Wei!"

Donté appeared out of nowhere, wedging his body between Kitty and Coach Creed. "Step off, Coach," he said, his voice steely.

"You're interfering with the law!" Coach Creed roared. His bald head shifted hues from red to burgundy to purple.

"And you're out of order," Donté replied. "You need to get out of here before someone gets hurt."

Coach Creed's eyes bugged out of his head. "Are you threatening me, Greene?" Without waiting for an answer, Coach Creed lurched forward and drove his arms into Donté's chest.

"Donté!" Kitty screamed. But she couldn't even hear her own voice over the melee. A shoving match had broken out between the 'Maine Men and the students gathered at the rally. Bodies flew as each side traded shoves. Kitty lost sight of Donté and Coach Creed in the chaos.

A blare of sirens floated above the shouts and cries of the brawl, and suddenly dozens of uniformed police officers swarmed the quad.

"Everybody, calm down!"

The fighting ceased as the police broke through the crowd; bodies grew still, voices fell silent. All except one.

"I'll fucking kill you!" Coach Creed screamed. "I'll do it! I swear to God!"

Donté held Coach Creed at arm's length, desperately trying to avoid the punches Coach was throwing at him. Sergeant Callahan vaulted onto the stage and hauled Coach Creed away. "Stand down!" he yelled, throwing an arm in Creed's face.

Coach Creed pointed at Donté. "Arrest this traitor!" he yelled. "By the authority of the 'Maine Men."

"You don't have any authority here," Sergeant Callahan said. Kitty could tell by his voice that the officer's patience was wearing thin.

"This is my school," Coach Creed said, jabbing his thumb at his chest. "Father Uberti has given me the authority to use the 'Maine Men as I see fit."

"What the hell are you talking about, Dick?" Father Uberti bolted up to the stage. He wrung his hands in front of him. "Sergeant Callahan, thank you for getting here so quickly. I think the situation has gotten out of control."

Sergeant Callahan turned his cool, appraising gaze on Father Uberti, and Kitty smiled as she watched the principal squirm under the scrutiny.

"Is it true?" Sergeant Callahan asked. "That you condoned the use of force by Coach Creed and the 'Maine Men?"

Father Uberti's hand flew to his chest and his eyes grew wide in mock horror. "Absolutely not! I have no idea what this man is talking about."

Coach Creed's mouth fell open. "But you said—"

Father Uberti cut him off. "Richard Creed, you are hereby suspended from Bishop DuMaine Preparatory School, effective immediately."

FORTY-ONE

MR. CUNNINGHAM STOOD CENTER STAGE AT THAT EVENING'S rehearsal, arms folded gravely across his chest. "Fourth period was a disaster."

That was the understatement of the century. Bishop DuMaine had been thrown into complete chaos after the rally as both sides pointed fingers. And as cool as it was to see students protest Father Uberti's tactics, Olivia couldn't help but think that everything DGM had fought for was beginning to unravel.

"Sorry, Mr. Cunningham," Donté said. "I didn't know it would get so out of hand."

Olivia turned around and beamed at Donté. He'd spent almost the entirety of fourth period sequestered with the police, and Olivia had been convinced that he'd be hauled off to jail after his confrontation with Coach Creed. There had been a few students put on probation—Theo and Mika for organizing the protest, and several 'Maine Men for throwing punches—but Donté appeared at rehearsal that night with nothing more than a warning on his "permanent record."

"It's all right, Mr. Greene. I can appreciate your motivation and your passion. But, people, there are only eight rehearsal days left until opening night. That's it. So I'm going to need all of your motivation and passion focused on this production for the next two weeks. Any questions?" He pointed to the back of the house. "Yes, Mr. Blaine?"

"Remember the prompter I told you about, Mr. Cunningham?"

Mr. Cunningham cupped his hands over his eyes, shielding them from the bright stage lights. "Excellent. Attention, everyone! We have a new member of the production. I'd like to introduce Margot Mejia."

Margot stepped out from behind Logan and stared at the ground.

"Miss Mejia has volunteered to assist me in running lines during rehearsals and to act as a prompter during performances. With so little time before our opening night, we need all the preparation we can get, and Miss Mejia appears to have a photographic knowledge of the play."

Margot had volunteered for drama? That seemed incredibly out of character. But now Olivia had an excuse to talk to her about the photo Ed the Head had mentioned, without it seeming strange or suspicious. She just needed to catch her in private.

"Now that we have most of the sets in, we're going to run through all the blocking again, starting with act one, scene one," Mr. Cunningham continued. "Since we lost fourth period, we need to get through the entire play tonight, so no one wander off.

Those of you not involved in a particular scene can meet with Miss Mejia in one of the dressing rooms and run lines."

Olivia poked her head into the dressing room Margot had commandeered. "Hey!"

Margot jumped as if caught doing something she shouldn't. "Hey."

"You're going to help us run lines?" she asked.

Margot nodded.

"Awesome." Olivia plopped down in the chair opposite and smiled. "I'm ready."

Margot raised her eyebrows. "You know this play backward and forward. You don't need to run lines."

"True." She should have known better than to try to con Margot. She reached back and pushed the door closed, then dropped her voice. "But this gives us an excuse to talk without anyone getting suspicious, you know?"

"Oh."

"So," Olivia said, trying to sound cheery despite her frigid audience. "How are you?"

"How am I?"

"Yeah, you know. With everything that's going on. How are you?"

Margot stared at her blankly. "Would you ask Bree or Kitty, or just me?"

"I . . ." Olivia flushed.

"Because I'm the weak one? Because I can't handle the stress?"

Olivia shook her head. "That's not what I meant," she lied.

The door opened, and Logan stuck his head into the room. "Margot, I—" He paused when he saw Olivia. "Oh! Sorry. I should have knocked."

"It's okay," Olivia said, trying to look and sound as if she and Margot hadn't just been engaged in the world's most awkward conversation. "We haven't started yet."

Logan nodded, then cast his easy, sunny smile on Margot. "I'm glad you decided to join our little freak show."

Margot bit her lip. "Me too."

So Logan had asked Margot to volunteer for the drama production? Interesting.

"She's the best at running lines," Logan said. "I've got half the role memorized already and we only had one session."

"Oh!" Olivia looked at Margot. One *private* session?

"I, uh, remember things easily," Margot said.

"I've got to get onstage," Logan said. "We still on for Sunday night?"

Margot flushed. "Of course."

"Awesome." Logan smiled again. "Later!"

Margot stared at the ground and an amazing realization dawned on Olivia: Margot had a massive crush on the new kid in school, and it looked as if the feeling might be mutual.

This was life-altering for Margot. Ed the Head and the photos could wait. Margot needed her help.

"Is he taking you to the Ledge for the Bangers and Mosh show?" Olivia asked.

Margot nodded. "But I might not go."

"Why? Logan's hot and clearly into you. You can't bail on that."

"I . . . I don't . . ."

"You've never been on a date before, have you?"

Margot looked up. "There are more things in life than boys, you know."

Olivia wasn't entirely sure that was true. "Of course there are," she said. "But not right now." She grabbed her makeup bag and dropped it on the dressing room table. "Never fear, Cinderella. The ball awaits."

Margot flinched away from the wand of lip gloss that Olivia held before her. It smelled like strawberries and algae, and it had the consistency of rubber cement. "I don't wear makeup," she said. "My parents don't allow it."

"You can wipe it off later." Olivia pulled a plastic bin and a brush from her bag, as well as a shiny stick that looked like gold lipstick. "Powder," she said, holding up the bin, "and highlighter. Learn them. Love them."

This time, Margot didn't recoil as Olivia swept the highlighter over her cheekbones and across her eyelids.

An internal debate raged inside Margot. One voice argued that Olivia was merely trying to be nice to her. The other was a harsh reminder of what happened when Margot trusted girls like Olivia.

"Okay," Olivia said after a few moments. She twisted Margot's heavy mane of dark brown hair away from her face and held it behind her neck with one hand, then swiveled Margot's chair to face the mirror. "What do you think?"

It could have been the soft glow of the bulbs that rimmed the dressing room mirror, or it could have been the shock of seeing her face so starkly silhouetted without the thick fringe of hair masking her features, but Margot gasped.

"I look . . ."

"You look hot," Olivia said, selecting a word Margot had never used to describe herself. "Here, hold this." She grabbed Margot's hand and placed it on the chignon of hair. "I think I have a clip in my—"

Olivia stopped midsentence and stared at Margot's hand gripping the mound of hair at the back of her head. With a tentative finger, she reached out and slid the baggy sleeve of Margot's sweater up to her elbow.

"Don't look so surprised," Margot said curtly. "Everyone knows I'm the girl who tried to kill herself."

Olivia nodded and continued to stare at Margot's scars.

"You were there," Margot said, trying to sound like the subject didn't bother her at all. "In junior high, I mean. I know you didn't hang out with her then, but you remember what Amber was like."

"Do you blame Amber for . . . for . . ."

"For making me slit my wrists?"

Olivia nodded again.

Margot opened her mouth to say yes, then hesitated. She'd spent so many years nursing her hatred of Amber Stevens, and though Amber's daily bullying had made Margot's life a misery throughout junior high, the photo that had been the catalyst for Margot's suicide attempt had apparently not been taken by Amber.

"I used to think Amber took the photo of me that night," Margot said slowly. Was she ready to share this with Olivia? "But I found out recently that it wasn't her."

"Do you know who did?"

"Not yet. I'm working on it."

Olivia stared at her. "How?"

Margot hesitated. She wasn't used to trusting people with personal issues, not even a member of Don't Get Mad. Margot glanced at her transformation in the mirror. Olivia had done that for her. As a friend.

"I got a photo."

Olivia's face was suddenly pale, her usually cheerful features drawn and tense. "What was it?"

"It was from the same night as the one that spread around school, but it proved that Amber didn't take the photo."

"And you got this photo in a plain manila envelope?"

Margot caught her breath. "How did you know?"

"Because I got one, too."

FORTY-TWO

MARGOT STARED AT OLIVIA, UNSURE WHETHER OR NOT TO believe what she was hearing. "A photo," she said.

"Yes."

"In a plain manila envelope."

"Yes."

Margot felt her stomach clench. "Left in your locker."

"In my bag," Olivia said. "But close enough."

It had been creepy to receive the envelopes, worse when Margot realized what they contained, but in her mind, she had separated them from her involvement with DGM. Still, 50 percent of DGM receiving similar deliveries could have been a coincidence, albeit a slim one. Seventy-five percent, however . . .

Margot bolted from the room without another word. Seventy-five percent would definitely not be a coincidence. It would mean someone was targeting the members of DGM.

"Where are you going?" Olivia cried, teetering after her.

"We need to find Bree."

◆ ◆ ◆

Bree studied the user manual for the theater's lighting control console. She'd already spent an hour with the designer, who showed her how to input cues. But the moment he left the control room, his instructions for fades and blinds, channels and dimmers got all jumbled up in her head.

"You'd think they could afford a professional," she muttered to herself, tossing the manual onto the table.

"Bree!" Margot barreled into the lighting booth, Olivia close behind.

Bree leaned back in her chair. "I thought we weren't supposed to make eye contact at school. Isn't that your golden rule?"

"Extenuating circumstances."

"Extenuating circumstances," Bree mused, tapping the side of her face as if contemplating the meaning of life. "You mean like the cute new guy in school asking you to join a theater production?"

Margot narrowed her eyes. "Any different than why you're here?"

"Touché." Bree squinted at Margot. She looked weird. "Did you do something with your hair?"

"Powder, highlighter, gloss," Olivia said with an impatient sigh. "You really should look into it."

Bree pursed her lips. "Yeah, I'll get right on it." She paused. "Did you guys come here to talk cosmetics?"

"Did you get an envelope?" Olivia blurted out.

Bree stiffened. Was this a trick?

"Mail comes to the Deringer estate every day," Bree said, unwilling to give anything away about John until she knew why they were asking. "Envelopes galore."

"Cut the jokes," Margot said sharply. "Olivia means, have you gotten any large envelopes left in your locker or your bag?"

So Margot and Olivia were getting them too? Interesting. She had assumed that a member of DGM had sent her the information about John's inquiries into the group, but maybe it was an interested third party?

Her mind raced with possibilities, and two of the three most logical ones were staring at her, waiting for an answer. Who else would have wanted to clue her in on John's hunt for DGM? Who else might have known that she was involved?

She looked from Margot to Olivia, who both stared at her expectantly. If she admitted to being in the manila envelope club, what would come next—the inevitable sharing of what they'd received?

Margot was already hell-bent on pointing a suspicious finger at John. Knowing that he was close to discovering DGM's secret might push her over the edge. No, she couldn't trust anyone else. She would be the keeper of John's secret.

"I don't know what you're talking about."

"That's it?" Olivia said as she traipsed down the stairs behind Margot. "You're just going to believe her?"

"She said she didn't get one." Margot walked quickly, desperate to get away from Olivia and end this conversation. "Did you want me to call her a liar to her face?"

"Kinda."

"Just drop it, Olivia."

Olivia scurried in front of her. "Do you want to know what was in mine?"

Margot glanced at the floor. This is what she'd wanted to avoid. She'd let her guard down with Olivia in the dressing room, lulled into a state of complacency by a small token of kindness. But Bree's caginess reminded her of how much was at stake, and how little she could trust DGM with her secrets.

"No," she said, turning her cold stare on Olivia. "No, I don't."

Without another word she quickly sidestepped Olivia and hurried back to the dressing room.

Olivia wandered to a darkened corner of the house and collapsed into a seat.

She'd thought she'd had a moment with Margot, the sort of friendly kindness she'd been hoping for ever since they both joined DGM. Margot was always so closed off, so cold and professional at DGM meetings, it had been impossible to break through. But today in the dressing room, she thought they'd taken a step toward friendship.

Apparently not so much. Whatever trust she'd elicited from Margot by doing her hair and makeup vanished the moment Bree lied to them.

Way to go, Bree.

Whatever. She didn't need them. Ed the Head was working on the mystery. He'd dig up something.

Olivia slouched lower in her seat. Somehow, that didn't brighten her mood.

Voices drifted in from the lobby.

"Dude," Shane White said. "Your shit is tight."

A laugh Olivia recognized. "Thanks, man," Donté said with his usual modesty.

"Where did you learn how to act?"

"Dunno," Donté said. "I guess I just picked it up along the way. You know how it is."

The voices grew louder, and Olivia shrunk down as Shane and Donté entered the theater.

"Cool, cool," Shane said. "So we gonna see you at the Ledge Sunday? Should be epic." He held up his hand for a bro grab.

Donté gripped Shane's hand and shoulder-bumped him. "Wouldn't miss it."

"Sweet! You won't be disappointed. Bangers and Mosh has a reputation for bringing out the honies, if you know what I mean."

Donté laughed sheepishly. "No need, my man. No need. Got my eye on the one and only."

Olivia's heart leaped to her throat. *The one and only.* Again, he was talking about their song.

"I dig it," Shane said. They passed Olivia without noticing her presence and sauntered down the aisle to the stage. "Can't wait to meet her."

"You definitely will," Donté said. "Sunday should be a special night."

Olivia huddled in the theater seat, heart racing. The one and only. Sunday should be a special night. Was Donté planning to make a move on her at the concert?

She pushed all thoughts of DGM and anonymous envelopes from her mind. None of it mattered. Sunday night. She needed a mani-pedi, lip and eyebrow wax, and bikini too. Her mind raced to her closet. The hand-me-down little black dress Amber had only worn once and the brand-new Jimmy Choo stilettos, also an Amber cast-off, still in the box. She had to look perfect. The night had to be perfect.

She and Donté were getting back together.

FORTY-THREE

MARGOT'S DAD GLANCED UP FROM HIS TABLET. "WHERE ARE you going again?"

"The Ledge," Margot said, praying they had no idea what she was talking about. "It's a social event for school. Part of the production of *Twelfth Night*."

"You joined drama class?" A look of concern passed over her mom's face. "Do you have time for another elective?"

"It's not a class, it's an extracurricular activity," Margot corrected. Then she launched into the speech she'd been practicing for days. "My counselor suggested at least three extracurricular activities for any Ivy League application. Since I have community service and academic outreach already, she suggested I look for one that focused on the arts."

"Margot, this is unacceptable," her dad said, his voice stern. "Your mother and I haven't corroborated the legitimacy of this production, or verified if your work there would even count toward an extracurricular."

"The production is being cosponsored by the Oregon

Shakespeare Festival," Margot said. "After careful research and consideration, I thought the affiliation with such a historic organization would stand out on my college applications."

"Perhaps." He sounded less than impressed.

"I don't like this," her mom fretted. "That boy at your school was murdered and the police have no one in custody."

There was an edge of panic in her mom's voice, as if letting Margot out of the house for a social outing was going to end with her daughter in a body bag. If she'd known exactly how involved Margot was in that murder, her mom would have yanked her out of DuMaine, locked her in an attic, and homeschooled her until she was eighteen.

But Margot wasn't about to give up. Unsolved murder or not, Logan would be waiting for her at the Coffee Clash.

"Dr. Tournay has suggested several times that I need to engage socially with my peers, as part of my recovery."

"I'm uncomfortable that this is the first we've heard of tonight's event," her dad said.

"The opportunity to be a prompter came up last minute," Margot reminded him.

Her dad sighed and glanced over at her mom. Margot hadn't been this adamant about anything since, well, ever. And clearly her repeated logical arguments in favor of being let off her leash had impressed her parents.

"Curfew is ten o'clock," her dad said with a nod. "And we'll expect a full rundown in the morning, as well as a list of the students involved in the production. Agreed?"

"Agreed."

Margot was out the door before they could change their minds.

A powerful horn blared from the street in front of Olivia's apartment. Peanut's BMW. Olivia took one last look in the mirror: dress, shoes, hair, makeup. Perfect.

"Where you going?" her mom slurred from the love seat as Olivia dashed through the living room.

There was one empty bottle of red wine on the kitchen counter, one open bottle on the coffee table. Her mom must have found out she wasn't cast in yet another role.

"There's a concert at the Ledge," Olivia said. "The band that's in our production of *Twelfth Night*. I told you about it."

"*Twelff Nigh?*" Her mom pushed herself up to a sitting position. "O, sssir," she began with a dramatic sweep of her arm. Drunk or sober, Olivia's speech from act 2 was her favorite scene. "I will not be so hard-hearted." She slapped the cushion next to her twice to accentuate her hard-heartedness. "I will give out diverschedules of my . . ." The words morphed into an elongated yawn. "Beauty," she finished.

"Right." Olivia grabbed a sweater from the coat closet and headed for the door. "I'll be home late. Drink some water, Mom."

"You get drink some water," Olivia heard her mom say as she closed the front door behind her. Monday was not going to be pretty.

"You look fierce," Peanut said as Olivia stepped into the car. "Every guy in a twenty-mile radius will be jonesing for you." She glanced down at her own outfit with disdain, as if suddenly realizing she'd worn a muumuu instead of adorable cropped pants and a sparkly one-shoulder top.

"Stop it," Olivia said. "You look amazing. No one else could pull off those harem pants. Not even Amber."

Peanut's face lit up. "You mean it?"

"Of course." Peanut may have been a blind minion most of the time, but when you got her away from Amber, she was cool. Too bad she wasn't confident enough to stay that way. Olivia smiled wryly as Peanut screeched away from the curb. "Now let's go see if we can land Kyle for you, shall we?"

The Coffee Clash was hopping when Margot pulled her mom's car into the mini-mall parking lot, a mix of high school and college students crowded into every available table, counter, or floor space. She spotted Logan's blond hair right away at a table outside on the veranda. He was reading, head bowed over the table.

She parked at the far end of the lot, shielded by an SUV the size of an urban assault vehicle, and pulled down the visor to check her face in the mirror. Time to do this.

Margot dumped the contents of a plastic shopping bag onto the passenger seat, the spoils of a quick stop at the drugstore: a tube of lip gloss, highlighter, and a round tin of face powder with its matching brush. The same combination Olivia had used on her in the dressing room. She applied each as best she could remember. Then with her fingers, she swept her hair back into a low ponytail, loosening a few curls around her face, and secured it with a hair band.

She turned her chin from side to side, examining her

handiwork. Her face was brighter, more alive, and even without a smile on her face, she looked happier somehow, as if the excitement bubbling within was seeping through her pores.

Last up, her outfit. She'd been careful to leave the house in one of her oversize sweaters, but instead of the usual boxy T-shirt underneath it, Margot had found a long-sleeved scoop-neck shirt in the bottom of a drawer, a remnant of the days before she'd gotten fat in junior high. Like most of the clothes that she'd outgrown, it had been shoved out of sight into the depths of her wardrobe. But much to Margot's surprise, when she shimmied into the body-hugging shirt, it fit almost perfectly. A little tight across the chest where her boobs had come in, but instead of looking like an overstuffed sausage, Margot noticed that her curves were softer, her waist more defined.

She lifted the sweater off over her head, careful not to disrupt the controlled chaos of her hair, and pulled the sleeves of the shirt down past her wrists. They were just long enough to hide her scars. She wasn't ready to tell Logan about that. Not yet.

With a fluttering in her chest that was either adrenaline or cardiac arrest, Margot stepped out of the car.

Bree rolled her dad's new Lexus to a halt in front of John's apartment building and hit Send on her pretyped text.

Your chariot awaits.

Ten seconds later, she saw the blinds in John's bedroom window separate as he peeked through, followed immediately by a reply.

I didn't ask for a ride.

Her answer was short and sweet.

Get your ass out here.

She was going to force them back into friendship if it killed her.

Bree waited a lifetime for a reply, and was starting to worry that John wouldn't come down. She picked up her phone and began typing another text when out of the corner of her eye, she saw the metal security gate in front of the building swing open. A figure emerged, dressed all in black—jeans, boots, and a low tank under a vintage pin-striped suit vest. He wore a matching pin-striped fedora cocked to one side, which cast a shadow across his face. Bree looked up, heart racing. She didn't know Shane was going to be at John's tonight. There was something sexy about the way he walked, a cocky swagger with a Fender case slung over his shoulder. . . .

Bree's eyes grew wide as the figure approached her car. Not just any Fender case.

John's Fender case.

Donté beamed at Kitty as she climbed into his car. "You look great."

Kitty smiled. "Thank you." It was amazing what a denim skirt and some low heels could do when everyone was used to seeing you in workout clothes.

He placed his hand on hers and his eyebrows shot up. "You sure you're okay with this?"

"Of course," Kitty lied. "Why wouldn't I be?"

"Your hand is shaking."

Stupid nerves. Kitty couldn't believe her lack of self-control. She could lead her volleyball team to the state championship, she could serve with the whole season on the line, she could shake hands with her idol Kerry Walsh. She could do all that without so much as a flutter of anxiety. But outing her relationship with Donté to the whole school? That gave her heart palpitations.

"Olivia and I are history," he said, reading her mind. "She knows that, and I know that. We even had a conversation about it the other day."

"You did?"

"Absolutely. I made it clear that there's someone special in my life right now."

"Did you mention who?"

"No." He leaned his face close to hers. "But after tonight, everyone will know."

Kitty smiled weakly. That's what she was afraid of.

The other members of Bangers and Mosh were already gathered in the broom closet that served as a dressing room at the Ledge when John and Bree slipped in through the stage door.

"Bagsie!" Shane grabbed John's fist bro-style and bumped his chest. "You nervous?"

"A little," John said. Bree could hear the excited tremor in his voice.

She stood quietly in the doorway while the other members greeted John in turn. Devil Dan, the drummer, wearing his old-fashioned bowler hat and his short dark brown beard with lightning bolts shaved into each cheek. Sitting cross-legged on the table behind him was Grizzly, the lead guitarist. Anything but a Grizzly Bear, he was a short, scrawny junior-college student with horn-rimmed glasses as thick as Coke bottles and a military buzz cut that made him look more like a lab technician than a musician.

And then there was Shane. He had ditched his conservative school digs for a blue bowling shirt—unbuttoned, exposing his tattoo-covered torso—with the name "Tito" stitched on the front pocket. His arms were also bare, and Bree could see that he'd gotten new ink on the inside of his right forearm—a flaming sword in hues of black and blue, stretching from the crook of his elbow to his wrist. Shane's hair was spiked up into a faux mohawk, and he wore skinny jeans tucked into lace-up knee boots.

Total rock star.

"Bree!" Shane said.

Bree jumped. Shit. Had Shane caught her staring at his tatted-up chest in a pervy way?

But he was all smiles. "You can come in, you know. Don't have to stand in the door." He walked over and gave her a friendly hug. "You're practically part of the band."

Bree's stomach tightened, and she felt like her intestines were playing Twister. He released her, but held on to her left wrist, then whipped a neon green wristband from his pocket. "VIP access," he said with a smile. "I'm so glad you and Bagsie got back together. Band members' girlfriends are always welcome backstage."

Girlfriend? Got back together? "I'm not John's girlfriend," Bree said automatically.

"Wait," Shane said, leaning into her. He smelled like cigarettes and perspiration. It was intoxicating. "You guys aren't a couple?"

Bree shook her head.

"Are you serious?"

"John and I are friends. Period."

Even as the words came out of her mouth, she could feel something shift within her. They felt hollow and, for the first time in her life, not entirely true.

"Dude," Grizzly said, stealing Shane's attention. "Can we go over the set again?"

"Same as we rehearsed," Shane said. "Open with 'Bangin' Love,' hit the two B-sides from the EP, then the new songs for the play. And I want to do the cover song Bagsie brought to rehearsal the other night." He nodded to John. "You cool with that?"

John cast a fleeting glance in Bree's direction. "Yeah, man. Totally."

"Sweet," Shane said. "Then we'll close with 'Bang It Out.' Kosher?"

Everyone nodded.

"Thirty minutes to showtime," Shane said with a smile. "Let's blow it up."

Shane, Grizzly, and Devil Dan headed to the stage to do an amp and mic check, but John lingered. He laid his case on a table, opened it, and stared at the shiny red-and-white bass.

"Are you okay?" Bree asked.

John continued to gaze at his Fender. "No reward is worth this."

"No *Star Wars*," Bree said. "Be serious."

"I can't believe I'm doing this."

Bree laughed. "You're the only one, then." She stood by his side, her eyes involuntarily tracing the sharp lines of his jaw. "Anyone who's ever seen you play knew it was only a matter of time before you got a chance like this."

John turned his head and gazed down at her. Bree was surprised to see sadness in his eyes. "You really believe that, don't you?"

"Of course."

John took a step closer to her. "Is there anything you want to tell me? Anything at all?"

Bree searched his face and saw worry, confusion. What did he want her to say?

"I don't think so."

John took a deep breath and slowly let it out. "Everything's about to change, Bree. After tonight, nothing will be the same."

Bree cocked her head. The combination of the distress in his face and the gravity in his voice worried her. "What do you mean?"

John was so close she could feel his breath on her face. She wanted to repeat her question, ask him again what he meant when he said everything was about to change, but as she looked up into his eyes, the words died on her tongue. John leaned closer and for a heart-stopping moment, Bree thought he was going to kiss her.

Then he stopped himself, grabbed his bass, and slipped out the door without another word.

She slouched against the table, out of breath. Why was her heart racing? Why did her skin feel cold and clammy?

Bree closed her eyes and replayed that last moment. Lips parted, his eyes half-closed as he leaned down toward her upturned face. Bree started, her eyes flew open. John had almost kissed her. Of that she was absolutely freaking positive.

Even more disturbing? Bree had wanted him to.

FORTY-FOUR

AMBER TAPPED HER FOOT IMPATIENTLY IN THE PARKING LOT as Olivia and Peanut rounded the corner. "Come on," she barked. "There's already a line and you know how I hate to be in the back."

"Yeah." Jezebel folded her arms, mimicking Amber's stance. "I hate to be in the back."

"Sorry!" Peanut scurried to her side, scuffing her wedges across the asphalt. "There was traffic."

"Mm-hm." Amber cast a searing glance at Olivia. "More like you had to make an extra stop."

Really?

"But I always pick Olivia up," Peanut pleaded.

Amber looked Olivia up and down. "My old Zac Posen. How very two years ago."

"You never looked *that* good in it," Jezebel muttered.

Amber ignored the dig. "Olivia's used to my leftovers," she said to Jezebel, planting a hand on her hip. "But sometimes she gets greedy."

Greedy? "What are you talking about?"

Amber's nostrils flared. "You think I don't know about you and Rex?"

So that's what this was all about. Amber thought Olivia was after Rex. The idea was so ludicrous, Olivia laughed out loud.

"What's so funny?" Amber said through clenched teeth.

"You think I want Rex? That's ridiculous."

"Is it?" Amber said. "I saw you. I saw you at the bonfire. When I told you to dump that loser Donté, I didn't think you'd go after my boyfriend."

Dammit. The bonfire. Amber must have seen her kissing Rex. How could she explain that she was trying to make Donté jealous after *he* had dumped *her*?

"You tried to take Rex from me," Amber continued. "And now I'm taking everything from you." Then she swung around and marched toward the line, Jezebel at her heels.

There would be no reasoning with Amber now, but she needed Peanut to believe her. "Pea," Olivia said. "I never went after Rex. You have to believe me."

"I'll try and talk to her," Peanut said. "If you get back together with Donté, that might help smooth things over."

Donté. That's right. She scanned the crowd, looking for him.

Peanut giggled. "He's not here yet." She tugged on Olivia's arm. "Come on. Let's get in line."

A decent queue had already formed at the door. Mostly Bishop DuMaine students peppered with a healthy dose of Bangers and Mosh fans of all ages.

Amber stared disdainfully at the line. "I can't believe how long it is."

"There's got to be someone we can cut with," Jezebel said.

"Ooooh!" Amber squealed, pointing near the front of the line. "It's Logan." She stretched her arm up in the air and waved it frantically. "Logan!" she cooed.

Olivia followed Amber's line of sight, and a smile spread across her face as she spied Margot at Logan's side.

She looked like a totally new person. Her hair was swept loosely back from her face, which was artfully framed by escaping curls. With a tiny amount of shimmer from the cosmetics Olivia had suggested, Margot looked radiant. Her face was glowing with happiness, and she'd traded in the bulky sweaters she used to hide her body for a form-fitting scoop-neck top and boot-cut jeans. Still not quite as fashion forward as Olivia would have liked, but it was a radical improvement over the clothes that hid her from the world. Finally she'd been able to do something nice for Margot.

"Hi!" Amber said, reaching out to hug Logan. He gave her a friendly pat on the back and began to pull away, but Amber wasn't having any of it. She entwined her arms around his neck and hung off his body. "I'm so happy you're here."

Yeah, happy you have a place near the front of the line.

"Me too!" Jezebel added.

"Me too . . . too," Peanut said.

Logan extracted himself from Amber and took a step back. "It's good to be here."

Amber touched his arm with her hand, clearly oblivious to

his body language. "It's nice to spend some real time together. You know. Outside of school."

Outside of Rex.

"Um, sure." Logan ran his hand through his long blond hair. Amber's attention seemed to confuse him. He wrapped his arm around Margot's waist.

"Have you met Amber?" he asked. "We're in the play together." Logan laughed uncomfortably. "Oh yeah. You already know that."

Amber gave Margot a once-over. "Who's your friend?"

"This is Margot," Logan said. His face lit up.

Amber glanced from Logan to Margot and back. "Huh?"

Logan squeezed Margot close. "From rehearsal? She's helping Mr. Cunningham run lines for *Twelfth Precinct*."

"Huh?" Amber repeated.

Olivia could actually see the moment when Amber recognized Margot. Amber's eyes grew wide and her face tensed up. Her jaw dropped a mere inch, and Olivia noticed an almost imperceptible intake of breath.

The shock lasted a moment, replaced instantly by a steely, hardened look that froze Olivia in place.

"Margot Mejia," she said, drawing out each syllable. "I didn't recognize you without all that . . . weight." She turned to Logan. "Did you know Margot used to be really fat in junior high?"

Margot's shoulders instinctively hunched, head lowered as if she were attempting to hide herself in plain sight. No way would Olivia allow Amber to crush Margot's spirit. Not again.

◆ ◆ ◆

Margot felt all the heat in her body concentrate around her face and was terrified that she was either turning a fluorescent shade of crimson or sweating like a turkey in late November. She was immediately twelve years old again, walking into school the day the photo of her encased in plastic wrap had gone viral. Logan would realize she was a loser, the fat kid who'd been bullied for so long that no one at school would be seen within a ten-foot radius of her. He'd practically fall over himself trying to get away from her. Shame, panic, and an instinct to flee that was so overwhelming her feet actually shifted position.

Quiet the mind, quiet the panic. Dr. Tournay's words were hollow and meaningless as the swell of bullying muscle memory swamped her rational mind. She felt her legs weaken, her knees buckle.

"Margot!" Olivia cried. "You were absolutely brilliant running lines with me this week. A real lifesaver."

Margot glanced up, the panic abating. "Thanks."

"And I love what you've done with your hair." She grabbed at the short curls that crowned her own head. "I can't wait until mine grows out so I can wear it like that."

Margot could have hugged her.

"Oh, that's rich," Amber said, wheeling on Olivia. "*You* sticking up for *her*?"

"She looks gorgeous," Logan said.

Olivia smiled at her, and Logan's arm pulled her into his body. Both gave her strength.

Margot faced Amber. "I have a line coaching with you after school tomorrow." With Olivia and Logan nearby, she felt emboldened in a way she'd never dreamed possible. "Mr. Cunningham says you have a *lot* of work to do, so if you want to come early I can probably manage that."

"I . . ." Amber's voice trailed off, and Margot saw the sheep beneath the wolf's clothing—vulnerable, weak. "I don't think I can—"

"Amber!"

Amber swung around. Storming across the parking lot were Rex and his buddies.

"Who the fuck are you talking to?" Rex asked as he wedged himself between his girlfriend and Logan. His left eye was still discolored from where Bree had punched him.

Logan stuck out his hand, affable and friendly as always. "Logan," he said. "Amber and I are in the play together."

Rex turned on him. "Oh yeah? And what makes you think you can talk to her in real life?"

"Dude, she talked to me."

Rex grabbed Amber roughly by the arm. "Really? I'm five minutes late and you're all over *Point Break* here?"

Amber shook herself free. "Five minutes? *I* was five minutes late. You're like thirty." She leaned in and sniffed his neck. "Drinking again? Really? You couldn't invite me along to raid your dad's liquor cabinet?"

Margot had to give Amber credit—no one could shift the focus of an argument quite like her.

"Babe, it's a guy thing."

Amber folded her arms across her chest. "Then you and your guy thing can go stand at the back of the line."

"Fine," Rex said. "If that's how you want to be." He turned to Olivia and gave her outfit the once-over with an overt expression of lust. Margot wanted to throw Logan's jacket around Olivia's shoulders to protect her from Rex's eyes.

"Liv, you're looking fierce tonight. Seriously making me pant over here." Rex reached out and grazed her bare arm with his finger. Olivia flinched. "I'll be seeing you later. That's a promise." With a glance at Amber, he marched toward the back of the line, head high, with Tyler and Kyle following in his wake.

"Dude doesn't know how to treat a lady," Logan said, his voice low, his lips inches from Margot's ear.

Somehow, Margot didn't think Logan had the same problem.

They stood awkwardly together, waiting for the door to open. Peanut and Olivia chatted away about clothes and the play, while Amber tried to look as uninterested as possible. Margot barely noticed. She felt so light and giddy she wanted to skip around in circles. She'd faced down Amber Stevens and won. Her life was about to—

An ear-splitting screech of tires jolted the crowd. Screams filled the air as a car veered erratically into the parking lot. Logan pulled Margot protectively against him, shielding her body from potential impact, but the car skidded to a halt just feet from where they stood.

The driver's side door opened, and Margot's jaw dropped as the driver toppled out of the car.

Coach Creed.

FORTY-FIVE

KITTY AND DONTÉ ROUNDED THE BACK CORNER OF THE CLUB to find Coach Creed stumbling through the parking lot.

"'Maine Men!" he cried to no one in particular. "We have an emergency." His face was bright red and slick with a layer of sweat.

"Coach?" Rex trotted up to him. "What are you doing here?"

Coach Creed gripped Rex by the shoulder. "The enemy is here," he said. "Hiding in plain sight, son. Basking in their victory."

"Um, okay."

"We can't let them have this triumph. It's time to take the enemy down." Coach Creed pounded on the front door of the club. "Open up! This is Major Sergeant Richard Creed. You are harboring a dangerous criminal and I demand you open this door immediately."

Donté tightened his grip on Kitty's hand, pulling her behind him for protection. "That suspension made him lose his damn mind."

The door swung open and a bookish guy dressed in black stepped into the doorway. "I'm the manager of this establishment," he said calmly. "Are you a cop?"

"I am Major Sergeant Richard Creed," he repeated.

"So you're not a cop."

Coach Creed jabbed his finger in the manager's chest. "You are harboring a criminal," he said. "I demand that you give him up to my custody immediately."

The manager arched his eyebrow. "A criminal, huh? And who would this be?"

"John Baggott."

The manager sniffed Coach Creed's breath. "Dude, you need to lay off the Wild Turkey."

"Either give him up or face the consequences."

Coach Creed tried to push his way past the manager, who straight-armed him square in the chest. "I seriously don't need this tonight," he said under his breath, then half-turned and called into the club. "Tiny? I need backup."

Someone jostled against Kitty as he squeezed through the crowd. "What's happening?" Theo asked. Where had he come from?

Donté shook his head. "I think Coach Creed is having a breakdown."

Theo bobbed his head. "Awesome."

Another figure stepped through the doorway into the parking lot. He was massive, six and a half feet tall and at least three feet wide, with shoulders so meaty it looked like he was wearing football pads under his black T-shirt.

The color drained out of Coach Creed's face as Tiny the Bouncer cracked his knuckles in wordless warning.

Coach Creed hesitated as if he was considering retreat, then suddenly pointed to the door of the club. "You!"

Kitty's eyes followed Coach Creed's finger to Bree.

"You're his accomplice," he roared. "You're protecting him."

"That bullshit may work at school," Bree said, fists balled up in defiance, "but not here. Leave us the hell alone."

Coach Creed breathed faster, his eyes still locked on to Bree. "I'm going to get you both," he yelled. "Make no mistake. You're both dead!"

All around Kitty, students gasped. First he'd threatened Donté, now John and Bree. It was over the line, even for Coach Creed.

He made a sloppy fake-out move and tried to dash around the double-wide Tiny, but the bouncer was too quick for him. With one fluid motion, he grabbed Coach Creed's wrist and twisted his arm around his back, then drove the coach forward and pinned him to the brick wall.

"How dare you attack an officer?" Coach Creed sputtered.

"Sorry about this, Tiny," the manager said, strolling up behind the bouncer.

"No prob, Boss,"

"Listen up, moron," the manager said. "This is my club, and no one comes in here threatening my customers or my bands. So unless you want the cops to bust you on a variety of counts, including but not limited to trespassing, disturbing the peace, and driving under the influence, I suggest you get the fuck out of here right now."

Tiny released Coach Creed, who immediately crumpled to his knees, his cheek indented with the rugged surface of the brick wall.

"And if I ever catch you here again," the manager said, following the bouncer back inside, "Tiny's fist will be the last thing you'll ever see."

FORTY-SIX

MARGOT COULD FEEL HER HAND TREMBLING IN LOGAN'S AS Coach Creed peeled his car out of the parking lot. He'd threatened to kill John and Bree. Had he taken it a step further with Ronny, who'd gotten him fired from Archway? She could see the madness in his eyes as he stormed the front door of the club. Not only did Coach Creed have motive, he had the ability—both physically and mentally—to commit murder. She'd seen it on his face when he spotted Bree in the doorway.

"I doubt he'll be back," Logan said.

Margot pushed all thoughts of Coach Creed from her mind. She wasn't going to let anything ruin this night.

Logan squeezed her hand as the line began to move. Once inside the club, he navigated them to the railing that separated the bar area from the mosh pit. It was the perfect spot: far enough from the action that she wouldn't get trampled in the pit, but two steps up from the dance floor, it had an unobstructed view of the stage.

"I'm going to the bar," Logan said, close to her ear. "Can I get you anything?"

"Just some water," she said.

"Okay." He nodded with fake seriousness. "Hold down the fort while I'm gone."

Margot sighed and leaned against the railing. She must have slipped into a coma and was living out some kind of repressed fantasy. There was no way this could all be real.

A body sidled up behind her, and Margot spun around, expecting it to be Logan.

Instead, Ed the Head glared at her coldly.

"So this is why you couldn't go out with me tonight," he said. "You already had a date."

"I told you I was busy," Margot said. "That wasn't a lie."

"Wasn't the truth, either."

Margot felt the heat of shame spreading across her chest. "I'm sorry. I should have told you."

Ed craned his head, scanning the club. "So who's your date? And why did he leave you alone to fend for yourself?"

"He's at the bar," Margot said defensively. "Getting me a bottle of water." She wasn't going to let Ed the Head disparage Logan.

"Ah." Ed stared at the bar in silence. "Logan Blaine, huh?" he said after a few moments.

"How could you possibly know that?"

He shrugged. "Easy. He keeps looking over here."

Great. "Can we talk at school tomorrow?" Margot asked, desperate for him to leave her alone.

Ed the Head ignored her. "What do we know about this guy?"

"We?"

"Yeah. I mean, he just transferred into this school and you're already boyfriend and girlfriend? Have you met his parents? His friends? Know where he lives? Done any sort of background check or extensive email hacking?" He eyed Margot. "This guy could be anyone."

Margot winced as thoughts of Christopher Beeman flooded her brain. *This guy could be anyone.*

Stop it. Coach Creed was clearly the prime suspect and Christopher Beeman, whoever he was, had faded into Ronny's backstory. "Is there something you wanted?" Margot asked.

"Actually, yeah." Ed the Head pulled a file folder out of his ever-present backpack. "Small lead on your photo."

Margot caught her breath. "Do you know who it is?"

"Not exactly." Ed the Head held the folder in both hands. "I tried everything. Even dusted it for prints. No one's but yours."

"You have a fingerprinting kit?"

"Why should that surprise you?"

Margot shook her head. "Anything else?"

"The photo was taken with an older iPhone model, maybe a 3G or a 3GS."

"Oh." Margot got the distinct impression this information could have waited until school Monday morning. "Well, that narrows it down to every single person I went to junior high school with."

Ed the Head clicked his tongue. "O ye of little faith." He opened the folder and pushed a photo into her hands. "I ran it through some filters and here's what I got."

The photo looked as if it had been lightened, color enhanced, and expertly contrasted. The face of the photographer was still a featureless blob, but Margot could clearly make out the light curly hair.

"Based on my estimations, the girl in the photo was about five feet tall, with midlength curly blond hair."

"Which describes most of the girls in my class," Margot said with a sigh.

"Not so much." Ed the Head slipped several more photos out of the folder and handed them to Margot. They were blowups of photos from her seventh-grade yearbook. "Taking into account hair length, height, and when these yearbook photos were taken, I've narrowed it down to five suspects."

Margot sifted through the photos. Tiffany Horne, Samantha Heisberg, Loretta Davis, Eleanor McGrath. As she stared at the fifth and final photo, her hand began to shake.

Olivia Hayes.

FORTY-SEVEN

BREE LEANED AGAINST A PILLAR NEAR THE BACK OF THE PIT and wrapped her arms tightly around her body. It was less her usual "don't mess with me" stance and more "I need to give myself a hug."

You're both dead, Coach Creed had screamed. And he'd meant it, of that Bree was sure. She'd never looked into the eyes of a killer, but the wild hatred she'd seen in Coach Creed was exactly what she'd imagined she'd see. It wasn't much of a leap to think that he'd turned his blind rage on Ronny as well. Now they just had to find proof before he followed through on his threats and went after John.

Another image replaced Coach Creed in her mind. John, lips parted, leaning down to kiss her. Just the memory of it caused an involuntary reaction: her pulse quickened, her stomach fluttered, her breath caught in her chest.

John had been right: everything was about to change.

Bree's eyes wandered aimlessly around the sellout crowd, tightly packed into the small club, all there to see John's band.

Maybe that was affecting her judgment? Her gaze lingered on a couple frantically making out in the corner. Maybe the rock-star vibe John was giving off had seduced her subconscious to the point where her hormones raged out of control like those two idiots?

As she stared at the make-out session with a mix of envy and horror, she realized the two figures were familiar. Holy shit, Kitty and Donté.

If Olivia didn't know that her ex-boyfriend was getting primal with their DGM leader, she would soon.

She glanced back toward the stage, searching for Olivia, and caught sight of her in the mosh pit, snaking her way through the crowd, practically on a collision course with the Kitty–Donté face-sucking display. It was only a matter of time before Olivia barreled into them.

Bree's instinct was to intercept Olivia, but she stopped herself. Why did she care? So what if Kitty and Olivia fought over the same guy; wouldn't it be more entertaining to watch her two friends go at it?

No. No, it wouldn't be fun to watch the fallout. She didn't want to see either of them get hurt.

Bree pushed herself off the pillar and shouldered her way through the crowd. "Olivia!" Bree cried out, but her voice was muted. Olivia never even paused. She was practically within sight of Kitty and Donté. Crap. This wasn't going to end well.

Just when Bree thought a Kitty–Olivia confrontation was inevitable, someone stepped between them, blocking Olivia's path.

Bree had never been so happy to see Ed the Head in her entire life.

"What is it?" Olivia asked. Her eyes shifted to either side of him, still in search of Donté. The concert was about to start. Where was he?

"I have some more information for you." Ed the Head leaned forward and dropped his voice. "About that photo."

Olivia arched an eyebrow, her interest piqued. "Spill it."

Ed the Head smiled wryly. "Perhaps we should discuss price first?"

Olivia threw up her hands, exasperated. "Ed, I'm not going out with you. Give it a rest."

"Olivia, Olivia, Olivia," Ed the Head sighed, shaking his head. "Not everyone at this school dreams of a date with you."

"What do you want then?"

"I want"—he paused dramatically—"a favor. To be named at a later date." He extended his hand.

A favor. Olivia had no idea what Ed the Head had in mind, but she'd deal with his request later. She accepted his hand and gave it a firm shake. "Done."

Immediately, Ed the Head was all business. "Barbara Ann Vreeland was expelled from Bishop DuMaine after the grade-fixing scandal broke two years ago, based on an anonymous tip. She was failing algebra, again, and her coach struck a deal with the math teacher."

Olivia pursed her lips. "I already knew that."

"Aha!" Ed the Head made a dramatic flourish with his

hands. "But did you know that Barbara Ann was the captain of the JV girls' volleyball team?"

"Yes," Olivia said slowly. "Because you told me."

"Oh, right. Wait, let me try that again." He bowed his head, like an actor preparing for a scene, then whipped his face up, totally in character. "Aha!" he repeated. "But did you know that after she was kicked off the team, our very own student body vice president took over as JV captain?"

"Kitty?"

"*And*," Ed the Head added, "did you know that Kitty was also failing algebra?" He didn't wait for her to answer. "*And* did you know that Barbara Ann was expelled because she was recruiting teammates for grade fixing?"

Olivia's eyes grew wide. "You think Barbara Ann told Kitty about the grade fixing, and Kitty turned her in?"

Ed the Head threw his hands up in faux innocence. "I'm just saying, it's an odd coincidence that now Kitty is the captain of the state-champion girls' varsity team with scholarship offers from every Ivy League school on the planet, while Barbara Ann brews lattes at the Coffee Clash."

Olivia couldn't believe it. Kitty had turned in her friend and teammate. Had she done it intentionally to gain the captain's position? Olivia thought back to their study sessions for the religion assignment freshman year. She remembered how affected Kitty had been by the whole scandal. At the time, she'd assumed it was because several of Kitty's friends had been put on academic probation or flat-out expelled, like Barbara Ann. But maybe her reaction had been more personal. Maybe it had been guilt.

"Worth the price tag?" Ed the Head asked.

"Yeah," Olivia whispered. "Thanks."

"Awesome. You'll be hearing from me." He backed away and flashed her two finger guns. "I am considerably out of here."

A cry went up as the band took the stage. There was a rush forward in the mosh pit, and Bree lost sight of Olivia and Ed the Head. Oh well. At least Olivia had been derailed from her search.

Devil Dan was the first one out, followed by Shane and Grizzly, with John trailing behind. He kept his head down as he picked up his bass and gave a few quick strums before getting into position. Without a word, Devil Dan counted off with his drumsticks and they launched into "Bangin' Love."

John attacked the opening bass line and Bree held her breath. Within two bars, the crowd went absolutely apeshit.

The rest of the band joined the song and the club literally erupted in movement and sound. The screeching guitars and vicious cymbal hits were deafening, and even Bree, veteran concert goer that she was, fought the urge to plug her ears with her fingers. The mosh pit writhed like a living, breathing organism. In the front, girls and guys alike were reaching their hands out toward Shane, who straddled his guitar with a ferocity that had always turned Bree's insides to Jell-O. Usually, Bree couldn't keep her eyes off him at a Bangers and Mosh show. But tonight she could only see John.

When the chorus kicked in, John and Grizzly joined with

harmony, and every single person in the audience, including Bree, sang along.

> *Don't you know I want you?*
> *Don't you know you know you want me?*
> *Don't you know you want my*
> *Bangin' love?*
> *Don't you know you need my*
> *Bangin' love?*

As the song crescendoed to the finale, John reprised his solo bass line, then jumped up and landed the final note of the song.

The crowd exploded.

"Thank you!" Shane said. He took a swig of water from his bottle as the noise died down. "Thank you guys for coming out tonight. We're so thrilled to be back at the Ledge, the best fucking all-ages club in Northern California."

The audience roared in appreciation.

"We're doing a mix of old and new tonight," Shane continued. "If you haven't noticed, we've got a new member of Bangers and Mosh to introduce. On bass now is Bagsie, who just threw down the wickedest rendition of 'Bangin' Love' I've ever heard. Seriously, how epic was that?"

Again the crowd roared, even louder than before. John held up his hand in thanks, but looked totally and completely embarrassed by the attention. Bree wasn't sure if she wanted to hug him or slap him across the face and tell him to man up.

"Bagsie and I have been working on some new songs, some of

which we'll be debuting tonight. So . . . yeah. Fuck it. Let's play."

The band started their second song—another classic Bangers and Mosh tune—but before Bree could enjoy it, she noticed a face coming toward her in the crowd. She was easy to spot: while everyone else was watching the band onstage, Olivia was aiming for the back of the club again.

One second Olivia was searching in an unfocused way, the next, her eyes were locked on to something in the corner. Bree was close enough to see the color drain out of Olivia's face as her eyes grew wide and her jaw fell slack.

Shit.

Then, by some weird psychic connection, Kitty broke away from Donté's tonsillectomy and looked toward the stage. She saw Olivia right away, and Bree watched the same look of horror overcome her.

"Olivia!" Kitty mouthed, her voice lost in the music. She broke away from Donté and ran toward her.

But Olivia didn't wait. She swung around and disappeared into the crowd.

FORTY-EIGHT

BREE BROKE FREE OF THE CROWD IN TIME TO SEE KITTY FOLLOW Olivia into the ladies' room. Thankfully there was no line as Bree squeezed in behind them.

"Olivia," Kitty said. "I'm so sorry. I thought you knew."

Olivia leaned close to the mirror and dabbed at her face with a paper towel. Her eyes were already red and overflowing with a flood of tears.

"Knew what?" she said, her voice cracking with emotion. "That you're boning my boyfriend?"

"I'm not sleeping with him," Kitty said.

Not yet, Bree wanted to say, but she kept that little nugget to herself.

"I saw you," Olivia said. Her lower lip trembled. "I saw the way he touched you. You can't possibly tell me that you're just friends."

To her credit, Kitty was amazingly calm. "I won't tell you that, because it's not true. Donté and I are dating."

Olivia gasped and a tsunami of tears cascaded down her

cheeks. "How could you do this to me?"

"Donté said he told you about it at rehearsal and that you were okay with it."

Kitty tried to touch Olivia's arm, but she jerked away. "Don't touch me!"

The door flew open, momentarily flooding the room with the ear-splitting sounds of the band, and Margot marched in. *Oh, thank God*, Bree thought. Margot would know what to do.

Margot pointed at Olivia. "It was you."

Olivia swung around, gripping the sink behind her. "What are you talking about?"

"You took the photo," Margot said. Her voice was more forceful than Bree had ever witnessed. "You were the one with Amber that night. You were the one who ruined my life."

So much for an ally. "What are you talking about?" Bree asked.

Kitty seemed to know what was going on. She put a hand on Margot's shoulder. "You mean *the* photo. The one that—"

"The one that precipitated my suicide attempt," Margot said. She pulled up the left sleeve of her shirt, exposing several dark, parallel scars.

"Holy shit," Bree said.

Margot laughed. "You didn't know, did you?"

Bree shook her head.

"Yeah, well, I'm the crazy girl who tried to kill herself after an embarrassing photo circulated in junior high. A photo that up until a few days ago, I'd assumed was taken by Amber Stevens. Turns out, it was Olivia."

No wonder Margot had kept DGM from going after Amber. She wanted that revenge for herself.

Olivia's lip trembled. "I can explain, Margot. I swear I didn't know—"

"Didn't know that taking a photo of me naked and bound in plastic wrap would ruin my life?"

Olivia swallowed. "I didn't know what Amber was up to. She said we were going to a party. Then she told me she wanted to pose for some photos in front of Rex's bedroom window. I had no idea it was your house."

"Sure you didn't," Margot said.

Kitty stepped between them. "Why didn't you say something?" she asked Olivia. "Why would you keep Amber's secret?"

Olivia laughed. "Oh, you're one to talk about secrets. Were you ever going to tell us about Barbara Ann Vreeland?"

That name was familiar. "She was one of the students kicked out of school freshman year, right?" Bree asked.

"Yep." Olivia turned to Kitty with a wide smile. "Do you want to tell them who was responsible for getting her expelled, or should I?"

Bree's jaw dropped. "You blew the whistle?"

"I . . ." Kitty started.

"Holy shit," Bree cried for the second time in as many minutes. "You totally did!"

Olivia's eyes narrowed, giving her face a nasty Amber-like quality. "She threw a friend under the bus so she could be captain of the volleyball team. Makes you wonder what she'd do to us."

"It wasn't like that," Kitty said. Her voice was flat. "I was failing algebra and my coach said if I didn't go along with it, they'd kick me off the team. I had to do something." She turned to Margot, then Bree. "I didn't think they'd expel her."

"Did you know she was involved before you narced?" Margot asked.

Kitty dropped her eyes to the floor. "Yeah. She was the one who told me about it."

"See?" Olivia cried. "At least I didn't know what Amber was going to do with that photo."

"If you didn't," Margot said, "then you're stupider than I thought."

Olivia twisted the faucet on, hanging her head so no one could see her face reflected in the mirror. "I can't believe this is happening. My life is ruined."

"Yeah," Margot said. "The same way you ruined mine."

"Look," Bree said, stepping up behind Olivia. Time to put years of listening to Dr. Drew to good use. "Your life isn't ruined. You and Donté broke up. He moved on. It's not that big a deal."

In the mirror, Bree saw both Kitty and Margot wince.

"Not that big a deal?" Olivia shook her head. "How would you feel if she'd been making out with your boyfriend?"

Not again. "I don't have a boyfriend." This time, the words made her cringe.

"It's not always about you, Bree!" Olivia said.

"Wait, *I'm* the drama queen here? Are you kidding me?"

"Stop!" Kitty held up her hands. "We can't turn on each other."

Bree couldn't help herself. "Too late."

"Enough with the sarcasm, Bree," Kitty said.

Why were they trying to shift the blame to her? "I'm not the one getting the competition kicked out of school."

Kitty raised her chin, clearly irritated by Bree's accusation. "I told you, I didn't know she'd get . . ." Her voice trailed off, then Kitty caught her breath. "Hold up. Olivia, how did you find out about Barbara Ann?"

Olivia squared her shoulders. "Anonymous tip."

"I'm serious," Kitty said.

"So was she," Margot said. "Someone sent her a photo of you and Barbara Ann."

"A photo?" Kitty asked Olivia. "In a plain manila envelope?"

"You got one too?" Olivia asked.

Kitty nodded.

"Try to keep up, Princess," Bree said, exasperated at Olivia's slowness. "We all got one."

Olivia looked utterly confused. "But the other day in the lighting booth you said you didn't?"

Bree shrugged. "I lied."

Silence fell in the bathroom as the girls looked at one another.

"It could be any of us," Margot said. As always, straight up and to the point. "Any of us sending the envelopes."

"But why?" Bree said. "Makes more sense that someone's fucking with us."

"Who?" Kitty asked. "Who would know about our connection?"

Bree tilted her head. "The same person who killed Ronny and planted our card on his body?"

"Coach Creed," Kitty said. "Or Rex, or Amber, or Theo, or John."

John? "Hold up."

Kitty ignored her. "Or Christopher Beeman, who literally could be anyone since we have no idea what he looks like."

"Or one of us," Margot said quietly.

Kitty nodded. "Or one of us."

Bree couldn't believe what she was hearing. "You were the one who said we had to stick together."

Kitty whirled on her, her face reddening by the second. "Then find us some proof, Bree, okay? Find proof that it's someone else. You're the one who went to school with Christopher. How convenient is it that you don't remember what he looks like?"

Bree set her jaw. "What the hell is that supposed to mean?"

"She's implying that you're protecting someone," Margot said.

"It's not John, okay?" She eyed Margot. "You want to know who's the best candidate for Christopher Beeman? Try your new boyfriend on for size."

The color drained out of Margot's carefully made-up face. "Logan?"

Bree shrugged. "New kid in school, don't know shit about him. Totally fits."

Kitty glanced at Margot, who'd begun to tremble. "Theo," she said. "Christopher could also be Theo. He was new last spring."

The door handle turned as someone tried to get into the bathroom.

"I don't know what's going on," Olivia said, gathering her purse from the top of the paper towel dispenser.

Bree rolled her eyes. "Shocking."

Olivia ignored her. "But I'm out of here." The tears welled up again. "I don't want to talk to you ever again. Any of you."

A knock on the door. "Hurry up in there!"

"But—" Bree started, then stopped dead.

A new song started. Grizzly's lead guitar played a lonely strain of melody that was at once strange and familiar. The band joined in, and finally the vocals. But it wasn't Shane's voice this time.

It was John. And he was singing "The Promise."

"But what?" Olivia's hand was on the deadbolt.

"John's playing that for me."

Olivia sniffled. "Of course. He's in love with you. Everyone has someone in love with them but me." She threw open the door and dashed into the hallway.

Bree should have gone after Olivia, but she couldn't. Her feet had a mind of their own.

She ran down the hall to the club, shouldering her way up to the railing in front of the bar. It was definitely John singing. He stood at the microphone in the blue glow of a spotlight. His eyes were half-closed, as if he didn't want to look at anyone in the audience, his body tight and angular. But he sounded fabulous. It wasn't intense like Shane's vocals, or even ferocious like the way John played the bass. Instead, his voice was delicately plaintive over the revved-up punk version of the song.

"And if I had to walk the world, I'd make you fall for me. I promise you, I promise you I will."

There was no way he could have seen her, the club was too dark and he would have been blinded by that spotlight, but Bree couldn't help but feel like he was singing directly to her.

FORTY-NINE

KITTY SHOULD HAVE FOLLOWED OLIVIA OUT THE BACK DOOR of the club, grabbed her by the shoulders, and talked some sense into her. She was the leader of DGM, and it was her job to remind Olivia that they all needed to stick together.

The problem was, none of it was true. Kitty couldn't trust them, not anymore. And they clearly didn't trust her. The team was broken.

"What do we do now?" Margot yelled over the music.

Suddenly, Kitty didn't care about the team, didn't care about anyone but Donté. It was time for Kitty to put herself first for a change. "Go home," she said.

"What?"

Kitty stepped into the hallway and shook her head. "It's over."

"You okay?" Logan asked when Margot made it back to him.

Margot nodded and forced a smile. Don't Get Mad was no more, and she wasn't sure how she felt. "Long line for the restroom."

She turned to the stage, where John Baggott was crooning away at the microphone. Logan slipped his arm around her waist and held her close.

You want to know who's the best candidate for Christopher Beeman? Try your new boyfriend on for size.

First Ed the Head, now Bree, both echoing a possibility Margot had already acknowledged. Logan could be Christopher Beeman.

Logically, she couldn't dismiss the possibility. But even if he was Christopher, did it matter? Coach Creed had killed Ronny. All she needed to do now was prove it and then the entire nightmare would be over and it would be time to forget Don't Get Mad, forget the girls and the missions and the wounds that would never heal. She had Logan now, and things would be better. Life would be better.

The song ended, and the crowd went wild. Shane leaned over to John and gave him a high five before he took his own microphone again. "How fucking awesome is this guy?" The audience cheered like maniacs. "And, ladies," Shane said coyly, "I hear he's single so, you know, there's a chance for you after the show."

The girls in the club screamed as if Channing Tatum had rushed the stage. One of them jumped up, threw her arms around John's neck, and gave him a sloppy kiss.

"Exactly," Shane said, as the girl bounced back into the pit. "Okay, last song, you guys. Thank you so much for coming out and supporting Bangers and Mosh!"

Just as they were about to start, the door of the club flew open, flooding the stuffy interior with a sharp blast of cold air, and Margot felt a chill race down her spine as the blare of dozens of sirens filled the air.

What now?

Olivia paused in the alley behind the Ledge. Her eyes stung from a mix of humiliation, shame, and smeared eye makeup, which only added to the deluge of tears. She leaned against the wall and, gritting her teeth, pressed the back of her head into the rough, jagged bricks. Olivia could have seen Amber going after Donté, or even Jezebel. But not Kitty. The only person less likely to try and date a friend's ex was Margot.

Margot. Olivia had worked so hard to put that night back in seventh grade out of her mind. She'd known, deep down, that Amber was leading her into something sketchy, but she hadn't been strong enough to speak up. She wasn't popular then, just a poor kid from a broken home, so when Amber started buddying up to her, Olivia was flattered. And too scared of having that kernel of friendship withdrawn to speak up when she realized what was happening.

Then the day freshman year when by some bizarre twist of the universe, she and Margot had been assigned to the same project in religion class. She'd wanted to say something, to apologize. But how do you say you're sorry you ruined someone's life? They don't exactly make a Hallmark card for that. When Kitty had approached them all about starting a secret revenge society, Olivia saw an opportunity. Maybe she couldn't erase what she'd done, but she could at least try to make up for it.

But that was over now. Done and finished. DGM was no

more, and all Olivia wanted to do was get away from the Ledge, away from the rest of DGM, and away from the site of her total and utter humiliation.

Slight problem. Peanut was her ride home, and Peanut was still inside the club. She had four dollars in her purse and her mom was passed out on the couch at home, which left only two options: walk or take the bus.

Walking five miles home on a chilly fall night sounded so romantic, like Kate Winslet caught in the rain returning from Willoughby's. Maybe she'd catch pneumonia too, and practically die. That would show Donté how much she loved him, how much he'd hurt her. Then he'd be sorry.

Olivia stared at her feet. The black lace peep toes were sexy as hell, exposing just a hint of her scarlet toenails. But the skin around those toenails was rapidly turning a matching shade of red, and the backs of both of her heels were raw from the friction of an unfamiliar pair of shoes. Blister city in the morning. Walking was out of the question.

With a sigh, Olivia pushed herself off the wall and picked her way down the darkened alley, the shortest distance to the bus stop. It was creepily atmospheric, like something out of a movie set, and Olivia found herself tiptoeing past ominous Dumpster bins and piled-up garbage bags. She kept her eyes on the broken pavement, a necessity if she didn't want to trip in an asphalt pothole and break her ankle. The light from the waning moon illuminated the cracked surface, veined like the parched desert as she forced herself to put one foot in front of the other.

Just a few more feet. But as she neared the end of the alley, something caught her eye. Not a garbage bag, or discarded furniture. It looked like a shoe, lying at a strange, unnatural angle. Like it was still attached to something.

Like it was still attached to a leg.

Olivia's brain registered this fact too late. She stumbled around the corner of the building and stopped cold.

Lying facedown in the alley was a body.

Olivia had a split second to take in the camouflage pants, the bald head splattered with blood, before she started to scream.

FIFTY

LOGAN SHIFTED HIS CAR INTO PARK AND KILLED THE ENGINE. "Are you sure you're going to be okay?"

"Yeah." Margot stared out the passenger window at her mom's silver Prius sitting alone in the abandoned Coffee Clash parking lot. It was well past midnight, more than two hours after her parents' arbitrary curfew, and though she'd called to tell them about Coach Creed's murder and how the police kept everyone in the club until they could secure the scene and ask questions, it hadn't mattered. She wasn't sure if they were more upset that she was out past ten o'clock or that she'd somehow gotten mixed up in a murder investigation the first time they'd allowed her to venture out alone. With any luck, she'd only be put on lockdown until she was eighteen.

But the potential parental freak-out was nothing compared to Coach Creed's death. A teacher—and another DGM victim—had been murdered, and since he'd been Margot's prime suspect in Ronny's death, all of her theories were officially blown out of the water. Logan laid his hand on top of hers. "I sure didn't picture our first date ending like this."

"You mean you didn't plan on a murder investigation?"

He laughed. "Yeah, I planned that just for you. Guy's got to impress a girl." He leaned in closer. "I was hoping for something a little less police procedural, and a little more romantic."

Margot's heart might technically have stopped beating momentarily as he tilted his head, easing his lips close to hers. He was going to kiss her. He *wanted* to kiss her. No one had ever wanted to kiss her in the history of boys kissing girls.

Logan's lips brushed against hers, and Margot's mind fell instantly silent. All she could focus on was the tingling sensation. Logan paused, waiting for the green light. She smiled a fraction.

That was all he needed.

Logan kissed her, and her legs went limp. He nuzzled her upper and lower lips separately, then pulled back and cupped her face with his hand. She gazed into his eyes, desperate to feel his lips on hers again. Instead, he kissed her eyelids, left then right, as if he was afraid she was going to break.

He might be a killer.

No. She'd read Christopher's emails. She knew his voice, the way he talked, the way he acted, and it was nothing like Logan. Besides, he'd been by her side most of the night, his body pressed against her own. Best alibi ever.

Something stirred deep within her. She didn't want soft and romantic, she wanted to feel every piece of him. She pushed herself up in the seat, hooking one leg underneath her, and launched herself into his arms.

Logan easily met her ferocious kiss with one of his own.

Then his hands were in her hair, pulling the clip out so he could run his fingers through her long, tangled curls. Margot had no idea what she was doing with her hands: they seemed to have developed a mind of their own as they caressed Logan's chest.

Nothing mattered. Not Coach Creed or Ronny DeStefano or DGM. Certainly not her parents impatiently awaiting her at home. The whole world had disappeared, leaving just Margot and Logan and the interior of his SUV, the only sounds she could hear, blood rushing through her ears and the sharp pounding of her own heart.

Without warning, Logan pulled away.

"What's wrong?" Margot panted.

"Nothing," Logan said, panting too. "Just realized that your parents might ban me from ever seeing you again if you're this late for curfew."

Margot rested her head on Logan's shoulder. "They don't know I'm out with you."

"They don't?" Logan sounded hurt.

Margot sighed. Normally she would have been terrified that she'd offended him, but for some reason, she was oddly calm.

"Baby steps," she said. "They're not exactly lenient."

Logan brushed her cheek with his hand. "I don't scare easily."

As he kissed her, Margot swore she'd never be scared again.

Bree pulled her dad's Lexus into the garage and sat in the driver's seat until the door had fully closed behind her. She was exhausted, so tired the backs of her eyeballs felt like they were made of lead and were threatening to drop out of her skull into her lower intestines if she didn't get herself into a prone position as soon as possible.

Yet as she sat there in the darkened garage, her hands shook uncontrollably. Coach Creed was dead. The killer was still on the loose. A *serial* killer, who apparently held all of DGM's secrets in his or her hands. And the suspect list was a short one: Theo Baranski, Amber and Rex, Christopher Beeman, and John.

John had decided to get a ride home with Shane, and Bree hadn't fought him on it. Ever since the show ended, things had been super awkward between them. He'd avoided her, easy enough in the chaos that ensued once the police arrived. John had been the first person they'd questioned, since Coach Creed had showed up at the Ledge like Salome screaming for John's head on a platter. They'd sat together in the dressing room, an uncomfortable and seemingly impenetrable silence between them. Shane and Grizzly talked a mile a minute about the show, what had worked well and what hadn't, while Devil Dan nervously air drummed so obsessively that after about an hour of nonstop movement she had wanted to rip the drumsticks from his hands and break them over her knee.

John had spent the time doing anything to avoid looking at, talking to, or interacting with Bree in any way. Normally, she would have broken the tension with some well-timed *Star Wars*, but tonight she'd let it go. She wasn't interested in having a conversation with him because, shit, what would she say?

Even now, sitting in the car by herself, her stomach dropped as she remembered John leaning in to kiss her. But that wasn't the worst. The female scream that went up when Shane said, "And, ladies, I hear he's single." It had felt as if someone had punched her in the kidneys with a pair of brass knuckles.

Bree forced the memory from her mind. She wasn't going to deal with it, wasn't going to think about it. Avoidance was a coping strategy, wasn't it?

She was about to get out of the car, when her eye caught something in the rearview mirror. A yellow envelope in the backseat.

Kitty wasn't even remotely tired as she traipsed down the hallway to her bedroom. Coach Creed was dead. Their main suspect. She thought back to the look on his face in the parking lot, the murderous rage in his eyes, then to the list of suspects. Did they have two murderers on their hands, or just one? And how did the anonymous envelopes factor in?

Thoughts of Barbara Ann haunted her. As much as she'd told herself over the years that she'd done the right thing, hadn't forming DGM been an admission of her guilt? Like she was attempting to make up for her own misdeeds by helping others?

And while Kitty never thought for a second that Barbara Ann would get expelled from Bishop DuMaine, she'd believed—no, worse, she'd *hoped*—that Barbara Ann's involvement in the scandal would get her suspended from the team for at least a semester, during which time Kitty would take over as team captain. . . .

Olivia was right. It had been selfish. And she'd ruined Barbara Ann's chances at the same scholarships Kitty was vying for.

Kitty sighed as she slowly pushed open her bedroom door.

Even a hundred DGM revenge missions couldn't absolve her of that.

She was about to collapse into bed when she saw the envelope propped up against her pillows.

Olivia stared at the envelope. Another one. The sleeping pill she'd taken was already making her brain thick and fuzzy, but she wasn't hallucinating.

What would it be this time? She wasn't sure she could handle the contents after everything that had happened that night.

With a trembling hand, Olivia placed the envelope on her nightstand, vowing not to look at it until morning. But as she lay there, desperate for sleep to overtake her, she couldn't shake the nagging voice in her head. A quick peek. Nothing more.

Fine. Olivia sat up in bed and opened the envelope.

Another photo. It was from a newspaper; the image of four girls seated around a library table was blurry in its grayscale, but the girls' faces were distinct and recognizable. Margot, Kitty, Bree, and Olivia.

Beneath the photo was a line of text.

Turn yourselves in or else. You have until opening night.

Margot stared at the photo. She felt no panic, no fear. As if she'd known this was coming. She turned off the light and lay back against the pillows.

"And so it ends," she said out loud.

FIFTY-ONE

BREE SPENT ALL OF MONDAY THINKING ABOUT THE MYSTERIOUS envelopes, squirreled away in her bedroom since classes had been canceled. They were the key to finding a murderer, she felt it in her gut; if she could figure out who sent them, she could exonerate both DGM and John.

Basically, it came down to two options: either there had been two killers—Coach Creed, who killed Ronny, and someone else, who'd killed him—or both murders had been committed by the same person, who'd just been upgraded to serial psychopath.

Personally, she leaned toward the second option. "Serial psychopath" fit in better with the anonymous envelopes, especially the last one. *Turn yourselves in or else. You have until opening night.*

Two killers or one, the result was the same—a murderer was still out there. And she was tired of letting him or her call the shots.

Bree returned to the list of suspects. Rex and Amber were the next logical choice after Coach Creed, and then there was

Margot's broken-record hypothesis: the killer was a member of DGM.

She had to admit Margot had a point. They had all been inside the club when Coach Creed was murdered, but how hard would it have been to lure him into the alley, slip outside, and clobber him without anyone noticing? Not exactly rocket science.

A few days ago, Bree wouldn't have thought Olivia, Kitty, or Margot capable of such a crime, but last night's blowout in the ladies' room had made her think. How well did she really know them? She hadn't known about Margot's suicide attempt or about the photo that had precipitated it. A photo Olivia had taken. And she certainly would never have imagined Kitty would have stabbed one of her teammates in the back, even unintentionally. If she'd do it to a volleyball player, wouldn't she do it to a member of DGM?

And then there was John. As much as Bree hated to admit it, the photo that had been left in her car was the same one John had torn from the *DuMaine Dispatch* last week. And he had been in her car last night, placing his Fender case in the backseat while they drove to the Ledge. Could he possibly be the one pulling the strings?

Bree forced the thought from her mind. She absolutely, positively refused to believe that John murdered anyone. Even Coach Creed.

Despite all the options, Bree's mind kept drifting to Christopher Beeman. So many clues pointed in his direction. Could her junior high crush have returned to Menlo Park as a cold-blooded killer?

She thought of Theo Baranski. Like sixth-grade Christopher, he was short and overweight, and like Christopher, Theo was an observer, the kid who was always watching what everyone else was doing. But there was something off about their personalities, something that didn't jibe in her mind. She couldn't bring herself to believe that Theo and Christopher were one and the same.

Logan Blaine, however, was a different story. True, he didn't look much like the Christopher that Bree remembered, but puberty did that to boys. Could he have returned from Archway a taller, leaner, blonder version of himself? He was starring in the school play, after all. Maybe he was a better actor than anyone realized? She wasn't sure. She needed a second opinion.

Perhaps it was time to tell the girls about Christopher.

The thought of reliving the events of sixth grade made Bree's stomach churn. Christopher had been her friend, in the way that most sixth graders of the opposite sex are friends, which is to say that Bree had an enormous crush on Christopher, to which he was totally and completely oblivious. She'd tried everything to get his attention, from sitting next to him at weekly mass to joining his solitary play at recess. He was a loner, picked on by the boys at school as he was a little overweight, preferred art to sports, and had, according to the ruling posse of boys led by Rex Cavanaugh, a "raging case of gay face."

Which had become his nickname. "Hey, Gay Face!" was a common mode of getting Christopher's attention, and in typical Catholic school fashion, no adults who caught wind of the name-calling stepped in to correct it.

So after months of hanging out with Christopher, Bree had

finally told Christopher that she really, really liked him.

It hadn't gone over so well.

Christopher had physically recoiled from the idea of romantic feelings for Bree, his face horrified. Humiliated and despondent, Bree did something that she was still so ashamed of, the memory of it made her hands go ice cold. She'd joined in the bullying.

She still remembered the look on Christopher's face the first time Bree called him "Gay Face" in the cafeteria. As if all the hope had been stomped out of him. His eyes weren't sad or angry, just disappointed, which was somehow worse than the other two combined. He'd shaken his head and stared at his uneaten lunch.

It was the last time Bree had seen him.

That night, Christopher had made a stunning confession to his parents. Or so the rumor went. He told them about the bullying at school, about the name-calling and the gay shaming. And then he told his parents that he thought he was bisexual, and had already experienced an "encounter" with another boy at school.

A shitstorm ensued. The Beemans pulled their son out of St. Alban's faster than the Pope could grant absolution. Before Bree could even call him, Christopher's cell phone number had been changed, his Facebook account deleted, and when their sixth-grade teacher finally addressed the class about what happened to Christopher, Bree learned that he'd been sent away to a military academy in Arizona. Archway.

And it was Bree's fault.

Now two people were dead, and Christopher Beeman seemed

to be the key to the killings. Would he kill again? Would a member of DGM be next?

Bree clenched her fists. She wasn't going to let that happen.

She may have ignored 95 percent of what her father said, but one piece of advice had stuck with her: in politics, the best defense was a good offense.

It was time to fight back.

When school resumed Tuesday morning, Olivia's first thought was that she needed to talk to Margot.

She'd looked for her in the halls between class and in the quad at lunch, but without any luck. Rehearsal after school would be her next opportunity, and with an hour to kill before her first scene run-through, Olivia headed backstage. Margot usually camped out in a dressing room, taking sign-ups for line coachings. But today, the dressing rooms had been requisitioned for costume fittings.

The hall that led into the rehearsal room was filled with actors, sporting the various gang uniforms from the movie *The Warriors*. There was a group in striped shirts and denim overalls, another in shiny purple vests and feathered pimp hats, and still another in orange gis.

Peanut stood in front of a mirror in the rehearsal room, staring dejectedly at her reflection. She was wearing a pin-striped baseball uniform, complete with stirrups and matching cap. The costumer pinned the pants to be hemmed below the knee, while Mr. Cunningham looked on appreciatively.

"Why am I dressed like Derek Jeter?" she asked.

Mr. Cunningham made a note on his clipboard. "You're a member of the Baseball Furies gang," he said, without looking up. "Don't you remember the film?"

Peanut grimaced. "Am I going to have to paint my face like a mime?"

"Yep."

Peanut's eyes met Olivia's. "I hope your costume isn't this heinous," she said.

"Sleeveless denim vest and camo pants," Olivia said.

Peanut sighed. "Figures. You'll probably look ridiculously hot in it too."

"Mr. Cunningham," Olivia said, changing the subject. "Do you know where Margot is? I wanted to run the final scene with her."

"She's in my office." Mr. Cunningham looked at her quizzically. "But she told me you didn't need any more coaching."

"She did?"

Mr. Cunningham nodded. "This morning. She told me specifically not to schedule any sessions for you."

"Oh."

Olivia wandered out of the rehearsal room and back into the wings of the theater. Margot clearly did not want to talk to her. And did she blame her? At the end of the day, she'd wounded Margot in a way that did not deserve forgiveness.

"Psst!" someone hissed from the darkened wings behind her. "Olivia."

"Bree?" Olivia said, turning around.

"We need to talk." Bree grabbed Olivia by the arm and

dragged her to the corner, behind the curtain that lined the back wall of the theater.

"We shouldn't be seen together," Olivia said.

Bree snorted. "It's a bit late for that. Did you get another envelope last night?"

Olivia hesitated. Was there any point in keeping it a secret? "Yeah."

"See? Whoever's behind this already knows who we are and how we're connected."

Olivia peeked behind the curtain. "What do you want?"

"It's time we played a little offense," Bree said, her eyes gleaming. "Fight back against whoever's been pulling our strings."

"Fight back?" Olivia dropped her voice. "*Turn yourselves in or else*," she quoted. "What do you think that means, Bree, huh? This guy is a lunatic. He's already killed two people. What makes you think he won't come after one of us next?"

"Don't get hysterical."

"Hysterical? There are cops stationed in every hallway. I was patted down on my way to rehearsal. Father Uberti's getting an armed escort back to the rectory every day after school because they think he might be the next victim." She felt her voice getting higher and higher as the panic set in, but she didn't care. "If the cops can't stop him, what makes you think I can?"

Bree pursed her lips. "I have a plan. All we have to do—"

"We?" Olivia shook her head. "DGM is finished. Besides, what if Margot's right? What if the person sending all those clues is one of us?"

"Do you really believe that?"

Olivia couldn't look Bree in the eye. "I . . . I don't know."

"All I'm saying," Bree continued, "is that we can't let this anonymous tipster go on murdering people. The best way to avoid that 'or else' is to call him out."

"I . . ." Olivia's voice trailed off. She looked around the theater. This was her home; this was the place she felt the most alive. Not with DGM. Once they graduated from high school, all of their missions would be a distant memory, and Olivia's real life of theater could begin.

But she had to get that far.

"I can't," she said at last, stepping out from behind the curtain. "I'm done."

FIFTY-TWO

LOGAN'S VOICE SOUNDED FARAWAY AS HE RECITED THE OPENING of act 2, scene 4.

"Now, good Cesario," he said. "But that piece of song, that old and antique song we heard last night."

"The song" made Margot think of the Bangers and Mosh concert, which made her think of Coach Creed's murder, of Ed the Head and his skeptical attitude toward Logan, of Olivia and how all of Margot's illusions about their friendship had been shattered in one horrid moment.

"Hey," Logan said, placing a hand on her knee. "Are you even listening?"

Margot shook herself, discarding the anger. "Where were you?"

"Never mind." Logan squeezed her knee through her jeans. "I think I'm good enough."

Margot sighed. "I'm sorry. I was—"

"Reliving Sunday night?"

"Yes."

"Look, I'll make it up to you," Logan said quickly, misinterpreting her mood.

This guy could be anyone. Ed the Head's words lingered in her mind.

"Another date," Logan added. "A better date. One without dead bodies."

Margot smiled, despite herself. Coach Creed's death was far from hilarious, but the way Logan was trying to cheer her up made her smile. Like it was his fault someone had been murdered outside the club that night.

"You don't have to," she said, feeling guilty about even suspecting Logan might be involved in the murders. "Take me out again, I mean."

Logan tossed the hair out of his face and leaned closer. "I know I don't have to. I *want* to." He pecked her quickly on the cheek. "I have to be onstage in five. See you at the break?"

Margot was still smiling after he disappeared from the office.

It didn't last long. "Hey, Margot."

Bree leaned against the door frame.

"I have a coaching in five minutes," Margot said coldly.

"Good, then you have four minutes to talk." Bree stepped into the room and closed the door behind her. "Did you get an envelope last night?"

"*Turn yourselves in or else,*" Margot recited. "*You have until opening night.*"

"We need to do something."

Margot shook her head. "What are you talking about?"

"This murderer, whoever it is, is controlling us. Dictating

our actions. He sends us anonymous clues, and we all react. And so far we've been taking it because we were more concerned with keeping our secrets. News flash, this guy already knows our secrets. In fact, he knows things about us no one is supposed to know. Secrets time is over."

Margot stared at a giant promo poster for *Chicago* box-framed on Mr. Cunningham's wall. Bree had a point, however crudely made.

Margot tilted her head to the side. "Where do we start?"

"Why are you calling me?" Kitty snapped before the first ring had been completed. "We have a strict rule against contact by phone."

"Yeah, yeah," Bree said. Why was Kitty so paranoid? They had bigger things to deal with. "Did you get another envelope last night?"

"Obviously," Kitty said. Bree had never heard her so irritated. Kitty was usually the calm one.

"Okay," Bree said, leading her toward what should have been a logical conclusion. "Don't you think we need to talk about it?"

Kitty sighed, a loud, audible grumbling kind of exhale that was meant to transmit annoyance. Message received.

"Margot and I," Bree said quickly, hoping the implication that Margot was with her would capture Kitty's attention, "we think it's time to fight back."

"We've *been* fighting, Bree. We've been fighting the system for two years, and where did it get us? Vilified, hunted, possibly framed for murder, and now targeted by a serial killer."

"What do you want to do, then? Turn yourself in?"

Bree thought that might spur Kitty into action, but as she waited for Kitty to say something, the silence seemed to last an eternity.

Margot's eyebrows pinched together as her lips silently formed the words "what's going on?"

"The most likely answer," Kitty said at last, "is that one of us is behind the envelopes."

"And the murders," Bree said. "That's what you're saying, Kitty. You're saying one of us is a killer."

Again, silence.

So much for their fearless leader. Bree couldn't hide the disappointment in her voice. "I guess we're on our own, then."

"Bree," Kitty said.

"Yeah?"

"Be careful."

Bree clicked off her phone and shoved it back into her pocket. "Kitty's out," she said simply.

"So I gathered."

"You going to bail too?"

She firmly expected Margot to drop out. She'd taken the hardest hit in the last week, reliving the pain of a seventh-grade humiliation so horrific it had driven her to attempt suicide. It made sense if Margot wanted out, and of all of them, Bree wouldn't have blamed her for ejecting.

"Logan," Margot said quietly. "Rex and Amber, Theo, Christopher Beeman, or . . ." She paused and glanced up at Bree.

"Or John," she said. She needed to be open about the

351

possibility, even if she refused to believe he was a suspect.

"Or John," Margot repeated. "Whoever it is, we need to stop them before they kill anyone else."

A wry half smile crept across the right side of Bree's face. She could have hugged Margot. "It'll be hard with just the two of us."

"We'll need help."

"Yeah? You got someone in mind?"

Margot nodded. "Meet me in the computer lab at lunch tomorrow."

FIFTY-THREE

BREE WAS ALL SMILES AS SHE SAUNTERED BACK TO THE theater. Olivia and Kitty might have been out, but at least Margot was willing to fight. It felt so much better to have a plan than to lay low and hope that their anonymous friend would stop killing people and leave them alone. Nope, Bree was taking matters into her own hands. For the first time in days, she was in control. She felt so giddy she practically skipped as she rounded the corner into the back entrance of the theater.

Where she ran smack into John.

"Hey!" she gasped, the wind momentarily knocked out of her.

"Hey."

He was in costume, or at least Bree hoped so. He wore a black biker's vest, completely open with nothing underneath, and low-slung black jeans barely held in place by an enormous silver belt buckle. A leather headband crowned his black hair, making him look like a cross between Tonto and Jimi Hendrix, and his wrists were bound with matching leather cufflets.

"How are you?" Bree said. She tried to keep her eyes on his face, but they kept drifting south. Despite two years of friendship, she'd never seen John with his shirt off. Though skinny, he was more muscular than Bree would have guessed based on his almost total lack of physical exertion, and there was a trail of dark brown hair below his belly button that disappeared into the hip-slung pants, igniting an absolutely inappropriate feeling deep within her.

"I'm good," he said. "And you?"

Bree forced herself to focus. John was a suspect. She had to remember. "Good."

John turned to leave. "Yeah, well, I've got to get back to the dressing room."

"John, I think we need to talk."

He paused, but didn't face her. "About what?"

About what? That was such a loaded question. Bree had about a million things she wanted to talk to him about, but all she could manage was—

"Stuff."

Stuff? Really? Bree's face burned.

"Stuff? Really?" John asked.

Damn, was he inside her head?

Bree opened her mouth to clarify her brilliant statement, but no words came out. She was desperately trying to keep her eyes above John's equator, failing miserably, and her brain was getting all jumbled in the process.

What is wrong with you?

"Look," John said with a heavy sigh. "What do you want,

Bree, huh? Do you want things to be like they were between us? Because that isn't going to happen."

"Why not?"

"Because things have changed. Can't you see that?"

"What's changed? You're still my best friend in the whole world. Hell, you're my only friend." It felt so pathetic when she said it out loud like that.

"I'm not your only friend," John said quietly. Something about the icy calmness in his voice caught her off guard.

"What do you mean?"

Instead of answering, John shook his head. "You accuse me of keeping secrets from you, Bree. But are you any better? Haven't you been doing the exact same thing?"

Bree swallowed. "I don't know what you're talking about," she said automatically. She'd lied about DGM for so long it was second nature.

John turned away. "I can't do this anymore."

Bree clutched his hand. She felt like she was losing him forever, and the panic almost blinded her. "I'll be a better friend, John. I promise."

"I don't want a better friend."

"Huh?"

John set his jaw. "And I can't be your consolation prize."

What a mess. Something had changed, shifted in her brain and her heart. But how could she even explain that to John if she wasn't sure what it was?

"I care about you," she said.

Dear God, that sounded lame.

John looked at his hand still clasped in her own; then his eyes traveled up her arm to her face. She gazed into his eyes, framed by that ridiculous seventies headband. He wasn't her geeky best friend anymore. He was something more. Something she'd been yearning for without even knowing it.

"You care," John said softly. "But not enough."

"That's not true!" Bree blurted out. "I—"

"John!" Amber came tearing up the aisle into the lobby. Like John, she was in costume. Also a seventies monstrosity, but significantly more on the streetwalker side. She wore high-waisted short shorts with a white patent leather belt and a pink, midriff-exposing halter top that tied together between her boobs. Her sky-high crushed-velvet platform sandals made her lean legs look about ten miles long.

"John," she repeated, grabbing him possessively by the arm without even a glance in Bree's direction. "I've been looking for you."

John didn't shake her off. "What's up?"

"Mr. Cunningham wants to sign off on your costume." She leaned back and scanned him from tip to toe. "If you want my opinion," she added, "meow."

"Ew." Bree couldn't help herself. The idea of Amber looking at John with anything even resembling a sexual interest made Bree want to throw up.

Amber casually looked Bree up and down, assessing her outfit. "Wow," she said with a laugh. "Thrift-store dress *and* jeans? Couldn't make up your mind this morning?"

Bree curled her lip. "It's so I can be stylish *and* comfortable when I kick your ass."

"Stylish?" Amber said, her hand languidly stroking John's arm. "Try again."

Instead of coming to her defense, John turned toward the theater. "I'll talk to you later, Bree," he said. Then he marched back down the aisle with Amber hanging off him like tinsel on a Christmas tree.

Bree watched them go, John's words from Sunday night ringing in her ears. *After tonight, nothing will be the same.*

He'd been right on more levels than perhaps he'd known at the time. She realized with a stabbing pain somewhere between her heart and her spleen that if Amber was all over the new rockstar version of John, then half the girls in school would be too. He was no longer Baggott the Faggot, but one of the cool kids. Like Shane. And it was only a matter of time before he forgot about Bree entirely.

Bree bit her bottom lip to keep it from quivering. Just when she realized that John was more than a friend, she'd lost him forever, and she'd have to stand idly by at school while he dated someone else—Cordy or God forbid Amber—and pretend like it wasn't ripping her heart to pieces.

Worst of all, it was entirely her fault. She'd spent so much time denying that there was anything between them, ignoring the very real connection she felt with John because she'd labeled him as a friend. She'd hurt him in the process, and now he could never forgive her.

Bree swallowed and took a deep breath, forcing the self-pity back to the depths of her mind. There was one thing she could do, one way she could still protect John, even if he was lost to her forever.

Find the killer before he struck again.

FIFTY-FOUR

ED THE HEAD CROSSED ONE FOOT OVER HIS KNEE AND LEANED forward, resting his pointy chin on his hand. "Tell me again why I'm giving up my lunch, the most profitable fifty-five minutes of my day, to be holed up in the computer lab with you?"

"After all the money I've made for you in the past year," Margot said, organizing papers on the desk in front of her, "I'd think you'd be elated to do me a favor."

"I already *did* you a favor, remember? And you stiffed me on payment."

Margot thought of Logan, eating lunch in the quad by himself. "It's not a concert," she said with a shrug. "But consider this a lunch date."

Ed the Head stretched his legs in front of him. "I guess it'll do in a pinch."

Margot had had a difficult time lying to Logan about why she needed to be someplace else at lunch. But with the opening of *Twelfth Precinct* in just over twenty-four hours, Don't Get Mad was running out of time. She and Bree had to act immediately if they were going to prevent another murder, and she didn't want to get Logan involved in what they were about to do. It was too dangerous.

"Are we waiting on someone?" Ed the Head asked. "Or are you just relishing my presence too much to get down to business?"

"Ha, ha."

"Because if you don't have anything for me," he said, rising to his feet, "then I am considerably out of here."

As if on cue, there was a knock at the computer lab door. Margot threw the bolt and Bree slipped inside.

She did a double take at the sight of Ed the Head. "This is your contingency plan?" she asked.

Margot shrugged. "You said we needed help. I got us help."

"Can we trust him?"

"For a price."

Ed the Head raised his hand as if waiting to be called on by the teacher. "Hello? In the room!"

Despite her usually rabid concern for safety, security, and secrecy, for whatever reason Margot trusted Ed the Head. He had no love for the administration at Bishop DuMaine, and besides, they weren't actually revealing DGM's secrets to him—just tasking him with some information discovery.

"I trust him," Margot said.

Bree nodded. "Good enough for me." She pulled a manila envelope out of her bag and slapped it on the table.

Ed the Head's eyes grew wide. "You got one too?"

"Yep," Bree said, offering no explanation.

Ed the Head eyed the envelope. "You, Margot, Olivia. What is it the three of you have in common?"

Margot stared at him coldly. "That's not important, Edward."

He cocked an eyebrow. "You sure about that? Could it possibly be three little letters known as DG—"

"What's important," Bree said, interrupting him, "is that there's a killer on the loose and what's in this envelope could be the key to stopping it."

Ed the Head nodded. "Proceed."

Bree took a deep breath. "Let me tell you a story about a boy named Christopher Beeman."

Olivia sat in the back of the house, watching Amber and Donté on the stage. The final dress rehearsal was in just a few hours, and Amber was still stumbling over her words every few lines. As much as Olivia secretly wanted Amber to fall on her face onstage, she didn't want the show to suffer as a result. But at this rate, it would take another month of rehearsals to get Amber up to par.

Soon all of Olivia's dreams could be coming true. Or blowing up in her face.

Maybe she'd been too hasty when she shot Bree down? Whoever had been sending the envelopes was clearly on to them, and Bree had a point. If they just sat around and waited for something to happen, they were giving this person all the power. Striking back at least meant they weren't giving up.

Still, if they got caught, Olivia faced expulsion, arrest, prosecution for murder, juvie. She wasn't sure which was worse at this point. No, she had to be selfish right now. She had to focus on herself and her performance tomorrow night. Her entire future was riding on it.

Olivia's phone buzzed. She had an email.

She picked up her phone, and froze the moment she saw the sent-by address: DGM@bishopdumaine.edu.

Olivia opened the email and realized it had been sent through the all-school email system, which meant that every student, teacher, and administrator had just gotten the same message.

> You had us at an unfair advantage, knowing so much about us when we knew nothing about you.
>
> Now, we've evened the playing field. It's our turn to dictate terms.
>
> We know who you are, and we know what you've done.
>
> We'll keep your secret as long as you keep ours. And if anything happens to us—or anyone else—all bets are off. Get it?

Had Bree and Margot just called out a killer?

Margot exhaled slowly and closed the lid to her laptop. It was done, the email sent.

"And that went to everyone?" Bree asked.

Margot had only explained this to her about twenty times.

"I hacked into the main contact database," she said once again. "Everyone at school got that email."

Bree grinned. "Then I'm sure our friend got it too. Do you think he'll buy it?"

Margot shook her head. "I'd say there's only about a forty-five percent chance."

"Crap."

It was a bluff, of course. But they had to buy some time so Ed the Head could work his magic.

"Still," Margot said slowly. "It'll give him pause. Whoever this is, cockiness drives him. A belief that he's a step ahead of us all the time. If this email shakes that confidence even a little, it should give us enough time to actually find out who's behind it, and gather some evidence that links him to both murders."

"I hope Ed the Head comes through."

"He will," Margot said. She'd assigned Ed the task of tracking down any and all information about Christopher Beeman. All roads seemed to lead to him, just like the list Bree had found in Ronny's room: Theo, Rex, Coach Creed, and Ronny were all connected to Christopher.

"Guess we'll just have to wait and see," Bree said, rising to her feet.

The dressing room door flew open and Olivia burst into the room. "What did you do?"

"Saved our asses," Bree said.

"But you just emailed the entire school!"

"They'll think it's another prank," Margot said. She couldn't even look at Olivia.

"Oh." Olivia plopped down in the empty chair and stared at the floor. "You were right, you know. About fighting back. Sorry I was such a wuss."

"Not the first time," Bree said.

The room fell silent. Out of the corner of her eye, Margot caught Bree making eyes at Olivia, nodding in Margot's direction.

"Right," Olivia said to Bree's unspoken comment. She swallowed, then shifted her chair to face Margot. "I'm sorry, Margot. I know you can't ever forgive me for what I did, but I want you to know that I'll spend the rest of my life trying to make it up to you."

Margot wanted to hate Olivia. And right up until that moment, she truly thought she did. But maybe too much time had passed. Maybe Margot was in a happier place in her life. Maybe she realized that Olivia had also been one of Amber's victims. Whatever the cause, as Olivia stared at her, pleading silently with her enormous blue eyes, Margot realized that despite the tremendous sense of betrayal, she didn't hate Olivia. And she was ready to forgive.

On one condition.

"Tell Kitty she can date Donté," Margot said.

"What?" Olivia asked.

"Tell her you want them both to be happy. That's how you can make it up to me."

"Really?" Olivia glanced at Bree. "That's it?"

Margot raised an eyebrow. "You have to mean it."

Olivia stared at her for a moment, then nodded slowly. "Okay."

As if on cue, the tall figure of Kitty slipped inside the dressing room.

"What did you do?" she asked, panting. She wore her workout clothes from volleyball practice, complete with knee pads.

"Took matters into our own hands," Bree said.

With a determined nod, Olivia sprang to her feet, head thrown back, and hugged Kitty fiercely. "I forgive you," she said dramatically.

Kitty stood there in shock, Olivia's arms still wrapped around her midsection. "What did you guys do to her?"

Bree laughed. "I think she's trying to apologize. Right, Olivia?"

"Yes!" Olivia squeaked into Kitty's stomach. "I'm sorry I was a bitch the other night." She pulled back and embraced Kitty's shoulders. "I want you and Donté to be happy and get married and make babies. Okay? I really, truly mean it."

Margot hid her smile. Leave it to Olivia to go completely overboard.

"Okay." Kitty leaned back against the door. "I've got ten minutes till I need to be back in practice. You guys want to fill me in on the plan?"

"Gladly," Margot said.

The gang was back together.

FIFTY-FIVE

MARGOT TRIED TO MAKE HERSELF COMFORTABLE IN THE
prompter's box.

It was actually a corner of the stage left wing, set up with a
stool and a music stand, complete with a small light shuttered
and caulked with electrical tape so that the only direction the
meager beam could shine was directly on Margot's copy of the
script.

There had been an alarming number of slipups and missteps
during last night's dress rehearsal, and though Mr. Cunningham
assured the cast that "a bad dress rehearsal foretells a grand opening night," Margot couldn't help but worry about her ability to
keep the actors on the script.

Especially since she was having her own focus issues.

She checked her phone approximately every one hundred
and twenty seconds. She couldn't help herself. Ed the Head had
sent her one tantalizing text around lunch time and had then
gone incommunicado.

He was supposed to dig into Christopher and Ronny's past at

Archway Military Academy and hopefully find a clue that would shed some light on the killer's identity. But she never guessed he would go above and beyond, and his text had caught her off guard.

Hi, Sunshine! Don't wait up for me. Had to take a field trip to Arizona.
Be back in time for the big show tonight.
Have a surprise for you that you'll never see coming.

All her follow-up texts to him had been left unanswered, all her calls went straight to voice mail.

Based on the speed limit, current traffic and road conditions, the reliability rating on Ed the Head's 2008 hatchback, and the personal reliability rating Margot had assigned to him based on their years of acquaintance, Ed the Head still should have hit the Bay Area an hour ago with the information he'd managed to dig up at Archway. Could he possibly have discovered the identity of the killer? Would they be able to put an end to the ordeal once and for all?

The rest of the girls clearly thought so. After Margot had briefed them, Bree had sent her a text approximately every thirty minutes, asking if she'd heard from Ed.

No, Bree. If I did, I'd have told you.

Another buzz from the music stand as a text came into her phone. Margot sighed as she picked it up. "Yes, Bree. I know," she said out loud. "You want to know if—"

In Gilroy. Refueling. Should hit DuMaine in an hour. Meet you at the theater.

Bring your big girl panties because you aren't going to believe what I've got.

Ed the Head. Finally.

Margot replied right away, typing as quickly as her virtual keyboard would process.

Meet us backstage. Prompter's corner, stage left.

She was about to text Bree with the good news when she felt someone's breath against the back of her neck. For an instant, she tensed, then she heard Logan whisper in her ear.

"You're going to be amazing tonight," he said.

Margot smiled as she spun around on her stool. Logan wore the same tight-fitting black jeans as the other members of the count's gang, and through his low scoop-neck tank, Margot could still see the contours of his surfer's body. Over that, he wore a silk brocade dressing gown, indicating his leadership.

"Aren't I supposed to be saying that to you?" Margot asked.

Logan winked. "I've done this before."

"And I'm the rookie?"

"Exactly." He sidled up to the stool and placed both hands around Margot's waist. "So . . ." He kissed her, sending a shock of electricity racing through her body. When he pulled away, she leaned into him, desperate to keep his lips against her own. "Have a great show. I'll see you on the flip side."

Bree was starting to despair, when she finally got the text from Margot.

> He'll be here in an hour.

She wasn't sure if she was going to hug Ed the Head when she saw him, or throttle him. Probably depended on what kind of information he brought back from Arizona.

Either way, they finally had a leg up on the killer. In an hour, they might actually know who they were dealing with, hopefully with enough evidence that they could turn him over to the police and exonerate Don't Get Mad once and for all.

At least, she hoped so.

The frazzled voice of the stage manager buzzed through her earpiece. "Five minutes. We're at five minutes, everyone."

Bree pressed talk on the headset. "Five minutes, thank you."

They just had to get through this performance.

Olivia let out a tremendous sigh as she read Margot's text.

> Good to go. Break a leg.

Ed the Head had come through. With any luck, by the end of the evening Olivia would have an internship with the Oregon

Shakespeare Festival and a captured killer to her credit. Not too shabby.

"More shading under your cheekbones," her mom said, scrutinizing Olivia's face in the mirror.

"The theater's not that big, Mom," Olivia said. "I don't want to look like a drag queen."

"Don't you think I know how big the theater is?" Her mom sat back down, pouting. "Haven't I been to every single performance you've given at this school?"

Yes, you have. Without a word, Olivia picked up the contour brush and added several additional swipes of the dark beige powder below her cheekbones. It wasn't worth the argument.

"So much better." Her mom blew her a kiss. "Shall we go over your blocking for the duel again?"

Olivia turned around to face her mother. "Honestly, Mom, I'm good. I know it backward and forward."

Her mom raised an eyebrow. "Even the final scene?"

"Even the final scene."

Her mom sighed, then grasped Olivia's hand and squeezed it. "You know I just want you to be perfect."

"I know." Of course it was easier just to give in to her mom, but all she could think about was the pack of Ding Dongs in her bag, which she planned to bust into the second her mom left the dressing room.

Her mom straightened Olivia's pleather vest. "My own *Twelfth Night* meant so much to me . . ." Her voice trailed off and Olivia wondered if her mom was going to launch into her favorite scene from act 2 yet again. Instead, she gripped Olivia by

370

both shoulders and smiled.

"Your career is just beginning, Livvie," her mom said, oddly serious. "So much promise. I remember—"

A knock at the door interrupted her mom's reminiscence.

"Hello?" Mr. Cunningham cooed. He cracked the door and stuck his head into the dressing room. "Everyone decent?"

"Reginald!" Olivia's mom squealed.

Mr. Cunningham threw the door open and genuflected before Olivia's mom. "June! My mistress, dearest; And I thus humble ever," he said, breaking into Shakespeare's *The Tempest*.

Olivia's mom didn't miss a beat. "My husband, then?"

"Ay," Mr. Cunningham said solemnly. "With a heart as willing as bondage e'er of freedom: here's my love."

"My *hand*," someone corrected from the hallway. His tones were round and mellifluous. "Ferdinand's line is 'here's my hand.'"

A short, stocky man stepped into the doorway. He had a shock of white hair, close-cropped above the ears and tapered upward to allow the thick waves some space to poof up in a semi-obvious attempt to give him more height. He wore a black turtleneck under a black sports jacket, both loose but not ill-fitting, and pointy leather shoes, polished to within an inch of their lives.

"Fitzgerald!" Mr. Cunningham squeaked.

Olivia's breaths came more rapidly. This was *the* Fitzgerald Conroy!

Mr. Cunningham scrambled to his feet. "Sorry. I got carried away."

Mr. Conroy's eyes were fixed on Olivia's mom. "As one would with such a lovely creature." He sidestepped Mr. Cunningham. "Fitzgerald Conroy," he said, his eyes locked on to hers. "At your service."

Olivia was shocked to see the color drain out of her mother's face. She looked as if she'd seen a ghost, and her hand trembled as Fitzgerald raised it to his lips.

"Fitzgerald, let me introduce Ms. June Hayes," Mr. Cunningham said, oblivious to Olivia's mom's discomfort. "Her daughter, Olivia, is starring in our production tonight, ironically as Viola."

Fitzgerald tilted his head to the side. "June Hayes?"

"Livvie," her mom said hurriedly, "I really should find my seat for the performance." She tried to extricate herself from Fitzgerald's grasp, but he held her hand firm as he scrutinized her face.

"Public Theater," he said at last, bobbing his head. "Summer 1997. You were my Olivia in *Twelfth Night*."

Olivia's jaw dropped. Fitzgerald Conroy had directed her mom's production of *Twelfth Night*? Why hadn't she ever mentioned it?

Fitzgerald pulled Olivia's mom closer to him. "You were magnificent."

"Yes," her mom said, blushing up to her hairline. She looked flustered as she scurried out the door. "Well, I'll see you all after the performance. Break a leg, Livvie."

Fitzgerald's eyes followed Olivia's mom out of the room. Then he seemed to remember Olivia. "If you're half as good as your mother," he said, his piercing blue eyes boring into her own, "then I'm very much looking forward to tonight."

Kitty slipped into the seat next to Mika and tried to keep her hand from trembling as she read the front of the program. *Tonight's performance is dedicated to the loving memory of Ronald DeStefano.*

And in his loving memory, they were about to unmask his killer.

Mika eyed her for a moment, then laughed. "I'd think *you* were the one making your stage debut, not Donté."

"Sorry," Kitty said sheepishly.

"He's going to be fine," Mika said, misinterpreting Kitty's nerves. "Tonight is going to be perfect."

The lights dimmed, signaling the beginning of the performance, and Shane White, John Baggott, and the other members of Bangers and Mosh slipped out from behind the curtain, taking their places at their instruments in front of the proscenium on stage left. Once they were in place, the lights faded to black.

Kitty took a deep, controlled breath. "I hope you're right."

FIFTY-SIX

"YOUR MASTER QUITS YOU," LOGAN SAID, TAKING OLIVIA'S character by the hand. "And for your service done him, so much against the mettle of your sex . . ."

Margot didn't need to look at the script during Orsino's pen-ultimate speech. Logan had never so much as stumbled over a line, let alone forgotten one, which meant she got to pay close attention to his performance, instead of hovering over the lines in the prompter's corner.

He looked down at Olivia during that speech with so much love and tenderness it made Margot's heart ache. Logan was amazing: smart, funny, talented. Margot still didn't understand what he saw in her.

She flipped to the last page of the play as the actors prepared for the final musical number. Opening night was almost over, and no one had been attacked. Perhaps their bluff had worked?

Now they just had to figure out who they were dealing with, and gather enough evidence to turn him over to the police. She wondered what Ed had found out about Christopher Beeman that had made him so excited. Margot's eyes drifted to Logan onstage, leading Olivia through the final dance sequence, smiling out at the audience. Suddenly, his face clouded, the smile replaced by a cross between confusion and fear, as if he'd seen something in the house that disturbed him.

The choreography shifted and Logan disappeared from her view. That nagging doubt about Logan flared up. Was it her logical brain telling her that Logan was the best candidate to be Christopher Beeman? Or was it her insecurity trying to sabotage her new relationship?

A creak from behind her broke Margot's concentration. She spun around in her stool, but there was no one behind her. Clearly, thinking about a killer had made her paranoid, jumping at each and every sound.

She turned back to the stage. The play was almost finished and no one had been attacked. DGM had won.

Another creak. Closer this time.

Margot turned her head in time to see a dark shadow lunge at her.

As the final strains of the last Bangers and Mosh song faded into the heights of the theater, the applause washed over Olivia like sunshine piercing through the grayness on a cloudy day. She and Logan held their final pose from the dance finale for a count of three, then along with the rest of the cast, they lined up, hand in hand, across the stage for a group bow before breaking in the center and opening the stage for their individual curtain calls.

Olivia felt as if she'd emerged from a dream. From her first entrance until the final applause exploded throughout the house, Olivia's memories were hazy and indistinct, as if they'd passed by her eyes on the opposite side of a foggy lens.

The band jammed on a reprise of the final song as one by one the cast members cycled through their individual bows. It had been a bone of contention at the final dress rehearsal as to who got the last bow. Usually it was reserved for the character with the largest role in the play, in the case of *Twelfth Precinct*, clearly Violent. But as with everything else in this production, Amber had pulled a variety of strings, and with a rambling explanation that no one quite understood, Mr. Cunningham had informed the cast that Amber would be getting the final bow, with Olivia directly preceding.

The audience was clapping along with the beat of the music, crescendoing politely as each cast member took their turn. Logan got a nice round of cheers and whistles, which made Olivia smile. He'd given a tremendous performance, one that actually made Olivia's better, and she was glad the crowd recognized it.

Then it was her turn.

There was always a part of Olivia that expected crickets when she took center stage under the spotlight, that never assumed she'd touched the audience in the way that she'd hoped and would therefore be booed off the stage for her lackluster performance.

So when the audience vaulted to their feet for Olivia's curtain call, her eyes welled up with tears. She bowed as a boy, since she was still in her boy's costume, and took the opportunity to wipe the tear streaks from her cheeks.

Then she relinquished the stage to Amber, who swept in like an opera diva at the Met, and brandished her arm over her head before sinking into a deep curtsy.

Olivia noticed right away that though the crowd remained standing, their reception was politely enthusiastic at best.

Mr. Cunningham glided onto the stage, taking Amber and Olivia each by the hand to present them for one last bow. He led Amber forward first; the nasty look she shot him over her shoulder adequately expressed how she felt about that. Then with a wink, he brought Olivia forward.

The reaction was instantaneous. The applause, the whistles. In that moment it didn't matter if Fitzgerald Conroy chose to work with her or not.

Olivia had already won.

Bree almost felt bad for Amber. She'd given a good performance, based on what Bree had seen in rehearsals, especially considering her notorious inability to remember her lines. Olivia, on the other hand, had literally stolen the show. Bree didn't know shit about acting, but she knew watching Olivia under the lights that she was in the presence of something special. Whatever damage had gone down between them, Bree could say without prejudice that Olivia was an amazing actress.

As Olivia finished her second bow, a short older guy, dressed all in black with blindingly white hair, took the stage. This must have been the British director everyone had been drooling over since the start of production. He approached Olivia and took her hand, pressing it to his lips.

Even from Bree's vantage point way up in the spotlight crow's nest, she could see Amber turning bright red, a mix of embarrassment and rage. She stormed off the stage, much to the amazement of the rest of the cast, but Mr. Cunningham didn't even bat an eyelash. He joined hands with Olivia and brought the cast together for another group bow, then gestured to the band.

Shane's fist shot into the air, while Bangers and Mosh continued to jam. John didn't look up, just focused on his Fender, but even he couldn't ignore the riotous applause. His songs had been perfect, his performance immaculate.

Mr. Cunningham now started throwing nonverbal shout-outs to the crew, pointing to the stage manager, the lighting booth, even Bree in the crow's nest, while the music and applause continued. In the end, Olivia, Shane, and John had all gotten what they wanted. Even Bree, in her way. She'd managed to keep their anonymous friend from ruining opening night. Now she just had to make sure—

A scream ripped through the theater.

FIFTY-SEVEN

KITTY ROCKETED TO HER FEET THE INSTANT SHE HEARD THE
scream. It wasn't a cry of triumph but of fear, and as the actors
milled around onstage, trying to figure out what was going on,
Mr. Cunningham marched into the wings.

He was back onstage in a split second. "We need a doctor
backstage immediately. There's been an accident!"

Accident? No way. Nothing that had happened in the last
few weeks had been an accident.

"Where are you going?" Mika said, grabbing Kitty's hand.
"You're not a doctor."

Kitty shook her off without a word. She was safe, Olivia was
onstage, Bree was in the back of the house manning a spotlight.
That left only one person unaccounted for.

Turn yourselves in or else. You have until opening night.

Kitty's stomach clenched. She'd assumed the "or else" was
that their secrets would go public, or their roles in DGM would
be exposed. But could the killer have meant something more
ominous?

The cast had gathered in the wings as Kitty sprinted up the steps at the far side of the stage.

"Margot?" Logan cried. "Margot, can you hear me?"

Kitty's stomach dropped as she approached the crowd. Logan was on his knees beside Margot's unconscious body, grasping her hands in his. A stool and music stand had been knocked over, and a pool of blood had formed beneath her head. From where she stood, Kitty couldn't tell whether Margot was breathing.

"The paramedics will be here any second," Mr. Cunningham said, taking Logan by the shoulders. "Let them do their job."

Logan's face shot up. Tears streaked his stage makeup. "Who would do this? Who would want to hurt her?"

Kitty wished she knew.

Olivia stood behind Mr. Cunningham, her arms wrapped tightly around her body as if trying to protect herself from what was happening. She looked up and found Kitty in the crowd. The look on Olivia's face was unmistakably helpless.

Bree was the last to arrive, her face a mix of pain and guilt. Kitty couldn't even comfort them; she was totally and completely at a loss.

She stood there in shock with the rest of the cast until the paramedics arrived. The good news: no body bag, which meant Margot was still alive, for now. The bad news: they hustled her out on a gurney faster than she'd seen in most medical trauma shows on TV, which meant Margot was in critical condition.

"Will she be okay?" Logan asked the last paramedic as he followed the gurney off the stage.

"I don't know yet, son. Only time will tell."

Logan and Mr. Cunningham hurried after the paramedics, followed by some of the cast members. As the crowd thinned, Kitty found herself staring at the stricken faces of Bree and Olivia. They were lost. Scared. They needed a leader.

And that was Kitty's job.

She nodded toward the wings and dashed to a corner of backstage, obscured by set pieces and curtains.

"This is my fault," Kitty said as soon as Bree and Olivia joined her. She wasn't so much looking for someone to contradict her, but saying the words out loud made them real, and steeled her for what she needed to do next.

"Did you attack Margot?" Bree asked.

Kitty rolled her eyes. "Of course not."

"Then I don't know how this is your fault."

"We all know," Olivia said, between sniffles, "that this is *my* fault."

Bree sighed. "How do you figure?"

"Well." Olivia paused, thinking through her reasoning, then seemed to come to a conclusion that pleased her. "It's my fault she joined Don't Get Mad in the first place," Olivia said, sounding very satisfied with her argument. "If it wasn't for me, she never would have been involved."

"If I hadn't started Don't Get Mad," Kitty said, "she never would have gotten involved."

"Oh, come on, guys." Bree stepped in front of them. "If her parents hadn't birthed her, if God hadn't rested on the seventh day. It's ridiculous. None of us are to blame for what happened to Margot. We all knew the risks."

"You shouldn't have taunted our anonymous friend," Olivia said. "I told you it was a bad idea."

Bree set her teeth. "At least I *did* something. If it had been up to you two, we'd have sat around and let that guy turn us against each other while he continued killing people. I'm sorry, but I wasn't going to let that happen."

"That's hilarious, coming from you," Olivia said.

Olivia and Bree and their endless bickering. Kitty couldn't take it anymore.

"Bree was right," Kitty said. "We should all have been in it together from the beginning. We let that asshole tear us apart. And this is what happened." She squeezed her eyes shut and pictured Margot speeding away toward an emergency room, her status and chances unknown. "We should have been a team on this one. I'm sorry."

Bree looked taken aback by the apology. "It's okay," she said, all the fight gone out of her.

Kitty's eyes flew open. "Tell that to Margot."

The girls stared silently at one another as an ambulance siren faded into the distance.

"Any word from Ed the Head?" Kitty asked.

"Nope," Bree said. "His cell phone goes straight to voice mail."

"And you have no idea what it was he found in Arizona?"

Bree shook her head. "I wish."

"Do you think he's the killer?" Olivia asked.

"It's possible," Kitty said.

"But I've known Ed since fourth grade," Olivia said. "He

can't be Christopher Beeman."

"But he could have known about Christopher," Kitty said. "And used that knowledge to throw us off the scent." She sighed. "I'd say at this point, we can more definitively say who *isn't* the killer."

"Oh," Olivia said.

Bree nodded. "You were onstage, I was manning the spotlight, Kitty was in the house."

"And Logan was onstage with me," Olivia added.

"And John was playing with the band," Bree said quickly. "Which leaves Theo and Rex unaccounted for."

"And Amber," Kitty said. "She stormed off the stage before Margot's body was found."

"Or," Bree added, shifting her feet, "someone totally off our radar." She shook her head. "Whoever it is, the killer is still out there."

"And coming for us," Olivia added.

Kitty turned to them. "Not necessarily."

Olivia looked confused. "What do you mean? Do you think he'll just give up?"

"No." Kitty set her jaw. She was the team leader. It was up to her to make the tough decisions and, if need be, the sacrifices. "I think he'll give up if one of us turns ourselves in."

Bree held up her hands in front of her. "Kitty, no way."

"What are you talking about?" Olivia asked.

"You can't do this," Bree continued.

Olivia looked from Bree to Kitty and back. "You want us to turn ourselves in?"

Bree stared at her. "No, Olivia," she said slowly, as if speaking to a child. "She wants to turn herself in."

Olivia gasped. "But your college scholarship!"

"It is what it is," Kitty said. "I started this with Don't Get Mad. Now, I end it." She turned to Bree and stuck out her hand. "It's been a pleasure having you on my team."

Bree opened her mouth to say something, thought better of it, and took Kitty's outstretched hand. "Thank you for putting up with me."

Olivia threw her arms around Kitty's neck. "Don't do this. There has to be another way."

"There isn't."

"But—"

Kitty pried herself loose. "I won't give them your names, so don't worry. I'll go to Father Uberti in the morning and confess. Just do me a favor."

"Anything," Olivia said impulsively.

"Don't give up." Then Kitty turned and marched out of the theater before either of them could convince her otherwise.

She prayed she'd have the strength to go through with it.

FIFTY-EIGHT

THE SURPRISE ALL-SCHOOL ASSEMBLY THE NEXT MORNING was less "surprise" and more "duh" as far as Bree was concerned. Actually, as far as the entire school was concerned. No one in first-period religion even unpacked their bags; they just waited for the perpetually flustered Sister Augustinia to make the announcement before they lined up and filed into the gym.

She passed Olivia in the bleachers. She was nervous, Bree could tell right away. She was biting her lower lip with a savagery that threatened to take off a layer of perfectly pink skin. Olivia was paler than usual too, with purple circles under her eyes that indicated how little sleep she'd gotten the night before.

John walked behind Bree in line, slow and steady, and shimmied onto the bench next to her. She wanted to breach the hideous silence that had descended between them. But what would she say? Sorry I've been such an idiot? I know I've lost my chance with you, but I hope you don't hate me? It all sounded hollow and pointless and lame.

The gym was electric, but not in the same chattery way it

had been on the first week of school when a similar assembly had played out. Today it was more like the entire student body was tensed, preparing for a punch in the face. No one more so than Bree.

It was surreal, in a way. Total déjà vu—Mr. Phillips setting up the microphone, the cadre of police officers, Father Uberti and members of the administration huddled together in conversation. Bree sat in practically the same row, John by her side, with the same knots in her stomach. And yet the world had changed so drastically in the last few weeks as to make the gym almost unrecognizable, and the excitement Bree had felt then had been replaced by sickening dread.

Bree spotted Kitty as soon as they took their seats. She was standing near Father Uberti, her hands clasped before her. Bree wondered when she planned to turn herself in.

Father Uberti left the school officials and approached the police officers for a quick chat. Looked like things were about to get hopping. Bree slipped her cell phone out of her pocket and looked at the prewritten text she had prepared. Yep, that would do nicely.

"If everyone would quiet down and take their seats," Father Uberti said. The announcement was needless. Every butt was on a bench, every mouth was closed, every set of eyes trained on the microphone.

"Good," he said. "Before we begin today, our student body vice president, Kitty Wei, has asked to say a few words."

Shit. She was going to do it right this freaking second. *It's now or never.* Bree hit Send on her phone, and sent two little words barreling out into the cybersphere.

My turn.

"What are you doing?" John whispered.

But Bree ignored him. She watched Kitty with bated breath, registered the moment her phone vibrated in her pocket, the instant she decided to see what it was.

"Kitty?" Father Uberti said, none too patiently. "We're waiting."

Then, the moment Bree had been waiting for. The moment Kitty realized what Bree was about to do.

Olivia turned around at the exact instant Bree shot to her feet.

"Don't!" Olivia cried out. But it was too late.

Bree shouted into the silent gym. "I'm the one you're looking for. I'm DGM."

The entire gym pressed in on her at once. Voices shouted—some angry, some congratulatory, all extremely loud.

"You crazy bitch."

"I knew it was you!"

"Way to go."

"Free DGM! Free Bree!"

Bree felt her body being jostled in every direction as people reached out and patted her on the back. Didn't they believe she was a killer?

Then Olivia's face, tears streaming down her gorgeous cheeks. "Why?" she mouthed.

But Bree just smiled. She had the least to lose, and Kitty had said it herself: this was the only way. Mr. Anonymous would be satisfied. For now.

Fingers laced between her own, and Bree turned to find John looking down at her. "Why didn't you tell me?"

"I couldn't," she said, desperately hoping he wouldn't hate her forever. "It was too dangerous for you to know."

"But . . ." His voice trailed off and Bree watched as weeks of emotion cycled rapidly across his face—anger, frustration, sadness, pride, understanding. "Your dad won't bail you out this time," he said at last. "You'll be on your own."

"I know."

Then he pulled her to him as the police pushed their way into the bleachers, enveloping her fiercely with his arms as if he'd never let her go. "I know you didn't kill them," he whispered in her ear.

Several pairs of strong arms pried her away from John, but she hardly felt them. The only thing in the world was John's body pressed tightly against her own, as she gazed up into his eyes.

"Bree Deringer," an officer said. "You are under arrest for the murders of Ronald DeStefano and Richard Creed." They wrenched her from John's arms, but her eyes never left his face. There was so much she wanted to say, so much she needed him to know. Her Miranda rights faded into the background as they pinned her arms behind her back and handcuffed her. Still, all she could think about was John.

"I love you," she said.

John stared at her silently, then a grin spread across his face. Lopsided and wicked, and every inch Han Solo. "I know."

She smiled as the police led her away. John had been right all along.

Nothing would be the same.

DGM

ACKNOWLEDGMENTS

There is a reason *Get Even* is dedicated to my agent, Ginger Clark, and editor, Kristin Daly Rens. These two amazing women are the reason *Get Even* exists. They've supported me, encouraged me, and fought for me every step of my career. They dose out tough love and shiny praise as needed, and their enthusiasm and encouragement inspires confidence, even when I have none. I am truly the luckiest of authors.

Of course, it takes a village to make a book, and I am indebted to the following people:

To my Balzer + Bray/HarperCollins team—Alessandra Balzer, Donna Bray, Kelsey Murphy, Caroline Sun, Olivia deLeon, Stefanie Hoffman, Emilie Polster, Michelle Taormina, and Melinda Weigel.

To the rock stars at Curtis Brown, Ltd.—Jonathan Lyons, Holly Frederick, Sarah Perillo, and Kerry D'Agostino.

To the hardest working book blogger/marketing guru around Amber Sweeney, who single-handedly managed all of my giveaway and promo efforts. I literally could not do this without you.

To Laurel Proctor Jones, without whose mad beta skills this book would still be a series of note cards scattered across my living room floor.

To my Bacon Sisters—Elana Johnson, Stasia Ward Kehoe, Jessi Kirby, Carrie Harris. Because you know where the bodies are buried.

To the amazing friends who pitched in to make my wedding happen while I was buried in revisions for this book: Brigitte Hagerman, Tara Murphy, Rachel Hunter, Cameron Russell, Amy Romero, Julia Shahin Collard, Roy Firestone, and Donald McCarthy.

To the best group of fans around—Kayla Keefer, Giedrė Šliumbaitė, Christine LaRue, Jenelle Riane Yu, and Debbie from Snuggling on the Sofa. My Army of Ten lives on!

To Michael Feldschuh, who graciously opens up his home to us every time we're in New York.

To my mom, who is, without a doubt, the most supportive and patient parent on the planet.

And last but never least, my husband, John, who has patiently held my hand through more insane writing deadlines than either of us can count. You are my reward at the end of every day.

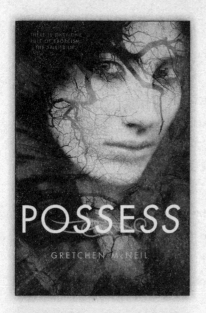